SUBMITTING TO THE RANCHER

RANCHER

Cowboy Doms Book One

BJ WANE

Published by Blushing Books
An Imprint of
ABCD Graphics and Design, Inc.
A Virginia Corporation
977 Seminole Trail #233
Charlottesville, VA 22901

BJ Wane
Submitting to the Rancher

Print ISBN: 978-1-64563-042-5
v1

Contents

Submitting to the Rancher

COWBOY DOMS, BOOK ONE

Published by Blushing Books®,
a subsidiary of

ABCD Graphics and Design
977 Seminole Trail #233
Charlottesville, VA 22901
The trademark Blushing Books®
is registered in the US Patent and Trademark Office.

BJ Wane
Submitting to the Rancher

EBook ISBN: 978-1-61258-923-7
Cover Art by ABCD Graphics & Design

Chapter 1

Why now and, more importantly, why me? The headlights of Sydney Baker's Mustang offered just enough illumination driving down the tree-lined road to cut through the pitch darkness of late evening. Her tires crunched over gravel and dirt, the narrow lane a vast difference from the smooth, four-lane highway she exited five minutes ago. Gripping the steering wheel, she squinted her eyes, peering ahead when she spotted a small glow of light. "Thank God," she muttered. Wasn't it bad enough she'd taken a wrong turn out of Billings that had resulted in her missing the three-o'clock report time for her new job by three hours? By then, hunger had forced her to take the time to eat something. Then she had to get a different set of directions to the Dunbar Ranch than her GPS spewed out and pray her poor sense of direction wouldn't steer her wrong before it became too late to meet her new boss, and that he wouldn't fire her on the spot for being tardy. She possessed two vices her family despaired of her ever getting under control: a penchant for always getting lost and getting herself into difficult situations.

Okay, in her defense, she'd tried to learn the art of following maps and directions from her phone or the GPS coordinates, of acquainting herself with the directions of east, west, north and south no matter where she was, but finally had to admit defeat by the time she'd hit her mid-twenties and still hadn't mastered the skill others found so easy. "So I can't find my way around sometimes. Sue me," she grumbled to no one. The worst part of being alone and away from her family the past six weeks was having no one around to gripe to. If nothing else, her beloved grandmother and sympathetic cousins were always available to lend an ear.

Sydney breathed a sigh of relief when the road ended at a gravel parking lot filled with vehicles parked in front of a lit-up barn. The large window set above the wide double doors was too high to see inside, but from the number of trucks and cars, there had to be a substantial crowd inside the well-kept barn. Maybe it was a barn dance, or some kind of fund-raising ho-down. What the heck did she know about what went on in the boonies of Big Sky Country? Cutting the engine, she pondered what to do now because it was obvious this was not the sprawling ranch house where she'd accepted a job as the new chef for a crew of twenty cowhands. Checking the time, she swore. If she didn't find her new employer soon, it would be too late tonight to show up, jeopardizing her position that much more. After working the last five years as the star chef in St. Louis' top restaurant, throwing together a pot of chili or batch of spaghetti to appease a group of hungry cowboys wasn't a position she craved to jump into. But, as the saying went, beggars couldn't be choosers, and since she was down to her last hundred bucks, she couldn't give up on the position yet, and didn't dare attempt to access her savings.

Getting out of the car, Sydney hugged her light jacket against the cold breeze. Early October in Montana blew as brisk as January in Missouri, just another reason to bemoan the circumstances that forced her to flee her home and family a few weeks ago. With any luck, someone inside would tell her she was only a ten-minute drive from the ranch and would give her detailed directions. Grabbing the front door's frigid metal handle, she pulled and damn near fell backward when it didn't budge.

Shit. Couldn't anything be easy? Stomping around the side, looking for another entrance, she came across a lower, wide window first. Feeling like a Peeping Tom, or Thomasina, she stood to the side and peeked around to see what she might be dealing with. Shaking her head, Sydney blinked, the scene inside catching her completely off guard and unlike anything near what she'd expected.

Oh, wow, just... wow. Crouching under the window, she hugged her jacket around her and tried to get a better view of the cavernous room that resembled nothing like the inside of a normal barn. It wasn't the circular bar centered in the middle of the wood-planked floor that left her agape, but the naked woman sitting on top of it. Leaning back on her hands, the woman's eyes widened, along with Sydney's, when the man standing at her side poured his beer between her bent, splayed legs and then dipped his head to lap up the spilled, tangy brew.

Swallowing past her suddenly dry throat, Sydney shifted her gaze, taking in the round tables and chairs then the gyrating bodies on a dance floor, the women wearing little to nothing. A staircase in the far corner caught her eye and she looked up into the loft to see another woman bound on a padded, wooden X, her sweat-glistening body pink-striped from the wicked looking flogger dangling from a tall man's hand. Damn, did they make all the men in this state that big?

Sydney wasn't a prude by any means. She'd read her share of smutty romances and drooled over every explicit, erotic word. She enjoyed sex as much as anyone, and since she'd tipped the scales over thirty three months ago, she'd discovered the truth to women reaching their sexual prime in this decade of their lives. Heck, she'd even asked a few of her lovers to slap her butt during sex. Only one granted her request, just a light tap that didn't even sting. But she could still recall how the slight burn that lingered afterward spread, surprising her by fueling her lust.

It never entered her mind she might be into voyeurism, but the longer she crouched at that window and the more she saw, the longer she wanted to stay and the more she wanted to take in. Suddenly, the night air didn't feel as cold. From what she could tell, the upper level held all the bondage equipment, and from her limited viewing position, those apparatus were being put to good use by willing women and some of the sexiest men Sydney had ever set eyes on. Then her breath lodged in her throat when she clapped eyes on a tall man whose scowl at something his attractive partner said drew Sydney's nipples into tight puckers. And that was before he yanked the short blonde over a bar stool, shoved down her shorts and peppered her upturned buttocks with a volley of ass reddening swats.

A shiver racked Sydney's body, one that had nothing to do with the cool temperature. Would she lie there and take such a punishment, and respond with a wiggle of her hips for more as the other woman just did, or would she blast the son-of-a bitch and stomp off in a fit of pique? God help her, she believed her response would be a hell of a lot closer to the former than the latter, if the warm gush between her legs was any indication. Then her heart rolled over as the stern cowboy lifted the blonde with large, gentle hands, sat on the stool and pulled her onto his lap. Cuddling her to his massive chest, he ran his hand up and down her quivering back in a soothing caress, his head bent to whisper in her ear. Whatever he said calmed the woman, and she shifted on his lap before slowly spreading her thighs as far as her lowered shorts allowed.

The pleased, tender look on the man's sun-leathered face as he drove two fingers inside the blonde cut Sydney to the quick. No one, not one man who had come and gone from her bed ever gazed at her like that, not even the few she'd grown closest to and most fond of. Is that what had been lacking in her relationships

6

that kept her from responding with the blatant enthusiasm the young woman exhibited as he drove her toward climax? She blew out the breath she'd been holding as the woman climaxed, and then the man patted her labia, the proud look crossing his rough-hewn face setting off a series of butterfly flutters that tickled her lower abdomen. What Sydney would give to have him gaze upon her like that after being driven mad with lust through pain induced pleasure. His tall frame had to top her own five-foot-six height by at least eight or nine inches, which she loved, and his thick, wavy mahogany hair curled around his nape in the most enticing, finger-itching way. She couldn't detect the color of his much lighter eyes, but the way his rugged face and previously stern mouth softened spoke volumes.

Sydney knew she needed to get going and at least find the closest town to book a room for the night since it'd become too late to arrive at her destination. But this was the most fun she'd indulged in since fleeing St. Louis, and the first time she'd been able to relax and shove aside her worries long enough to enjoy herself. With effort, she tore her eyes away from the compelling man who got her fired up on all cylinders just from eying him and took a few moments to spy on the other goings on. By the time she worked her way around the room and back to the bar where she'd left her jaw-dropping, panty-dampening hunk, he was nowhere to be seen.

With a sigh, she started to stand but the deep, irritated voice coming from behind her wiped away Sydney's disappointment and sent a frisson of heated awareness down her spine. Before she even turned around and looked up, she knew who stood there.

"You're trespassing on private property and snooping where you don't belong."

CADEN DID NOT APPRECIATE HAVING the first hours of relaxation away from the grueling task of running his thirty-thousand-acre ranch all week interrupted by an encroaching Peeping Tom. Mindy had been a soft lapful of teary-eyed submission he'd been looking forward to relieving his lust with when his brother, Connor had pointed toward the pale face peering in the window with wide eyes that didn't shy away from the BDSM activities going on in their private club.

Those big eyes rounded even more when she stood to face him, her red head tilting back to gaze up without flinching. Hell, he had to admire her for that.

"Sorry." Her small shrug signaled she wasn't *too* sorry, and he found himself fighting back an urge to smile. "I'm lost, and this is the first place I came to. Your front door is locked."

The accusation in her tone erased the brief flare of humor. "For good reason. Like I said, this is private property, and this," he waved toward the barn, "is a private club."

In the dim, outdoor lighting, he barely caught the quirk of her soft lips. "I noticed," she drawled.

"Most people," he stated, clasping her elbow and steering her toward the front, "would be shocked and apologize, and *wouldn't* take the time to stare in the window."

"I don't know what you're so peeved about," she returned calmly. "From what I saw, nobody inside minded an audience, including you."

Caden blew out a frustrated breath. There was no talking to the woman. "Where's your car?"

She pointed to a small sporty vehicle that must've given her a bumpy ride from the highway. "Right there, but I need directions." He opened the driver's side door and the interior light lit up her long, bright red hair as she folded her lean frame behind the steering wheel. Bracing his arm above the door, he looked down when she gazed up at him with vivid, moss green eyes and added, "*Explicit* instructions."

"Get lost a lot, do you?" He nodded toward the only road that led to the club, the one she had to come in on. "Just follow the same road back to the highway. A left will take you into Willow Springs, the closest town. Turn right if you're headed to Billings, but that will be a much longer drive, close to an hour at night."

Those pretty eyes lingered on his face for a moment, as if memorizing every detail, the look filled with interest he appreciated but refused to acknowledge. The girl had trouble written all over her attractive face with its smattering of freckles across her small nose, and he possessed neither the time nor the patience to deal with her further. He'd had a hell of a week and the weekend looked to be just as busy and aggravating.

"Thank you... Sir."

Shutting the door on her cheeky grin, Caden shook his head as he watched her turn around and disappear down the road. The hint of sarcasm she attached to sir had carried a thread of humor with it, telling him she didn't take him, or the activities she'd stumbled upon inside seriously. Too bad. If she were a member, he would've enjoyed spanking that insolent smirk off her face.

Heading back inside, he saw Connor manning the bar and strode over looking for Mindy. He spotted her climbing the stairs, already hooked up with someone else, but that didn't bother him other than now he'd have to spend time seeking another willing partner to join him for the rest of the evening. Sliding a tall, foamy brew across the sleek bar top toward him, his brother eyed him with a raised brow.

"What did our interloper have to say for herself?"

"How do you know her gender?" He hadn't been sure from the quick glimpse he'd gotten at the window before tromping outside.

Connor's blue eyes, identical to Caden's own, twinkled with humor. "Too pretty to be otherwise. At least, I'd hoped so. Why didn't you invite her in? She didn't appear shy about what she was seeing."

Caden snorted. "She wasn't." Taking a hefty swallow, he relished the tingling, cold glide down his throat as his mind filled with the image of laughing green eyes and a smart mouth. "Said she was lost, and I didn't see any reason not to believe her. She's not from around here or we would've either seen or heard about her. Where's Annie tonight?" His brother and Annie had been together long enough to make him wonder if his younger sibling would be the first to settle down until Connor's jaw went rigid and he looked away before uttering an evasive reply.

"She's busy tonight. I'll see her tomorrow, if I have time after we bring the herd down from the north pasture." Connor busied himself wiping non-existent dampness off the counter but Caden wasn't fooled.

"She was busy last weekend, both Friday and Saturday night as well," Caden pointed out. "Anything you want to talk about?" The two of them were close, but when it came to personal issues, they took after their father and tended to hold things in.

"No." Connor looked back at him with a shrug. "Not yet anyway."

Caden nodded, sipped his beer and then offered, "I'm here whenever."

"Good to know. Since Mindy has ditched you, maybe you should give sweet Nan some attention."

Swiveling his head, Caden spotted the nicely curved brunette who enjoyed long sessions with a flogger or cane followed by rough fucking. "You know, I think she would be perfect to end the night with. Later."

Connor's low chuckle followed him as he walked over to the table where the experienced sub and long-time member sat nursing an Amaretto Sour, her favorite drink. "You interested in accompanying me up to the loft tonight, darlin'?" No sense beating around the bush, not with her. They'd played together often enough to know what the other wanted.

"Yes, sir, I would." Her brown eyes lit with excitement when she took his hand, but it was a pair of twinkling green eyes he thought about as Nan followed him toward the stairs.

SYDNEY PULLED into the one motel in the town of Willow Springs thirty minutes later, grateful it was right there on the outskirts where her GPS said it would be. She ached with exhaustion, her nerves frazzled over missing the arrival time for her new job. The only thing keeping her going now was the adrenaline high that started the second she stood so close to the hunky cowboy Dom. He'd been just as tall and big as he'd looked from the window, his massive body emitting enough heat to defuse the chill of the cold night air. His chiseled jaw and cobalt blue gaze had drawn shivers of awareness that had nothing to do with the temperature outside and everything to do with the growing warmth inside her body.

"I just miss sex, that's all this is," she mumbled, opening the car door and sliding out. "Orgasm deprivation and stress would make anyone react in such a way to that deep, commanding voice." She figured a quick finger job ought to do the trick in getting both the man and the activities he liked to indulge in out of her mind so she could concentrate on a job and making it through another week or two while she struggled with her dilemma.

But when she slid naked between the cool, clean sheets on the motel's double bed twenty minutes later and ran her hands over her breasts, all she could think about was how a pair of larger hands, likely with calluses, would feel kneading her small plumpness, and imagining rough fingers plucking at the sensitive tips of her nipples. With a groan of frustration, she slid one palm over her abdomen, recalling the little flutters that tickled her insides as she'd watched him spank the other woman and the way her own buttocks clenched in response, as they did now just thinking about him tossing her over those hard thighs. Hell, she didn't even know the man's name and still couldn't quit thinking about him, fantasizing about him.

Tracing over the thin line of hair on her mons pubis, the only strip she opted to leave from her last wax job, she wondered if *he* preferred a bare mound and labia. It had been her last boyfriend who had talked her into waxing, and she loved it as much as he professed to, but when she ran her fingers over the damp, bare flesh now, the sensations weren't as strong as usual. Swearing in frustration, she spread her legs and plunged two fingers knuckle deep between her slick folds, aiming for her clit and a quick release.

A few strokes over the swollen bud sent her hips bucking against her pumping hand, the pinch to her nipple an extra boost just as her climax erupted with strong grips around her fingers. Breathing heavy, she rode through the pleasurable sensations, but it wasn't until she pictured a dark, rugged face with bright blue eyes watching her every thrust and jerk that the pleasure skyrocketed her into orgasmic orbit.

"*Holy shit,* what a look can do," Sydney whispered in the dark, waiting for her body to cease trembling. A coyote howled, and she shuddered from the lonely sound that reminded her of her circumstances. Sitting up, she snatched her nightshirt and panties from the foot of the bed and donned them, wishing she had someone to hold her, to tell her everything would be all right, that she could return home soon without fear. She drifted asleep thinking with regret of a man she would never see again, and a tucked away barn filled with all kinds of naughty indulgences she'd never get to try with him.

"THERE'S NOTHING FOR IT, I have to give it a shot," Sydney told her reflection in the bathroom mirror the next morning. Odds were, the cook's job on the Dunbar ranch was no longer hers, but maybe they were desperate enough to give her a second chance, if she could find the damn place. She'd come across the job opening when she stopped in a computer café on her way through Boise, Idaho last week and filled out the application using her grandmother's maiden name instead of Greenbriar. She'd traveled a long way from the Midwest where her family name was synonymous with their chain of all-natural grocery stores but wouldn't take the chance of her Uncle Mike finding her, not until she found a way to defuse his intentions without letting her beloved grandmother know just how low her youngest child had sunk.

Thirty minutes after sending the application, she'd gotten a call from Jase Wiggins, the ranch manager, who told her she was hired, and they needed her to arrive Friday by three p.m. The salary was more than she'd imagined and included room and board. It would be the perfect place to lie low until she figured out a way to keep her uncle's greedy hands off her shares of the company and her grandmother, as well as her other two uncles, in the dark about Mike's nefarious deeds that would break their hearts.

Sydney checked out of the motel thinking with optimism and followed the clerk's directions back down the highway. "Everyone knows where the Dunbar Ranch is. You can't miss it," he said, rubbing salt into the wound from yesterday's mishap. Only, it turned out he was correct. She came upon the turnoff just a mile past the one she was sure she'd taken the night before. This road was wider and a little smoother, although not by much. There weren't as many trees lining the way, and the glimpses of wide-open range she caught in between them spread as far as she could see. Dotted with cattle and a few horses, the vastness of the ranch stunned her until she rounded a bend and the house came into view.

Pulling into the circular drive and stopping in front of the sprawling ranch home, she took a moment to admire the wrap around porch, cute rocking chairs facing several barns surrounded by neat, white-fenced corrals and a garden that made her hands itch to explore. Just as she slid out of the car, the front door swung open and a tall man wearing a Stetson pulled low over his eyes stepped outside. It took only a second to recognize the imposing height and broad shoulders, the curl of dark brown hair around the collar of a blue, long-sleeved work shirt tucked into a pair of snug, thigh molding jeans and a voice that haunted her dreams last night.

"Don't tell me. You're lost again," he drawled, coming down the steps toward her with a swagger that spiked Sydney's pulse into racing. Stopping in front of her, he tipped back his hat, those enigmatic blue eyes holding a hint of pleasure even though he frowned down at her.

Running sweaty palms down her thighs, Sydney sucked in a fortifying breath to calm her rapidly thudding heart, the open car door between them doing little to block the heat generated from his nearness. "Nope, not this time." Holding out her hand over the door, she introduced herself for the first time. "I'm Sydney Baker and I apologize for being so late, but as you know, I got a little turned around last night, and then," she flipped him a sassy grin, "I got a little distracted."

Chapter 2

J ust when Caden thought the weekend problems looming ahead of him couldn't get any worse, *she* shows up again. Not only does she land on another one of his doorsteps but claimed to be the new employee he'd been desperate for ever since Mattie, the ranch's cook for the last twenty years, broke her hip, cementing her decision to retire. The same green eyes filled with open curiosity and a glint of teasing humor that plagued his dreams last night gazed up at him with guileless unconcern. Too bad the slight tremor when he clasped her hand revealed she wasn't as sure of herself as she tried to pull off.

"Caden Dunbar. First rule, don't be late. Since you're new to the area, I can let that infraction lapse this time. If you're late on meals, you'll not only answer to me, but twenty other hungry hands. I don't have a lot of time and need you to have something ready for the noon lunch break, so let me show you your room first then I'll walk you over to the dining hall and kitchen." He released her hand and immediately missed the contact. The uncharacteristic reaction was another mark against her. He needed to set aside whatever it was about Sydney Baker that kept pulling at him and needed to do so fast. Mixing with his employees outside work was something he never did, and he always kept work, including those on his payroll, separate from his pleasures.

The relief on her face couldn't be missed even though she tried to hide it by turning away. "Thank you. I'll grab my bag out of the back…" Before she finished, he had the door open and her one suitcase in his hand. "Or, you can get it," she finished with another one of those small quirks of her mouth, her very soft, tempting mouth.

Pivoting, Caden shoved that observation aside and strode back up the steps, expecting Sydney to follow. Holding the front door open, he said, "Your quarters are in the north wing, just past the kitchen." When she stood in the tiled entry without turning in the right direction, he released a frustrated breath and pointed. "North is that way."

"Hey, I had enough trouble finding your place. Don't expect me to know my way around anytime soon. Not happening, boss." The emphasis she put on 'boss' almost drew his smile, but it wouldn't do to encourage her.

"As long as you stay away from my personal quarters on the *far* south end of the house and can find your way to the dining hall, you'll be fine. Just don't go wandering out after dark. There are too many pitfalls around the ranch for someone unfamiliar with the property." He couldn't help feeling miffed she didn't appear in awe of his spacious, six thousand square foot home as he led her through the open great room with its wall-dominating stone fireplace, large dining area and state-of-the-art kitchen, down the back hall to a bedroom with an attached bath. "You should be comfortable in here." He set her suitcase on the queen size brass bed covered with a multi-patterned quilt and nodded toward an antique cupboard. "The dresser is empty so feel free to use it." Pointing to another door, he added, "There's a linen cabinet in the bathroom with extra towels and sheets. Laundry's off the kitchen."

Sydney padded over to the bathroom and looked inside, and Caden couldn't prevent his gaze from wandering to the snug fit of her jeans molding a very nice backside. He liked her height, not too short, not very tall. And why he was musing over her attributes when he had work to do, he didn't know, but it needed to stop.

"This is nice. Where does that door lead to?" She strolled past him toward the French door that opened onto a small, covered patio. "Oh, what a beautiful view."

The awe in her voice as she gazed out at the snow-capped mountain vista drew his eyes over her bright red head to a sight he never tired of seeing. Born and raised on the ranch, Caden had never desired to live anywhere else, to do anything except run the homestead he and his brother took over when their father retired several years ago. Breeding cattle was in his blood, and when he and Connor expanded the ranch's operations to include raising Quarter horses, the extra work had paid off in spades.

"Wait until it snows. It's even prettier then." Her shoulders slumped, and he wondered if she didn't care for snow, or if there was another reason she wasn't looking forward to the winter months. Newcomers to the state often found the long, cold winters intolerable. "Come on," he ordered in a gruff tone, annoyed with his curiosity and a growing need to learn more about his new cook. *She's an employee, remember that.* Why did he think he would need to repeat that reminder a lot in the coming days and weeks?

SYDNEY RELISHED the morning sun on her face when they stepped back outside, the warmth helping to dispel the coldness inside her when she thought of still being so far from home come winter. She'd been enjoying listening to Caden's deep voice and looking around the rustic but appealing interior of his home so much, she'd forgotten for a few moments the reason she was here in the first place. At least being stuck cooking boring meals for a bunch of cowhands came with the benefit of having Caden as her boss. Tall, dark and handsome didn't begin to do his sex appeal justice, which the constant quickening of her girly parts could attest to.

"So, what do you do with all those cows?" she asked, nodding toward the pasture strewn with black grazing animals as they walked toward the clump of buildings a good city block from the house.

"Cattle," he corrected. "And we breed them then sell them to either other ranches or farms or drive them to market." Two large collies came bounding out of the closest barn and he stopped a moment to greet the friendly dogs.

"Oh, they're so cute!" Stooping, Sydney laughed when wet tongues attacked her face and she sank her hands into their long, soft fur. "What're their names?"

"Sadie is the tan and white. The black male is Spike. They're working dogs, not pets, so don't spoil them," he warned, taking her elbow and steering her over to a dark green, one story building with neat white trim.

"I wouldn't dream of it, boss." Caden tossed her a suspicious look as he opened the door, but Sydney kept her expression bland. What he doesn't know wouldn't hurt either her or the dogs.

"This is where the hands gather for meals. Only five of them bunk overnight in the attached room, in case of an emergency and Connor and I need the help. You can fix breakfast and dinner for the seven of us up at the house. The others arrive by eight a.m. and work until five, some days a little longer. They expect a big lunch, not a salad or sandwich. Lots of carbs and calories. This hall is only used for the noon meal, or the large gatherings we hold with friends."

The sparse, wood-planked big room held three long tables with chairs, a fireplace against the back wall and a door labeled 'Restroom'. It was a far cry from the five-star restaurant where she enjoyed cooking gourmet meals from scratch, using nothing but all-natural ingredients. To take her mind off missing her job and friends, she resorted to teasing him again. "Friends?" Sydney drawled when he led her toward the large, industrial kitchen in the rear. "I saw how you like to entertain your friends, boss."

Caden faced her, a scowl drawing his dark brows together. "The young woman you saw me with last night is not a friend, she's a play partner, and you're an employee. I don't mix business with pleasure, Sydney. Remember that, and we'll get along fine."

Bummer. Her new boss sure could be a stick-in-the-mud. Turning her mind to her job, she admired the large kitchen and restaurant-grade appliances. At least she'd find some pleasure working here, even if the meals wouldn't allow room to utilize her skills and preferences. Maybe she could play a little with the smaller breakfasts and dinners.

"I get along with everyone," she told him as they left the building. Caden rolled his eyes but said nothing until he stopped at a corral and reached out to stroke the nose of a pretty, brown and white horse that trotted up.

"This is Daisy. She's a sweetheart. Do you ride?"

Sydney wondered why she wanted to keep riling him. Maybe it was hormones, or lack of sex, or plain old attraction prodding her to goad him, to get under his skin the way he had hers. Looking up at him, her heart stuttered at his direct, blue gaze under the low brim of his hat. *Shit.* What the man could do to a girl's insides with just a look ought to be illegal.

"I love to… ride," she drawled with blatant innuendo.

His jaw tightened, his reply stated in a low, controlled voice. "Horses, Sydney."

"Oh, well, no, I've never been on top of one of those. But it couldn't be too hard. You said she's a sweetheart." She reached out a tentative hand to stroke the mare's soft neck, enjoying the ripple of muscle under her hand.

"When I have time, I'll take you up, give you a few lessons. Until then, don't even think about it," he warned.

"Another rule?" she quipped, beginning to chafe under the weight of his restrictions.

"Safety is high on our priority list, along with no employee membership, or even visits to our private club," he stated, laying it on the line in blunt terms.

Sydney blew out a frustrated breath and gripped the rail. She may just end up as lonely on this busy ranch as she'd been traveling alone for the past few weeks. "You sure know how to suck the fun out of a new job, boss. I guess I'll have to come up with other ways to enjoy my time off."

CADEN WANTED his reply to confirm his distrust of the innocent look on Sydney's face when she uttered that last question. He needed to squash her interest before he caved, and *he* was the one to break his own, steadfast rule. "You saw how I deal with little girls who let their mouths run away with them. Same goes for those who break the rules." Which wasn't true for employees, of course, but she didn't know that.

"I'm not a little girl," she returned, unfazed. He should've remembered how she hadn't shied away from watching him spank Mindy, and how there'd been no reasoning with her last night.

"Then don't act like one and we won't have a problem," he growled in frustration, doing his best to ignore the way the twinkle in her eyes stirred his cock.

Caden didn't hear Connor come out of the barn until he spoke behind him, his voice laced with amused curiosity. "Is big brother giving you a hard time?"

"Connor, meet our new cook, and yes, she's also our trespasser from last night. Sydney Baker, my brother, Connor."

"Thank God." Pushing his way between them, Connor held out his hand. "We may have had a mutiny on our hands come noon if the guys had to eat one more catered meal from the deli in town. It's so frigging nice to meet you, Sydney."

The smile Sydney bestowed on his brother lit up her face with pleasure, the look drawing Caden's hands into fists to keep from giving in to the urge to shove Connor away from her. How the hell could she get to him so fast, and in a way no other woman ever had?

"It's nice to be greeted by a friendly face, Connor. Caden was going over the rules with me, with an emphasis on safety and no more spying in the window of your 'other' barn." The finger quotes she put up when she said other drew a reluctant smile from Caden. The girl didn't give an inch and damned if he couldn't help the thread of admiration that trait elicited.

"That's funny. Caden was always the one to tell me rules were made to be broken when we were growing up and getting our butts walloped," Connor drawled.

Since he couldn't fight both of them at once, Caden yanked on his hat in exasperation. "We have work to do and Sydney has a meal to prepare. I suggest we all get to it."

"Sydney, again, nice to meet you. See you at lunch." Connor tipped his hat to her before catching up with Caden in the barn.

Why it should grate that his brother was so friendly and showed an interest in Sydney, Caden didn't know, and didn't care for the fact it did. Under any other circumstances, he'd enjoy the attraction, the interest in kink, and act on it. But he couldn't afford to sour a much-needed employer/employee relationship by giving in to her and indulging in a brief fling.

"You could cut her a little slack. She seems nice."

He flicked his brother a sharp glance. "She is nice, but rules are put in place for a good reason."

"Yeah, I know," Connor sighed in agreement. "But some-times bending the rules doesn't hurt anything and can be a hell of a lot of fun."

THE DUNBAR BROTHERS together certainly packed a punch, Sydney mused, watching the pair stride off. They were of the same height, but Connor had a leaner build than Caden, his hair a lighter, tawny shade of brown worn long enough to pull back in a short ponytail compared to his brother's shaggy, collar-length, dark mahogany. The twinkle in Connor's matching blue eyes belied the whole scruffy, rugged look he had going on with the shade darker beard that was sexy as hell. But the horny, perverse side of her only tingled when Caden drilled her with his irritated, cobalt gaze and warmed from just an innocent touch of his callused hand, leaving her no choice but to jump him if given the chance. Since that prospect seemed unlikely, she'd have to suck it up for now and concentrate on her job.

As she suspected, the pantry and large refrigerator/freezer in the mess hall held only the basics, ingredients that lacked imagi-nation. After finding everything she needed for a large batch of spaghetti, which would take no time, she indulged herself by sinking her hands into yeasty dough for fresh, homemade bread. She just pulled the golden loaves from the oven when she heard the outer door open and voices heralding the arrival of the hands.

Snatching up the mitt hot pads, she lifted the heavy pot of spaghetti and meatballs off the stove and carried it into the dining hall. A lanky young man rushed forward and took it from her with a beaming smile, his tanned face shadowed by his Stetson.

"Billy Joe, ma'am. Welcome to the Dunbar Ranch. Oh, man, this looks fu... er, darn good."

Amused, Sydney smiled at him. "Thank you. I'm Sydney. I'll grab the bread."

Another young hand swiveled his blond head toward her, his blue eyes widening at her announcement. "Bread? Is that what I smell?"

"Yes. Hold on." She rushed back into the kitchen as several more guys strolled in, all hurrying to take a seat. Their youth surprised her, and as she returned to set the bread and butter on the table, the rest welcomed her with unreserved comradery.

"Thank God," a dark skinned, dark-eyed guy said with an appreciative sigh as he scooped spaghetti onto his plate. "If we had to eat deli sandwiches one more time, I was going to protest."

"They weren't that bad, Diego. I'm Tyler, miss." He held out his hand and she shook it, bemused by the show of respect that was rare anymore in young men their age.

"Nice to meet you. If you'll excuse me, I need to finish up in the kitchen."

She was so pleased with their welcome, and their enthusiasm and praise for the simple meal and homemade bread, she was able to ignore the tightness in her chest when Caden walked in fifteen minutes later. Only midday, and already a sexy shadow darkened his swarthy cheeks, and she'd bet he shaved that morning. His eyes zeroed in on her all the way into the kitchen for a split second, just long enough to produce an instant rush of heated pleasure to pool between her legs. That reaction proved harder to set aside.

Sydney returned with another pot and passed on several offers to sit and join the hands, none of which came from her boss, opting instead to eat in the kitchen while cleaning up. She wanted to explore a little before raiding the house kitchen for something to fix for dinner later. There was also the lengthy list of ingredients she needed to make, but thought to save that chore for later tonight, assuming Caden would spend his Saturday night the same as he had Friday night, leaving her to entertain herself.

It took no time for the twenty hands to devour both huge pots and all of the bread, and she sent them back to work with brownies and beaming smiles of gratitude. At her job in St. Louis, she didn't get the chance to mingle with the customers she fed and only got wind of compliments second-hand. She rather enjoyed receiving praise first-hand, even if it was for a simple meal anybody could toss together at home. Sydney spent the afternoon walking around the acres surrounding the house, investigating the barns, playing with the dogs whenever they came rushing by, petting a few friendly horses. The ranch hands all stopped to chat a few minutes if she wandered into their area, taking the time to answer her questions and gave her directions with a smile when she'd get turned around. Despite the cool fall temperature, the sun felt good and the view of sweaty, hard-working young guys a nice diversion from the looming, lonely night ahead of her.

Her mood improved even more when she inspected the large garden and brought in enough ripe vegetables for a salad to serve with the meatloaf and mashed potatoes she planned for dinner. She missed getting fresh produce from the farmer's market back home, and from the looks of the garden and feel of the air, she doubted she would get many more days to pluck from the home-grown supply.

Right at six o'clock, the five hands that stayed full-time on the ranch came in with Connor and introduced themselves before taking a seat at the extended dining table. "Don't worry, Sydney," Connor assured her, squeezing her shoulder. "You'll learn every-one's names in no time. Grab a seat."

She flicked an uneasy glance toward Caden, who had just entered and stood in the doorway. "Oh, I don't think…"

"I do. Ignore my cranky big brother and join us. I insist." Conner sent Caden a challenging look.

Caden shrugged. "Fine by me."

Pleased to not be eating alone, she sat between her two bosses, but her mind, and body, couldn't drum up any interest in anyone except Caden. What was it about the rancher that pulled at her with such a forceful tug? She wondered if her infatuation stemmed from watching him in such an erotic setting or if the loneliness and stress of the last weeks were getting to her in a different way.

"Great meal, Ms. Baker," Jim, a short, stocky-built man commented as he rose, donned his hat and tipped it to her. "Nice to have you on board."

"Thank you," she beamed. The appreciation he and the others voiced over another simple meal pleased her in a way compliments for her more extravagant dishes never had.

They especially enjoyed the chocolate cream pie she'd baked hoping to mellow Caden's attitude toward letting her at least visit their private club as a guest. The longing to explore, up close and personal, the happenings she'd stumbled upon last night continued to increase during the time she spent around the rancher, as did the need to discover why he did it for her on every level, more so than any other man. She'd never experienced such a quick, strong reaction to a man before, and she didn't know whether she found him different from other men due to the sexual arena she'd first seen him in or his larger-than-life appearance and dominating air.

As soon as the ranch hands departed, Caden and Connor started discussing leaving for the club while helping her clear the table. "You'll be fine here while we're gone, Sydney," Caden said, handing her his plate at the sink. "I showed you the line on my desk that goes directly to the bunk house if you need anything."

"Why can't I go?" she asked, hating the tremor and whine in her voice. The thought of facing yet another long, lonely night depressed her. "Don't you ever allow visitors, those who want to check things out for the first time?"

"All the time," Connor put in before glancing at his big brother with a raised brow. "Surely we can make an exception to the no mixing employees with pleasure rule. I hate to think of leaving poor Sydney all alone tonight."

Caden frowned and shook his head, dashing the surge of gratitude and hope Connor's words elicited. "No." He pinned her with those laser blue eyes and her body's instant reaction made her want to both smack him and jump him, and she wasn't sure which was stronger. "I don't bend the rules for anyone. That would be a bad habit to get into. Other than my private quarters, you have free run of the house. Find a way to amuse yourself." Slapping his hat on his head, he started for the door, tossing over his shoulder, "You coming, Con?"

"Right behind you." Connor squeezed her shoulder, his eyes sympathetic. "I'll work on him, Sydney. We've never hired an outsider before. All of our employees have been locals, including our cook for the past twenty years. They have their own homes, and own lives and friends away from the ranch, unlike you. He knows that."

"Thanks, Connor. I just want to socialize, and watch," she added with a cocky grin. "I've never…"

"Submitted to bondage, erotic pain, dominance?" he supplied for her when she paused, unsure how she wanted to phrase her inexperience with kinky sex.

Her face warmed. "Right. My… past doesn't include any of those things, but I'm not opposed to experimenting… but, not with…" She floundered again, her face heating even more as she wondered how she could tell him her lust seemed to center on just his brother. From Connor's low chuckle, she figured maybe she didn't have to explain.

"Got it, Sydney. And don't worry." His eyes clouded, and his smile slipped. "I'm in a relationship, at least for the time being."

Sydney followed him onto the front porch and spotted Caden sitting behind the wheel of his huge black truck, Connor's matching vehicle parked behind him. "I hope it works out for you," she told him softly, reaching out and squeezing his hand before he jogged down the steps. Folding her arms against the chilly night air, she stood on the porch watching until their taillights disappeared around the bend, a heavy weight pressing on her chest.

The dogs bounded up on the porch and, ignoring Caden's orders not to pamper them, she held open the door to let them in. "You're better than no company," she told the pair, following them inside. In a fit of irritation and despondency, she cut up the leftover meatloaf Caden mentioned saving for lunch tomorrow and fed it to the grateful pups.

By the time she slipped into the comfortable bed a few hours later, the howling wind emphasized the loneliness of the big, empty house, stretching her already taut nerves. She drifted asleep aching for a large rancher to take her over, divert her thoughts from missing home and worrying over her relatives with his hard hand and even harder body.

Sydney blinked, the realization something was wrong hitting her like a ton of bricks. She cast Uncle Mike an accusing look as she tried to stand. Dizziness assailed her, sending the room spinning out of control and turning her blood to ice in her veins with the sudden dread infusing her. Why did I trust him?

"What... what have... you done?" she whispered, shrugging away from the hand he reached out to her.

"I'm sorry, Sydney, really I am, but you left me no choice." He snatched her arm with one hand while pulling a folded piece of paper from his back pocket with the other.

She shook her head, knowing what it was, what he wanted. "I... I told you... no... way..." The sharp yank on her arm to force her hand down to the coffee table where he tossed the paper drew a cry from her numb lips. She knew if he succeeded in coercing her signature, he would have her shares in their family-owned company sold before she could do anything about it. "No!" With a burst of strength born of desperation, she pulled free and stumbled toward the front door of her apartment. Why, oh why did I let him in?

He took her down before she could grab the handle, the impact with the hard wood floor jarring her body and wrenching another cry from her. The floor swam before her eyes as she struggled under his weight, his heavy breathing sending goosebumps racing over her skin. She wasn't the only one in a distressed state.

"C'mon on, kid. Cooperate and it'll be over. I promised I would pay you back, didn't I?" he growled as he hauled her back on her feet.

Sydney shook her head again, flashes of her grandmother's pain-filled face dancing in her head. Nana could never learn of her youngest son's deceit; it would kill her. She pulled on her arm again, refusing to let him drag her back over to the table. Reaching out with her free arm for balance, she connected with the small end table lamp and, without conscious thought, grabbed hold and swung. The metal base just grazed Uncle Mike's temple, but it was enough to draw a trickle of blood and startle him long enough for him to loosen his hold. This time, she managed to make it out the door with no thought in mind except run... run.... run.

Sydney jerked awake, shaking and sweating from the nightmare that wouldn't leave her alone, no matter how far she traveled from home. The night her Uncle Mike stopped by with a bottle of wine as a peace token to mend the bridge between them had ended with her drugged, struggling against his powerful hold as he tried to force her signature, signing the shares left to her by her mother over to him. Drowning in a gambling debt his two older brothers and mother knew nothing about, his only option, he'd been telling her for months, was to invest her shares and, with luck, turn enough of a profit to pay her back someday. She'd refused his first few, polite offers and then avoided him as much as possible after he resorted to nasty threats. His final act of drugging her and trying to force her hand ended with her fleeing in the middle of the night, aching, devastated and determined not to hurt her grandmother with what Uncle Mike had done. Nana had already suffered the trauma and grief of losing her only daughter, a tragedy followed by her husband's untimely death just two weeks later.

Sliding out of bed on trembling legs, she stumbled into the kitchen and flipped on the small light above the sink. Gazing out into the inky darkness, her mind jumped to Caden, her imagination picturing him with that curvy blonde. She was so engrossed in her thoughts, the sudden sound of the back door swinging open startled her, causing her to fumble with the glass she'd been reaching for when she turned and saw him standing in the door.

GUILT, coiling through him like an insidious snake, kept Caden from enjoying himself once he arrived at The Barn. Instead of seeking a willing sub to spend the evening with, he'd sat at the bar brooding over a pair of hurt, green eyes and a lonely figure standing on his front porch as he'd driven away. Connor hadn't helped, accusing him of being too hard on Sydney, not giving enough consideration to her new arrival in the state. Finally giving up on getting any enjoyment out of the night, he left it to his brother and best friend, Grayson Monroe to close up and returned home to check on their new cook.

He hadn't expected to find her up, standing in the dim light of the kitchen wearing nothing but a skimpy nightshirt hiked up to reveal the edge of pink panties as she reached for a glass with a shaking hand. "What's wrong?" he barked, striding forward and turning her to face him. Her slender body shook under his hands on her shoulders and her face was paler than usual, but those arresting eyes snapped with green fire when she jerked away from him.

"Nothing, I got up to get a drink and didn't hear you come in."

"The house is well-insulated against the harsh winters. What's wrong?" he asked again, some insane part of him needing to know despite the way she crossed her arms in a belligerent stance of stubbornness.

"I couldn't sleep."

The evasive shift of her eyes gave away that untruth, drawing his scowl. "Do your hands always shake when you can't sleep?"

She avoided his question again with a point-blank one of her own. "Did you have fun with your blonde?"

Exasperated, Caden swore and demanded, "Are you going to tell me what happened to upset you?"

Sydney tilted her head and regarded him with a probing stare before asking, "Are you going to let me into your club?"

She's like a damn dog with a bone. "No."

"Then goodnight, boss."

Sydney moved to brush by him and, unable to let her go just yet, Caden gripped her arm and hauled her against him. Frustration with the entire, fucked-up night ripped through him. Fisting his free hand in her red hair, he tilted her head sideways and dipped down to nip at the soft, tender flesh of her neck. Her gasp went straight to his cock; her low moan when he stroked his tongue over the bite jerked him into a semi-erection. Lifting his head enough to coast over her lips with his, he warned in a low voice, "Be careful what you wish for, Sydney. You may just get more than you bargained for." Before he could give into the temptation to toss her down and bury himself inside her slick heat right there on the kitchen floor, he released her and stepped back.

"Goodnight." Caden left her standing there with a bemused expression, but that was better than the stress lining her face from whatever had kept her awake. He needed to learn to remain calm and unaffected by her, to remind himself she was just another employee, here to do a job, and that was the extent of their involvement.

Chapter 3

Sydney smiled to herself as she cleaned up the kitchen in the mess hall. She'd served homemade rolls with today's beef stew and set out an array of desserts it had taken her all morning to bake. The guys couldn't praise her enough, a few even offered marriage proposals in jest. Going by her boss' scowl, she guessed Caden didn't appreciate their humor, but Connor's sly wink and grin said he did.

She relished the friendly banter and camaraderie today after spending Sunday mostly by herself after Caden informed her he didn't have time to teach her to ride before taking off for Billings. Other than to approve her grocery list and grumble about feeding *his* meatloaf to the dogs, he had made himself scarce after returning in the late afternoon. She'd killed some time strolling around the barns and learning her way around the buildings, petting the horses in their stalls and throwing sticks for the dogs. Compared to the hustle and bustle on Saturday, the ranch had been quiet and lonely yesterday and made her enjoy the activity and noise of a working ranch even more this morning.

When the hall finally grew quiet, she stretched, more than

ready for some fresh air. With luck, maybe a long walk like the one she'd taken yesterday would help her sleep well again tonight. She refused to credit Caden's presence in the house for the previous good night's rest. Grabbing her jacket off its hook, she slipped out into the pleasant afternoon sun and brisk breeze. She followed a path of worn down grass through the closest field, catching sight of a few ranch hands working the cattle from afar. Annoyance slithered under her skin when she realized her eyes kept seeking one cowboy in particular, and she cursed her inability to stop pining for more attention from her boss. *I'm just lonely, and horny,* she repeated over and over as she increased her stride and concentrated on keeping her head down.

An hour later, that strategy proved to be a piss poor one. "Damn, damn and double damn," Sydney cursed while trying to disentangle her snagged jeans from the barbed wire fence she had attempted to climb over. The sound of a horse thundering toward her drew her attention just as she felt a painful, sharp scrape ripping through the sock covering her ankle. Shielding her eyes, Sydney groaned when she recognized Caden galloping up to her, his horse puffing from exertion.

"I should've known you were where you're not supposed to be," Caden sighed as he dismounted and tipped his Stetson back with a thumb. "Don't tell me, you got turned around, right?"

"Can I help it if your land stretches on and on with nothing to break it up?" The cut stung, and she could feel blood dampening her jeans, which didn't improve her mood.

"Hold still." Gripping her pant leg with both hands, he ripped the bottom three inches of denim off, freeing her before he caught sight of the cut. "Son of a bitch." Whipping out a bandana from his back pocket, he tied it around the cut and lifted her off the fence, his arms gentle, his weathered face taut with frustration. "When was your last tetanus shot?"

Sydney racked her brain and cringed. "Uh, over ten years

ago." Thinking of going to a clinic and the forms she'd have to fill out, she shook her head. "I'm fine, it's just a scrape."

"Out here, we don't take chances. Let's go." He swung up on his huge horse and before she knew what he was about, reached down and hauled her up in front of him as if she weighed no more than twenty pounds.

Then his muscle-hard arms wrapped around her and Sydney forgot about the problems going for a doctor's visit would cause her. Leaning against his wide chest, she turned her face up to his with an impish grin. "Is this my riding lesson?" she asked as he prodded the horse into a trot that bounced her on his lap in a very enticing way.

"Hell no," he returned with a frown.

She couldn't help it. It felt too good to be held again, to set aside her worries and problems and enjoy a pleasant afternoon and the nearness of one hunky rancher to stifle the urge to needle him again. Gripping his thick forearm, she wiggled her butt against his crotch and felt the press of his growing erection as she told him with a laugh, "That's okay. I like riding with you."

Caden tightened his arm around her waist and snapped, "Sit still."

Unperturbed, she shook her hair back, turned and put her mouth on his throat, his earthy scent making her ache as she taunted, "Or what?"

Shifting the reins to his hand at her waist, he gripped her hair and pulled her head back, the steed never breaking stride as he bent and nipped her lower lip. "Have I mentioned my belt?" Her instant stillness drew his chuckle. "That's what I thought. Behave, Sydney."

The man either had no idea what he did to her or didn't care. Sydney ran her finger over her throbbing lip, struggling to keep from rubbing her crotch against the leather saddle to alleviate the warm ache that small sting brought about. She shuddered when she thought of how his belt would feel snapping on her bare butt, and then recalled the blonde's contented face after Caden spanked her. Was it any wonder her boss had her tied up in knots she craved to untangle?

HE HAD BETTER things to do on a Monday afternoon, Caden reminded himself as he tried to ignore the way Sydney's soft ass cushioned his hardening shaft. When she'd left for one of her walks and hadn't returned within a few hours, he and Connor had taken out in different directions to look for her. As he would for any of his employees, he'd feared for her safety and when he'd come across her tangled in the barbed wire fence she'd foolishly tried to cross over, the relief at finding her safe switched to annoyance from the worry and trouble she'd caused him.

"You have a cell phone, don't you? Why didn't you call the ranch when you got into trouble?" He looked down into her flushed face and grew suspicious when she averted her eyes. The girl carried secrets he normally wouldn't be interested in prying into. His life had been anything but normal the past few days.

"I left it in my room. Besides, what good would it have done? I couldn't tell anyone where I was because I didn't know."

Her excuse was both logical and feasible but he wasn't buying it. "From now on, take your phone with you, or, better yet, limit your walks to around the buildings instead of taking off through the fields." Caden told himself he was not disappointed when he halted Ranger at the corral next to the horse barn and lost the feel of Sydney's soft body swaying with his as he dismounted. "Come on." Lifting her down, he stepped back as soon as her feet touched the ground and couldn't miss the regret crossing her face. For his sake, he wished she would be more like other women and at least try to hide her interest.

"I honestly don't think I need to get the scrape looked at," she protested as he clasped her elbow and led her over to his truck.

"Yes, you do." Opening the passenger door, he waved his hand inside. "Get in. Willow Springs has a twenty-four-hour clinic."

"Look, the truth is I'm low on funds until payday. I can't afford a doctor's bill." He could tell she didn't like being forced to make that admission. Tough.

"You're covered under our insurance since you were hurt on our property while in our employ. Why don't you have insurance?"

She ignored his question and hopped up onto the seat with a relieved smile. "In that case, let's go."

The next afternoon, Caden returned from the fields in time to stroll around the side of the big barn and catch a view of Sydney's upturned ass as she stood leaning over the rail enclosing the pigpen. *Way over*. With a squeal, she toppled into the sty, landing in a mud puddle from the previous night's rain. With a glare toward two hands laughing on the sidelines, he strode toward her, snapping at them, "You didn't think to stop her?"

"Ah, c'mon, boss," Tyler drawled as he and Carl came forward to help. "You gotta admit she's cute."

"And entertaining," Carl put in.

Ignoring them, he reached over the rail for Sydney's hand. "I dare you to find humor in your current position." Mud caked her hair and splattered her face, yet she grabbed his hand with a beaming smile.

"I have no one to blame but myself. The big one distracted me when he bullied Princess."

Tyler chuckled. "You named her?"

Sydney shrugged, climbed over the railing and hopped down. "Sure, why not. Thanks for the hand, boss." She flipped Caden one of her cheeky grins, leaving him itching to spank her mud-caked butt as she sauntered up to the house.

Turning to his other employees, he growled, "Get back to work."

Sydney was driving him fucking nuts, Caden groused when he found himself searching for her again the next day. If he didn't fear the hands would stage a walkout, he'd fire her and wash his hands of her. Unfortunately, she'd had the gall to endear each and every one of his hired help to her with home-made breads, fantastic meals and an array of baked sweets that had the guys practically eating out of her hand. So, that option was out, no matter how much she continued to burrow under his skin.

She'd treated the lost, fence-snagging incident on Monday as a fun adventure, drawing smiles from the guys and adding to Caden's frustration over a growing attraction he couldn't get a handle on. Yesterday, when she'd grinned up at him with that irrepressible smile stretching her mud-splattered face, he'd struggled with an urge to either kiss her or toss her over his knee. Thank goodness she had walked away before he could do either.

Now, he and Connor were once again out looking for her after no one could find her by late afternoon. "I swear, if she's wandered into a field again, she'll have trouble sitting tomorrow."

His damn brother had the gall to laugh at that threat. "Be careful. She may end up liking your discipline enough to egg her on instead of deterring her."

"There is that, isn't there?" What the hell was it about the woman he couldn't get a handle on? In all his thirty-nine years, he'd never experienced such a constant pull for one woman, and wouldn't you know it? It would have to be for an off-limits employee with a penchant for suspicious evasiveness.

A few minutes later, Connor slowed and pointed east across a field. "There she is. What is she doing?"

Spotting her, Caden's blood ran cold as he swore, "Un-fucking believable!" Spurring Ranger into a gallop, he prayed he reached the idiot girl before one of their orneriest bulls followed through with his hoof-pawing threat and charged her. Why the hell did she just stand there with her hand out? "Head him off," he shouted to Connor.

"UH, OH." Sydney took her eyes off the enormous cow that didn't look happy with her and cast a quick glance toward the sound of approaching riders. She winced when she recognized the Dunbar brothers coming to her rescue. Caden was not going to be happy with her. Again.

Was it her fault she'd been daydreaming about her boss and ended up completely turned around? No, her mistake was in thinking she could just retrace her steps and find herself close to the house. Oops. The 'bigger than life' cow had charged out of nowhere, snorting his displeasure and shaking his massive head at her as if to say, how dare you tread on my turf! He couldn't even be bribed into a friendlier attitude with a sugar cube she'd been saving for Daisy, the little mare she'd grown fond of.

Thank goodness her cowboys knew what they were doing. Caden came trotting up behind her while Connor rode between her and the cranky cow, his horse herding the heifer away from them as Caden leaned over and scooped her up with one hard arm around her waist. Her relief at their timely rescue changed to startled, breath-stopping unease when she found herself lying face-down in front of him and the grassy ground shifting in dizzying circles below her.

Before she could get her bearings, he swatted her wiggling backside hard enough to feel the discomfort and burn through her jeans. "What... *oh!*" The next smack cut off her complaint, the dull ache and warmth spreading to her quivering pussy rendering her mute with astonishment.

"I'm spanking some sense into you," Caden growled, delivering one more slap before shifting her upright and leaving her sitting sideways as he nudged his horse back into a trot.

Sydney was too stunned from her body's response to what should have been a humiliating set-down to wonder much what Connor meant when he pulled alongside them and, after one look at her face, called over with humor lacing his voice, "I think you lost that gamble, brother."

The rumble of Caden's low-voiced swearing vibrated against her shivering frame, and she enjoyed his frustration as much as she was shocked by the low-level arousal those few swats generated. She couldn't even find it in her to be embarrassed from Connor witnessing his brother's actions. With a wave, Connor took off ahead of them and Sydney braved a look up at her boss' handsome, rugged face, exasperation swirling in his cobalt eyes.

"I can explain," she offered.

"Really. How?" he mocked.

"I intended to stay within sight of the barns, but... got distracted and then turned around." She wasn't about to tell him she'd been fantasizing about being spanked and then fucked by him. He may fire her over such an infraction. As much as she missed her family, she was stuck here until she came up with a plan to return home and keep Uncle Mike and his desperate actions from hurting her grandmother and uncles.

"And, why didn't you call this time?"

She looked away from those probing eyes that saw too much. Her lack of funds didn't allow for her to add minutes to the pre-paid cell phone she'd been using since fleeing Missouri. She couldn't reveal that without raising his suspicions about her even more than her refusal to tell him why she didn't have insurance to charge for the medical bill the other day.

"I don't carry it with me around the ranch." She shrugged. "I didn't think I needed to."

"And now you know otherwise. You're disrupting my work

with your irresponsibility," he chastised her as they neared the barns.

"If you would teach me to ride, like you promised, I would have something to do in the afternoons," she argued in defense despite finding it difficult to concentrate on what he was saying while being held snug against him, his cock pressed against her thigh, her butt still tingling from those swats. Even the girls were on board, her nipples puckering into tight nubs.

"Maybe I'd have time if I wasn't constantly riding to your rescue." Caden dismounted at the barn and lifted her down. With his hat pulled low over his forehead, she could barely see his eyes, but his tight jaw told her she shouldn't risk pushing him further today.

"I should see to dinner. Thanks for the ride, boss." Her buttocks clenched when she felt his eyes on her as she strode across the lawn to the house, making her wonder what her response would be if he were to slap her bare butt. Just the thought drew a shiver down her spine and a heated throb between her legs. She bemoaned the desperate state stress and loneliness forced on her and despaired ever getting out of.

Sydney spent that evening making thick sandwiches the ranch hands could pack in their saddlebags the next day after Caden informed her most of them would be out on the range all day. After waving them off this morning, she'd grown unsettled with the stillness. She didn't even have the dogs to keep her company. By the time the noon hour rolled around, and she still found herself at odds with her melancholy and itching to get away, she hopped in her car and drove all the way into Billings, using gas she could ill afford to use before payday and spent the last of her cash on lunch, a sexy romance novel and ten minutes on her cell phone.

She returned to the ranch broke, full and eager to hear her grandmother's voice. But after using up her entire airtime and listening to Nana's tearful questions about when she'd be home, she didn't feel any better. Pulling her jacket on, she stepped outside intending to visit Daisy when she heard a high-pitched neighing coming from the far side of the barn. Rounding the corner, she saw an aggressive stallion and shy mare in the rear corral, the pair dancing around each other with tails held high. Out of the corner of her eye, she spotted one of the older ranch hands inside the stables, tossing down bales of hay from the loft, and felt better knowing someone else was near. The horses continued to prance around each other, nipping at each other with their large teeth, their sexual organs swollen and needy. When the stallion mounted the mare from behind, Sydney gasped and flushed from the sheer dominance of the larger animal.

Leaning her arms on the rail, she couldn't look away from the carnality of the mating ritual between the two equines. The large male sank his teeth into the little mare's neck while bucking against her hindquarters. She responded to his aggression by tossing her head and shifting on restless legs as he took her with pounding intensity. Sydney couldn't help but picture Caden fucking her in much the same way, taking her with ruthless possession, his pistoning cock bringing her to climax over and over. She shuddered at the image in her head, her body breaking out in a sweat despite the cool afternoon temperature, her nipples and sheath tightening with pent-up lust.

"I really need to get laid," she muttered, turning away from the now prancing horses, both animals looking quite pleased with themselves.

"THERE'S no telling what the damn woman will get into today with almost everyone out in the pastures," Caden grumbled to Connor as they rode through the east pasture looking for strays. They were slowly making their way through the grazing fields, herding cattle closer to the homestead before the winter months bogged them down with snow.

Connor chuckled, tipped his hat back and looked over at him. "I think you like her. I know damn well you want her."

"What's your point?" No sense in denying the obvious.

"Just saying. Oh, shit." Connor's gaze had shifted over Caden's shoulder, and he knew his brother had a clear, long-distance view of the barns and corrals. "She wouldn't, would she?"

"What?" Whipping his head around, Caden spotted Sydney's bright red hair where she stood perched up on yet another rail, this one around the horse corral. Saddled and tethered in front of her, stood one of their bad-tempered saddle horses that refused to let anyone sit on him. "Fuck if she wouldn't. She's been pestering me to give her a riding lesson, but I haven't had time. Come on."

Spurring their horses, they both knew they'd never arrive in time to stop her and fear for her safety lodged in Caden's throat, nearly strangling him.

SYDNEY RAN her hand down the silky nose of the black horse, receiving a soft nudge in return. "Well, you're friendly, aren't you?" The afternoon hadn't improved, ending another day on the job that hadn't gone smoothly. She blamed Caden for that. For some, inexplicable reason, she'd set her sights on her boss and couldn't seem to look elsewhere or keep her mind off him. She wouldn't have gotten so turned around on her walks if she hadn't been fantasizing about Caden tying her to that padded cross she'd seen in the loft of their club and doing whatever he wanted to her vulnerable body, or picturing herself over his lap, her bare butt on display in front of all those strangers as he smacked her cheeks. The small neck bite he'd given her the other night stung just enough to breathe life into her imagination, and coupled with those swats the other day, filled the last few nights with erotic dreams that woke her shaking for a whole different reason than the previous nightmare.

Her latest mishaps did nothing to endear her in his eyes as his continued refusal to teach her to ride proved, and she was so put out by that, not to mention bored and lonely, she developed the sudden urge to take the matter into her own hands. "The heck with waiting for him," she told the horse, throwing caution to the wind. Worst-case scenario-he paid her the wages she'd earned and then fired her. Ignoring the pang that possibility stirred in her gut, she checked to be sure the saddle was cinched, something she'd seen the hands doing. "You're already saddled, so you must be okay to ride. Now," she cautioned the horse as she swung a leg over the rail, "be nice. I'm a newbie." Stepping on the bench inside the corral, she grabbed the pommel and lifted one leg over the saddle, the sudden shift of the horse's hooves catching her off guard. "Whoa, mister." Sydney soothed him with a hand down his quivering neck and when he settled, reached in front to untie the reins, missing the comforting feel of Caden's big body behind her. "Well, this isn't so hard," she boasted, trying to convince herself as the horse turned on its own. He'd only taken two steps before startling her by lifting his head with a loud neigh followed by a body-tossing buck of his hindquarters. Loud, male shouts reached past the roaring in her ears as she went flying then landed with a body-jarring thud.

Blinking her eyes against looking up into the glaring sun, Sydney struggled to catch her breath while testing to make sure she could move her legs. Relief swept through her before trepidation took its place when Caden's big frame appeared in front of her, blocking the warmth from the sun.

Stooping, he ran his hands over her body, checking for broken bones. Sydney would've enjoyed his impersonal touch more if it weren't for the rigid set to his jaw and his nerve-racking silence. Satisfied, he pushed to his feet and reached out a hand to help her stand. "Do you hurt anywhere?" he asked in the quietest, calmest voice she'd ever heard him use with her, one that didn't bode well for her immediate future.

"Just my pride." Hoping to defuse any repercussions, she quipped with a teasing grin, "I gotta tell you, boss, that toss was kind of fun, flying like that, but the landing leaves a lot to be desired."

Those blue eyes stayed on her as he brushed her off with gentle swipes, lingering on her backside long enough to have Sydney's toes curling inside her sneakers. "Can you take care of Ranger, Connor, while I have a word with Sydney up at the house?"

"Of course. You should've waited for someone to help you pick a mount, Sydney," he admonished, and she cringed at the censure she'd never heard in Connor's tone.

"I…"

"Quiet."

Caden's cold, demanding voice accompanied his tightening grip on her hand. Wariness mixed with excitement as he led her across the yard. "I don't have time to keep bailing you out of trouble. You were told, repeatedly, not to attempt to ride without me."

Miffed, she glared at his back as they entered the house. "I never told you to take time away from work to come to my aid. There's always someone in the barn…"

He spun around so fast, Sydney stumbled back a step and would've fallen if he hadn't yanked her forward to land against his rock-solid body. "Do not speak to me of my ranch hands. It's bad enough you spoil the dogs, now I have to contend with those kids following you around, drooling, which they were not here to do when you just pulled that foolhardy stunt."

A pleased smile split her face. "Do they really? *Aww*, that's sweet."

Caden gritted his teeth. "No, it's not, and neither are the consequences I warned you about for breaking the rules."

Before she realized his intentions, he hauled her into the den, had her jeans unsnapped and shoved down with a few quick movements, and yanked her over his lap as he sat on the sofa. Both startled and thrilled, Sydney reared her head up, shoved her hair out of her eyes and asked him in a tone a lot calmer than her racing heartbeat, "Do you know what you're doing?" She prayed he said yes because the exposure of her bare butt under his heated gaze was enough to fill her pussy with moisture, to bead her nipples into tight pinpoints and to send her blood flowing through her veins in a hot, molten rush. And that was before he rested one wide, callused palm on the rounded curve of her bottom.

"I disciplined my first sub fifteen years ago when I was only a few years older than the employees you have eating out of your hands. What do you think?"

Throwing caution to the wind, in for a penny, in for a pound and all that, she tossed back, "Okay, then do your worst."

THE CHEEKY GRIN Sydney flipped Caden shouldn't have surprised him, or her easy compliance when she turned her head back down and waited for his retribution. Had she kicked and screamed for him to let her go, he would've done so, but when had the girl reacted as he thought she should? Knowing it was a mistake and may very well end up crossing a line he couldn't cross back over, he swatted her right buttock, the red imprint he left behind showing with vivid brightness against her lily-white skin. The terror that sent him speeding down to the corral wouldn't abate, his mind still reeling from all the injuries she could've sustained with that foolhardy stunt. He spanked her other cheek and enjoyed the bounce of the soft globe and her shifting hips way too much. "Had enough?" he asked, rubbing his hand over the warm, smooth flesh.

"Would you stop if we were at The Barn and I was your sub?" she returned with a slight catch in her voice.

"Hell, no." He refused to lie even if doing so would be in his best interest.

"Then pretend I am and don't stop… *please.*"

He sighed, her whispered plea sealing both their fates. "Remember, I warned you to be careful about what you ask for." Caden proceeded to give her what she thought she wanted ever since he'd caught her spying and caved to what he'd been itching to do.

With a volley of sharp smacks, he peppered Sydney's ass until the pink tinge turned a deep red, her warm skin grew hot and her quiet mewls erupted into louder cries. She shifted with a moan when he stopped to rub the abused mounds. After soothing the sting, he gave her time to adjust to the soreness by palming the plump curve of one crimson cheek. She had a perfect shaped ass with soft, malleable buttocks that had clenched with each spank then softened as she adjusted to the pain. Then she shifted again, lifting into his hand, and he barely heard another whispered entreaty of *'please'* that drew his eyes to her glistening seam. "You continue to surprise me, darlin'."

Sydney whipped her face around, shaking her hair out of her drenched eyes. "Does that mean…"

Caden squeezed her buttock and drew a yelp from her by delivering a final, blistering swat. "You're new to this and don't realize how sore you'll be. Sit up." Her face mirrored the color of her ass, but it was the blatant need reflected in her dilated eyes that tempted him to change the tone of this lesson and reward her, and that would not do. His actions were meant as a deterrent, not a pleasurable interlude. "Next time you disobey a rule, you'll get a taste of my belt." Ignoring the desire to sink his fingers between those enticing, plump, damp folds, he stood her up and pulled up her panties and jeans. Standing, he lowered his Stetson and headed to the door, saying without looking back, "I have work to do."

Connor stood waiting for him by the corral when he stepped outside, a knowing grin playing around his mouth as he handed Caden the reins to his steed. "Not a word, got it?" Caden snapped in warning.

"Wouldn't dream of it, brother."

Chapter 4

Sydney stood rooted by the sofa, her body humming with unfulfilled arousal as she watched Caden saunter out. Squeezing her thighs together, she tried to still the heated pulses between her legs that mimicked the lingering, warm throbbing encompassing her butt. Nothing could have prepared her for the surprising pleasure/pain of her first, bare-butt spanking, or the longing she'd felt for him to increase after his erotic abuse. There'd been a certain intimacy to lying over his lap with only her bottom exposed. The rough abrasion of his hard, denim covered thighs against her soft abdomen added to the exciting strength of his control; the roughness of his leathery palm connecting with stinging force against her cheeks demonstrated who had the upper hand and who was the boss, and she liked it.

Shaking her head at her own foolish mistake that had inadvertently given her what she'd been pining for, Caden's hands on her, she wondered where they would go from here. Somehow, she doubted this meant he'd have a change of heart and would allow her into his club, but hope springs eternal, and all that. She'd just have to keep working on him until he caved, or fired her, whichever came first. Heading to the kitchen to start dinner, she shied away from delving into the reason behind the way her heart contracted from that last thought.

The next morning, Sydney rolled over in bed, the slight pressure on her tender backside tickling her with a frisson of pleasure. Shaking her head at the unaccustomed responses still making themselves known, she padded into the bathroom, cooled her heated cheeks with a splash of cold water and winced as she pulled her jeans up over her butt. "It's going to be a long day," she muttered, brushing out her hair before strolling into the kitchen to whip up breakfast.

She had just poured the eggs into a frying pan when Caden beat any of the others inside. "Almost ready," she tossed over her shoulder, wishing her pulse rate wouldn't kick up every time he looked at her with that intense, probing stare. "What?" Wariness colored her voice.

"I wanted to check on you before anyone else came in." Striding across the tiled floor to stand in front of her at the stove, he lifted her chin with two fingers. "Are you okay this morning?"

"Are you inquiring about my fall from the horse or your punishment for that infraction?" she asked dryly.

"Both and be honest."

The nearness of his tall, imposing body unnerved her, in a wholly good way. She turned back to the eggs, stirring them as she assured him, "I'm fine, boss. Thank you for asking."

"Good," he replied.

She felt his pause and then heard him sigh before he moved away as the door opened, and several others tromped inside. With a mental headshake, Sydney finished putting breakfast on the table, wishing she could figure out what made her rancher tick.

That evening, she stood at the kitchen sink again, rinsing dishes and fighting back frustration and a sweep of overwhelming despair. Caden had spent the entire day either keeping his distance or treating her with aloof politeness, the same as any boss would behave toward an employee, damn it. Every step she'd taken today, every time she'd sat down, the lingering soreness from his spanking had made itself known and her sheath still wept in response. Her agitated, needy state didn't faze him however, since, after the hands left the house following dinner, he wouldn't even discuss allowing her to visit the club tonight. Instead, she watched him walk out with Connor without a word after getting called to the barn on an emergency birth.

"Stubborn, frigging moron," she muttered, snapping off the faucet.

"More like a fucking ass," Connor injected from behind her, surprising her with his return. "You know, Sydney, I'm equal partners in the club."

Whirling, she gaped at him before a slow smile stretched her cheeks. "You are?"

He nodded, returning her grin. "I am, and I say you're welcome to attend as a guest tonight. I'll let the other Doms know you're there to observe first, and that you're a newbie. You can take it as far as you'd like. But I suggest we leave before big brother gets wind of it. It won't take him long to tend to that birthing."

Tossing the towel on the counter, she threw her arms around Connor and hugged him tight. "I can be ready in a few minutes. Don't leave without me."

"Since I don't want to spend a good portion of the night looking for you, I'll give you five minutes. After that, offer's off the table."

She heard him chuckle as she dashed into her room. Changing into a skirt and low-cut, long-sleeved tee, she met him at his idling truck with time to spare. "Made it!" she exclaimed, tossing her hair back and slamming the door with a quick glance toward the barn.

"So, you did. Caden's still tied up out there, but let's hope he doesn't take a strip off both our hides when he shows up at the club."

THE BARN, as they'd named the club, proved to be even more pulse-pounding exciting inside than it had been watching from the window. Sydney figured there were around thirty people gathered on the first floor when she and Connor entered, with several others already up in the loft, enjoying the BDSM equipment she'd only gotten a glimpse of last week. Connor handed her a one-night punch card for her two-drink limit then led her over to the bar and introduced her to the drop-dead gorgeous man eyeing her with piercing grey-green eyes filled with speculative interest, a toothpick dangling from the corner of his mouth.

"Grayson, this is our new cook and my guest tonight, Sydney Baker. Sweetie, Grayson is Willow Springs' sheriff and the third owner of the club."

"Nice to meet you, Sheriff." Sydney held out her hand, surprised at the warm tingle his grip elicited. She put her reaction down to a normal response, given her long celibacy followed by her frustrating, unrequited lust for her boss this past week.

"The pleasure's mine, Sydney. Have you taken a tour yet?"

"No, but I think I'll stick to this level for now." She glanced toward the dance floor, noting a few, bouncing bare breasts before scanning the rest of the spacious room. Her face warmed as she caught sight of a woman slipping to her knees, her hands and mouth reaching for the jutting cock of the man standing before her. "Then again," she stated with a rueful grin, "down here may not be any tamer than the loft for a newbie like me."

The midnight-haired sheriff winked and drawled, "Trust me, sugar, upstairs, any Dom here can take you much further." He stood to his impressive height of six-four and clasped her hand. "Connor, if you don't mind, I'd like to dance with your guest."

"Feel free." He looked from Grayson to her. "Sydney, the only thing you need to remember tonight is that red is the club's safeword. Say it, and whatever is happening will stop immediately, including something innocent like dancing."

From the little she'd seen, even dancing wasn't so innocent, but Sydney nodded, too thrilled with the sheriff's attention after a week of pining for a man who wanted nothing to do with her outside her job to wonder if she was in over her head. "Got it, thanks."

CADEN ENTERED the club in a pissy mood. As if the memory of a world-class ass with soft, malleable buttocks that reddened to a beautiful hue under his hand wasn't enough of a burden the past twenty-four hours, he'd also developed another bout of guilt to contend with. The thought of leaving Sydney alone for another long night kept biting at his ass during the difficult breech delivery of a calf. When he'd returned to the house intending to offer to stay home with her and found her gone, his first thought was she'd gotten herself lost again. A quick call to Connor had set his mind at ease over that possibility but hearing his brother mention her whereabouts took his mood from tepid to boiling in the blink of an eye, effectively erasing the guilt.

He spotted her bright, waist-length hair across the room, her slim body swaying too damn close to her partner, keeping perfect time with the upbeat country western song. Stomping over to the bar, he ignored the questioning looks from friends and glared at Connor across the bar top. "Explain."

Grayson, whom he hadn't noticed sitting on the stool next to him, slapped him on the back none too gently. "Lighten up. We're keeping an eye on her. She's having fun and is a damn good dancer for a city girl."

Connor shrugged, just as unperturbed over Caden's anger as

Grayson. "I have every right to invite a guest and don't need your permission."

"Fuck." Running a hand through his hair, he looked over at Sydney again and had to admit they were right. His gut tightened when she laughed up at Dan, a long-time friend and member, her green eyes alight with pleasure. The tight band of her skirt hugged her slim hips before flaring out around her thighs, her twirls revealing creamy, soft flesh he itched to touch again. Small breasts swayed braless under the cotton tee, and his eyes weren't the only ones enjoying the rigid outline of pert nipples.

"How long are you going to sit there stewing?" Connor asked him.

Ceding to the inevitable, Caden dragged his eyes from Sydney to his conniving brother. "Your turn is coming. Don't forget that. You too," he included his best friend, Grayson, before turning his back on their smirks.

Nudging his way onto the dance floor, he tapped Dan's shoulder. "My turn with our guest," he stated without giving the other man a choice. Thankfully, Dan was a good sport and nodded with a small grin curling the corners of his mouth.

"No problem, Caden. Thanks, Syd." Dan bent and kissed her on the mouth before sauntering toward the bar.

Moving in, Caden drew Sydney next to him, enjoying the way the quick flare of ire in her eyes changed to a gleam of excitement as he pressed her close. "Someone should've warned you of the consequences of playing with fire, darlin'."

"Oh, they did, but I found getting singed could sometimes be worth it, for the right reason," she returned with a smug look.

The brush of those pert nipples against his chest turned out to be a good example of getting singed, Caden thought. He could swear the turgid tips left imprints on his chest when she shifted away.

"Yes, but that doesn't negate the higher risk of getting a

third-degree burn." That saucy smile prompted him to make a snap decision and try to thwart her persistent come-ons with a harsher taste of what she thought she wanted from him. The spanking yesterday seemed to have done nothing but spur her on. Knowing his luck, this may not work either, but he'd be damned if he'd stand by all night and watch her flirt with others. He would save questioning the prick of jealousy that poked him when he saw her with Dan for later.

Grabbing her hands, Caden drew them behind her, cuffed her wrists together in one of his hands and hauled her tighter against his gyrating pelvis. He ground his thick erection against her mound, watched her eyes widen and eyed the rapid beat of her pulse in her neck with relish. His little cook wasn't as sure of herself as she let on.

Bending down, he ghosted his lips over hers, whispering, "You want to play with me, Sydney?"

SYDNEY SHIVERED from the unexpected light brush of Caden's mouth, the warning in his tone bumping up the heat pulsing in her sheath. She liked the tight clasp of his hand around her wrists, the way the restraint bound her to him, stripped her of choice and gave him complete control. "Yes, I mean... all I know is I can't stop thinking about..." *Wanting you.* "Hell, Caden, I don't know, but I want to give it a try."

The resigned look crossing his sun-bronzed face was not flattering, but she'd take what she could get as he ground out, "Then come upstairs, and we'll see if you can take what I like to dish out, and we'll both know, one way or another."

He brought her hands in front and kept a tight hold of both as he tugged her along behind him toward the stairs and then up. The sense of urgency he displayed would thrill her if she didn't think his sole intention was to drive her away rather than introduce her to the pleasures he indulged in. She was getting good at shoving aside the pangs of hurt he caused her.

The dim lighting in the loft cast eerie shadows around the space, but Sydney could still get a clear picture of various apparatus scattered around and barely make out the row of spanking implements hanging on the far wall, some of which drew a frisson of unease down her spine. The faint strands of music were over-ridden by the sounds of leather-slapping flesh and high-pitched cries from either pain or pleasure, or both. Caden didn't give her time to gawk at the scenes taking place as he led her over to what looked like a gymnastics vault until she got close enough to see the thick dildo attached in the middle.

Stumbling to a halt, she tugged on her hands. "Uh, what…"

Turning, he drilled her in place with his vivid gaze. "You've been pestering me for a riding lesson, haven't you?" he reminded her with a slow lift of one brow before commanding without pause, "Strip."

She struggled to swallow past the sudden lump constricting her throat as she glanced around to see if anyone watched. "On this?" She waved to the vault. "Just like that, huh?"

He nodded and crossed his arms. It was the 'I told you so' confident smirk on his face that galvanized her into action. Moving fast, she shimmied out of the skirt, whipped her top over her head and toed off her shoes. Standing in just a pair of bikini panties, Sydney swore she could feel the heat of his blue gaze seeping through her skin. Her nipples puckered under his intense regard and her pussy warmed and swelled, reactions she was starting to get used to. God help her, but she wanted him any way she could get him.

Waving his fingers, he cocked his head, asking, "Do you need help with those?"

"No." Sydney slid the last barrier to complete nudity off and then gasped when he clasped her waist and lifted her astride the wide, padded vault.

"It's called a Sybian." After placing her feet in stirrups on the sides, Caden wrapped her hands around the pommel set a few inches in front of the long, wide dildo that was giving her heart palpitations. "I'll leave your hands free since you're new at this." The light brush of his callused fingers up her slit drew a full-body shudder as he nodded and then grasped her hips and lifted her, leaving her little choice but to lower onto the phallus or say the safeword.

A low groan spilled past Sydney's compressed lips as the sheathed, lubed toy speared her vagina, stretching the under-used muscles until she sat with it fully embedded. She tossed him a look of triumph he cut short with the flick of a side switch and a sardonic curl of his mouth.

"Oh!" The slow roll of the Sybian accompanied small vibrations against the long-neglected, ultra-sensitive nerve endings deep inside her. Sydney was so intent on concentrating on rocking with the apparatus and dealing with the fast spiral of arousal curling up through her pussy, she didn't notice Caden retrieving a slim rod from underneath, or the square, silicone slapper attached on the end until he snapped it against one buttock. The immediate sting snagged her attention and her eyes flew to his.

"Either ride or say the safeword. Those are your two choices. Anything else will earn you a punishment I guarantee you won't enjoy." He flicked his wrist and struck her other cheek, the sudden burn fueling her lust and whipping her into a frenzy of need that outweighed the urge to kick out at his smug look.

Pressing down with her feet, she rose with the forward sway of the machine and lowered when it righted itself. Closing her eyes, she pictured herself astride Caden's wide body, pretended it was his cock she gyrated on with increasing vigor, his hair-rough-ened thighs against her softer ones as she gripped his sides tight. A few more strikes peppered her buttocks, the painful heat spurring her on until he switched and shocked her by blistering her right nipple with a snap of the rubber square.

"*Ow!*" Reaching up with one hand, she cast him a reproving look while rubbing the abused tip. Too bad her indignation fell flat when the throbbing, painful burn executed a straight beeline south to take up residence between her legs, the added pleasure spurred on by her hand caressing her nipple.

"Do you have anything else to say or are you ready to continue?" he drawled, one corner of his mouth kicking up in a taunting smirk.

Sydney returned her hand to grip the pommel and gave in to his mastery and the need rippling around the ridged toy filling her. "Do your worst, boss. I can take it." At least, she prayed she could.

Shaking his head, he delivered a strike onto her left nipple, but this time she was prepared for the bite, and for the heated streak of pleasure. She closed her eyes again, this time against the cobalt blue of his knowing gaze and rode the dildo for all its worth. If he wanted a show, she'd give him one, and get a little payback along with her pleasure in return.

She shivered as the thick phallus abraded her slick, swollen tissues and her inner muscles clamped around the toy. Pushing down with her feet again, she dragged her pussy up the pulsating, silicone cock, moaning as she contracted around it with the slow glide over her clit. Arching her head back, she lowered once more, feeling the stretch and burn, glorying in the fiery pleasure. The clit rasping up and downs were accompanied by snaps of the spanker back and forth between her breasts and buttocks, leaving behind the most delicious zing of pain/pleasure.

Unable to hold back any longer, Sydney gasped, arching her sweat-slick body and grinding down on the fake cock with all the finesse of a panting bitch in heat. Her body bucked under the onslaught of pleasure coiling up through her core with the vibrator's increased pulsations. Muscles spasmed, her juices seeping around the intruding phallus to pool on the seat as her sheath convulsed with rhythmic pulses. Her cry reverberated around the room, but she kept her eyes closed, basking in the release that soaked her mind as well as her body, through it all, conscious of Caden's eyes on her.

CADEN'S MOUTH went dry watching Sydney splinter apart, her soft, glistening body undulating on the Sybian a sight to behold, guaranteed to drive a man to his knees with lust. Tight nipples thrust up, begging for a touch, the areola puckered around them, giving away her heightened state of excitement the cream coating her slippery folds confirmed. Her labia wrapped around the dildo like a loving glove, and he couldn't look away as her body clutched at the toy with tight grips meant to contain both the vibrator and the pleasure. Her abdominals quivered as she strained for release and he succumbed to the urge to touch, lightly tapping on her mons pubis with the slapper while strumming one turgid nipple with his finger.

By the time he shut off the vibrator and the machine and watched her come down from the high by slow degrees of awareness, he wasn't sure who won this round. All he knew for certain was it wasn't him, not when his cock remained a steel rod of discomfort in his pants and he refused to bury himself between her slick folds and allow her fiery heat to take him up in flames. Even if her responses to his control were every Dom's fucking dream.

Setting aside his own need to see to Sydney's well-being after such an intense experience, Caden lifted her perspiration-slick, quivering body into his arms and carried her over to a chair nestled in a corner. Without talking, he cuddled her on his lap, stroking her damp hair back, running his hands over her soft skin as he gave her time to work through what she was feeling. For him, he would need more than these few moments of aftercare.

His brother had a lot to answer for, but could he honestly blame Connor for the riot of emotions Caden couldn't get under control? Only two things had become clear as a bell tonight; he couldn't continue to straddle the line between employer/employee and Dom/sub. And he couldn't let her go.

SYDNEY SNATCHED her purse off the hook by the front door and skipped out into the crisp afternoon. Bounding down the steps, the dogs came loping toward her. She smiled at their eager welcome and stooped to feed them the leftover bacon and sausage from breakfast. Too bad she didn't see or hear Caden come up behind her until his deep voice revealed his frustration with her continued spoiling of the collies.

"Sydney."

Spinning on her heels, she shielded her eyes and looked up at him, catching the glimmer of amusement in his eyes despite being shaded by the low brim of his hat. "You're not mad," she accused, pushing to her feet. "It's just a few meat scraps. See, they're back to work already."

They both watched the dogs answer a call from a hand on horseback before Caden noticed her purse. "Where are you off to?"

"Willow Springs, and get that look off your face," she chided. "I know my way there and back. I didn't find whole fryers in either the mess hall's freezer or yours and the guys have been asking for chicken and dumplings."

He nodded toward the chicken coop attached to the horse barn. "Give me a few minutes and I'll save you a trip. How many do you need?"

Sydney stiffened with a wave of incredulity at his suggestion.

Indignant, she fisted her hands on her hips and sputtered, "We are *so* not eating Clara or Betty or Tandy..." He closed his eyes and his lips moved but nothing came out. Cocking her head, she asked blandly, "Are you counting?"

"It's either that or wring *your* neck. You've named the damn hens? Please tell me you haven't been making nice with the chickens like you have the dogs." He tipped his hat back and his eyes held the same disbelieving surprise she'd felt riding the Sybian at his command, only now there was also a hint of humor tugging at his mouth.

"Well, I couldn't very well keep calling them 'hey you', now could I? And all I've been doing is tossing them some of the rotting vegetables from the garden. Besides, *my* meat comes already dead, plucked and ready to cook. Later, boss." With a small finger wave, she strolled to her car, feeling the heat of his gaze through her jacket.

Last Saturday, Caden, Connor and the weekend hands had been called away from the ranch on an emergency involving a lost herd and hadn't returned until sometime after midnight. Part of Sydney had been relieved at the call of duty that kept Caden from going to the club that night, but his attitude toward her hadn't thawed a whole lot since he'd seen her naked and his orders had driven her to a height of ecstasy she'd never achieved with anyone else. A few times in the past five days, she'd caught him looking at her with an expression that brought on a heated rush through her veins that compelled her girly parts to sit up and beg for attention. Just from him. But he'd covered it quickly and treated her with the same friendly indifference as he did all his employees, damn it.

Still, those few looks were enough to inspire a thread of hope he would come around in two days and ask her back to the club himself. If not, she wouldn't be above cajoling another invite from Connor. She'd enjoyed dancing last weekend, flirting with the men who all bore the same dominant air about them that tickled her in more ways than one. Just socializing had helped dispel the loneliness she'd lived with the past few weeks. The weekly calls she'd been making to her grandmother were both difficult and heartwarming. She loved hearing Nana's voice and catching up on what her cousins, aunts and uncles were doing. But they always ended with nostalgia pulling her down, and an ache for her world to be put to rights.

Driving down the highway toward the small town of Willow Springs, she pulled up the few memories she could still recall about her mother. Sydney had only been eight-years-old when Nana's only daughter died from an undiagnosed aneurysm, leaving her grandparents and her devastated. She'd never known her father, and no one spoke of him. That had been fine with her; she had everything she wanted with her mom, and afterward her grandmother and two oldest uncles did everything in their power to keep her happy and well-grounded. Only Uncle Mike, the youngest and most spoiled of Nana's four children, never bothered with her, always too busy with his self-centered life to mess with a young, clinging niece who lived in fear of losing someone else.

"Be careful what you wish for," she mumbled, pulling into a parking space in front of the only grocery in town. When Uncle Mike finally got around to paying attention to her, she'd found out it had only been for his own, selfish purposes. She didn't know how much longer she could keep the truth from the rest of the family as they kept threatening to track her down and drag her home. But until she figured out a way to prevent hurting her grandmother with the news of Mike's attack on her, she would continue to struggle with balancing her growing fondness for her temporary new life with the longing for home and loved ones.

Winding her way through the aisles of the small, family-owned grocery, Sydney filled the cart with items lacking in both kitchens at the ranch, smiling inside as she imagined Caden's face when she showed him the receipt for the amount she would put on his account. Then again, he didn't appear to be struggling financially, so maybe it wouldn't faze him. She was trying to think of another way to get under her rancher's skin when a man stepped in front of her, his sudden appearance bringing her to an abrupt halt with a hand braced on her cart. His hold prevented her from moving and the cold look in his dark eyes sent a ripple of unease slithering under her skin.

"Excuse me," she said in a polite tone, wondering what his problem was.

"I have a message for you, Ms. Greenbriar. Go home, or else."

The wave of apprehension turned into cold dread as she stared at the stranger who not only knew her real name, but just threatened her. "Who... who are you?" she whispered past the tightness of her throat.

"An associate of your uncle's. Unless you want to be responsible for what happens if you don't heed my warning, I suggest you get on the road soon." Tipping his hat in mock politeness, he walked away without a backward glance.

Sydney stood rooted in disbelief, her hands shaking, her abdomen cramped with fear. What did he mean by 'what happens'? Her blood turned to ice in her veins as she stood there in indecision. He'd have trouble getting to her on the ranch; there were always men about, and rifles in all of their trucks. Surely that alone would be enough to keep her safe from the stranger's cryptic remarks. God help her, she just realized how much she longed for more time at her temporary home. The thought of leaving Caden and the friends she'd made brought an unaccustomed ache to her chest. The stranger didn't know it but delivering the threat from her uncle only reinforced her belief she couldn't return home yet. Besides, if she left, where would she go?

With fear and despair clawing at her insides, she struggled to make her way to the checkout, stopping just once more to toss a six pack in the cart. So engrossed with her thoughts and the over-whelming decision she needed to make, she didn't see the sheriff entering the grocery as she headed out.

Clutching the two heavy bags with her head down, Sydney ran into Grayson, recognizing his deep voice when he grabbed her arms to steady her. "Whoa there. Let me take one of those for you. Sydney, right?"

Startled, her eyes flew to his face, and she cringed at the sharp look he gave her followed by the slow removal of the tooth-pick in his mouth. "Are you okay?"

"I… yes, fine. I'm sorry, I wasn't watching where I was going." She cast a frantic look down the street but didn't see the man who turned her inside out with a few words. "Thanks, but I'm parked right there, so I can get these."

"I'll get your door." His tone, so much like Caden's, didn't leave room for argument.

Sydney set the bags on the back seat then schooled her features into a bland expression before facing his assessing gaze again. "Thank you, Sheriff. It's nice to see you again."

He nodded, his gaze remaining keen despite the small smile softening his hard face. "I hope you'll join us at The Barn again tomorrow night. Have a good day, Sydney."

Oh God. The longing to return to the club with Caden shook her. Gripping the steering wheel with damp palms, she struggled with her decision all the way back to the ranch, weighing the need to stay a little longer, to cajole a few more exciting memories from her rancher before she went back to being alone with keeping him in the dark about her problems. Never in a million years could she have guessed Mike would stoop this low, not even after he'd drugged her and tried forcing her signature. She should have known the happiness starting to blossom wouldn't last.

Sydney drove home in a state of turmoil and indecision. If Uncle Mike was desperate enough to send someone after her, would he go so far as to instruct his henchman to act on his threats? He had sworn he hadn't planned on physically harming her in any way the night he showed up at her apartment and tried to force her signature, but that was weeks ago, and she didn't have a clue how much his dire situation might have escalated since she'd been gone. God, she really hated being in the dark about her family, and especially her mother's youngest sibling.

By the time she returned to the Dunbar ranch, fixed dinner and then hid in her room instead of joining the others at the table, she still hadn't decided whether she should stay or flee. The plate she'd brought with her sat untouched on the small, bedside table, the tightness in her stomach too painful to try to eat. So far, she'd stayed clear of Caden and his all-too-knowing eyes, and she missed even that small contact. She didn't know if she cared that much for him or just craved more of his dominant, sexual control before leaving, but whichever one it was, it hurt to think about it.

The house grew silent, and she knew Connor had left for his own home and the hands for the bunkhouse. Caden spent most evenings holed up in his office, and she assumed that's where he'd gone off to. Unable to sit still or watch television, she left her too quiet room, grabbed the six-pack from the refrigerator and slipped out into the inky night. Walking around outside after dark would break another one of his rules, but Sydney didn't care. At this point, she didn't have all that much to lose.

Chapter 5

"**T**hanks, Grayson." Caden hung up the phone and pushed away from his desk, unaccustomed worry settling like a rock in his gut. His friend's call bothered him as much as Sydney's absence from the dinner table earlier and galvanized him into leaving his paperwork to confront her. He couldn't believe how much hearing from the sheriff that something, or someone had upset her bothered him. For Grayson to take the time to express concern for her distraught appearance in town, she would have had to appear noticeably overwrought. Later, he would need to delve deeper into why the thought of Sydney in distress caused a tightness in his chest he'd never felt before over a woman.

When he found her room empty, a plate of untouched food sitting on the nightstand, and couldn't locate her anywhere else in the house, anger mingled with worry as he went to scout around outside. Damn it, she knew the rule about wandering around outdoors after dark. It took him almost twenty minutes of fretful searching, but he finally found her in one of the barns, propped on a stack of hay bales, halfway through a six-pack of beer.

"What are you doing out here, alone in the dark?" he barked. Only one small, overhead light offered any illumination and the meager glow left most of her in shadows. But he could see well enough to notice the slight stiffening of her body, her sudden, indrawn breath another clear sign whatever happened in town was still affecting her.

"I was talking to the dogs, but they have this bad habit of not talking back. What're you doing out here?"

"Looking for you, wondering why you've broken yet another rule." Striding forward, he snatched the beer from her hand before it reached her mouth. "You've had enough. Tell me what's upset you. Did someone harass you in town?" The instant panic crossing her face drew a surge of protectiveness Caden didn't know he possessed and an undeniable urge to strike back at whoever was responsible for that look. Reaching down, he clasped her upper arms and pulled her against him with a 'need to know' demand. "Tell me."

"No... I mean, it's nothing," she stammered with an evasive-ness unlike her.

Caden had seen her teasing grin, her frown of irritation and her green eyes glow with pleasure, but he'd never seen her afraid, or hear her lie, and neither sat well with him. Instead of shaking her, like he was tempted to do, a better plan came to mind. Grabbing her wrists, he backed her toward a low rafter, snatched a coil of rope off the wall and made short work of tying her wrists together.

Sydney tried to pull away from him as he lifted her hands above her head and looped the end of the rope around the beam. "What *are* you doing?" she squealed, yanking on her arms, her pale face reddening either from the slight exertion or the flare of excitement reflected in her eyes. Both were better than the fear.

"Making sure you don't fall when I do this." He slid his hands under her shirt, shoved her bra up and scraped his thumb nails over her already turgid nipples. "Tell me what's wrong."

She shook her head, her wild, red hair flying around her shoulders even as she arched her back and pushed her breasts into his hands. "I promise; it was nothing. Just a little… misunderstanding. *Oh God.*"

Small white teeth sank into her lower lip when he tugged on her nipples and then drew the tips out, elongating them with a tight pinch. "I can keep this up all night, darlin'."

A flare of resentment tightened her face. "I'm not on the clock now, *boss*. You can't order me to talk."

"No, you're right about that." Releasing her nipples, he kept his eyes on hers as he slid his hands down to the waist of her jeans. "But I can punish you for disobeying another rule by coming out here alone after dark. Same safeword applies here, by the way." Caden yanked her jeans down along with her panties, the narrow strip of pubic hair drawing his gaze straight to the enticing view of delicate, plump bare folds already damp with arousal. He wasn't sure how far he would take this, he only knew he couldn't stand to see her hurting or hear her evasive replies to his inquiries.

"Caden, please." A hint of desperation laced her whispered plea and he fought against caving to both it and the way her hips shifted toward him in silent supplication.

"Are you going to tell me what I want to know?" He lifted his hands to release his belt. Her eyes widened as he pulled the soft leather through the loops, but if he wasn't mistaken, and he rarely was, the sudden increase in her breathing had nothing to do with fear.

"I told you, it's nothing. I'm over it already." Since she averted her eyes with that statement, he doubted the truth of it.

With a quick twist, Caden spun her toward the wall and didn't pause before snapping the belt across her quivering buttocks. "Like I said, I've got all night."

SYDNEY'S HEAD BUZZED, and not just from the beers she'd downed on an empty stomach. Caden hadn't struck her hard. Instead, the stroke of leather over her butt induced tiny, pinpricks of pain that disappeared fast, too fast, and left her aching for more. Right now, she'd take any diversion from the decision she needed to make, more than willing to accept anything he would give her at this point.

"Nothing, huh?"

She heard the swoosh first, felt the burning sting second. This time he'd struck a little harder, and the heated pain zipped straight down between her legs, increasing the moisture already seeping from her pussy. Shaking her head, she gave him a non-verbal answer and held her breath as he delivered a blow a little lower.

"Fuck, but you're stubborn," he groused.

Any other time, before she'd gone into town, she would've relished the frustration in his voice. But all she yearned for now was to forget the threat of a stranger and the lonely weeks ahead of her if she left and to bask in the heated throbbing spreading across her butt and filling her sheath. "Fuck me, Caden," she begged, keeping her eyes pinned to the wall so she couldn't see his rejection.

He answered her plea by delivering three, quick slices across her quivering buttocks, leaving behind a more painful burn and deeper throbbing. She both heard and saw the belt drop at her feet before his hands came to her hips. Her breath caught as he slid one hand between her legs and cupped her soaking flesh while he squeezed one, warm pulsating cheek with the other. An unprepared for, deep, three-fingered thrust into her pussy brought her up on her toes with a gasp, the invasion accompanied by the startling probe at the entrance to her back hole.

Taken off guard, she stuttered without looking around, "What… I'm not sure about…"

"Are you saying red?" A small prod with his wide, calloused thumb breached her sphincter and sent a riot of new sensations spreading up that untried orifice.

"No, it's different, is all," she panted, struggling to acclimate to the new sensations and surprising pleasure while wondering if there was nothing he could introduce her to that she would shy away from trying.

"Good," he returned smugly, satisfaction coloring his tone. "I like knowing I'm going where no man has been before. Deep breath, darlin'."

Caden brushed her clit while thumbing her ass with short, jabbing prods, the dual assault driving Sydney to the precipice within seconds. Just as the small tremors heralding an orgasm began, he frustrated her by pulling back. Leaning against her, his mouth at her ear, he uttered the four words she'd been pining for since meeting him. "I'll fuck you, Sydney, not because you asked, but because I can't hold back any longer. But make no mistake. This isn't over."

Everything he said after 'I'll fuck you' barely registered through the roaring in her head and the surge of hot blood straight to her groin, swelling her vagina. She heard him sheathing himself then held her breath as he grabbed her hips again and kept her still for his possession. One deep thrust, and every delicious inch of his thick girth slid in a smooth glide through her slick channel and lay embedded deep inside her, leaving her to relish the burning pleasure of being jammed full. Feeling as if she'd been waiting forever for this, Sydney moaned in protest of his withdrawal and then embraced the next forceful plunge with a soft cry. His tight grip prevented her from moving, which increased the heat building from his pumping rhythm. Every rub against swollen tissues, every brush against her clit inflamed the sensitive nerve endings until she threatened to combust.

Arching her head back, she closed her eyes and begged, "More, please, *don't stop.*"

———

CADEN HAD REDUCED submissive women to pleading before, but none of their pleas affected him as strongly as Sydney's soft, achingly desperate voice. The urge to take, to stake a claim by pounding into her until she splintered apart and then revealed what had upset her, wouldn't let up. He'd never wanted to go after someone with such anger as he did the unknown person who'd left her troubled. How the hell had she gotten under his skin so fast, and so deep?

Digging his thumbs into her red-striped buttocks, he spread the plump globes to gaze upon the puckered opening into her ass before sliding his thumb back inside the tight orifice. Wet as a dewy morning and giving off as much heat as an Arizona desert, her pussy gripped his shaft with small clutches sure to drive him over the edge way too soon. His lust turned into a greedy bitch, clawing at his balls with a voracious need, hardening his cock into a tortured demand. He pounded into her with jackhammer thrusts, Sydney's small grunts followed by soft mewls egging him on. Her cry of release echoed in the cavernous barn as she spasmed around his girth so hard he had trouble pulling away from the tight clutches. Then his brain fogged as his climax spewed forth, nearly driving him to his knees with the powerful ejaculations and mind-numbing sensations.

It took Caden several blind moments to return to earth and loosen his tight grip on her hips. "You good?" he breathed in harsh inquiry as he pulled with slow reluctance from her snug, still spasming clasp.

"More than," she admitted with her usual candor, followed by a small laugh and full body shudder.

Disposing of the condom in the corner trash, he zipped his jeans then bent to pull hers back up. "I'm glad to hear that. I was rough."

"Yeah," she sighed, turning her head and flipping him one of those cheeky grins he enjoyed, the shadows in her eyes replaced with a sated glow. "And I liked it. Now, aren't you sorry you made me wait?"

Shaking his head, Caden released her hands and slung his arm around her shoulders as he led her out of the barn. "You're incorrigible. I think I need to work on that. You'll accompany me to The Barn tomorrow night as my sub."

"Gee, Caden," Sydney drawled. "You have such a sweet way of asking a girl out."

"Who the fuck's asking? I learned just minutes after meeting you that doesn't work."

———

THE WEEKEND, *that's all I want.* Sydney kept telling herself that all day on Friday while trying not to read too much into Caden's announcement that she would go to The Barn tonight as his sub, or the thrill it had given her. He'd come to mean a lot to her in such a short time, and *God*, every time she thought of leaving her stomach cramped and her eyes filled with tears. Telling herself this wasn't home, that she had a life in Missouri that she loved didn't work, regardless of how much she missed her family and job. Last night, while lying in bed enjoying the pleasurable after-shocks of submitting to Caden, she'd fretted over what she should do about this recent threat to her happiness. Maybe she should head back home on Sunday, drive at a snail's pace to allow her more time to think of an excuse for taking off like she had that would sound plausible to her grandmother and uncles.

As long as she stayed away from Uncle Mike, refused to be alone with him, she should be able to avoid a repeat of the way he'd come to her apartment on the pretext of making amends and then drugged her to force her hand. Hiring that thug proved how desperate he'd become for cash though, and if her shares continued to be his best option, avoiding him would only work for so long.

Her last option might be to come clean with her other two uncles, relying on their genuine love for her and stable home lives to come to her aid while sparing her grandmother the heartache of learning about her youngest child's duplicity. "Between a rock and a hard place," she muttered as she went through her limited wardrobe searching for something to wear tonight. Caden mentioned he liked the skirt she'd worn last week and considering how fast he had talked her out of it, she decided it didn't much matter what she wore. Of course, his succinct command, 'No panties or bra,' was another hint she would be stripped naked soon after entering his club. Donning a light-weight, fall sweater that buttoned down the front, she ran trembling hands down her sides as she replayed last night.

What was it about the way Caden simply took her over, just like last week in the club's loft, that was such a freaking turn-on? Granted, there had been something missing from her previous sexual encounters, but that hadn't kept her from enjoying the time she'd spent getting sweaty between the sheets with her partners. But *nothing* compared to the off-the-charts responses her sexy boss could evoke. No climax had ever come close to rivaling the heights he'd driven her to with his painful swats, penetrating blue eyes and deep-voiced commands. She savored every second under his dominant control, longed for more and despaired over where that would leave her once she left the ranch, and her Dom rancher.

"Sydney, let's go," Caden called out, his impatient voice spurring her on. She didn't know what had occurred to change his mind about her and wasn't about to ask. If only he hadn't insisted on keeping his distance those first days, she'd have that many more memories to keep her warm at night after she left. If only the circumstances that brought her here weren't the same ones driving her away. If only this were her home. *If only...*

"CONNOR LET you slide on a few things last week since you were a guest. Tonight, you'll need to observe all the rules," Caden stated while holding open the door to The Barn for her.

Sydney shivered, but not because of the cool, night air. His look alone was enough to keep her warm, but the sounds of BDSM play seeping through the entry door into the club as she stepped inside the large foyer also helped dispel any cold she might feel from walking around without panties. The air wafting up under her skirt teased the sensitive skin of her bare labia and heightened her awareness of her near-naked state, keeping her on that tantalizing edge of sexual anticipation.

When she'd accompanied Connor last week, she'd been too excited, as well as anxious over Caden's reaction to discovering her here, to take much notice of the foyer. Now, Caden filled in the blanks by pointing to a row of large cubbies then nodding at her feet. "You can store your shoes in one of those." Opening a door opposite the cubby slots, he showed her a huge, walk-in closet. "This is where we hang the coats come winter. Remember to address me as Sir, or you could face consequences you're not ready for," he warned in a mild tone.

Slipping off her shoes, she smiled up at him with a raised brow. "Is that supposed to scare me, boss?"

Her deliberate use of boss instead of sir drew his scowl before he shook his head, clasped her hand and opened the door into the club room with a smirk. "If you want to start racking them up, then by all means, do so."

Probably not a wise idea, she admitted even as her heart rate picked up speed as she peeked inside the playroom. The same as last week, the sheer pulse of the place seeped under Sydney's skin the moment she stepped inside. A good crowd already filled the space, and as Caden drew her toward the bar, he stopped to say a word or two to friends and to introduce her. She didn't try to keep track of names, or even say much in return to the friendly greetings and welcomes. What would be the point of making new friends when she might be leaving soon? Another pang tightened her stomach, but she shoved it aside in favor of getting the most out of Caden's attention as possible.

Sheriff Monroe beckoned them over to the bar as he nudged a stool out, and it took Sydney a moment to stifle a flare of resentment over the way he'd tattled to Caden after his keen observation locked on to her upset state yesterday. She understood the two of them were close, but that didn't lessen her disgruntlement. Connor manned the bar, his Stetson tipped low, shielding his eyes, but the tight set to his jaw revealed he wasn't in his usual, light-hearted mood tonight.

"What's wrong?" Sydney asked him before Caden distracted her by pulling her in front of him on the stool, his arm coming around her waist to draw her back until her buttocks nestled against his groin.

"Let me guess," Caden drawled above her head, his voice carrying a hint of concern. "No Annie again tonight."

"We're no longer seeing each other," Connor clipped, his tone discouraging further inquiry. "What can I get you, sweetie?" He held out his hand for the punch card that would limit her to two drinks.

"A beer, anything light, please." Even though the previous night's excess kept her from wanting to indulge again tonight, Caden's fingers toying with the top button of her sweater until it popped, prompted her to order something with a kick.

Conscious of both Grayson and Connor's eyes on her,

Sydney peered up at him with a quirk of her mouth. "You're not wasting any time, are you?"

"You're the one who addressed me improperly right after I told you the correct form of address." Caden kept his eyes on hers as he slipped open the next button and brought his beer to his mouth.

"I have a feeling this one will keep you on your toes," Grayson commented as Caden released the third button.

"She's run me ragged for two weeks, and now she's keeping things from me. What should we do with you, Sydney?" Caden murmured in a low, seductively conversational tone. The last button popped free and he spread the sweater open, exposing her bare breasts, when one word registered with a fiery response between her legs.

"We?" Sydney's gaze flew to the sheriff's, and his stern frown didn't bode well for what they planned for her. Yet, instead of becoming leery, she thrilled to the prospect of another new experience. She didn't lust after the other man, not the way she had Caden from the moment she clapped eyes on him through the window. But she doubted there was a woman alive who didn't fantasize about two men doling out double the pleasure.

Running a rough finger over one turgid nipple, Caden replied, "You also refused to come clean with Grayson, so I thought it only fair he takes part in your punishment."

With a nod from Caden, Grayson leaned forward and plucked the beer from her hand. She didn't get a chance to ask why before Caden leaned her back, over his arm. With a glint in his eyes, he slowly tilted his beer bottle over her up-thrust breasts, leaving her just enough time to suck in a deep breath before the cold trickle drew a startled gasp. The sheriff leaned forward, shackled her wrists in one hand and dipped his head to lap at the spilled alcohol, stroking everywhere except over her aching, rigid nipples.

Caden bent to her ear. "Isn't it nice of him to clean up my mess, Sydney?"

Nice? Not when he continued to avoid two of her most sensitive areas that throbbed for a touch. Connor's low chuckle earned him a glare from her. "You too?" she asked, her face heating even though she couldn't resist the urge to shift her torso toward Grayson's lips. The not so innocent maneuver brushed one nipple against his stubbled cheek, the abrasion sending sizzling sparks of pleasure straight down to her core.

"I always enjoy a good punishment scene." Connor thumbed back his hat, his look both caring and disapproving.

Caden delivered a sharp slap on her thigh, diverting her attention with the quick, painful burn. "It looks like we have to restrain more than her hands, Grayson, since she can't be still."

Lifting his head and licking his lips, he nodded in agreement. "She did make it difficult for me to concentrate."

Bemused, turned on and a touch miffed, Caden caught Sydney off guard again when he righted her, slipped off the stool and tossed her over his shoulder as if she weighed nothing, one arm wrapped in a tight band around her legs. But her mortification and indignity didn't stop there.

"Here, let me," the sheriff offered, flipping up her skirt.

"Caden!" The only thing her squealed protest earned her was another sharp slap on her thigh. Adding to both her embarrassment and arousal, he brought his free hand between her legs and teased the entrance to her pussy with light strokes while they ascended the stairs to the loft. Sydney kept her flaming face down, her eyes on Grayson's jean covered legs as he followed them.

When they reached the upper floor, Grayson caressed her buttocks, saying, "I'll pick out something that'll decorate this pretty ass nicely."

"Meet us at the Wheel of Misfortune," Caden said.

Sydney refused to ask him what that was, instead closing her eyes as he walked across the loft, stopped and lowered her to her feet. Blood rushed south then swept back up to her face as she opened her eyes and saw a large wagon wheel hanging a few inches off the floor. All but four spokes had been removed, these spread wide enough apart to provide large spaces in between. A smaller wheel with writing along the spokes and a flap attached in the center sat propped next to the bigger apparatus.

Turning questioning eyes up to Caden, he spoke before she could voice her misgivings about the contraption. "You have me worried about you, and I'm not used to fretting over a woman. It's your fault you've come to mean so much to me, and your fault for pushing until you ended up in this position. Remember the safeword and either say it or strip."

He didn't look happy about his feelings, and neither was she. Not because he too meant more to her than she'd planned for, but because she knew better than him this couldn't go anywhere. Removing her clothes, she avoided looking at Grayson when he returned carrying a round leather paddle that made her buttocks clench. She would deal with the repercussions of her feelings when she left. Tonight, she yearned for as much attention from her rancher as she could get.

Caden looked at Grayson and nodded toward the smaller wheel. "You can do the honors while I prep my sub."

The sheriff removed the toothpick from his mouth and slipped it into his pocket. "Glad to."

Grabbing her hand, Caden tugged her next to him and cupped her breast, his thumb strumming her nipple. "He'll spin the wheel and whatever position the flap lands on will be the one we'll restrain you in on the wagon wheel. Don't worry, the spokes were sanded smooth to negate the risk of splinters. Now, bend over and grab your ankles. Any time you want to tell us what happened yesterday, say so and we'll stop."

Humiliation heated her face, but Sydney refused to utter red, no matter how much that order tempted her to. She didn't know which disconcerted her the most, bending over or the different prospects awaiting her with the apparatus. Grabbing her ankles, she was grateful for the way her hair shielded her face from what they were doing. She heard the small wheel spin then held her breath as Caden spread her buttocks and inserted a row of greased, cool balls inside her. Unable to hold still against the strange invasion, she swayed her hips, the move rolling the foreign objects against the tight walls and ultrasensitive nerves along her rectum.

"What the heck are those things?" she gasped as Caden helped her upright, her entire body quaking from the tiny sparks of pleasure the anal toy produced.

"Vibrating anal beads, but I haven't turned them on yet." He glanced at the smaller wheel as the fast twirling slowed and then stopped. "It looks like you'll be starting in the ideal position." Caden and Grayson exchanged identical smirks, leaving her to wonder if the sheriff hadn't taken liberties with his spin.

Sydney didn't protest when they bound her facing the wheel, stretching her arms up and out along the top spokes before cuffing her wrists and then doing the same with her spread ankles. She had little time left with Caden and planned to soak up every minute of his attention she could get before she moved on, even if she trembled inside over what they might do because of her silence about her troubles.

"Perfect." Caden stepped in front of her and her heart turned over at the tight set to his mouth. With her arms bound on the two spokes, her breasts were thrust forward, aligned just right to it make it easy for him to tug on her nipples.

"Ca... Sir," she corrected when he scowled. "What..." She broke off with a startled cry, the smack Grayson delivered with the paddle catching her unaware. Hissing in a deep breath, she struggled with the burn before the painful pleasure took hold.

"The paddle is worse than my belt, but not as bad as a flogger, or cane. We can switch to one of those if you don't tell us what we want to know." Caden reached into a pocket and in the next instant, small pulsations rippled up and down her rectum as the beads set up a vibration against sensitive tissues she could feel in her sheath through the thin membrane separating the two orifices.

"*Oh… crap.*" Sydney's low moan followed the next swat, both cheeks now throbbing along with her rectum. Caden's fingers plucked at her nipples, adding to the bombardment of sensations slowly robbing her of cognizant thought. She averted her eyes from his rugged face, not trusting his probing gaze, or her ability to resist giving in to him.

"Talk to me, darlin'," Caden insisted before bending and drawing one beaded tip into his hot mouth.

She could feel the strong, suctioning pulls on the tender bud all the way to her toes, the warm pleasure overridden by the next, painful smack of the paddle. "Please, I… can't," she pled, wishing different circumstances had brought her to the Dunbar Ranch, and to her rancher.

"Why?" Grayson nipped the soft spot where her shoulder and neck connected, his hand caressing her heated buttocks.

Shaking her head, Sydney fought off the desire to share her burden and remained silent. They couldn't help her out of her dilemma back home. Despair dampened her eyes and need threatened her determination to keep from revealing her uncle's machinations. That need increased when Caden swore and delved between her legs to tug on her swollen clit and the sheriff delivered yet another blistering blow to her ass, and her sanity.

"I just can't… Caden, Sir, *please.*" Unable to voice her concern over her plight or the desperation to lose herself in the pleasure only he could drive her to, she yanked on the restraints and looked into his eyes. "*Please.*"

Chapter 6

Caden's frustration with Sydney's stubborn silence rose another notch. The need to learn what could have happened to upset her so much warred with the driving force to lay claim to her once and for all. She surprised him with the way she'd maintained her stoic resolve to keep him in the dark given what he and Grayson were putting her through. Since his patience was wearing thin, he deemed it time to up the ante.

"My turn to spin the wheel," he said, yanking on her hair and then stepping over to the smaller wheel. He spun it, the odds in his favor of it landing on a position convenient for what he wanted to do next. Smiling at where it stopped, he moved in front of her again and reached up to rotate the large wheel. "Head down, literally," he warned before turning the apparatus until she dangled with her head a few inches off the floor. "Perfect."

"For what?" she gasped, her heart thumping in rapid rhythm beneath his hand as he reached down and squeezed one breast. The bonds were snug enough to hold her without undue pressure or discomfort, at least not on her limbs. Both her libido and sanity were another matter.

"Oh, a little of this," Grayson interjected, nipping one reddened buttock.

"And a little of this." Caden flicked the anal beads up a notch and bent his head to lick up her damp seam and then dip inside her slick pussy to tease her clit before pulling back. "Ready to talk yet, Sydney?" He pinched her ass when she shook her head, her breathing escalating as he added a finger to his tongue delving inside her. Grayson kept his own hands busy on her breasts while tracing his mouth over her butt. The two of them had enjoyed many years tormenting reluctant women into submitting to their demands and knew what they were doing. The curl of jealousy in Caden's abdomen took him by surprise however, but then, it shouldn't have. He should be used to the unexpected emotions she pulled from him by now.

Sydney quit pleading aloud, but her body spoke in eloquent demand for her. A light sheen of perspiration coated her soft skin, her pussy's slick, grasping heat, and the little mewls of pleasure that accompanied each stroke over her puffy clit all telltale signs of her heightened state. Caden nipped at one smooth fold, enjoyed the catch in her throat, and then plundered her depth with three fingers.

"Anytime you want to spill the beans, we're all ears," he said above her saturated flesh. Wrapping his lips around her clit, he drew on the delicate, hypersensitive nub until her whimpers turned into cries and a gush of liquid heat filled his mouth.

"I don't know," Grayson put in as he took another bite out of her ass and reached down to squeeze her breasts. "I'd hate for her to stop my fun now."

"I...*God!*" she exclaimed as Caden upped the vibrations of the anal beads one more time and plowed her pussy with deep, forceful plunges. He tortured the tender flesh of her clit with a scrape of his nails and then pulled back as her damp muscles contracted with small spasms. "Okay! I got a message from...

back home I didn't... like," she stammered, her confession easing his guilt, her next pitiful, whimpered plea shredding his need to push for more. "*Please.*"

Caden nodded at Grayson and stepped back, even though he suspected there was much more to Sydney's upset yesterday. She'd never spoken of her family or hinted at where she hailed from. Understanding family dynamics, and the desire to keep them between family members, he relented in pushing for more as there was always tomorrow to delve deeper if he found it necessary.

With a slow spin, he righted Sydney's body and they both worked to get her down. Her flushed face revealed a combination of relief, irritation and desperate need, all of which he planned to do something about without his friend's help.

Grayson cupped her face and kissed her slow and deep and then nodded at Caden. "Later," was all he said before strolling away, leaving Sydney to fall against him when her legs refused to hold her up.

Scooping her up, he carried her over to a spanking bench, laid her down and released his engorged cock. Her thighs fell open as he sheathed himself, the blatant invitation also reflected in her eyes and in the cream oozing from between her swollen labia. Grasping under her knees, he brought her legs over his shoulders and leaned forward to thrust inside her grasping pussy. "Now, darlin', right now," he growled in demand, withdrawing and then plunging, over and over, his vigorous assault inching her up on the bench until he grabbed her ass and held her groin tight against his. He could feel the pulses of the anal toy through the thin membrane separating her orifices, the tight clutches of both holes pushing him to the edge. His grunts mingled with her pants, the glaze in her eyes matching the mindless ecstasy spinning through his head. The bench shook from his hard, carnal fucking. The unexpected pain of Sydney's small teeth sinking into his shoulder caused him to see stars with his explosive climax, the exalted pleasure more than anything he'd experienced before.

CADEN AWOKE TO AN EMPTY BED, missing the warm softness of Sydney's body curled against him. One night, the only entire night he'd spent with a woman in his bed, and the longing to repeat it couldn't be denied. A door opened and closed, followed by low voices echoing from down the hall. Glancing at the time, he couldn't believe he'd slept past seven a.m. The only mornings he indulged in an extra hour of sleep were Sundays when the ranch chores consisted of feeding the livestock not already grazing in the pastures. Rolling out of bed, he dressed and padded into the kitchen to find Connor and the live-in hands already eating.

Sydney stood, picking up her empty plate and smiling at him. "Don't worry, we saved you plenty." She breezed by him as if nothing had changed between them, and that just pissed him off because *everything* had changed. By the time he discussed the day's agenda with his brother and then ate, he was the last one to remain. He carried his plate into the kitchen where he found her at the sink, gazing with an expression of longing out the window.

"I didn't want to ask in front of the hands," he said, setting his plate down and wrapping one arm around her waist to pull her back against him, "but how are you this morning? Any problems?"

"Just a little sore." She turned her head up to him, her look now teasing. "But I kind of like it, even if you were mean last night."

He quirked an eyebrow. "Don't keep things from me and I won't have to be."

A shadow crossed her face, but she smiled and drawled, "Really?"

"Yeah, okay, I still might be, but only for fun, not to pull answers from you." He kissed her before pulling back. "I've got to run…" A shout from outside drew his frowning gaze out the window to see several of the younger hands riding in from the north pasture, their faces masked with anger and concern. "What the hell? Excuse me, darlin'."

A COLD KNOT of dread settled in Sydney's abdomen as she followed Caden outside. The lingering pleasure and contentment she'd felt since returning to the ranch last night and waking with his massive body curled around her vanished in the time it took to hear Austin, one of the younger hands, tell Caden, "It looks like poison, boss. We've already lost three heifers, several more are showing signs of sickness."

"Call the vet," Caden snapped to Connor who had just pulled up. His blue eyes turned to ice as he scanned his employees' faces that were gathering in the yard. "You guys bring in the sick as fast as possible. Connor and I will look for the source. Let's hope whoever did this only messed with the water supply in one pasture."

Sydney's hand went to Spike's scruff and she sank her fingers into the collie's soft fur to anchor herself against the pain sweeping through her. This was her fault; she brought this trouble to Caden's ranch, his livelihood and the ranch hands that had embraced her with such friendliness. Without a doubt, she knew the stranger sent by her uncle to threaten her was behind the vandalism. She'd never dreamed he would try to get her cooperation by harming the livestock. If she didn't leave, would he go after Caden, Connor or one of the hands next? Oh God, she couldn't bear it if anyone was harmed because of her. It was bad enough several cows had already suffered because she put her selfish reasons for staying a little longer first instead of doing the safe thing and leaving.

She reached out to snag Caden's arm as he started toward the barn. "What can I do to help?" she asked, not realizing the need to be of assistance in her voice was also reflected in her eyes.

"We'll need food when we get back, sandwiches if you can because we likely won't have time to sit down to eat. And watch for Grayson. I'll call him and report this and he'll need to come out and investigate with us." He strode off without another word, his face stiff with anger, his cobalt eyes swirling with frustration.

Sydney walked over to the mess hall on leaden feet, her heart heavy in her chest, praying she was wrong but knowing she wasn't. She wouldn't leave until she helped them through this crisis, which was the least she could do. But she refused to return home. Where she would go, she didn't know. Caden had paid her a week's wages, so she had enough money to last a few weeks if she stayed frugal. Despair threatened to overwhelm her as she entered the kitchen she'd grown to enjoy cooking in, memories of the hands teasing her about her penchant for getting lost and complimenting her cooking filling her head. She couldn't believe how much she would miss everyone after such a short time.

As she put together thick sandwiches filled with ham, roast beef, turkey and cheese, she stewed over her circumstances. The more she thought about her uncle and his lackey, the faster her despondency changed to anger. How dare they interrupt the first peaceful weeks she'd been enjoying since fleeing Missouri. Damn it, wasn't it bad enough Uncle Mike's actions forced her from her home, a job she loved and far away from the rest of her family, whom she adored? She thought of Caden, the way his blue eyes lit with fondness even when he'd been exasperated with her behavior or how they would darken when arousal outweighed his determination to keep her at arm's length. He'd introduced her to new sensations that had led to heights she'd never achieved before, never imagined were possible, and she didn't want to give that up, or him. She wanted him more than she missed her family, and that acknowledgement shed a whole new light on what she needed to do next.

"I'll show you, you son-of-a-bitch," she muttered aloud as she got out ingredients to make brownies. "The sheriff just might be interested in hearing about what I know…"

"I wouldn't advise that," a cold voice said from behind her.

Sydney whirled to face the doorway, fear clogging her throat when she saw the same man who threatened her in town last week leaning with negligent nonchalance against the doorjamb. With a shaking hand, she reached for the large knife lying on the counter separating them and let him see she wouldn't cower from him this time, even if her insides were jelling into a quivering ball of nerves. "Get out of here before…"

He cut her off with a slice of his hand, his eyes going to slits in his lean face. "Everyone's out trying to save their precious cattle, I made sure of that. You can put that down; I'm not here to harm you, just to deliver one final warning. Your uncle needs you back in Missouri by the end of the week, and since you have a two-day drive ahead of you, I suggest you leave no later than Tuesday."

"And if I don't? You'd be a fool to try anything on this ranch again after I talk to the sheriff." She didn't know where her sudden bravado came from; she only knew she was tired of her uncle controlling her life.

He shrugged, as if unconcerned by her threat. "Maybe, maybe not. It's your word against mine, and I assure you, I left no evidence that could be traced back to me. It's a huge spread, a lot of places where one of those young cowboys or your rancher can meet with an untimely accident."

The very softness of his voice chilled her to the bone. "You wouldn't," she whispered. Fear for the people she'd come to care so much for spread throughout her quaking body, turning her hands clammy and her throat dry. With those few words, anguish over her hopeless situation returned tenfold, demolishing her brave front.

"Tuesday, at the latest, or you'll find out." With a mock, two-fingered salute, he spun about and disappeared as quietly as he'd snuck in.

With a sob of defeat, Sydney slid to the floor, buried her face in her hands and wept. No way would she risk anything happening to Caden or anyone else on his ranch. Two days, that's all she had with him, and then it was back to long days and lonely nights while she searched for a way to keep her plight from hurting her family.

She managed to pull herself together by the time the first riders returned with some of the sick cattle. The veterinarian team was waiting for them in the barn where they immediately started pumping stomachs to rid the poor animals of the toxins poisoning their bodies. From what she could gather, only the three cows had died so far, a small boon considering how many could have succumbed before help arrived. The other good news was that pasture held less than twenty head of cattle that hadn't been driven closer to the ranch yet. To help keep the line for treatment moving steady, she brought the food out to the hands and the veterinarian staff, enabling everyone to continue administering first aid while eating. The guys mentioned they'd fenced off the two watering holes and samples were en route to a lab in Billings. By the time Caden returned with Connor and Grayson, the cattle had been treated and were resting quietly in the corral behind the barn.

"I don't know about you two, but I'm beat," Connor sighed as he, Caden and Grayson entered the house after the hands left for home. "I'm heading back to my place for a quiet night."

Sydney looked at their tired faces and her heart ached for

what she'd inadvertently put them through. "I made chili, since it turned so cold this afternoon." The clouds that had rolled in with the increasing north wind dropped the temperature ten degrees in an hour and didn't stop there as afternoon slipped into dusk. "Can you stay for dinner?" She included the sheriff in her invitation.

"You wouldn't have to twist my arm, Syd. Thanks," Connor accepted, squeezing her shoulder. She swiveled her face sideways to hide the tears pricking her eyes.

"Unless you want to open the doors tonight, Grayson, I say we close the club and warm up with Sydney's cooking. I can send out a group text to members." Caden gave her a grateful look as she turned back around. "You had me as soon as I came in and took a whiff, darlin'.""

Grayson nodded. "Chili and a quiet night works for me. Thanks, Sydney."

The full-time hands started trickling in, and she didn't question their early arrival for dinner. Their faces were etched with exhaustion, their eyes still conveying their anger over the senseless vandalism. Her stomach cramped when she thought of them turning on her if they discovered their woes today were her fault. She couldn't bear to lose not only their friendship, but their high regard.

For the first time since Sydney arrived on the ranch, Caden spent the evening with her instead of barricaded in his office. She cuddled against him on the big, leather sofa in front of the large-screened television while they watched a movie, her mind racing from having to tell him the next day she would be leaving. As much as she wanted to go home, her job at the expensive, fancy restaurant in downtown St. Louis no longer appealed to her. As nice as her two-bedroom, two-bath condo was, she knew the space would feel cramped after living on the ranch with its wide-open spaces. She missed her grandmother, her two oldest uncles and her cousins, but knew she'd miss Caden, his brother and the ranch hands just as much. Why couldn't anything be easy?

By the time Caden tugged her down the hall into his bedroom, stripped her and tucked her into his wide bed next to him, tears blurred her vision at the thought of leaving. Before he caught sight of them, she dove under the covers and took his straining erection into her mouth.

"Sydney?"

Shaking her head against his tight abs, she refused to answer the question in his voice, instead, moaning from the masculine taste of him as she stroked over the smooth cap, catching a drop of pre-come on her tongue. He fisted a hand in her hair, his low groan rumbling under her ear, the sound curling her toes as she took him deep with a tight suction of her mouth. The veins along his shaft pulsed under her tongue, his sac weighed heavily in her palm as she cupped him, and his thick length threatened her gag reflexes while she worked to suck on as much of him as possible.

"Had I known how talented you are at fellatio, darlin', I may not have resisted you for so long," he growled above her.

Cocooned in the darkness, buried under the cover with the warm flesh of his rigid cock stretching her lips, Sydney basked in his praise and sought to drive him crazy. She wanted to make sure he didn't forget her after she left, so she tormented him by bringing him right to the brink of orgasm, waited for the telltale jerk of his cock and spew of more pre-come before pulling back, replacing her mouth with her hand. She laughed against his cockhead when he cursed and tightened her hand around his girth before shifting to rub the damp crown back and forth, over her nipples.

"What? You don't like to be kept waiting? Now you know how I felt last night." She sighed at the lovely sensation of his sex brushing over her tender tips and then dipped her head again to lave under the rim of his cap, putting pressure on the sensitive area until his fisted hand in her hair pulled.

"Enough. Come up here."

Sydney shook her head, ignoring his demand, too afraid of what his astute gaze might pick up on her face in the moon-lit room to obey him. Sliding her palm down to his base, she engulfed him in her mouth again, this time scraping her teeth along his silk-covered, hot flesh. Caden reached down with his other hand and cupped her breast, rolled the damp nipple between two fingers then delivered a sharp pinch to the tender bud. She gasped at the nip of erotic pain that caused her sheath to spasm and gush, her attention diverted just long enough for him to haul her up his body using his grip on her hair. Why she found that so heart-pounding thrilling, she didn't know, and didn't have time to evaluate as he spread her thighs over his big body, clasped her hips and pushed her onto his cock.

"As much as I enjoyed your mouth, this," he surged up inside her, "is much better. Ride me, Sydney."

Slamming her eyes shut, she arched her head back until she felt her hair brush her lower back, praying he didn't read anything more into her actions than a need to be with him. Bracing her hands on his shoulders, she rose until only his cock-head remained nestled inside her folds before lowering slowly, taking him back in one slow inch at a time. She shuddered from the pleasure of him filling her again, relishing the way his thick-ness stretched her to the point of discomfort before she adjusted to his possession. His fingers dug into her buttocks as he tight-ened his hold and took over after her next rise and fall.

"Fuck but you feel good. Let me…" He rammed up into her, bumping her womb before lifting her with effortless ease and slamming her back down with a deep groan. "Like that, just…" another lift and downward plunge, "like that."

Tightening her hands on his shoulders, Sydney cried out with the third controlled thrust, a cry that ended in a whimper as he released one cheek to root out her clit and press the aching piece of swollen flesh against the hardness of his ravaging cock. They splintered apart together, their heavy breathing sounding harsh and meshing with the rigorous smacking together of their pelvis' in the otherwise silent darkness. By the time her mind was starting to clear of the engulfing pleasure shaking her body, Caden was drawing her down on top of him, his voice heavy, his breath warm as he whispered, "Go to sleep, Sydney. We'll talk in the morning."

CADEN WAITED until he heard the shower come on before sliding out of bed and slipping on his jeans. Shirtless and barefoot, he padded down the hall into his office, closing the door behind him before dialing Grayson's number. Ever since he'd seen a look of horror cross Sydney's face when she heard the news about his poisoned cattle yesterday, followed by a flash of fearful guilt in her green eyes, his worry and suspicions about her had increased. He now regretted not running a background check on her before instructing his manager to hire her after their phone interview. Everyone on the ranch had been desperate for a new cook, but that was no excuse for him not being more diligent. From the moment she'd turned her face away from peering in the window of the club to gaze with undisguised unrepentance at him, his gut had told him she could wreak havoc on his life. She had, and he'd grown to like it. Something told him his girl was in trouble and since she refused to talk to him, she left him no choice but to go around her stubbornness to get the answers he needed to help her.

"It's too damn early for you to be calling," Grayson grumbled with irritation upon answering.

"I need a favor." As Caden knew he would, Grayson listened quietly as he explained his worries and what he wanted before he gave him Sydney's license tag number to run the search, or at least start it.

"Give me ten minutes," was all he said before hanging up.

Sydney averted her gaze when she emerged from the bathroom as he returned to the bedroom, her damp hair appearing darker around her pale face. "Hey. I'll get breakfast started. I imagine you're anxious to check on the cows."

"Cattle," he corrected her for about the hundredth time. "And yes, I'll need to get out to the barn early." He strode toward her and clasped her narrow shoulders, feeling the small tremble of her body at his touch. Bending his head, he nipped her lower lip before asking, "You okay this morning?"

"Yeah, sure." Stepping back, she inched around him with a smile that didn't reach her eyes. "I better get in there."

Caden watched her scurry out, more determined than ever to get to the root of what was bothering her. He'd known all day yesterday something was up with her, but he'd been too busy seeing to his cattle and property to question her. Last night, he hadn't wanted to disturb the pleasant interlude of having her snuggled next to him as they both relaxed after the long grueling day. She'd been hiding from him when she ducked under the covers to treat him to a hell of a blowjob, and by the time he'd come so hard inside her he was seeing stars, they were both too exhausted to do anything but fall asleep. Now, he wished he had pushed her for an explanation last night.

Ten minutes later, after receiving Grayson's return call, he swore under his breath and stomped to the kitchen, armed with the information from Grayson's first run on her. But as soon as she saw him, she turned from the stove with determination etched on her face and sadness clouding her eyes, one hand keeping a white-knuckled grip on the spatula she'd been stirring eggs with.

"I have to leave in a few days. I'm sorry."

Surprised, Caden stared at her for a moment, speechless.

Fuck. "Why?" he demanded harshly, struggling to rein in his temper and loosen the tight clutch around his chest her words evoked. For the life of him, he couldn't think of a single reason for her to tender her resignation, unless it was because of what she wasn't telling him.

"I… I need to get back home. Something has come up." She shifted her green eyes out the window over the sink, her slim shoulders drooping.

"Damn it." Grasping her shoulders, he turned her to face him. "You pestered me until you got me, now you owe me more than 'I have to leave tomorrow'. What has happened that requires your immediate return home? Are you in trouble or does this have something to do with your family, whom you refused to share anything about?" Frustration colored his voice, but he didn't care. Her evasiveness about her past and family grated on him. "Can't tell me that? Maybe this will be easier for you. Why did you lie about your last name? Your license plate is registered to Sydney Greenbriar from St. Louis." He didn't think it possible she could turn any paler, but she did as she struggled to free herself from his grip. Releasing her, he stepped back, the anger and betrayal swirling in her eyes cutting him to the quick until he remembered she wanted to leave.

"You checked up on me? Don't I have enough to deal with without you betraying me also?" she wailed, the despair in her voice forcing him to reach for her again. She sidestepped his grasp with a glare. "Don't." Her breathing hitched. "I can't do what I have to if you touch me. Hell, I can't even think straight."

He didn't have time now to question why that statement pleased him so much, or how she'd gotten to him so quickly. First, he needed to discover what had occurred to cause those flashes of fear he'd caught on her face yesterday, and again just now. "You're my employee, and that means you're under my protection. Do you honestly think I, or anyone else on this ranch, wouldn't stand between you and any trouble you're facing?" He stepped toward her again, this time ignoring her efforts to wiggle away from the press of his body against hers. Fisting her hair like he did last night, he brought her up on her toes and kissed her long and deep.

"Let me go, Caden," she demanded in a breathless whisper when he released her lips.

"No." He couldn't, not without answers, not without knowing what brought on this sudden announcement and why she was so scared.

Frustration ripped through what little composure she had maintained as she jerked against him and cried out, "Damn it, he'll come after you next if I don't leave!"

"Who?" he returned, his concern more for her and the anguish written on her face than for himself.

"I can't say anything else. There are people I love dearly, my family who will be unbearably hurt if they find out why I had to leave home." That stubborn look he knew so well returned. "I owe them and won't do that to them. I thought I had more time to work this out, but yesterday," she turned her head away again, "yesterday proved I don't. Now, let me go."

Caden didn't want to, but he wasn't into forcing women. He stepped away from her, folded his arms and asked, "Do you know who's responsible for poisoning my cattle?"

Sydney's incredible green eyes turned bleak. "Yes, and no. He threatened me in town last week, but I swear, he never hinted he would come after you or your ranch, only me. I'm sorry. I know you and the others can never forgive…"

He cut her off with a scowl and two words. "Shut up." Caden fought to get himself under control, just the mere mention of someone threatening her threw him into a tailspin of worry and anger. "No one here will blame you. I take it you don't have a name?"

"No, he's a stranger, sent by… that's all I can say." She squared her shoulders and looked him in the eye.

He knew when he'd run up against a brick wall, but just because he couldn't get anywhere with her, didn't mean Grayson wouldn't come up with something else. "You're determined to leave?" he asked.

She turned back around to gaze out the window and replied in a soft voice, "I have to, Caden."

"What if I said I want you to stay, and not because you're an employee I don't want the hassle of replacing?"

Her voice wobbled, and she gripped the counter with white knuckles. "I can't. I'm sorry."

Exasperated with her obstinacy, he snapped, "I don't need you to protect me. My family's been safeguarding this land for decades and I have the utmost confidence in the loyalty of my hands. You can't trust me enough to tell me anything else?"

Sydney rubbed her temples, still refusing to face him. "There's nothing you can do," she sighed. "To reveal what's going on would irrevocably hurt those I care about very much."

Caden understood the love of family, which was why he could admire the hell out of her willingness to sacrifice herself for those she cared deeply for even as he resented that was the very trait forcing her to leave. Stomping toward the back door, he snatched his hat off a hook then pivoted back around to see her still gazing out the window, her shoulders slumped with an air of abject sadness that tore at him. "I can't stop you from running tomorrow, but damn it, you'll face me now, while you're still here."

She spun about and there it was, that familiar spark of defiance backed by a flare of heat she didn't bother to hide. Even though he preferred it when she pushed his buttons with her teasing candor, he'd take this look over the misery etched on her face a second ago.

"I'm thirty-nine years old. I've enjoyed women I've been fond of, but I've never felt for anyone an iota of what you mean to me.

For me, that's worth fighting for and worth taking risks for. Just so you know."

Slamming out of the house, he pressed Grayson's number on his cell as he strode toward the barn. As soon as he picked up, Caden snapped at his friend, "Anything else yet?"

Chapter 7

Sydney's heart executed a slow roll at the hint of possessiveness in Caden's gaze, the touch of caring that went beyond concern for an employee's welfare for the first time. His gruff words were everything she'd wanted to hear without realizing it and only added to the burden of having to leave. He walked out without a backward glance and she turned back to the window to watch him cross the space between the house and barn with his phone at his ear.

She wanted to confide in him, but how could she without him insisting she confront her family? The death of her grandfather from a stroke brought on by grief over her mother's unexpected death occurred less than two weeks after the funeral of their only daughter. The double blow almost cost Sydney her beloved grandmother also, and she couldn't, wouldn't subject her to yet another heartache. Not if she could help it. Her only hope for her own current desolation was to find a way to return to the ranch, and her rancher, once she found her way out from under Uncle Mike's threats.

The afternoon was more difficult to get through than she'd imagined. She didn't see Caden, and when Connor showed up followed by the sheriff, neither came up to the house to talk to her. Instead of going on her usual midday stroll, she started to pack and then took scraps out to the dogs one last time. It was almost six p.m. and dusk had fallen when she started back up to the house and saw an unfamiliar car pulling into the drive.

Sydney's heart jumped into her throat as her two oldest uncles, Robert and David, got out and glared at her from across the yard. With a crook of his finger, Uncle Robert beckoned her over. Unable to help herself, she ran to them, throwing her arms around Robert and promptly bursting into tears.

"Well, hell, Syd, how can we lay into you if you're going to turn on the waterworks?" He squeezed her tightly before handing her over to his brother.

"You have a lot to answer for, girl." The strain in David's voice went with his damp, green eyes as he hauled her next to him.

She burrowed deeper against his shoulder, whispering, "I'm sorry… what're you doing here? How'd you know…"

"I called them."

She stiffened and then whirled at the sound of Caden's rough voice. "But… how…"

"You know," David drawled, slinging his arm around her shoulders. "I don't think I've ever had the pleasure of hearing Sydney stutter in front of a man. Good job." Holding out his free hand, he introduced himself. "I'm David Greenbriar, and this is my brother, Sydney's other uncle, Robert."

"Nice to meet you both. Let's take this inside."

SYDNEY JERKED AWAY from her uncle. "What have you done?" she hissed as Caden drew her away from David and hugged her close before ushering everyone inside, with Connor and Grayson joining them. Her breathing grew short as she fretted over what the sudden appearance of her relatives might mean.

"It pays to have friends with easy access to government records. It didn't take Grayson long after running your license plate this morning to unearth where you're from and more about your family. About an hour after our talk, he called back with your uncles' names and numbers. The only thing he wasn't able to learn is why you took off two months ago." Caden nodded toward her uncles. "I called them this morning. I have to say, they made damn good time."

"We grabbed the first available flight," David said.

She had trouble wrapping her mind around Caden's subterfuge and determination until a sudden thought added to her concerns. "Did… did you talk to anyone else?" She prayed he hadn't contacted her grandmother and upset her.

Robert faced her as soon as they entered the den, hands on his hips, eyes snapping with impatience as he answered, "You're the one who has caused her grief. And we're," he nodded to his brother, "guessing this has something to do with Mike and the substantial debt he owes. He's been scarce ever since you took off."

"You know?" Sydney sank onto the sofa in shock. "But, he told me no one in the family knew, or could find out as it would break Grandma's heart."

David crouched in front of her and clasped her hands. "Lucille Greenbriar is tougher than you think, sweetheart, and a gambling debt incurred by Mike won't surprise her. He's always been bad with money, and lazy to boot. But none of that is why you left. He threatened you for help, didn't he?"

She shook her head, not wanting to be the one to reveal how immoral and corrupt in his desperation Mike had become. "I don't want to hurt you, or anyone else. It's bad enough Caden's ranch has suffered because of him, and me."

"Don't make me turn you over my knee in front of your relatives," Caden warned, his stern look saying he wouldn't hesitate if she didn't stop with the self-blame. "While it's damn admirable for you to want to spare your family's feelings, darlin', in this case it's no longer wise," Caden growled in his usual impatient, caring way. "The truth has to come out sometime. And I say now."

"Taking on that burden alone was never a smart thing to do," David admonished. "Magnanimous and selfless, but wrong, nonetheless."

Sydney wanted to hide from everyone's nods, but now wasn't the time to turn coward. Caving to the pressure bearing down on her, she relayed Mike's desperate actions at her apartment and the thug he hired to threaten her into returning. "For months, he'd been pestering me to trust him with the shares Mom left me, saying he could invest them and turn a nice profit for both of us. I may not know much about such things, but enough to know he was conning me. When he became really desperate, he let slip he owed a lot of people, some who didn't like to be kept waiting for payment." She shuddered at the memory, but when she looked up into Caden's cobalt gaze and saw the anger on her behalf, that warm, fuzzy sensation in her chest she first experienced when he'd found her spying through the window of his club, returned.

For the first time since Mike's hired bully had approached her, Sydney felt a spurt of optimism and giddy glee. Flipping her rancher one of her cheeky grins, she quipped, "I'm an idiot, aren't I?"

"Yes, but a very caring one," David answered with a smile as he rose. Caden just lifted one eyebrow, as if to say, 'you damn well are'.

"We knew it was bad, but not how bad," Robert sighed, running a hand through his thinning hair. "But there's no excuse for his behavior. Under the circumstances, I think it's best if you stay here while we dish out some tough love to our baby brother."

"What about Nana?" Unbidden, tears welled as she thought of all her grandmother had endured already.

"You're a good girl, Sydney. We'll give her the details on his debt, but just say he wanted your shares and leave it at that. That'll be enough for her to come down on Mike like a ton of bricks. Don't worry, you'll be able to come home soon, I promise," David assured her.

"In the meantime, give me a description of the man who accosted you in town," Grayson said as he took a seat next to her and pulled out a small notebook. "Was that the only time you saw him, last week?"

This isn't going to go over well, she mused before telling the truth and bracing for Caden's wrath. "No. He showed up at the mess hall yesterday, while everyone was out. That's when he admitted he'd poisoned the water and suggested it could be someone on the ranch who got hurt next time."

"Son-of-a-bitch," Connor muttered.

Caden remained silent, but his glacial look spoke volumes. Her uncles' faces were creased with concern, and guilt slithered under her skin again, making her regret her choices.

Funny, Sydney thought fifteen minutes later as Caden showed her uncles the guest rooms they could use tonight before catching their flight in the morning. Somehow, in the past few weeks, her desire to return home had shifted into second priority, while remaining here on the ranch, with her rancher, slid into the first slot. She made it through dinner and the evening of catching up before she turned to Caden with a beaming smile as he shut them into the privacy of his room.

Keeping her eyes on his, she slowly unzipped her jeans and shimmied out of them. "It looks like you're stuck with me a little longer, boss."

Arms crossed, he replied in a cool tone, "Looks like."

Her top went sailing onto a chair next, followed by her bra and panties. "Gee, what *will* you do with me?" She cupped her breasts, a shiver rippling down her spine at the raw lust stamped on his sun-bronzed face.

He reached out, hauled her up against him and took her mouth in a deep, tongue-stroking kiss before swatting her ass, hard.

"*Ow!* What was that for?"

"For not trusting me or your family sooner." With a small push, he sent her toppling onto the bed. "Continue." He placed her hands back on her breasts then rid himself of his clothes.

Sydney's arousal skyrocketed by the time he draped the full length of his rock-hard body on top of her, clasped her hands and held them above her head. The relief of having shared her burden and her uncle's promise to take Mike in hand brought a whole new level of excitement to submitting to Caden.

"This can be your home, if you want it to be, Sydney," he said, shoving her legs apart. "I want you." He worked his cock inside her, one slow inch at a time. "I need you." Pulling back, her breath caught as he took his time filling her again. "This," he bumped her cervix, "is now home for me, *you* are home."

The tears returned as she wrapped her legs around his hips and dug her heels into his flexing butt. Who said she couldn't call two places home? Only this one, here, with her rancher, was the one she longed to plant roots.

"Well, since you put it like that, and given my poor sense of direction, I probably couldn't find my way back to Missouri, at least not without you. I would love to stay." Tomorrow, she'd tell him she loved him. Tonight, she'd just show him.

Epilogue

Two months later

Sydney stood at the kitchen sink, staring out the window at the light snow falling in large, soft flakes. The afternoon had darkened early due to the cloud cover, and she worried Caden wouldn't get back tonight like he promised. He and Connor had been gone for five days at an annual ranching seminar in Wyoming, and she missed him dreadfully.

The last several weeks had passed in a blur of changes. The sheriff had found the man sent by her uncle, using her description, and with Uncle Mike's sworn statement, had been able to make charges stick against him. For his part, her uncle had shown true shock at the man's threats and actions, swearing he never asked him to harm anyone and never intended for him to take his persuasion to get her to come home so far. With no choice left to him, Mike agreed to rehab and counseling in exchange for the family paying off his debt, but only after they made it clear it would be his last chance. Robert and David also threatened him with expulsion from the family if he stepped out of line again.

She'd returned home for two weeks, Caden accompanying her for the first week. He'd won her grandmother over in spades and nothing could have made Sydney happier than having her beloved relative's blessing to move to Montana for good, especially since they all promised to visit often. Now, if only her rancher would get his butt back here. The nights had been cold and lonely with him gone.

The sound of his large truck tires crunching over the frozen ground reached her ears before the bright headlights crossed in front of the window. With her heart beating in a wild tattoo of excitement, she braced her hands on the counter ledge and leaned forward to watch his tall frame striding up to the front door.

Turning as he entered the kitchen, she beamed at him. "You're home."

Caden's eyes gleamed as he tossed his Stetson onto a kitchen chair and shrugged out of his coat. "Not yet, darlin." Striding toward the minx who had turned his life upside down, he gave her a cold kiss before spinning her around and placing her hands back on the edge of the counter. After making short work of yanking her jeans down, releasing his cock and sinking into her wet, slick depths, he breathed in her ear, "Now, I'm home."

The End

Submitting to the Sheriff

COWBOY DOMS, BOOK TWO

Published by Blushing Books
An Imprint of
ABCD Graphics and Design, Inc.
A Virginia Corporation
977 Seminole Trail #233
Charlottesville, VA 22901

BJ Wane
Submitting to the Sheriff

ebook ISBN: 978-1-61258-960-2
v1

Chapter 1

The flashing outline of the neon red motel sign bled through the curtained window, shedding an eerie glow into the darkened room and distracting Avery Pierce from glaring at the cell phone she'd tossed onto the bed beside her. Propped against the headboard, she tightened her clasped hands, trying not to panic over her current destitute circumstances, which had just worsened after her first attempt at this new job ended in such a failed, embarrassing fiasco. With a mental headshake, she wondered why she'd ever thought she could pull this off. *Relax, would you? You're so fucking uptight you're as rigid as a fucking virgin.* She could still recall Darren's comments the first time they'd had sex, and how they'd made her feel inept and unappealing, the same as her first caller had just made her feel.

A phone sex operator. What the heck had she been thinking? Her lack of experience with both sex and men in general had been glaringly obvious to her ex as well as to the man who hung up on her after less than a minute. At that rate, the extraordinary high hourly pay she'd been promised would take weeks to earn instead of the day or two she'd been hoping for. Heck, she bemoaned on a sigh, if her next caller ended their conversation that fast, she might not get a third chance, and then how would she get out of Springfield and continue with putting as much distance as possible between herself and Darren?

Avery's minimal college dating experiences had taught her most guys didn't go for brainy geeks with mousy brown hair best left worn in a braid and wearing black-framed glasses, and those who did didn't stick around. By the time she'd reached the age of twenty-nine, the only man she'd let herself trust after those depressing break-ups had been Detective Darren Lancaster, and her chest tightened against the instant up kick of her heart rate just thinking about him caused.

The phone pealed again and she jumped, her palm growing clammy as she picked it up. With less than a hundred dollars left of her meager savings and not knowing whom she could trust, she needed enough cash to get out of Illinois altogether. Two weeks and the two hundred miles she'd put between her and Chicago and the corrupt cop who had played her for a fool wasn't nearly enough. As sleazy as this job was, it was the only thing she'd found that would pay in cash and that she could do quickly without having to fill out traceable paperwork. Between being an avid connoisseur of suspense novels and working at the police department, she at least knew of a few things to do, and not to do, to stay hidden for as long as possible. She also knew nothing was failsafe or could last forever.

Taking a deep breath, Avery followed a tip Esmerelda passed on when she hired her and draped the thin scarf intended to disguise her voice as huskier than it really was over the phone given to her by the agency. Pressing the green button, she answered, praying she could do a better job keeping this person on the line longer than she had with her first attempt at seducing a stranger over the phone.

"Midnight Whispers. How can I pl... please you?" Avery winced at her stutter, those words tripping her up the same as with the first call. She chilled at the slight pause, but when the voice finally came through, the deep, amused rumble sent an unexpected wave of warmth through her.

"Excuse me, sugar. I must have dialed wrong."

"Wait!" Panic and desperation turned her voice reed thin as she tried to stop him from hanging up. "Please, can you just… talk to me for a minute?" How stupid, she moaned, knocking her head against the headboard. At the price per minute they would charge him why would he stay on the line? He paused again and then asked her a question that threw her for a loop with his astuteness.

"You in some kind of trouble, sugar?"

"I… why do you ask that?" Was the man a mind reader?

"Let's say I'm good at listening to women, hearing what they need without them saying so. It can help to talk, even to a stranger," he offered, surprising her yet again.

Not in this case. If only she could. Confiding in someone, anyone would be such a relief. But telling anyone how Darren had used her and ensured she would fall under suspicion should his evidence stealing ever be discovered was not an option, at least not until she could find a way to keep her name clear.

"N… no, there's nothing I need to… talk about." She sighed in despondency. "I… I'm just desperate for money," she admitted. Why not? At least that much was true, and at this point she had nothing to lose by revealing that personal tidbit to a stranger. Damn it, there he went with another pregnant pause, leaving her struggling to swallow past the lump of dread lodged in her throat as she waited for the buzz of a disconnected call to ring in her ear.

"And this was your only option?" Doubt colored the rich tenor of his voice before turning to one of regret. "I'm sorry. I'll let you get back to work then."

"Wait!" she gasped again, not believing she was about to do this. Given how nice he'd been so far, what could it hurt? It wasn't like they would ever meet. And what other choice did she have? "Would you mind giving me… some pointers? You know, on what I could say that might…" Avery winced, gripped the phone tighter and rushed to say, "make you want to keep talking to me?"

Amusement crept back into his voice as he returned in a dry tone, "You really are desperate and out of your depth, aren't you?"

"Yes," she breathed. There was no point in denying the obvious.

"I'm much better at telling and showing women what they want, what turns them on. Let's go with that and then you can turn it around for your next caller. Are you somewhere private?"

He wanted to turn *her* on? Good luck with that. Her responses to sex had always been lukewarm, at best, and ever since discovering Darren's shocking betrayal, the thought of any kind of intimacy left her cold. But Avery was so thrilled with his willingness to stay on the line, she didn't hesitate to go along with him. What he didn't know about her couldn't hurt either of them. "I'm alone, at my place." She fudged the location but figured the motel room where she'd stayed holed up for the last twelve days was her place as long as she paid the rate.

"Good. One thing," he cautioned with a hard edge to his voice that drew a shiver. "I insist on honesty. Deal?"

"Deal," she readily agreed, deciding it wouldn't be her fault if he failed to get anywhere with her. The closest she'd come to relaxing enough to let go with a pleasurable release were the times Darren's frustration with her in the bedroom had brought out his take-charge attitude. His succinct 'flip over' or 'ride me' commands had enabled her to shove aside worries over whether she was pleasing him or doing something he didn't like. Those few times always left her wondering if her orgasm would have been stronger if his focus hadn't then switched to himself and his pleasure.

"Then we'll start with something simple. Tell me what you're wearing."

She glanced down with a grimace at her baggy jeans and plain pink tee shirt. Well, he did insist on honesty. "Nothing exciting, I'm afraid. Just jeans and a tee."

"Clothes don't need to be sexy or tantalizing. It's how you obey my instructions on getting out of them that will please me. Are you wearing a bra, panties? You didn't mention those."

Avery frowned at the light note of censure behind his last statement. "I wasn't aware you wanted every item."

"And now you are. If I were there with you, you would have earned five swats for the sarcasm I heard in your defensive voice."

Swats? "As in spanking?" she squeaked, a sudden rise of heat covering her face. He must have been joking.

"As in."

"You can't be serious," she returned, still unsure over whether or not he was putting her on.

"As a heart attack, sugar. But since I don't have that discipline option, watch your tone if you want this to continue," he warned, his tone now lacking all humor.

Oh, wow. She was more out of her depth now than when she'd first taken his call, only in a better way financially, she mused, surprised at how much time she'd already clocked on this call. Doing the math in her head, she figured she could get through anything he ordered without balking as long as he was willing to stay on the line.

"Sorry," she replied. "This is all so… strange." That truth was an easy admittance.

"Good girl. Your honesty pleases me." Warm approval softened his tone, but her delicate shiver in response to his voice remained the same. "Now, finish telling me what you're wearing."

"A bra and panties. No shoes or socks, no jewelry." There, that should cover all possibilities.

"Excellent. Remove your top without setting the phone down."

Even knowing she was alone, Avery couldn't keep from casting a quick glance around the room and then toward the curtain-covered window. "I'll try," she stated, cocking her head until the phone sat pressed between her shoulder and ear. Pulling her arms through the sleeves, she maneuvered the shirt over the right side of her head and then grabbed the phone with her right hand before shaking the tee down and off her left arm. "There! I did it!" she exclaimed with a pant, rather proud of herself.

His low chuckle drew goosebumps of pleasure along her arms. "You have potential, sugar. That also pleases me. Describe your bra."

The inherent demand in his voice kept her from asking what he meant by the word potential. Since she didn't want to risk him hanging up, she shoved aside her curiosity to keep him talking. Remembering his insistence on the truth, she replied, "I hate to disappoint you, but it's plain white, nothing fancy, no padding." She injected humor behind her next words. "That's what you get for demanding honesty."

"Your ceding to my demands turns me on more than what you're wearing. Remove it and describe your breasts."

"You want me to talk about my own breasts?" Avery never imagined herself doing such a thing, but then, she also never dreamed she would be conversing like this with a stranger.

"Since I can't see them, yes." When she hesitated, he added, "Remember, your job is to excite me."

Avery blew out a breath and shrugged out of her bra. Her nipples beaded from the brush of cool exposure, or maybe because of the tremors his deep voice induced. She'd never experienced such a strong effect from a man, let alone from the deep timbre of his voice. Add in his air of authority and sex-backed demands that seemed to stir something new, exciting and a touch unnerving deep inside her and was it any wonder her body perked up and took notice?

"I'm waiting."

Guilt sluiced through Avery. He was kind enough to instruct her at a high financial cost to him, she shouldn't push her luck or his generosity. "Sorry. I'm not sure what to say. I'm a size thirty-four C, and fair skinned."

"Very good. Is your skin pale all over, or do you never sunbathe topless?"

A giggle burst free. She would have to gain a ton of courage before she'd ever be brave enough to parade outside showing more than a hint of cleavage. "Both, and since I don't draw a lot of male appreciation, I've never imagined doing anything so risqué. Besides, it's too cold outside."

"Don't bring practicality into it; that's a sure way to lose your caller's interest." He grew quiet again, and she held her breath. When he spoke, his next instruction cut off her sigh of relief. "And your nipples? Describe them, please." Despite the polite phrasing, his words still came through as a command.

"Uh, they're pale pink, not small but not big either." Damn, this wasn't easy, she thought, wondering about his reaction to that vague description.

Avery quit worrying when he said, "I would enjoy fucking your breasts, stroking between the fleshy mounds as you held them together. Tug on your nipples."

The erotic image he'd implanted in her head sent another rush of heat over her face, only this time the warmth invaded her pussy, leaving her with another surprising response to question later. As she reached up to pluck her right nub, the stimulating touch added to the cocoon of intimacy he'd drawn around her with his smooth, deep voice. Avery no longer heard the night traffic outside the window or the loud voices coming from the

adjoining room, only the deep timbre of his voice and the stac-
cato thumping of her heart.

"Feel good, sugar?" he crooned, leaving her to wonder if he'd
caught the shallow sound of her increased breathing as she toyed
with her nipple.

"Y… yes. But what about you?" How mortifying it would be
if he were completely unaffected by this conversation.

"I like that you think of me as you're playing with yourself,"
he returned without answering her question. "Now, grasp your
nipple between thumb and forefinger and pinch until I tell you to
stop."

"Why?" she asked even as she obeyed the order. Her nipple
warmed and pulsed under her grip, the sensation soon repeating
itself deep inside her core.

"Because I want to test your threshold for discomfort, and
your response to something alternative. A little tighter. Your
breathing hasn't turned to shallow pants yet."

That astuteness shook Avery as much as the pinch of pain
she delivered to her tender bud. To her shock, instead of turning
her off, the sharp, needle prick induced a surge of pleasure that
engulfed her entire breast and tickled her pussy into quivering.
"*Oh,*" she breathed, startled at the exalted sensations.

"Oh good or bad?" he insisted on knowing.

"Good, in a strange way." *Very strange.* Who would have
thought?

"I'll take that," he said, his voice laced with satisfaction. "Let
go and we'll move on."

Avery released her nipple and gasped as blood rushed to the
engorged tip, adding to her discomfort with sharp pinpricks of
stabbing pain. "You could've warned me," she snapped, disconcerted by her immediate reaction to the pulsating ache.
Clamping a hand over the throbbing, tortured bud, she rotated
her palm to ease the soreness. She wasn't sure what would alleviate the reciprocating palpitations between her legs.

"I could do a lot of things, sugar, like hang up. Apologize for your tone."

The hard-edged, stern rebuke reminded Avery of the huge favor he was doing her and drew her attention to her escalated aroused state, a result of that tight grip on such a tender part of her body. "I... I'm sorry. That was... unexpected."

"I'm guessing all your responses to this conversation have been unlike anything you've felt before. It excites me to know I've gifted you with a new experience and opened your eyes and mind to new possibilities. If you want to continue, remove your jeans and panties."

Did she want to go further? She was much more relaxed and comfortable having a sex-charged conversation with a stranger, but now there was more going on with her than just insecurity over her ability to entice a man over the phone. Her body clamored for something she couldn't define, her mind awash with a need to grasp whatever relief and pleasure she could now because tomorrow wavered with uncertainty. The thought of losing the deep rumble of his voice in her ear or talking to anyone else tonight turned her cold, and she knew both need and curiosity demanded she continue.

"I want to keep going, if you do." Her conscience and gratitude demanded she at least warn him about the financial cost he was incurring. "But in case you don't already know, you're being charged by the minute. A lot." Avery held her breath, praying that wouldn't matter.

"I do, and yes, I know that, sugar."

SHERIFF GRAYSON MONROE leaned back in his home office desk chair and shifted his hips to ease the tight press of his erection against his zipper. With the phone to his ear, he glanced at the time and winced, wondering what the hell he was doing.

What started as a good deed would leave him with a hefty financial price to pay, as she'd just cautioned him. Still, there had been something in the woman's frantic voice when she'd asked him to hang on that had alerted him to trouble, and the longer he spoke with her the more her soft, breathy tone of uncertainty and fear tugged at his dominant instincts. The sparks of irritation with his instructions she let slip out tickled him and he was glad she hadn't allowed whatever trouble she was in to beat her down completely.

The rustle of clothing and her increased breathing whispered through the phone. Pressing one wrong digit on the toll free number he'd been dialing was proving to be an entertaining, if costly mistake.

"Okay. They're off."

"So, you're naked?" He tried picturing her body and wondered if the rest of her was as lush as her description of her breasts sounded.

"Yes." That small catch in her voice stirred him again. *Fuck*, but that sound got to him.

"Excellent. Now, since it's your job to excite your caller, you'll want to entice him, or her to touch themselves with the goal of getting them off. But, not too fast since your pay depends on you keeping them on the line as long as possible."

"What do you mean 'or her'?"

Grayson rubbed his brow in bemusement at the surprise in her tone. *Phone sex with a newbie. Who would have thought?* He had figured this outlet of sexual diversion had gone out with the internet, but here he was, trying to use his knowledge as an experienced Dom to give a scared stranger instructions on the job. He didn't mind and was enjoying himself even if the whole scenario would have sounded incongruous before tonight.

"Men aren't the only perverts out there, sugar," he drawled with a touch of humorous sarcasm. Imagining what he would order her to do if she were a sub at his club, he stated, "Bend your knees and widen them. Your position should leave your labia spread and display your pretty pussy."

"Okay, done," she breathed.

"Excellent. Now, bend over and name a fruit that best describes what you're eyeing between your folds."

"*Sheesh.*" Her muttered shock came through the line loud and clear.

"That and your delay would earn you another few swats. I'm waiting." He loved those small gasps that hinted her body was on board even if her mind wasn't. Those little signs of submissiveness would be a delight to explore under different circumstances.

"Fine, uh, watermelon. How's that?"

The whispered need for approval made Grayson wish he could give it to her in person. "Good girl. Your words have my cock hardening as I picture your juicy, dark pink flesh. Putting an image into your caller's head will egg them on. Now, using one finger on the inside of your thigh, up by your knee, start making small circles."

"Why?" she questioned him again, her breathlessness leaving Grayson to wonder if she was imagining the erection she caused.

"Because I said to." She huffed, but the sigh that followed told him she liked the light teasing touch. "Since your knee is bent, move downward, widening your circles with each shift toward your crotch. Does that feel good?" He spoke without pause to keep her from questioning herself too much. The time for introspection could come later, after they hung up.

"Yes, but sort of tickles. I'm… there with the next circle."

"Excellent. Once you hit the crease where your bent leg meets your pussy, your circle should be wide enough your finger will glide up your spread labia. Do it."

Jesus. That little catch in her voice was enough to turn his cock into a steel rod that threatened to bust through his fucking zipper. Biting back a groan of self-inflicted frustration, Grayson decided to reward her before turning her loose to fend for herself with the next caller. Although, after checking the time again, she may have just made enough with him to call it a night.

"Circle your clit next, pressing a little harder. Pretend I'm watching you and your main goal is to please and excite me. I want to hear you climax."

"Oh, God," she moaned, her low voice carrying a tortured undertone that tore at his composure and had him questioning, again, what trouble had landed her in such a desperate state.

"Harder now, sugar. A little faster." Her breath caught again, a small sound that ripped through him before her cry resonated in his ear, ringing of both surprise and relief. He gave her a few more minutes to come down from the pleasure, to clear her head and remember he was there with her.

"I..." She sucked in a gasping breath. "I... never... thank you," she ended on a long sigh.

"You're welcome." He paused a moment before asking, "Are you sure you don't want to tell me what happened that you ended up with this as your only option?"

"I'm sure." She didn't hesitate over that answer, and he'd done all he could to help her but couldn't resist offering one more boon before hanging up. "Look, if you're ever near Willow Springs, Montana, stop and ask for Grayson Monroe. I might be able to help you."

WITH HER BODY still shuddering from small aftershocks of pleasure she'd never achieved before, Avery gasped at his generous, unexpected offer. "Are you serious?" He couldn't be, she decided. He was just being nice. But his parting words gave her pause.

"As a heart attack, sugar. You take care."

The sudden dial tone buzzing in her ear cleared the remaining euphoric fog clouding her head. When she saw how long they'd been talking, a different kind of warmth spread through her sated, quivering body. Dialing the number Esmerelda gave her to both check in and sign off, she took her number off the list for the night before they put any more calls through to her phone. Even if she hadn't made enough with *his* call, after that experience, there was no way she could concentrate enough to talk with anyone else right now. Not only was she still reeling from a stranger's generosity of time, money and concern, but her limited and disappointing sexual past hadn't prepared her for such an explosive response to a deep, commanding voice giving erotic instructions.

He'd left her with just one burning question waiting for an answer. Where did she go from here?

Chapter 2

"We need to talk."

Chad Banks' voice echoed around the corner of the police precinct's parking garage, halting Avery in her tracks. She'd never cared much for Darren's partner and preferred waiting out of sight for him to leave before meeting the vice detective she'd been dating the last six months for dinner.

"What about?" Darren asked with clear irritation.

"I stopped in the evidence room this morning. Avery jumped and appeared unsettled at seeing me. When she left her desk to get the box I requested, I checked her computer to see what she'd been so engrossed with when I came in. You will not like it," Chad warned, the menace in his voice sending a shiver of unease down Avery's spine. She feared she knew what he would say next.

"Talk faster, Banks, she'll be out here any minute," Darren insisted.

"She had the Mendez interview pulled up along with the log-ins from that bust. I *fucking* told you Mendez's accounting during the D.A.'s plea bargain interview would come back to bite us." Anger vibrated behind every word Chad uttered.

Oh, God. Fear coiled through Avery like an insidious, slow crawling snake ready to sink its fangs into her. Detective Banks had entered her small office adjacent to the evidence room in his usual brusque, hurried and demanding manner earlier that morning. After insisting on her immediate retrieval of an envelope from the storage unit for his perusal, he left her no choice but to leave her desk unattended to obey his order. As a lowly IT clerk, all the detectives in Chicago's busiest precinct were her superiors.

Just those few words confirmed her suspicions there had been something off between the money-laundering con artist, Josef Mendez's testimony to the D.A. and what Darren and Chad had given her to log into the evidence room. She hadn't wanted to believe what she suspected, but now might not have a choice. Darren's silence unnerved her until he spoke again, and then his words chilled her to the bone.

"Damn meddling bitch. Hell, the only reason I'm fucking her is to keep her from looking too closely at things like that. It'll really piss me off if my sacrifice turns out to be for nothing, but let's not jump to conclusions."

"Yeah, well that plan isn't working so well, now is it? I say we need to fix this, and fast, before she goes digging deeper." Banks sounded as angry and frustrated as Darren as the two of them confirmed the suspicions she'd been praying were all wrong.

"Quit acting like a hothead. There's nothing to panic over yet. I'll feel her out. Once I get an idea of what she knows, we'll go from there."

"And if she knows, or even suspects too much?" Banks persisted in wanting to know.

Avery recognized Darren's contemptuous sigh. "I'm not keen on prison any more than you. If necessary, we'll arrange an accident and that'll take care of the problem."

The casual indifference behind his coldly phrased suggestion sent Avery reeling back a clumsy step. She bumped into the trash container, the metal bin thumping against the concrete wall reverberating in the cavernous garage, the loud report increasing her already escalated heart palpitations. Oh God, oh God, oh God. How could she have been so stupid? Men never took notice of clumsy, muttering geeks and none had ever shown interest in her past a few dates or one round of sex. Why hadn't she remembered those hard-learned lessons when Darren started taking her out?

With her heart lodged in her throat, mind-gripping terror sent her fleeing *back into the elevator, the doors swishing closed before either man came around the corner. That small boon in her favor was short-lived as she fretted over what to do and where to go. It would be her word against two seasoned detectives, so it didn't take much thought to know she couldn't turn them in without solid proof that couldn't just as easily point the finger her way. After all, she was the one in charge of all evidence brought into the precinct and stored, as well as for logging everything into the computer.*

One word kept pounding in her head as she dashed back to her office. Run... run... run

Avery jerked awake with a gasp, her perspiration-soaked body shivering from the remnants of the dream still too vivid in her mind. Sucking in a deep breath, she looked around the dingy motel room and tried to remember which city she was in, and what happened to set off the nightmare. And then it came to her in a fearful rush. *I broke the law, I'm now a hacker.*

She'd left Springfield three days after getting the job at Midnight Whispers, unable to continue talking with strangers who wanted nothing from her except enough titillation to get themselves off. She'd tried turning everything her benevolent mystery man taught her around the other way but had continued to fumble her way through short conversations that left her humiliated, despondent and feeling more alone than ever.

In Des Moines, she had been lucky enough to land a waitressing gig at a highway diner, the owner more than happy to pay her less than minimum wage in cash. After visiting the public library and using their computer lab to see what, if anything was going on in Chicago, she'd stuck around for ten days when nothing incriminating showed up in the papers. Since she'd left her phone off with the batteries removed after sending a quick text to her foster mother, Marci Devers in Florida before fleeing, she didn't know if anyone else had tried to contact her and was too afraid to check. She couldn't take the chance of Darren tracking her through her phone or taking a call from him. Not even a text. Her acting skills were nil; as Marci often pointed out,

Avery wore her thoughts and emotions on her sleeve. There had always been few people in her life who mattered, or whom she mattered to, so there had never been a reason to learn the art of hiding what she was feeling.

And then, on her last day there, despair over having to move on again with no destination in mind or ability to get her life back prompted her to do the unthinkable; return to the library to hack into the precinct's logs. Using her skills and some creative maneuvering, she unearthed another discrepancy between the items Darren and Chad turned into evidence and the suspect's accounting of his stash. After noting the two similar inconsistencies were both from busts Darren and Chad had worked alone, she'd copied the data and fled, a new fear stemming from breaking the law pushing her to get out of Des Moines as fast as possible.

Sliding out of the lumpy bed, Avery hugged herself against the chill and peeked out the window to see light snowflakes falling. Shivering, she now recalled arriving in Sioux Falls, South Dakota yesterday afternoon, her first stop another library. A quick check of her email revealed the third message from her supervisor questioning her abrupt family medical leave request and sudden disappearance, but nothing indicating her snooping had been discovered. She felt bad for putting Susan in a bind; her boss had always been a pleasure to work for, understanding and supportive. But it was obvious Susan's generous consideration had been wearing thin when she let Avery know she would offer her position to the temporary young employee filling in for her if she didn't return on Monday.

Sighing, Avery rested her forehead against the cold glass windowpane. One of the hardest things Darren's manipulations had forced her into was answering Susan with her resignation. At least she'd been smart enough, and quick enough to copy all of Darren and Chad's evidence deposits, as well as the one transcribed interview of their suspect onto a flash drive before she'd fled after hearing them in the garage. If those files were erased or altered in her absence, she still held proof something was off with one, and now two of their raids and that the two were dirty cops. Not that it would stand up if it came to her word against theirs if they claimed *she* stole the evidence after they turned in the entire contents of their busts.

Start over, that's what she needed to do. Find someplace new, far from Chicago, begin a new chapter in her life and pray Detective Darren Lancaster would forget all about her in time. Not that *she* would be memorable, only what she might, or might not know would be. Only one man had shown genuine interest in *her*, had given her his undivided attention, listened to her, cared enough to help her even though they were strangers over the phone. That accidental call had been the only shining beacon during the last weeks of living with never-ending fear and uncertainty and what still aided in getting her through the long, lonely days and insecure nights.

Padding across the room to the miniscule bathroom, Avery flipped the shower on and stripped off her sleep shirt. Stepping into the small, steaming cubicle, she leaned against the wall and lathered her hands, remembering how he'd ordered her to touch herself and her response to his commands. The memory alone warmed her, much more than any other time when she'd indulged in masturbation. None of her previous self-induced climaxes had come close to rivaling the off-the-charts response he'd led her into that had left her stunned and steeped in pleasure.

If you're ever near Willow Springs, Montana, stop and ask for Grayson Monroe.

With each day that had passed since that night, the temptation to take Grayson Monroe up on his offer pulled stronger. The echo of his deep voice and her responses to both it and his commands still played through her head. Since being on the run, the only time she'd felt safe, the only time she hadn't suffered the pangs of loneliness had been those two hours spent with him on the phone. Did he mean it, or had he been sending her off with a comment neither of them expected her to follow up on? And was she desperate enough, brave enough to find out?

Going to Marci was out of the question. The social worker who had been the only stable adult influence in Avery's life as she grew up with an alcoholic single mother would welcome her with open arms, just as Marci had done every time Avery's mother ended up in rehab. But Darren knew about her close ties with Marci and she refused to put the woman who had always been more of a mother to her than her own in jeopardy.

Avery dried off, got dressed and opened the bathroom door to scan the bleak motel room and wonder how much longer she could keep up with moving around, going from one meaningless job to another. She was a geeky IT tech, quiet and reserved unless playing online video games with people she didn't know. She'd tried switching her wide-framed glasses for contacts and wearing her wavy, unruly hair down, but the small discs had irritated her eyes and her hair kept falling in her face as she'd worked, annoying and distracting her. Darren's betrayal still cut her to the quick, but that was on her as she should've known the precinct's hottest cop had to harbor an ulterior motive for seeking her out and pursuing her with dogged determination and flattery she'd never gotten from another man.

As the approach of dawn lightened the pearl gray sky to a warmer amber glow, Avery made a snap decision, counted her cash and figured her expenses between here and Montana before she could chicken out. The bulk of her savings had gone to purchase the fifteen-year-old, clunky sedan she still couldn't get used to after opting for public transportation the last ten years. She was okay out on the highway, in clear weather, but city traffic still made her a nervous wreck. She couldn't afford to draw attention or questions by getting a ticket or into an accident. With just over an eleven-hour drive ahead of her, she figured she had enough to last her a week or two if she continued to live frugally and could pick up work soon after arriving in Willow Springs. Considering everything else, what did she have to lose?

THE SOFT CRY reverberating down from The Barn's converted loft drew Master Grayson's attention. His lips quirked around the toothpick nestled on the right side of his mouth as he caught sight of Sydney, Caden's submissive strapped to the St. Andrew Cross, her petite white body attractively displayed, the light pink stripes decorating her skin from his flogger discernible even in the dim lighting shining from the rafters. Both he and Caden's brother, Connor still found Caden's recent tumble from bachelorhood amusing. Watching his friend succumb to her charming insistence a few months ago had entertained everyone in the club.

"I never tire of watching him with her," Grayson said, flicking his gray/green gaze to Connor who stood manning the circular bar in the center of the lower floor. The rough-hewn walls of the old barn had been whitewashed, insulated and reinforced; the floors sanded and refinished to a glossy shine. The bathrooms were just one of the amenities they'd added when they'd undertaken the huge task of turning the dilapidated structure into a private club over seven years ago.

Connor didn't bother tipping his Stetson back to get a better view of his brother when he glanced that way. "I'm happy for him, even if I did have to push him in her direction. She keeps things lively on the ranch."

"I bet." Grayson often listened to Caden's constant grumbling about Sydney's penchant for getting lost and pampering the farm animals with amusement, the way his rugged face would soften whenever he looked at her giving him away every time. They were all happy and relieved to hear her uncle, who had caused her such grief, was doing well in rehab and with keeping the new position in the family's whole foods company his brothers had given him. It had taken aligning himself with the wrong person to wake him up to his destructive ways, but at least he was trying to make amends to the family, and niece he had wronged.

Swiveling on the barstool, Grayson leaned his elbows on the shiny, mahogany top and eyed Connor. "He's a lucky man. Are you going to follow in his footsteps?"

Connor snorted and nodded to Master Dan seated at the end with his play partner for the night. "Coming up," he called down when Dan signaled for his second drink. Drawing the beer, he answered Grayson with slow-drawled sarcasm. "Not hardly."

"You know what they say when you fall off the saddle; it's best to get right back on." Grayson felt for Connor when he split with his long-time girlfriend, Annie last fall, but no woman was worth pining over for months.

"I can still ride just fine, thank you. Besides, I don't see you hooking up with anyone for more than a scene or two," he pointed out, sliding Dan's beer down to him.

"Okay, you've got me there." No use denying the truth, Grayson mused. He might limit his submissive picks to only a night or two of his dominance, but he made sure he gave them everything they desired, and often what they didn't know they wanted. Which made the edgy dissatisfaction marring his recent enjoyment unexplainable. Hoping for a better outcome tonight, he asked, "Speaking of which, who's still unspoken for?" He shifted his eyes to the dance floor where several couples pressed close together for the slow country western ballad pealing through high-tech speakers.

"Cassie was asking for you right before you came in." Connor smirked with a glint in his blue eyes.

Grayson scowled at him. Connor was well aware he'd been avoiding the persistent blonde ever since she'd turned demanding and clingy after two scenes with her. "I'll pass, thanks." He spotted another sub, Nan, whom he knew enjoyed pain play and rougher scenes, just what he was in the mood for. "I see a leggy brunette who needs me."

Connor looked across the room and saw the submissive everyone knew was not interested in settling down with one Dom. "Yeah, your bachelorhood is safe with her." With a two-fingered tip of his hat, he added, "Have fun."

Grayson slid off the stool and offered some parting advice before strolling over to claim his playmate for the evening. "Maybe you can try to do the same."

As sheriff of Willow Springs and the surrounding area, Grayson was well known with the town folk. As a partner with the Dunbar brothers in their BDSM club, he enjoyed socializing with members and friends from as far away as Billings, who didn't mind the one-hour drive for a night of indulging in their favorite sexual proclivities among others of like persuasions. Taking the time to wind his way through the tables and seating areas spread around the cavernous, first floor space, he spoke or nodded to acquaintances as he questioned his lack of enthusiasm in approaching Nan. He'd enjoyed her before, as had almost every Dom in the place, and never ended a scene with her without walking away satisfied. In fact, she was the only woman he'd broken his rule of not being with more than twice. Since she was of like mind in not desiring a full-time, committed relationship, he deemed her a safe bet to return to on occasion.

So why wasn't he anticipating putting her through her paces as she greeted him with a warm, interested smile, her pretty breasts propped up and put on display in the tight corset? Large dark nipples puckered as he eyed her bountiful mounds and unbidden, the memory of a soft, hesitant voice describing pale, pink-tipped breasts intruded on the enticing view. *Fucking A.* He couldn't understand why that misdialed phone call still popped into his head at random times, even now, over two weeks afterward.

"Master Grayson." Nan's deep, husky voice blocked out the faint echo of the mystery woman's soft hesitancy and stirred his interest.

"Nan." Removing the toothpick, Grayson slipped it into his shirt pocket and held out his hand in silent invitation while fingering the thin cane attached to his waist. He hoped he hadn't misread the invitation in her brown eyes or the fact she still sat alone.

Her gaze brightened as it drifted from eying the cane up to his face. "Glad to," she purred, rising and giving him a clearer look at the red, lacy lingerie that cupped her full breasts, cinched her waist and showcased the miniscule red thong barely covering her naked labia.

"You never disappoint, sugar," Grayson complimented her as he led her to a padded bench in the far corner by the wide glass doors that opened onto a back deck and spa.

"Neither do you, sir."

Maybe not in the flesh, but he couldn't help wondering if he shouldn't have done more to help the woman whose dire straits had left her no choice but to get work as a phone sex operator, a profession clearly out of her depth. Her hesitant and then frantic floundering over the line had hinted at someone in a desperate situation and worry over what might have happened to her still gnawed at his conscience.

"Lie on your stomach first," he instructed Nan, nodding to the bench. "I want you to feel the ache of your stripes when you turn over." He knew her, and her pleasures well. The flush of arousal spreading over her chest and up her neck matched the damp glistening on her denuded folds as she slid off the thong.

"Yes, sir," she replied, facing the bench and bending at the waist, leaving the corset, garters and stockings on. Her three-inch heels put her at about five ten, still five inches shorter than him, and arched her ass higher in this position.

Unclipping the cane, he reached out with his other hand and caressed her smooth, round buttocks, enjoying the soft, malleable flesh, her small quivers hinting of both excitement and unease. "Relax. I know your limits. Reach above you and grip the top of the bench. Do not let go until I say. Is your safeword still panda?" She once mentioned she collected stuffed pandas which was why that word was easy for her to remember.

"Yes, sir." Turning her face up to his, she quipped, "Why change now?"

Exactly. Maybe he was just going through a late-thirties funk, he considered as he traced a finger down her crack and tickled the damp seam of her pussy. She groaned, shuffled her feet and shifted her hips and he snapped the rod across one thigh. The sharp reprimand elicited a soft cry, but she stilled. He liked seeing those immediate responses to his heavy hand as much as he had relished his naive mystery woman's obedience. *Fucking A.* He needed to keep his head in this game and quit returning to one that should have no further meaning or bearing on his life.

Grayson tuned out the music, low-voiced conversations and high-pitched cries of pain-induced climaxes as he worked the cane over Nan's upturned ass, concentrating on the fleshiest part of her buttocks. Crimson stripes blossomed across her cheeks, but she kept herself quiet and immobile by tightening her hands above her and locking her knees against the urge to dance away from his swinging arm. Her breath came in rapid puffs among tiny mewls as he shifted to the sweet under curve of those plump mounds, but his pleasure in her response dimmed as another voice filtered into his head.

Disgusted with himself, he brought an end to the first part of their scene. "Excellent, sugar," he praised her after adorning her thighs with a few final strokes. Reaching for her hand, he helped her up, held her close when she wobbled and felt the rapid beat of her heart against his chest, the pointed drill of her turgid nipples through his black tee shirt. "You good?"

"Oh, yeah," she moaned on a sigh. "Thank you, sir."

"Don't thank me yet," Grayson warned, nudging her to sit on the end of the bench. He smiled as she winced with the pressure on her abused buttocks and assisted in laying her back. "This should help you maintain your admirable acceptance." After wrapping the cuffs attached to the sides of the bench around her wrists he did the same with her ankles to the outside bottom corners, leaving her legs in an enticing spread. "Nice," he commented, running his hands up the insides of her thighs.

"Sir, please."

"You beg nicely, Nan, but your pleasure will come when I'm ready, and not before." Her eyes flashed with frustration and darkened with need, both of which he ignored as he flicked the cane in a light snap across the underside of her breast. She closed her eyes and bit her lip, arching her chest upward in a silent plea for more.

Grayson found himself warming to the scene and her responses, his cock growing from a semi-erection to a full-blown hard-on as he striped her breasts until slick cream seeped from her gaping pussy. Setting aside the cane, he padded to the end of the bench and took up residence between her splayed legs. Leaning over her glistening body, he cupped her shoulders and stroked his open palms over her breasts. Pausing, he rotated atop her puckered nipples before gliding down her soft waist to palm the insides of her thighs. "So needy and ready for me, aren't you, sugar?" A sudden desire to move this along once again intruded on his concentration and pleasure, frustrating him anew.

"Yes, always Master Grayson. You know how to get me going," she complimented him as her muscles clenched under his hands.

"What a nice thing to say." Releasing his straining cock, he made short work of sheathing himself before using his thumbs to spread her folds even wider. With his eyes on the swollen, pink tissues all but begging him to take her, he slid slowly inside her convulsing vagina. The immediate, tight clamp of slick muscles around his girth drew a hissing breath. "Fuck, but you're hot and tight. Fast and hard. Ready?"

Nan nodded, her eyes glued to Grayson's pummeling cock, her breathing ragged as he plowed her moist depths with rigorous strokes, just as he had warned. She met each ramming thrust with a lift of her hips, each jarring plunge with a soft gasp and every withdrawal with a low moan of denial. He remembered what a delight she was to fuck and enjoyed the hell out of using her willing body, so why, when he drove Nan into a cock-gripping orgasm was he thinking about another voice crying out in climax, this one filled with both surprise and despair? Shaking off the haunting memory, he gave the woman with him what she deserved, his undivided attention, straining to bring her to another release before letting go and embracing his own pleasure.

Fifteen minutes later, Grayson stepped out back, into the cold snap of a Montana January night to clear his head. He needed to get his head straightened out and back in the game before he returned to play in the club again. He was a strict but generous Dom, and the subs willing to trust him with their needs deserved more than having half his attention during a scene that resulted in a half-assed, rushed conclusion. The frigid air seeped into his bones, leaving goosebumps along his bare arms, but the self-inflicted discomfort was well deserved for his poor performance with Nan. Despite her needy complaints, she was a woman who craved the sting and pleasure of having to wait. He knew that and let her down by moving on too quickly. Maybe he could make up for it in a few weeks. She was a good sport, walking away from their scene with a grateful smile and kiss of gratitude, but that just made him feel guiltier for not doing better by her. There was always more to a sub's needs than simply getting off, and he should have prolonged Nan's torture a little longer, taken her deeper into that place some women strived to go before climaxing. His sudden desperation to get to his own pleasure and end their time together was unforgivable.

Retrieving a toothpick from his shirt pocket, he slipped it into the corner of his mouth as the sliders swished open behind him. It didn't surprise him when Caden joined him in leaning his arms on the railing, his gaze following Grayson's to the dark woods. "Nan looked content so why aren't you?" the rancher asked with his usual bluntness.

"She should've still been lost in subspace and unable to walk away from me so easily," Grayson snapped, irritated with himself and his friend.

Caden's low chuckle didn't improve Grayson's mood. "You're not God. None of us are."

"*Fucking A*, Dunbar, go pester your girl. She likes you."

"So do you, when you're not cranky. How about if I take your mind off your poor showing as a Dom and give you something to work on as the sheriff? I'm missing several more head." Disgust laced Caden's voice and his hands tightened into fists. All ranchers dreaded and hated poaching.

"Shit. Jason from the Barton spread was in my office early this morning. He got hit last night as well. We're on it, but I don't have the staff to stake out every ranch. Did you put anyone on watch duty?" he asked, not knowing what else they could do until they had a lead to go on. Poaching was hard to prevent and even harder to catch the perpetrators.

"Yeah, the hands all stepped up and volunteered to rotate, but these guys know what they're doing. They snuck in between shift changes and moved fast. We'll catch 'em," he vowed in a cold voice, "but likely not before they've already disposed of our cattle."

Grayson shook his head and straightened. "I've got a call into state patrol for extra help in keeping an eye out. Let's hope they don't get many more before we take them down. I'm freezing my balls off and done pouting. Come on."

Caden's dry response of, "You're welcome," followed him inside and earned his friend the childish gesture of the middle finger.

Chapter 3

Montana's vast wide-open spaces backed by white-capped mountains and towering pines contrasted dramatically with the crowded metropolis of jam-packed industrial high rises of Chicago, as well as the other cities Avery had recently passed through. Driving through Big Sky Country, she noticed two things the state boasted in abundance: pickup trucks and cows. Pulling into Willow Springs, she took note of their smallest commodity: people. Growing up in one of the country's largest cities, she didn't understand the draw of small towns and worried this might be an even bigger mistake than she'd been fretting over the last two days. It was much easier to blend in among the masses filling the bigger cities she'd been hiding in than it would be in this town of less than seven thousand, and that population was large compared to most of the places she'd driven through to get here. Even the capital, Billings was a fraction of the size of Chicago.

Glancing at the gas gauge, she decided to check in at the only motel she saw once she hit Willow Springs' city limits and prayed the downtown section where she hoped to pick up work was within walking distance. Public transportation wasn't cheap, but she'd been taken aback by how much gas cost after using the lion's share of her savings to buy a used car on her way out of Chicago. She supposed if all else failed, she could always give up on this ridiculous idea of searching out her mystery caller, getting to know him first to determine if he might have been serious about helping her and then, if he seemed trustworthy, taking him up on his offer.

An hour later, Avery set out on foot from her motel room despite the cold, brisk air and walked the half mile to the quaint downtown square the motel manager directed her towards. Standing on the corner, she glanced around the neat, four-sided shopping and business area surrounding a large fountain and wooden benches. She caught a glimpse of towering mountain peaks over the rooftops of some buildings dating back decades, the view making her feel as if she stood in the middle of nowhere.

Hugging her coat around her to ward off the cold that came more from feeling out of her depth than the frigid air, she strolled down the first row of stores and businesses, noting the absence of parking meters along the neat rows of on-street parking. Several quaint gift shops displayed an array of western gear, home décor and souvenirs but no help-wanted signs. She paused outside a bookstore, her mood lightening as she peeked inside and saw the rack of new releases. After hearing Darren's threat, she'd only taken time to rush back to her furnished apartment and throw as many clothes and toiletries into one suitcase as it would hold before dashing out again to clear out her meager savings and get as far away from him as fast as possible, leaving behind her collection of suspense novels.

With a sigh of regret at not being able to spare the funds to purchase one, she kept going, hoping for a sign of employment since she didn't dare risk filling out an application online. A glimpse inside the old-fashioned soda and sandwich shop revealed it was doing a good, late afternoon business, but with enough employees to handle it. The two-story police precinct and court house followed by the water company filled the next stretch of old brick buildings and she took a chance on filling out an application at the utility office.

By the time she finished, the lowering sun had disappeared behind the buildings, leaving only a faint, yellow/orange glow of illumination to add to the lighted street lamps. The Palace, the smallest movie house she'd ever imagined looked closed, so she headed down to the corner and the bright, lit-up sign of Dale's Diner. To her relief, a large red and white help wanted sign sat in the checkered-curtained window.

Feeling as if she'd stepped back in time, Avery stood in the entrance enjoying the warmth while taking in the old-fashioned booths, each displaying a juke box, as she waited for the older woman bustling behind the long counter to break from barking out orders to the two cooks behind her. She'd no sooner taken a seat on a vacated stool than a hand plopped down a menu in front of her and the woman snapped, "Be right with you."

Bemused by her brusque manner, Avery glanced through the offerings with no intention of ordering. Even at the reasonable prices, she couldn't afford to spend more than a few dollars a day on food, which limited her to the cheaper items at fast food places. As luck would have it, her stomach rumbled just as the woman returned, reminding her she hadn't eaten all day.

"You're new around here. Monday's special is chicken fried steak, mashed potatoes and green beans."

"Oh, thank you, but I just came in to ask about the job," Avery replied as she tried not to drool over the steaming plate holding the special one cook set on the ledge for delivery.

Tapping a bell, the short, balding man called out, "Order up, Gertie!"

"Stay put," the plump, gray-haired woman instructed before snatching the plate and setting it in front of the man seated several stools down from Avery. She returned to glare at Avery, hands fisted on wide hips, blue eyes way too shrewd for her comfort. "I'm Gertie. Eat something and we'll talk."

With heat spreading over her face, Avery stuttered in response, "I… can wait… so I don't keep you. You look busy."

"Nonsense." Turning her head, she called out, "Get me another special, Clyde." Avery swallowed, resigning herself to parting with twice the cash she usually spent on a meal as Gertie faced her again and snapped out, "Food's on me. How much experience you got?"

Fidgeting on the seat, she saw no way around the truth. "Not much, just a short stint at another diner, but I catch on quick."

Narrowing her eyes, Gertie questioned, "How short?"

Regret sliced through Avery and she started to slide off the stool. "I'm sorry to have wasted your time…"

Pointing to the seat, Gertie ordered, "Sit. How short?"

"Ten days," she returned with a defiant edge to her tone as she nudged her glasses up with a jab of one finger.

"Can you write down orders correctly and bus tables in a timely fashion?"

Her pulse picked up a beat of hope. "Yes, ma'am."

"Then you're hired and don't ma'am me. It's irritating."

Surprised and grateful, Avery smiled before she remembered the hardest thing about finding work since being on the run. "Uh… I have one request, though. Can… you pay me in cash?"

That shrewd look entered her new boss' eyes again and her stare was as unnerving as her next question. "You got trouble, girl?"

Avery debated for one second on whether to decline the job offer and walk away or go with a leap of faith. Her finances encouraged her to chance the latter. "You could say that."

Gertie nodded. "Then cash it is."

"Order up!"

Grabbing the large plate, Gertie placed it in front of her, the steam and tantalizing aroma teasing Avery's senses as much as

Gertie's blind support. "Eat up and then I'll show you around. Study the menu while you're at it. You're on the clock."

WILLOW SPRINGS MIGHT BE a small town nestled amid sparsely populated ranch country, but by the time Avery reported for her evening shift on Thursday, three days later, her aching feet and the boost in cash from tips alone proved small didn't mean desolate. Monday's crowd hadn't been a fluke. The diner, named, she'd learned, after Gertie's deceased husband was not only the go-to place for the best home-cooked meal around, but a gathering hole for residents of all professions and ages. Gertie, with her gruff, no-nonsense way about her, ran a tight ship resulting in the best meals Avery had ever enjoyed, exhaustion by the end of each shift that enabled her to sleep soundly and a good start on getting to know people in the area.

The name Grayson Monroe hadn't come up, at least not when she could hear it, and she hadn't thought of a viable reason for asking about him yet. She hadn't thought that part through before turning her car in his direction and had spent the past few days pondering what her next move should be.

"Thanks, Clyde," Avery said, picking up the two plates of hamburgers and fries. Thank goodness everyone wore jeans instead of a uniform and that Gertie had given her three long-sleeved shirts with the diner's logo on the breast pocket. With her plain brown hair pulled back in a braid, her face shone with a light sheen from nonstop movement.

A smile wreathed the cook's weathered, lined face. "Quit thanking me, missy. It's my job."

"Got it. I'll try to remember." Turning, she bumped into Gertie, almost dumping one of the burgers. "Sorry... sorry," she stuttered, embarrassed by her clumsiness.

Shaking her head, her boss grumbled, "For such a klutzy girl, you sure have quick reflexes. Go on. I seated table six with my favorite customers. See to them next."

Nervousness increased her ineptness and Avery sported the bruises proving how on edge she'd been lately. "Yes, ma'am." Watching her step, she dashed away before Gertie could reprimand her for the slip. She couldn't help it. Marci had drilled the politeness her mother lacked into her and old habits were hard to break.

"Here you go. Enjoy your meal," she told the young couple seated in a corner booth as she delivered their order.

Pulling a note pad from her back pocket, she pivoted toward table six, faltering in her steps when she saw the three men seated with an attractive redhead. Damn, were all the men in this state so big and rugged? The golden oldies pouring out of jukeboxes and loud conversations from the other customers drowned out their voices until she came within two feet of their table. Avery's hands started to shake and her legs turned to jelly as the midnight-haired, broad-shouldered man's familiar voice halted her steps with jarring abruptness the second that deep tenor reached her ears.

"Excellent idea, Caden. Do you have an estimate yet?"

Avery closed her eyes as that unforgettable tone washed over her with the same impact as when she'd heard it through the phone over two weeks ago. It was that same voice that compelled her to come to Willow Springs. Somehow, the warm flow running through her body that hearing it produced didn't surprise her. Struggling to get a hold of herself, she cast a swift look around to see if anyone noticed her frozen hesitancy. When it appeared no one had, she breathed a sigh of relief and forced herself to approach their table.

"Hi, I'm Avery. Are you ready to order?" she asked, not too worried about him recognizing her voice since she'd disguised it with a thin scarf over the phone. She tried not to stare, but found her eyes drawn to the man across the table, the one looking at her out of the most startling gray/green eyes. The black Stetson hooked on the corner of his chair matched his hair and the light blue, worn denim shirt stretching over wide shoulders emphasized the swarthiness of his weather-whipped complexion. A lump lodged in her throat as she realized just how far out of her league he appeared to be.

"Sydney, you go first. I'm still deciding," the equally big man seated next to the young woman said.

"I'll have the Rueben." She smirked and handed her menu across to Avery. "It's *almost* as good as the one I make." Leaving her hand extended, she introduced herself. "I'm Sydney Greenbriar. You're new."

Avery shook her hand, noticing the winking diamond adorning her ring finger. "I've been hearing that a lot this week." Pointing to her nametag, she only offered her first name. "I'm Avery." Conscious of that steady, penetrating gray/green gaze, she shifted on her feet and tightened her fingers on the notepad.

"This is my fiancé, Caden and his brother, Connor." Sydney nodded to the man on Avery's left.

Reaching across the table, the man she now knew was Grayson Monroe demanded her attention and delivered another jolt of shock with his introduction. "Sheriff Grayson Monroe." Cocking his head, he asked, "How did you slip into town without me knowing it?"

Avery released his hand, took a hasty step back and bumped into the patron walking behind her, causing her to fumble and drop her notepad. "I… excuse me, sir," she mumbled, bending to pick it up. Red-faced, she looked back at the man she'd come here to meet only to learn he was in law enforcement. She knew not all cops were bad, in fact few were. But now that she'd committed the crime of hacking, could she risk confiding in him? The surprise and uncertainty over hearing his title hadn't abated enough for her to compose a feasible reply. "I… *sheesh*," she muttered, "I don't know."

Grayson frowned, his brows lowering and his gaze turning even more assessing. To avoid another question, she asked, "Do you know what you want?"

"Double cheeseburger, fries and a shake. Thank you."

She jotted it down as fast as her shaking fingers would allow and then asked the silent man, Connor for his preference. His slow drawl and the twinkle in his blue eyes helped her relax.

"I'll have the same, sweetie. It's nice to meet you. I hope you like our little community."

"It's quite the change from where I'm from," she blurted before thinking it through.

"And where is that?"

Of course it would be the sheriff who asked. "Uh… about as Midwest as you can get… Kansas City," she lied, giving the same answer as she had at her two previous jobs. Something told her he wouldn't take anything she said at face value though, giving her something else to stew over. As if she didn't have enough on her plate. "I'll just… get this turned in." Whirling, she fled to the safety of behind the long counter.

Avery managed to serve Grayson and his friends without further mishap but getting through the last hour of her shift had never been so difficult. Finally putting a face to the man who'd had such a huge impact on her flight removed one barrier to enlisting his help. The biggest obstacle, getting to know him well enough to learn how much she could trust him still loomed. The friendly overtures from Sydney were both welcome and heart-warming. Other than Gertie, Clyde and Ed, the part-time cook, she hadn't visited a lot with other people. When not working, she was walking the main streets and shops or catching up on some much-needed rest at the motel.

When the three men walked up to pay their tabs to Gertie at the cash register, Sydney stepped over to Avery with a smile. "Would you be interested in getting together sometime, just us girls? I hope you don't mind my asking, but it hasn't been that long since I was a newcomer here and didn't know anyone, so I thought you could use a friend."

Boy, could she. Not only that, getting close to one of Grayson's friends could help Avery learn more about him. "I'd like that. Thank you. Being new is… difficult."

Sydney nodded. "Where are you staying? I have a few hours free in the afternoons and can show you around." She grimaced, adding, "Provided I don't get lost myself. My sense of direction isn't the best."

"To say the least," her fiancé drawled behind her, his blue eyes warm with humor.

"Hey, I'm getting better," Sydney defended herself.

Grayson stepped over and tugged on her long hair, a toothpick now nestled in the corner of his mouth. "Is that why I found you parked over on Charleston Street the other day looking for Forest Lane?"

Avery smiled at their banter, but the shiver of awareness the sheriff's nearness and gaze produced distracted her from hearing Sydney's answer. Was it the fact this man had wrung such a stunning orgasm from her without even being in the same room, or the potential of being an ally that made him so desirable? Despite her trepidation over his job, she still ached to find out. She just wasn't sure which possibility held the most appeal, or if he would be worth risking either her body or her safety.

"How about tomorrow, Avery? Nan's Tea Shop is a quiet place we can sit and visit," Sydney suggested.

"I'd like that, but I can meet you there…"

"Nonsense. Don't listen to these guys. I'll pick you up."

Seeing no way around it, Avery sighed and admitted, "Okay, I'm at the motel…"

Gertie turned, snapping, "Girl, why didn't you say you were forking out money every day for that dump?"

Uneasy with everyone's eyes on her, Avery fidgeted and replied, "I… I plan to look for a place soon."

"Nonsense." Looking at Sydney, Gertie stated, "She can meet you there after moving into the studio apartment upstairs in the morning. It's just a short walk from here."

Her new friend smiled. "Don't argue with her, Avery. It won't do you any good. Let's meet at one-thirty."

Why did she feel as if her life was spiraling out of control again? Thanking her boss, Avery finished her shift in a daze, trying not to get her hopes up too much.

CADEN AND SYDNEY said goodbye and strolled toward Caden's truck before Connor turned to Grayson and asked, "What are you thinking?"

Grayson glanced back at the diner they'd just exited and answered with a question of his own. "Does the new waitress seem familiar to you?"

"No, not at all, but she's a cutie."

He agreed with Connor's observation, finding large whiskey eyes behind black frames, a small straight nose and lush, bottom lip all attractive features in the waitress' flushed face, but the nagging sense of familiarity bugged him. "There's something about the way she talks that's teasing my memory, but for the life of me I can't figure out why. I know I've never seen her before. I would've remembered those eyes." And the way they shied away from direct eye contact with him.

Connor lifted a brow. "You could have toned down your Dom look, then you might not have scared her off."

Grayson shrugged as he fished his keys out of his coat pocket. "Just because you're on holiday from exerting your need for control doesn't mean the rest of us have to be." He regretted the remark as soon as his friend tightened up. "Sorry, Con. I know breakups are hard." Only a few months had passed since Connor and his long-time girlfriend split ways.

"Really? How?" he asked, Connor's tone as derisive as the look in his eyes. "You've never given a monogamous relationship a try."

Stepping off the curb, Grayson grasped the cold door handle of his police cruiser, looking back at Connor over the hood. "True, but years of friendship count for something. You should consider taking either Caden or me up on our offers to listen while you vent. It might help."

Just as he'd done whenever his brother or Grayson prodded Connor into talking about what caused his breakup with Annie, he shut him down. "See you tomorrow night." With a wave, Connor hopped into his truck parked next to Grayson's and pulled out without a backward glance.

Frustrated with his stubbornness, Grayson slid behind the wheel and cranked up the heat to dispel the chill of standing outside in the frigid air. As he drove down Main, heading out of town, he spotted Avery walking alone, hunched against the biting wind. Swearing under his breath, he pulled alongside her and lowered the window.

"Get in, I'll give you a ride." Hesitation replaced her surprise at his sudden appearance, but he wouldn't let her balk. Not only would the evening turn pitch-black once she left the lighted square, but it was too fucking cold to walk the distance to the motel. "I can escort you back to the diner so you can bother Gertie to drive you or you can take me up on my offer. I wouldn't be doing my job if I let you walk back to the motel alone at night."

She frowned, and it pleased him to see she was wary of a stranger even if he knew he could be trusted. He wondered what circumstances brought her to Willow Springs in the dead of winter as they didn't get many newcomers this time of year. She finally relented and, stumbling on the curb, hurried around to the passenger side. Shaking his head, he leaned over and opened the door.

"Th… thank you. It is cold," she admitted with an appreciative sigh at the heat.

"We're a good distance north of Kansas City. It would be best if you remembered that when going out, even during the afternoon when it's warmer. Seatbelt." Her quick obedience stirred Grayson's interest even more, and he liked the disheveled look of her with several strands of loosened, caramel hair falling around her face and clinging to her neck.

Avery seemed to weigh her answer before she replied, "It's cold at home, but we don't have these wide-open spaces with no tall buildings to provide a buffer."

"Would you like to share what brings you here? Other than during the summer tourist season, we don't get too many strangers coming to town." He eyed her askance, watching for a hint of evasion and found it in her tightened jaw and the shift of her eyes out the window.

"I found myself… in need of a change, is all. I'm in room two ten," she pointed out with obvious relief as he turned into the motel lot.

Putting the cruiser in park, he swiveled in his seat and pinned her with a pointed look before saying, "Get to know Sydney, she's a good person to have as a friend, as is anyone in Willow Springs. I hope you'll remember that."

"I will. Thanks, Sheriff."

"Good night, sugar." Grayson heard her sudden indrawn breath as she jumped out and wasn't surprised when she fumbled with her room key before dashing inside without looking at him again. The girl carried baggage, that's for sure. The question was, was she in trouble or just needing a fresh start, as she claimed?

Driving home, his thoughts remained on the skittish new waitress at Dale's. Not since his four-year stint in the army, including eighteen months spent in Afghanistan had opened his eyes to the plight of innocent women had he seen that look on a woman's face. Last fall, Sydney had arrived on the Dunbar Ranch avoiding her uncle's nefarious intentions, but she'd never exhibited the genuine distress he caught reflected in Avery's eyes, at least not in front of him. As soon as he had introduced himself to Avery, she had avoided eye contact with him, the same as just now on the ride to the motel, and the best he could figure his job as sheriff caused her worry.

Fifteen years ago, he had walked away from the army without regret, but he had never forgotten the faces, or the lessons learned that prompted his interest in exerting his sexual dominance along with his protective control when warranted. And he sensed Avery could benefit from both traits.

Pulling into the gravel drive of his log and stone, twenty-five hundred square foot cabin, he smiled when he spotted Lobo, the old wolf he had nursed back to health after digging a bullet out of its hind quarters when he'd been just a pup. Grateful for the rescue and scraps he often left out for him, the wild canine came around every so often to renew their acquaintance. Grayson never attempted to domesticate him even though he appeared to be a wolf hybrid, part Alaskan Malamute or German Shepherd, but had grown attached to the mangy critter over the last ten years.

"What have you been up to, old man?" Holding out his hand, he waited patiently for Lobo to reacquaint himself with Grayson's scent before scratching behind his ears. "You look good, but let's see what I can scrounge up for you in the kitchen."

After tossing him two steak bones, Grayson returned inside and shrugged out of his coat. With darkness came a quick drop in temperature and his thoughts once again strayed to Avery. Gertie's insistence the girl bunk above the diner had eased the concern he'd felt when he heard her mention staying at the motel. Not that his town wasn't safe, but a young woman alone, living in a place with no security and going back and forth to work at night was just asking for trouble. Knowing Gertie, she would have Avery ensconced in the studio apartment before her shift started the next day. Now, if the rest of his suspicions and concerns regarding Avery could be handled as fast and with as much efficiency, he could quit wondering why he found himself so drawn to a perfect stranger.

Chapter 4

S ydney entered the diner in search of Avery after waiting fifteen minutes for her at the Tea Shop. After meeting her there last week, she felt an immediate kinship with the woman who had done such a poor job of hiding her nervousness, and her interest in their sheriff whenever his name came up. Because of the time it had taken for Avery to move into Gertie's studio apartment, they had only thirty minutes for a cup of tea and 'get-to-know-you' conversation before both of them needed to report to work. Since their time had been short, Sydney strove to gain Avery's trust by staying clear of personal questions. But it hadn't been that long since she'd found herself alone in a new place with no one she could trust or confide in right away, and she had seen that same despair and worry reflected on Avery's face both times they'd been together. Sydney's heart went out to her, and she intended to not only continue befriending the newcomer but supporting her in any way she could.

Grayson's distracted manner at the club last weekend left Sydney wondering if he shared her interest in getting to know Willow Springs' newcomer. She didn't doubt *Master* Grayson could pull Avery's troubling secrets out of her, but that introduction needed to wait until she was sure of Avery's interest.

"Hey, Gertie. Have you seen Avery? She was supposed to meet up with me again this afternoon."

Gertie tossed her head toward the door marked 'Private' without pausing in carrying an armload of heaping plates by Sydney. "Still holed up back in my office. The girl offered to have a go at my computer."

"Mind if I go on back?" she asked, already stepping that way.

"Go and quit bugging me."

Smiling, Sydney padded down the short hall and found her new friend right where Gertie said she would be. Avery didn't notice her until she walked up to the desk, saying, "Did you forget or are you blowing me off?"

Startled by Sydney's sudden appearance, Avery jerked and then panicked to close the screen. Jumping up, she rammed her hip against the desk, wincing at the sharp pain before catching the time. "Sorry, sorry. *Sheesh!* Where did the time go?"

Sydney's chuckle relieved the tension from Avery's shoulders. "I tend to lose track of time when I'm cooking." She nodded at the computer. "What were you looking up?"

"Oh, uh, nothing." Running her clammy hands down her sides, Avery shifted her eyes away from Sydney's quizzical green stare. She didn't want to give away she'd taken a few minutes after fixing Gertie's problem to snoop around in the files of her old job at the precinct. "Um, Gertie's screen kept freezing. I found the problem and fixed it, at least for now. She'll need some new software to keep it from happening again. I can go now if it's not too late." She hoped it wasn't. She had enjoyed their short chat last week, and meeting the teashop owner, Nan Meyers. After weeks of keeping to herself, being surrounded by so many well-meaning people felt foreign and took getting used to.

"I still have time. Let's go." As they left the office, Sydney caught her by surprise when she tossed out, "You know, Avery,

I'm a good listener and won't judge, if you need someone to confide in."

Looking over at her, Avery gauged her sincerity and relaxed even more. If only Sydney knew how tempting her offer was. "You know, Sheriff Monroe said almost the exact same thing about you last week when he gave me a ride."

"*Oooh*, tell me more," Sydney insisted with a gleam in her eyes as they left the diner and headed down the sidewalk toward the quaint teashop.

She shook her head. "There's nothing to tell. He saw me walking back to the motel and gave me a ride." *After ordering me into his vehicle or back to the diner in that hard-edged voice that still disturbs my dreams.* Her easy compliance to the sheriff's take-charge manner backed by that penetrating gaze bothered Avery despite the warm ripple of pleasure it generated, a hint there might be more to her responses to the man than the fluke born of need, loneliness and desperation she'd first thought when they'd spoken over the phone.

"Too bad you moved above the diner." Sydney opened the door to the teashop with a taunting grin. "Otherwise, you could've enjoyed more rides from our sheriff."

"Who's riding our sheriff?" Nan wanted to know as soon as they stepped inside.

The tall brunette and owner of the teashop had welcomed Avery last week with as much open friendliness as everyone else. Well, she amended, Gertie had welcomed her, but not exactly with the enthusiasm the other two women displayed. She liked Nan's sense of humor even as she blushed from her jest. "He gave me a lift last week after telling me it was too cold and dark to be out walking."

"Well, girlfriend, if anyone can warm you up, it'd be Grayson. The man does have a way about him." The look that passed between Nan and Sydney drew Avery's curiosity, but she didn't know either well enough to ask about it. "Do you know what you want this afternoon?" Nan waved them to a small, wrought iron table near the glass encased counter behind which an array of decadent sweets tempted Avery.

Pointing to a small lemon tart, she replied, "I'll take one of those with a cup of the lemon green tea. Thanks." Since Gertie included her biggest expenses of room and board with her job at the diner, this small indulgence offered her spirits a much-needed boost.

"You appear more at ease today. Are you settling in around here now?" Sydney asked as Nan turned to fill their order.

"Everyone's so nice, it's hard not to." If only constant worry over what Darren might suspect or be plotting to deal with her sudden disappearance didn't keep her on edge, Avery could grow to appreciate her temporary home more.

"Thanks, Nan." Sydney waited until Nan set their tea and tarts in front of them and then moved away to check on the other two customers before turning back to her. "You know, Avery, when I ended up here, I was running away from one of my uncles and hiding out from the rest of my family to keep them from learning how low he had sunk. I knew no one except Caden, my new boss, whom I could turn to to get through the days of anxiety and loneliness, and he wasn't too keen on my attention at first."

Avery stiffened against Sydney's well-meaning intentions even as her revelation about her similar circumstances offered hope her friend would understand Avery's plight. Not that she didn't appreciate Sydney's consideration. Before coming to Willow Springs, Marci had been the only person to offer her unconditional support and knowing there was someone she could at least turn to helped loosen the stranglehold on her emotions. But, as with her occasional foster mother, Avery refused to put Sydney at risk by divulging what she knew about Darren and his partner. The ice-cold disregard for her life behind his calm suggestion of her meeting with an accident depicted how ruthless the man who had duped her was.

No, sticking with her original plan of getting to know Grayson well enough to decide if she could trust him with both her hacking crime and what she knew about two of Chicago's finest remained her best option, at least for now. Since both Sydney's and Nan's teasing innuendos about the sheriff hit upon her personal interest in him, she let that guide her into bringing him up.

Pointing to Sydney's ring, Avery replied, "It looks like he came around. Congratulations. Is he good friends with the sheriff?"

Avery tried not to squirm as Sydney appraised her with a steady look, sipping her tea before answering. "Yes, he and Connor both. In fact…" She glanced up at Nan who was listening from behind the counter and waited for her nod before continuing. "The three of them are partners in a club. That's where I first met Caden." Her lips quirked with a rueful twist as she admitted, "He caught me spying through the window, gaping at the goings on."

The suspicion that had formed in her mind about Grayson during their phone conversation just grew. She was confident her disguised voice had kept him from identifying her as the shaken, naïve woman he'd assisted over the phone, and somehow doubted he had mentioned that call to anyone else. That meant no one knew how he'd brought her to a shattering climax with his strict, detailed instructions or how she longed for a repeat of that respite from her worries. It didn't surprise her to learn of her mystery man's involvement in a kink club like the ones even a geek like her couldn't help hearing so much about. Even some of her colleagues at the precinct had hinted of first-hand knowledge of such places in Chicago.

Sucking in a fortifying breath, she got up the gumption to ask for clarification about what she was thinking. "Are you talking about one of those BDSM clubs?"

Nan chuckled. "She catches on quick, Syd. You don't have to whisper, Avery. Everyone in Willow Springs knows about The Barn, and what goes on there. Heck, most of us are members and we've learned to ignore the few who disapprove."

Sydney's grin widened into a beaming smile. "Well, it knocked me for a loop that night, but I was so desperate for a diversion from my problems, I latched on to what was going on real quick, pushing Caden's buttons until he caved and gave me a first-hand lesson into his kinks." Cocking her head, she asked Avery, "Are you interested in checking it out, and seeing what Master Grayson's into?"

It sounded like she and Sydney had a lot in common, but Avery shied away from the thought of trying to get to know Grayson at a public, sex-charged venue. Her nerves were already stretched thin. The only thing urging her to consider it was the memory of that one night, that one phone conversation she was sure meant more to her and had left a bigger impact on her than Grayson.

"I... don't know," she answered honestly. "I've never, I mean..." Embarrassed about her lack of experience, she blushed and stuttered to a stop.

"Don't worry, I never had either. But I have to tell you, *whew*!" Sydney fanned herself in an overdramatic response. "For me, there was no going back to vanilla after that first night."

"I've been involved a lot longer, and never tire of what a strict Dom can do for me," Nan put in, leaning her arms on the counter. "I can tell you Master Grayson would be an excellent tutor, if you decide to try a scene. I've never had a Dom read me as well as he, except," she flipped Sydney a mischievous grin, "maybe Caden."

Sydney narrowed her eyes in a playful fashion. "Don't go there or I might have to hurt you."

Avery let them banter back and forth as she considered her options. It would take months for her to get to know Grayson from serving him once a week when he came into the diner. Observing him at the club would likely give her a faster, deeper insight into his character. But she took the pang that tightened her abdomen when Nan mentioned being with him as a sign watching him with others wouldn't sit well with her. *Need, not possessiveness caused that reaction*, she told herself. A need he had stoked and left simmering for weeks to add to the burdens she already carried around with her.

"I have to get going. What do you say, Avery? How about coming to The Barn as my guest tomorrow night? I can clear it with Caden and maybe Gertie will let you come in early and get off sooner. No pressure, you can just observe and get a feel for things. I promise. There are several members who come just to socialize, some enjoy voyeurism more than exhibitionism," Sydney explained.

"And some of us love it all," Nan put in with a wiggle of her eyebrows.

Avery couldn't help but smile at Nan's unabashed, straightforwardness as she answered Sydney. "Let me think about it and talk to Gertie. Can you give me directions and a time?"

Nan laughed and held up a hand. "Sydney still can't find her way out there by herself. You don't want her giving you directions. Here, I'll jot them down for you."

Sydney glared at her. "I am getting better, you know."

"Sure you are, hon." Nan smirked.

It must be nice, Avery thought, to have close friends you could rib with good-natured fun. "Thanks," she told Nan, taking the paper she handed over.

"I also wrote my and Sydney's phone numbers. Call one of us when you get there and we'll come out to greet you. If you arrive after nine, the doors will be locked, so someone will have to let you in."

"Okay, but I'm not making any promises." She didn't tell them she didn't dare use her cell phone, but maybe she could pick up a pre-paid phone sometime tomorrow.

AVERY WAITED until Friday evening to call Sydney and accept her guest invitation to The Barn. In the last twenty-four hours, she had changed her mind ten times, going back and forth between wanting to satisfy her curiosity by observing the side of Grayson she'd only heard in his voice and running away from something so far out of her realm of experience the thought brought on a flurry of nerves skittering under her skin.

She almost missed the turnoff to the secluded club from the highway, but Nan's instructions were good enough she spotted the narrow, tree-lined road right before passing it. Each bump along the unpaved lane jarred the steering wheel under her grip, distracting her from second-guessing her decision. She slowed a little, more used to smooth, straight-forward highway driving than rugged back roads, but couldn't risk arriving too late. The busy Friday night at the diner had kept her longer than planned and she hadn't wanted to risk getting on Gertie's bad side by leaving her short-handed after her boss had been nice enough to change her schedule. With relief, Avery spotted a lighted copse as the dense woods opened into a gravel parking lot and large, two-story barn.

She sat for a minute, waiting until the couple heading inside entered. The woman's bare legs peeking out from under her winter coat gave Avery pause as she glanced down at her loose jeans and the nicest top she had brought with her, a button-up, teal blue blouse. Sydney neglected to pass on a dress code and now Avery wondered if she would stand out like the naïve newbie she was in her plain attire, giving her something else to fret over. *Why can't anything be easy?* Since there was no answer to that age-old question, she forced herself to get out of the car, hoping Sydney was waiting for her in the foyer beyond the double doors like she promised. *I'm just here to observe, nothing else.* That's the line she'd been falling back on every time she thought of ditching this idea and it worked again this time as she stepped inside the spacious entry. The tautness cramping her muscles eased when she saw Sydney standing in the foyer.

Smiling, she rushed forward. "I'm glad you didn't change your mind." Waving her arm toward a large closet, Sydney prompted, "Hang up your coat and place your shoes in a cubby and we'll go in."

Eying her friend's short skirt, bare legs and camisole top that revealed her braless breasts, Avery couldn't help blurting out, "Aren't you freezing?"

Sydney shook her head, her grin widening. "The guys keep it plenty warm inside, not to mention they're darn good at heating us up in other ways. Come on, you'll see what I mean."

Avery followed her into the cavernous space of the converted farm building, the inside resembling nothing like a barn except for the high rafters and open loft on both sides. The far, opposite wall of glass brought the outside in with the wide, dimly lit view of the surrounding woods. She couldn't resist the temptation to look for Grayson as her bare toes curled against the smooth, hardwood floor. She executed a quick scan of the tables and seating areas between her and the circular bar separating the room but didn't see him. Not until a flesh-snapping echo followed by a soft cry drifted down from the loft and drew her gaze to the upper level on her left.

"*Oh!*" Nothing could have prepared her for seeing the man who had haunted her dreams for so long wielding a wicked looking crop on a naked woman's buttocks. Strapped facing a large cross with her arms and legs spread in a wide V-shape, the red stripes crossing the poor girl's cheeks were noticeable even from this distance.

"Yeah," Sydney sighed, following Avery's gaze. "Master Grayson has a way about him that draws all the girls, vanilla and subs alike."

Avery could see why. Even with a whole level and several yards separating them, she could depict the intense focus etched on Grayson's face as he concentrated on the woman who appeared to trust him enough to allow him to bind and torment her in such a manner. What would it be like, she wondered, to have a man so attuned to her every movement, her every need, as he appeared to be? During their two-hour phone conversation, she'd basked in his undivided attention and the respite his hard-edged commands offered from her fears. An ache had formed for a repeat of that experience, one that had intensified since meeting him in person.

He paused in wielding the slim rod to brush his hand in a slow caress over the woman's quivering back. The quick knot of displeasure tightening Avery's abdomen surprised her. It would not do for her to become enamored of the sheriff or to read more into his friendship than he offered. She'd made enough poor decisions regarding men to last her a lifetime.

She sighed and answered Sydney. "I can see that."

"If you're interested, you won't find better than him or Connor to take you through a few introductory scenes. Except for Caden, of course, but I'm not sharing. Oh, crap, here comes Cassie."

Sydney's disgruntled tone drew Avery's sharp glance and curiosity about her scowl. She watched an attractive blonde stroll toward them dressed in a leather bustier that displayed her breasts while drawing eyes to the sheer black thong barely covering her denuded pubes. "Why do you sound as if that's a bad thing?"

"I don't know her well, but the little I've seen of her I don't like. She's pushy and seems to like causing trouble. Several of the other girls I've met here have warned me to stay clear of her, and

I have. Come on, let's get a drink while Caden is still monitoring upstairs." Leading the way, Sydney started toward the bar, but the other woman stepped into her path with an arrogant toss of her head.

"Sydney, be a dear and introduce me to your guest."

With a sigh, Sydney said, "Cassie, this is Avery. She just moved to Willow Springs."

Avery held out her hand, glad Sydney had kept the introduction short and minus any more details. Not that her new friend knew much else about her. She'd been careful about that with everyone. "Hi, Cassie."

Cassie shook her hand but the derisive curl to her mouth was nothing new for Avery. She'd met more than her fair share of girls who had looked down on her for her geeky appearance. "Avery, I'm surprised one of the Masters hasn't punished you for your wardrobe. They much prefer skin to..." she waved a hand at Avery's jeans with a sneer, "denim. You won't catch anyone's notice all covered up."

Avery's face warmed, whether from the derogatory statement or the reference to punishment she didn't know. Maybe she should have worn her hair down and tried the contacts again, and then shook those thoughts aside. As much as she needed to get to know Grayson before enlisting his help, she refused to be someone she wasn't. She'd tried that with Darren and look where it had landed her.

"I'm just observing, not here to catch anyone's notice. If I've offended someone, I'll go."

"*You* haven't," Sydney interjected with a cool, pointed glare at Cassie. "Excuse us; there are others I want to introduce Avery to."

Avery wasn't accustomed to such loyal support, especially from someone she'd known less than two weeks. Gratitude filled her, and she bumped into a chair as she followed Sydney by the tables. "Excuse me," she mumbled to the two men seated in the other chairs, her face heating from their amused expressions and the idle way one was stroking the nipple of the woman snuggled on his lap.

"No problem," the man on her right drawled with a wink. "Welcome to The Barn."

"Thanks," she managed before darting after Sydney. She resisted the urge to look toward the loft again, too reluctant to witness what Grayson was doing now or to face what her reaction might be.

Avery found the open displays of nudity and scenes she'd never imagined she would be privy to view up close and personal overwhelming, distracting her from making a note of the names of people Sydney stopped to introduce her to. Seeing a plump woman kneeling at a blond man's side, her head resting on his thigh as he absently stroked her hair while conversing with the other man seated at the table shook her in an odd, indefinable way, one similar to her reaction to Grayson's voice. Her sudden inattention caused her to run into Sydney who turned and smiled at the couple.

With a light touch on Avery's arm, Sydney introduced them. "Avery, this is the Thompsons, Master Brett and Sue Ellen. This is my guest, Avery. She's new to Willow Springs."

Master Brett nodded. "Nice to meet you, Avery." He jerked a thumb toward the sandy haired man seated next to him. "Master Dan."

"Avery." After a slow, appreciative perusal that drew a delicate shudder of awareness, Dan pinned her with dark brown eyes. "When you're ready for a tour, let me know. I'll be happy to show you around."

"I… thank you." Sydney took her arm and nudged her toward the bar before she could come across as a bigger idiot. Avery wasn't used to drawing men's attention. Shaking her head, she slid onto the barstool and muttered, "Why does every man in this state have to be so…"

Sydney smirked. "Sexy? Overpowering? Panty melting?"

Avery nodded. "Yes, exactly." Sydney hopped onto the stool next to her, wincing before shifting her hips. Concerned, Avery reached over and touched her arm. "What's wrong?"

"Well…"

A deep, amused drawl interrupted Sydney's hesitation. "She took off this afternoon without telling anyone and got lost, again, which earned her another trip over Caden's lap," Connor, her soon-to-be brother-in-law answered as he strolled over from behind the bar.

Sydney scowled at him. "I was only going out to the new calf barn and took a wrong turn on the path. I would have found my way if you and Caden hadn't gotten yourselves into a tizzy."

Connor's lips tilted at the corners, his blue eyes lighting as he nudged his hat back and looked at Caden's girl with fondness. "Admit it, sweetie. You like the way big brother takes you in hand." He winked at Avery. "Welcome to the club, Avery. What can I get you?"

Avery was still struggling with the image of Sydney draped over her fiancé's lap while she let him spank her hard enough to still feel the discomfort hours later to answer Connor right away. Her own butt clenched as she recalled Grayson's reference to such discipline and the heat spreading through her body had nothing to do with the warm temperature of the room. *Sheesh.* Either her stressful plight had rendered her more desperate than she thought, or her past sexual encounters were more pitiful than she recalled to produce such a reaction to the memory of that suggestive threat.

"Uh, I'm not much of a drinker. A light beer?" Before she'd started seeing Darren, Avery's social life consisted of gaming with on-line friends and going to an occasional movie with a co-worker or one of the few people she'd kept in touch with since college. Geeky computer nerds didn't do the bar scene.

"Coming up," he replied without commenting on her lack of social skills.

Attaining such easy acceptance from a man as eye-catching as the scruffy bearded rancher thawed the last of the outside coldness Avery still shivered with. Her eyes shifted to the dance floor and the unabashed gyrations of the closely held bodies. Her own nipples tingled as a man scooped his partner's breast free of her demi bra and dipped his head to suckle the pert nipple, all the while grinding his hips against hers. She switched her gaze to her friend's knowing look. "How long did it take you to get comfortable with all this?"

"Honestly? Not long. I was so desperate for both Caden and a diversion from my troubles, I latched onto this," Sydney waved her arm, "quicker than most, I imagine. Let's have a drink and then, if Caden is still busy, I'll show you around some more."

"No need, Syd. I'll give our guest a tour."

Avery closed her eyes against the immediate effect of heated awareness that deep voice wrought, the same one that drew her here with his selfless concern and an offer of help. Her body tingled from head to toe as she swiveled on the stool and looked up into Grayson's penetrating, vivid gray/green eyes, another toothpick nestled on one side of his mouth. Connor set her beer down as Grayson held out his hand. Unable to refuse, she snatched up the cold bottle and placed her other hand in his, praying he didn't notice the way her fingers shook.

Chapter 5

A surge of anticipation had shot through Grayson the moment he gazed down from the loft and spotted Avery looking like a deer caught in the headlights of an oncoming car as she took in what appeared to be her first glimpse of what BDSM offered; his concentration and interest in the scene with Leslie taking a nosedive. He'd spent the last ten days struggling to remember where, if anywhere, they'd met before. The way she continued to avoid direct eye contact with him whenever he saw her set off alarm bells, her evasive answers to his simple questions among other signs she was either hiding something or uncomfortable around him. He wasn't used to a woman preoccupying his mind unless he was in a scene with a willing, needy sub. The urge to get to the bottom of her reticence toward him rivaled the growing interest to strip her of that loose clothing and familiarize himself with the lush curves they failed to hide.

Eyes the color of his favorite aged whiskey widened behind her glasses as she turned toward him, pink blossoming on her cheeks as he held out his hand, waiting for her to reply. The urge to order her to come with him almost overrode his common sense. She was not only new to town but appeared naïve about this entire venue. Attempting to run roughshod over her wouldn't do to gain her trust.

"I... are you sure you don't mind?" she asked, her gaze skittering away from him as she scanned the room.

Taking a wild guess at who she was searching for, he replied, "I've finished the scene with Leslie and sent her off happy. Does that help?"

A small frown drew her brows together. "I just don't want to step on any toes."

"Trust us, sweetie, you won't be. Subs know we're here to play, nothing else," Connor drawled, a small grin tugging at the corners of his mouth. "Go with Master Grayson, he can explain anything you're unsure of."

Sydney nodded in agreement. "Caden and I can catch up to you when he's done monitoring. Have fun." She waved a hand to shoo Avery on.

Grayson tightened his grip around her smaller, softer palm as Avery took his hand. He almost smiled when her knuckles whitened around the beer bottle as she slid off the stool.

"Okay, thanks," she said.

"Most of the bondage equipment is upstairs, but back here we have a few spanking benches." Grayson tugged her toward the space opposite of the dance floor. They passed an as yet unconverted stall currently under construction. Pointing, he explained, "We plan to tile that in and turn it into a large shower with several nozzles."

Stumbling to a halt, Avery jostled against him, eyes rounding behind the dark frames as she peered into the space. He could almost see the wheels turning in her head with the possibilities. "You think people will use it? I mean..." She flicked a look around. "It's so... open."

"Most members don't come here to hide behind closed doors, sugar. This," he nudged her toward the first bench after receiving a nod of welcome from Greg, "is a regular spanking bench. You can see how Master Greg has restrained Cassie."

Avery winced, took a long draw of her beer and edged closer to Grayson's side as Greg brought a wooden paddle down on Cassie's already reddened ass, her throaty cry accompanying the lift of her head as she glanced back at them. He didn't care for the way Cassie narrowed her eyes when she saw him with Avery and decided not to linger.

"Over here is a fucking bench," he explained, leading the way to the next apparatus that sported padded side rests for knees and arms to prop a sub up in a perfect pose for fucking, as Leslie now demonstrated. The way the experienced sub had jumped into another scene with someone else didn't bother him. If only he could get Cassie to move on without constantly pestering him for more attention. Faint pink lines still shone against Leslie's pale skin from where he'd cropped her, and the view her spread knees offered revealed her puffy, glistening labia wrapped around a wide dildo,

"*Sheesh*," Avery muttered before swigging another gulp of beer and averting her eyes.

Grayson experienced another tug of familiarity at her mumbling; something about the way she uttered that word poking at his memory. Frustrated, he asked her point blank, "What's your last name?"

She jerked and tried to step back, but he held onto her hand, refusing to let her go far. "If that's a requirement for your… guidance, then…"

"It's not," he cut her off. "I still can't shake the feeling I know you, that we've met before." When she shifted her eyes over his shoulder, more suspicions kicked in. Reining in the urge to demand answers, he changed tactics, reaching out with his free hand to grab the thick braid of caramel colored hair resting between her shoulders and using it to pull her closer. She flinched, whether from the sound of wood smacking against bare flesh or from his hold, he couldn't tell, but she made no attempt to pull away from him. "Did Sydney mention the club safeword?"

She nodded, the top of her head ramming his chin. Her face reddened with her apology. "Sorry. Yes, she said it was red."

"Excellent. Remember it. And if you return after tonight, wear your hair down and change into a skirt or shorts." He watched her pulse flutter in her throat as he pressed her body flush with his and he ached to see what other responses he could pull from her with a simple order or touch.

Avery gulped and then nodded again. "Okay. Where are we going?" she asked as he released her hair and moved away from the other couple after catching another glare from Cassie. Under other circumstances, he would deal with her insolence in a way Cassie wouldn't care for but thought it best if Avery didn't see that side of their lifestyle yet.

Grayson had seen and dealt with his share of confused, reluctant women, but none more baffled than Avery as he led her upstairs to the loft and started to explain each piece of equipment. But curiosity kept her going, overriding embarrassment and confusion. "This is a fucking swing." He lifted a dangling strap attached to the webbed seat, a cuff hooked on the end. "I'm sure you can imagine how I can restrain someone on it. But nothing can settle the mind better than first-hand experience. Hop on." He patted the seat, challenging her with his gaze. She possessed the most expressive face, every thought and insecurity portrayed in her eyes and around her mouth. Small, white teeth sank into her plump, bottom lip, tempting him to deliver his own bite to that soft flesh.

Avery shook her head and tried to back away even though curiosity and interest shone in her eyes. Tightening his grip, he held her in place. "I was just going to watch, not participate."

"Watching is fine for titillation, but only goes so far to appease curiosity. Sit on it and I'll only restrain one wrist. That will be enough to give you a small example of what bondage is like, and if it might be for you."

Grayson held his breath as she looked back at the swing, even though he enjoyed watching her sort through her feelings and the option he presented her. When she nodded and handed him her now empty beer bottle, he released his pent-up breath with relief, surprising himself by how much he wanted to push her.

"I'LL... GIVE IT A TRY," Avery agreed before cowardice sent her fleeing.

Her long dormant libido had awakened in the last thirty minutes with as much ease and heat as when Grayson had guided her to a self-induced climax using just his voiced commands. Her curiosity about the dangling contraption stemmed more from what he would do to her, how he could bring her to another shattering release than from her interest in the kink going on around the loft. She'd known she might have to participate eventually in a scene with him if she wanted to get to know the man better, but as she settled on the swing and gripped the lines attached on each side that connected it to the ceiling, she couldn't stop trembling with apprehension from both the unknown and with giving up even a token of control. The number of people teeming around the loft was of some comfort. After succumbing to Darren's machinations without second-guessing why a man like him would all of a sudden be interested in someone like her, she'd learned to be extra wary of attentive men she knew nothing much about. If it hadn't been for their anonymous first encounter and Grayson's generous time and kind offer to help a virtual stranger, she wouldn't do this, no matter what her body was clamoring for.

"Excellent," he murmured, reaching for her right hand and lifting it above her.

As he attached the cuff around her wrist, he kept his eyes down, focused on her as she looked up and watched his every move. His fixated attention and the warm approval reflected in both his voice and eyes helped to ease the tremors racking her body, but also increased the rush of heat spiraling through her veins. Avery tugged on the restraint, sucking in a gasp at the vulnerability the bondage brought about. Before she could balk, Grayson gripped her braid and tugged her face up to meet his as he bent over her. The slight pull on her scalp elicited a curl of desire in her abdomen that threw her for a loop, the same as when he'd tugged on it downstairs.

His warm breath brushed over her lips as he asserted in a low, toe-curling voice, "Concentrate on keeping your eyes on me, nothing else." He rubbed his lips over hers, keeping her head immobile for the light touch she swore she could feel between her legs. "Trust me, Avery."

Grayson locked her in his gaze with those three, simple words, the need inside Avery branching out to include more than just her body. And then he covered her mouth with his own and all rational thought fled as he kissed her with a thoroughness she'd never enjoyed before. For the first time in weeks, tension rolled off her, fear and uncertainty slipping away under his potent command. What started out as a soft coaxing as their lips clung and tongues stroked, soon turned into a ravaging posses- sion of all her unsuspecting senses. Her breathing turned heavy, her body arching toward his of its own accord, as if it controlled her instead of the other way around. He swallowed her moan before running his exploring tongue along her tender gums. With harder pressure, he drew her air inside his mouth as he tickled the sensitive skin on the roof of her mouth in an oddly arousing maneuver.

Instinct forced Avery to jerk on her arm again despite the heated pleasure building inside her body. Shockingly, her inability to move had her pussy swelling, her thick cream pooling between her legs, preparing her for more, so much more, and rendered her oblivious to the soft moans of painfully induced pleasure echoing around them. With no other recourse left except to wrench free and cry a halt or sit there and enjoy, she let go, basking in the assault on her senses that stripped her anxieties away for a few moments of a mind-consuming new experience.

By the time Grayson pulled back, her lips were almost numb, yet she found it difficult to resist the urge to beg for more. Lowering his head, he yanked on her hair again, arching her neck. She expected to welcome his lips on the tender curve of her exposed shoulder, but instead felt the astonishing effect of a sharp nip. The arousal already humming through her body escalated from that quick prick of pain and left her shaking with need, a heated state only he had ever driven her to. Avery couldn't fathom what it would be like to have him controlling her whole body in such an intense way, or what her response might be to the harsher pain she'd witnessed others receiving tonight.

"C'mon, sugar," he stated, releasing her braid and reaching to free her arm. "You look like you're ready for your second drink."

Avery stood and leaned against his hard frame, needing a moment to gather her thoughts. The man possessed an air of authority that went beyond his position as sheriff, a manner that both drew and scared her. After viewing the few scenes downstairs, she imagined he would label that demonstration vanilla, whereas, for her, it had been a taste of decadent chocolate.

Wanting to learn more about him and his preferences, she conjured up the nerve to ask, "Would you mind explaining more of this?" She nodded toward the other apparatus in use behind them.

"Not at all." Latching onto her hand again, he steered her toward a contraption that resembled a gymnastic vault, until you saw it up close.

"*Oh.*" Stumbling to a halt, Avery stubbed her toe on the heel of his boot, but the throbbing ache didn't keep her from gaping at the woman riding the dildo attached in the center of the padded vault, her glistening body bowing as she struggled to maintain her balance with her eyes locked on the man next to her. Fascinated with both the equipment and the look on the woman's face as her partner flicked a small, leather strap on one nipple, Avery couldn't help shifting closer to Grayson. "Ouch," she muttered before curiosity prodded her into questioning the woman. "How can you let him do that?" The man's eyes whipped toward her, the censure aimed her way drawing a shiver down Avery's spine.

Tearing her eyes away from that cold frown, Avery flung her gaze up to Grayson. "What?" He shocked her by answering her confused inquiry with a sharp pinch to her own nipple. Without thinking, she slapped a hand over the throbbing tip, her face burning with her surprised utterance. "*Ouch!*"

"Sorry, Devin, she's new." Grayson pressed two fingers under her chin, tilting her face up to his. "Master Devin's sub is trying to concentrate on pleasing him. Speaking directly to a sub during a scene, or without her Dom's permission is distracting for both people."

"I don't…" She looked back and then pulled Grayson away from the other couple. "What do you mean? I need permission to *talk* to people, *that's* why you did that?"

"I pinched you to keep you from making a bigger mistake, and to give you a clue as to why she enjoyed nipple pain. I can only bend the rules so much when dealing with someone who has broken protocol. You need to get permission when watching a scene or if a couple is in a strict relationship that extends beyond sex and the Master insists. It's an unspoken rule to remain silent unless the Dom speaks to you or invites conversation."

"*Sheesh*, how many of these unspoken rules are there?" There seemed to be more to this stuff than getting together for a few hours of kinky sex, Avery mused as she dropped her hand from rubbing the offended nub. She looked away from Grayson's knowing eyes as she dealt with the soft pulsing of her nipple.

"Several." Grayson pinched her chin and turned her back around. Cocking his head, he asked, "If you're considering returning, I can go over a few more. Next time, you won't be given a pass on crossing lines."

"Like with my clothes?"

He nodded. "Yes, that's one. Another will be the way you address a Dom. The respectful title is Sir and not using it will earn you a reprimand."

Avery winced, recalling the painful looking, bright redness of the women's buttocks downstairs. "Is there like, a pamphlet or something I can study before returning?"

A broad grin split his dark face, the first she'd seen from him, and almost dislodged his toothpick. "No, sugar, all you need is a good Dom to guide you."

She desperately wanted that to be him, reminding her it wouldn't do to read more into his attention than warranted. From the little she'd witnessed of his scene with the other woman when she had arrived, he wasn't stingy with his undivided attention when with someone. As he steered her toward another strange contraption, she tried not to wonder if all his examples would result in pleasant, warm pulsations like the one encompassing her nipple.

Strapped on a wood-slatted A-frame, Nan's bound arms and legs, along with Master Dan's tight hold of her hips, rendered the slender brunette immobile and helpless against his rigorous fucking. Their harsh breathing and low grunts accompanied the slap of their pelvises together. Her rigid tipped breasts jiggled with his pounding strokes, her glazed eyes and copious juices coating his sheathed cock sure signs of her pleasure.

"This is our newest acquisition. Nan and Master Dan are demonstrating one way someone can use it." Grayson reached behind Avery and cupped her buttock, his tight clasp making her jump. "I'd love to see you up there."

Struggling with his grip of her backside, Avery tried picturing herself in Nan's position and couldn't. There was no way she could imagine herself being taken openly in a room full of people even if she couldn't deny her friend appeared blissfully unaware of her surroundings and seemed entrenched in her partner's rough possession.

"I think I'll leave now. I have a lot to consider before I decide whether to return," she told him even though she already planned on coming back. She couldn't appease her curiosity and the need he'd stirred inside her tonight if she didn't, and she still wanted to get to know him better before risking asking for his help with what she knew about Darren and his partner.

Grayson released Avery's buttock and blood rushed back to the small area, leaving her cheek to throb in tune with her nipple, the dual titillating sensations distracting her from the other couple. He squeezed her hand, his rough palm pressing against her quivering one; a comforting hold no one had offered her before and a balm against the new, rioting sensations he had stirred up.

"I'll walk you out." As he escorted her back downstairs, she relished the intimacy of the simple gesture of keeping her close using his tight grip. She couldn't recall any of the few men she'd dated, including Darren, doing something so simple yet so possessive as hand holding. One more thing that set Grayson apart from other men she'd known.

"Leaving already?" Connor asked as they reached the bar.

"Avery feels she's seen enough for one night. I'll be back after I walk her out."

Connor nodded to Grayson but tipped his hat to Avery. "G'night, sweetie. I hope you come back."

"Thank you." Turning to Grayson, Avery said, "You don't need to trouble yourself. Thank you for your time."

"It's no trouble, and I insist."

Now, why did that deep, authoritative tone affect her with such heat? Avery had been asking herself that question for weeks and still couldn't come up with an answer. As Grayson helped her on with her coat after she retrieved her shoes, the need to offer a sign of appreciation and willingness to hook up with him again took hold as they stepped outside. She waited until he held her car door open before saying, "Jenkins. My last name is Jenkins." What could it hurt to give him her mother's maiden name? Before her only parent's passing three years ago, Alice had been married four times, that Avery knew of. It would take some digging to connect the two of them.

His silent, probing look unnerved her until he nodded and replied, "Thank you. If you come back, I'll take you further, give you more to think about. Drive safe." He stepped back, removing his body heat and the temptation to return inside and take him up on that offer right now.

GRAYSON WATCHED until the taillights of Avery's clunker disappeared. He wondered how she had made it all the way to Montana in the old car and hoped she had the foresight to ensure the engine was sound enough to make the trip. Pivoting, he returned inside before the longing and confusion etched on her face tempted him to follow her and continue his initiation into kink in private. He couldn't help regretting not getting her number so he could ensure she arrived back in town safely. He shouldn't be so concerned about her—she was a grown woman, perfectly capable of taking care of herself—and then reminded himself he *was* the sheriff. Wasn't it his job to look out for the welfare of the people in his county? *Yeah, keep telling yourself that, Monroe,* his inner voice chided. A large whiskey, that's what he needed to get his head back in the game. With his interest centered more on a drink than playing, he didn't see Cassie's approach until she waylaid him before he reached the bar.

Remembering the glare she had leveled at Avery from her earlier position over the spanking bench, he was in no mood to deal with the ornery sub's pushy attempts to get his attention again.

"Master Grayson!" Clutching his arm, Cassie leaned against him, making sure her bare nipples pressed against his bicep. "I'm free now and would *love* to try the new frame upstairs," she gushed.

Clenching his jaw, he removed her hand and stepped back. "I don't appreciate your forwardness, or your rudeness to our guest earlier. Watch your step, Cassie." He walked away before he could make the mistake of encouraging her bad behavior and possessiveness by dishing out a painful punishment.

Sliding onto a barstool, Grayson ran a hand through his hair before signaling for Connor's attention. "Pour me a whiskey, would you?"

"Did our little waitress get to you?" Connor reached under the counter for a glass, his eyes reflecting amusement at Grayson's expense.

"She's hiding or running from something, and couldn't be more obvious about it," he growled in frustration. It didn't help to have his cock aching to get inside Avery's body as much as he desired to pull answers from her.

Connor shrugged, pouring a healthy dose of liquor. "None of our business if she is."

"You didn't use to be so callous or disregarding of others' troubles," Grayson pointed out, taking the glass and bringing it to his mouth for a hefty, throat burning swallow.

"I'm just not interested in prying into the personal lives of others. Nothing wrong with that."

"Nope, there's not, but it hasn't been that long since you jumped right in to push Caden toward Sydney and helped him get answers from her about her plight." Grayson could tell the reminder didn't sit well with his friend. Connor's usual, light-hearted, easy going manner had taken a turn since his break-up with Annie and he'd been keeping to himself when not rebuffing friendly overtures from friends and subs alike.

"That was different. She was stuck on the ranch and needed a friend, and big brother was too pig-headed to see it. It's your turn to monitor upstairs," he reminded him with a deft change of subject.

"Okay, I'm headed that way." Downing the drink, Grayson lifted the glass and then set it down with a click. "Thanks."

Skirting around the dance floor, he glanced out the back windows and spotted Caden and Sydney enjoying the hot tub. With her slim legs draped over Caden's shoulders, water sluicing off her bowed body, he fucked her with slow, measured strokes that brought a look of frustrated arousal to Sydney's face. Grayson paused, waiting until his friend rewarded his soon-to-be-wife with an orgasm that transformed her face to one of tormented ecstasy and then sated bliss as he brought her down by slow, measured degrees. He admired Caden's restraint in holding back until he'd brought Sydney to the pinnacle. Grayson pivoted toward the stairs, yearning to see those same expressions cross Avery's face.

Grayson awoke the next morning out of sorts after being plagued all night by dreams of that misdialed phone call and the mystery woman who had pulled at his conscience with her shy hesitations and soft, desperate voice. He couldn't fathom why he couldn't forget her, or that call and why thinking about Avery seemed to conjure up the memory. Maybe Avery's insecurities and the obvious fact she carried trouble with her reminded him of the nameless, faceless woman's plight. Avery had responded to his minor examples of the lifestyle with as much surprised interest as he'd heard over the phone from the other woman, so the two bore that in common as well.

Padding into the kitchen, he checked the time and winced. For the first time since he could remember, a woman had consumed his thoughts enough to put him behind schedule. Or, in this case, women, as it wasn't just Avery he couldn't get a handle on or put out of his mind when he wasn't around her. Since he was only thirty-eight, he couldn't blame this uncharacteristic obsession on a mid-life crisis, as much as he'd like to. That left placing the blame on Caden's shoulders.

The rancher's fast and relatively easy capitulation to Sydney's charming ways had spelled doom for the man he'd grown up with and had sent up red flags of warning for both Grayson and Connor. If it could happen to a confirmed bachelor like Caden, it could happen to anyone. Pouring a steaming cup of coffee, he carried it back to his bedroom, vowing he wouldn't let a pair of expressive whiskey eyes filled with a yearning for what he could give her tempt him beyond a few nights of introduction into kink and discovering her secrets.

TWO HOURS LATER, Grayson sat astride his bay, Thunder, huddled in his overcoat against the biting north breeze and gazing down on the recent tire impressions marring one of the Dunbar's fields. "Fresh," he commented even though vocalizing his observation wasn't necessary. Caden, Conner and Dan could all see the proof of trespassing from an unauthorized vehicle.

"I checked my place before joining you. Looks like the same bastards who tried to snatch from my herd," Dan said. "My foreman just got lucky and happened to be driving by that pasture at the time. That was enough to send them running." The lawyer owned a much smaller spread, but still valued his stock as much as the Dunbars. Looking over at Caden, his Appaloosa shifted under him as he asked, "Your guy didn't see anything besides the taillights either?"

"No, and not because he was slacking. These guys are good and were on the lookout for a sentry." Caden shook his head, his voice laced with anger and disgust. "It's a good thing we moved our cattle from this field last week."

"Yeah, but now we're overcrowded in the southeast pasture. We'll need to do more shifting around in the next few days." Connor didn't sound happy about the extra work the rustlers were causing everyone.

Caden nodded. "I've got Jim transferring about fifty head farther east, but they can't go too far, else we'll never be able to get feed to them when the snow hits."

Grayson didn't envy his friends the burdensome winter chores of moving livestock closer to the barns before the worst of winter each year. He'd chosen the military and then law enforcement over following in his family's footsteps working with his two brothers on the Monroe ranch and had never regretted his choice. He boarded Thunder at the local stables; his ten-acre plot where he'd built his house too wooded to leave enough grazing room for the stallion.

As the four of them followed the tracks all the way back to the highway, he said, "My damn computer was down again this morning, so I couldn't check for any other early reports, but I'm betting they made off with someone's cattle before the night was over."

"Well, I for one have had enough of the fuckers," Connor growled. "If I have to, I'll keep watch with my Winchester."

Caden's eyes snapped to his younger brother, as did Grayson's. "Who are you, and what have you done with my easygoing brother?"

"There's a time to remain calm and friendly, and a time to get down and dirty, and fight back," he returned, nonplussed by Caden's frown.

"Chill, both of you. I've got backup coming from Billings. We'll get them, *legally*," Grayson emphasized for Connor's sake.

"I sure as hell don't want to have to defend you in court, buddy." Dan squinted his dark eyes against the glare of the mid-afternoon sun. "Let's head back. There's nothing more we can do today, and that stew Sydney had bubbling smelled damn good."

Caden turned his horse and led the way, tossing to Grayson, "Talk to Avery about your computer. According to Sydney, she's a whiz."

"Good to know."

Grayson pondered on that revelation on the ride back to Caden's sprawling ranch home. Since it seemed waitressing wasn't Avery's only job skill, he speculated on other positions she might have held before coming to Willow Springs, and reasons why she would lie low at the diner instead of pursuing a job better suited to her skills. All scenarios came back to someone who was trying to keep off someone else's radar. The Dom in him was drawn to the challenge of uncovering her full potential as a submissive while the man who couldn't keep from worrying was intrigued by the evasive, wary woman—a heady combination he couldn't resist.

Chapter 6

After spending several, nerve-racking hours at a library in Billings, Avery drove back to Willow Springs Saturday afternoon maintaining a white-knuckled grip on the steering wheel. *I did it again.* That admission drew a frisson of alarm that sent her pulse spiking. What started as a simple search through Chicago news looking for any word of an investigation into Darren and Chad's illegal evidence thefts, had ended up with her turning desperate enough to hack into other interrogation reports of suspects from raids they had led. The discovery of two more cases where the defendant's accounting of either money or drugs didn't match the items Darren and Chad had turned in to the evidence room sent her fleeing back to the small town where she'd felt safer than anywhere else since overhearing her ex-boyfriend and his partner's confession.

A quick glance at the speedometer had her swearing and easing up on the gas. She'd been careful when driving so as not to risk getting pulled over. It wouldn't do to take that risk now, her lack of insurance just one of the things that could land her in trouble. The flash drive zipped into an inside pocket of her purse taunted her with the evidence of two dirty cops she carried around with her, her palms going damp as she weighed her limited options on where to go from here.

By the time Avery pulled behind the diner with only ten minutes to spare before reporting for her shift, she'd decided Grayson Monroe remained her best choice. If only she could get up the nerve to come clean with the sheriff, to work up enough trust to believe he would help. Now that she'd committed another crime, her task to do either of those things had become harder. She was still a newcomer in town, a woman he barely knew, and Darren's deceit was a hard-learned lesson that continued to haunt and scare her. She couldn't afford to misjudge another man, especially another one in law enforcement.

Speak of the devil. Avery paused in the doorway between the kitchen and the diner counter as soon as she spotted Grayson seated in her section along with the dark blond, Master Dan she'd met at The Barn last night. The two men were drawing every female eye in the place, the striking contrast between Grayson's midnight hair and Dan's much lighter coloring enough to catch their attention without adding in their rugged good looks and broad shoulders.

"Don't stand there gawking, girl," Gertie snapped as she whizzed by carrying three heaping plates.

"Oh, sorry, ma'am."

"And quit ma'aming me," she tossed back.

Grabbing her pad, Avery hurried to the men's table, trying to ignore the sudden increase in her pulse rate and the warm flush spreading up her neck as they greeted her with friendly smiles and piercing looks.

"Nice to see you again, Avery." Dan folded his menu, his gaze not as body encompassing as last night, but still just as approving. "I'll take the meatloaf special."

"Got it." After jotting it down, she shifted her eyes to Grayson, somehow not surprised to find herself tightening her thighs against the effect of his potent, gray/green gaze. "Sheriff, what can I get you?" Her silent prayer he hadn't caught her breathless tone went unheard, if she judged the tilt of his mouth correctly.

"I'll take the same, thanks. How are you today, sugar? You looked flustered when you came in." Cocking his head, he inquired, "Everything okay?"

Damn that astuteness, the casualness of his polite question not fooling Avery. Her gaze skittered away from the probing intensity in his eyes. "Yes... uh, thanks. Just running a little behind. I'll get your order turned in." She spun around so fast, she bumped into the other waitress and nearly caused her to drop her tray. "Oh, Barbara, I'm sorry!"

"I've got it, no problem." As they stepped away from the guys' table, Barbara leaned toward Avery and whispered, "Honey, I may have over twenty years on you and am happily married, but I'm not dead. I get it."

With a wink, the experienced server trotted off and Avery breathed a sigh of relief her clumsiness hadn't caused a big mishap. Without looking back, she rushed to turn in the order and get to her other customers. The busy Saturday night crowd kept her from thinking about whether Grayson would go to his club after dinner until she brought them their food. As he removed his toothpick, she couldn't help but be drawn to his mouth and remember the feel of his possession as she set a food-piled plate in front of him. From his look, he knew exactly what she was recalling.

"Thank you, sugar. Looks good."

She nodded and stepped back as if those few inches would put enough space between her and a temptation that seemed to grow the more she was near him. "Anything else I can get you? Either of you?" she hurried to tack on.

"Not right now," Dan replied without wasting time before digging in.

"Not with food, but when you have some spare time, can I

talk you into looking at my computer? Gertie sang your praises over fixing her problem."

Grayson's request caught Avery off guard; her first thought they would be alone at his place. As wary as that made her, she couldn't very well turn him down after helping Gertie. It may even speed up the timetable of getting to know him better, a possibility she couldn't afford to pass up.

"Uh, sure, I'd be happy to. I'm, uh, off tomorrow, if that works for you."

"Excellent. I'll pick you up…"

"No…" She sucked in a breath as his gaze sharpened at her flustered interruption. "I mean… I'd rather drive myself, if you'll give me directions. I… I'm trying to get to know my way around."

He picked up his fork and scooped a bite of mashed potatoes before answering. "I'll write down directions before I leave," was all he said before turning his attention to his meal, her cue to get back to work.

After living her entire twenty-nine years in Chicago, Avery thought she'd be used to frigid temperatures during the long winter months. But the windy city of Chicago had nothing on Willow Springs. The wide-open spaces of Montana didn't offer any buffers against the wind or cold, not until you entered a forested area, as she did the next day when she followed the narrow but paved road off the highway that led to Grayson's house.

The smooth pavement ended at a gravel driveway where Avery parked and sat for a moment, taking in the rustic appeal of the ranch home with its wraparound porch. A welcoming, enticing plume of smoke spiraled from the stone chimney separating the log wall along the side. Since the heater in her old car worked as poorly as everything else, she slid out looking forward to the promised heat inside. She'd only taken two steps toward the front door when a large wolf/dog lumbered to his feet at seeing her, his size and the slow curl of his lips revealing sharp teeth keeping her frozen in place.

Avery held her breath, too afraid to move, shivering from more than the cold. Gripping her purse, she prepared to swing it at the animal's head should he attack, her only choice for a weapon.

"Lobo, down!"

Grayson's sudden, hard-voiced command caused Avery to jump, but the wolf lay back down, his tail now swishing against the ground. She released her pent-up breath as he jogged down the porch steps wearing a sweatshirt and jeans that didn't disguise the bulge of his thigh muscles as he strode toward her. It was one of the few times she'd seen him without a toothpick stuck in the corner of his mouth, but that didn't keep her from zeroing in on those chiseled lips or remembering how they'd felt covering hers.

"He won't hurt you," Grayson assured her as he clasped her elbow and urged her toward the wild dog. "I'm showing him you're a friend. Once he gets your scent, he'll recognize it and warm up to you."

"You keep a wolf as a pet?" Wary but intrigued, Avery went with him, stopping a few feet from the gray and white coated wolf now cocking his head as he peered up at her out of beady, inquisitive eyes.

"No, but after rescuing him as a pup and nursing him back to health, he decided I wasn't so bad for a human and comes around every so often for handouts. Here." He handed her a good-sized steak bone. "Hold it out to him. Trust me, he'll take right to you."

Grayson's emphasis on the words 'trust me' sent her gaze flying up to his, but she only encountered his bland expression. As Avery took the bone, she sensed he was asking for more from her than trusting the wolf wouldn't harm her. "I can't believe I'm doing this," she muttered, taking one more step forward and stretching out her hand with the meaty treat. "I never owned a dog as a kid."

"That's a shame. They're loyal, bonding animals that can enrich your life, even crossbreeds like Lobo."

Again, Avery sensed an underlying meaning behind his comment, but as Lobo stood again and opened his mouth, it took every ounce of her willpower and nerve to hold her hand steady. "Oh!" she exclaimed as he took the bone with careful slowness, his black eyes glued to her instead of the tasty peace offering. She waited until he settled back down and started gnawing before looking at Grayson with a wide smile and sense of accomplishment. "You were right."

"I usually am, sugar. Come on, you're shivering." He led her up to the house, saying, "I've set my computer in front of the fireplace since I don't imagine your car puts out much heat."

Avery stopped at the threshold and gave him a quizzical look. "How do you do that? See beyond what's in front of you?"

"A tour overseas taught me a lot about not relying on only what was visible. Besides, your car is a piece of crap so that was a logical deduction."

Warmth stemming as much from entering Grayson's heated home as enjoying his company spread through Avery. Although he still wore a cloak of authority like a second skin, he appeared more approachable and less intense in this cozy environment than he had at the sex-charged club. To dispel the desire his presence stirred, she let him slip her coat off and asked, "What's the problem with your PC?" Looking across the spacious great room, she saw the desktop sitting on a small table by the floor-to-ceiling stone fireplace blazing with yellow/orange flames of crackling heat.

"It's slower than molasses and getting worse. It also shuts down when I'm in the middle of something." Waving his arm toward the computer, he said, "Help yourself while I fix some hot chocolate. I left my password written next to it."

She nodded, now eager to get started on the challenge. After spending so much time alone since fleeing Chicago, she enjoyed the daily interaction with people her job at the diner afforded her, but she relished the chance to pit her skills against technology again even more.

GRAYSON WATCHED Avery settle at the computer, her slim brows lowering into a look of intense concentration as her fingers flew over the keyboard with admirable skill. The only time she paused was to scoot her sliding glasses back up, her face tightening with irritation each time. Even though her eyes had stayed wary, her rise to the challenge of befriending Lobo and unquestioning belief in his promise the wolf wouldn't hurt her were two more signs of her willingness to submit. Now, if he could just get her to reveal what trouble had landed her here, he could deal with it, and her and then move on without constant, plaguing thoughts interrupting his nights and interfering with his days.

Carrying two mugs of steaming cocoa over to her, he heard her mumble, "*Sheesh*," and experienced that same sense of familiarity certain things she did and said always conjured up.

"That bad, huh?" he asked, setting one mug down next to her.

"You have no room to talk about my old car. When was the last time you upgraded?"

Grayson shrugged, settling on the arm of the sofa. "Sorry, I'm computer illiterate and like it that way. I prefer hands on interaction with people." His mouth quirked as a delicate shiver racked her body. She was smart to read more into some of his words than the obvious.

"Huh. I've always been the opposite. Aha – gotcha!" she crowed, delighting him with the beaming smile she flipped him. "I haven't met a computer yet I couldn't set straight. You'll need to download some new programs and upgrades, which will cost you. A new one might be better in the long run."

"Put on what's necessary for now and when you have time, maybe you can go with me into Billings to look at them." Instant hesitancy wiped off her smile, and she glanced away to reach for the mug. He waited until she took a sip and set it down before leaning forward and cupping her chin to turn her face back to him. Holding her still, he covered her mouth with his, kissed her long and deep, and then released her to sit back. "Give me the cost and I'll put it through when you're ready," he stated, letting her know trust was a two-way street.

Avery's small tongue came out and stroked over her plump, lower lip, a simple gesture made all the more potent by its innocence. Grayson needed space and perspective, in that order. Rising, he nodded toward the hall. "I'll be in my office, first door on the right."

It took her another hour, but when she called for him to pay for the upgrades and then showed him how well his computer now ran, he couldn't help but be impressed. He also couldn't help wondering what position she held before coming to Willow Springs and watched her closely as he walked her outside, commenting, "You know, sugar, with your skills you could likely land any IT position." She stiffened against him before reaching for the car door handle and ignoring his observation.

"Thanks for giving me the chance to help you out."

With his hand on the top of the open door, he waited until she settled behind the wheel before leaning down and expressing his desire to pay her again. "Your time and talent are worth something, Avery. Since you refuse to let me pay you and we only offer one guest pass per person to our club, feel free to return at my expense." He hardened his voice when he saw the immediate resistance on her face. "I insist." Shutting the door, he stepped away with a wave and then turned his back on her confused expression.

"I NEED A FAVOR," Avery told Sydney a few days later as they sat in Nan's tea shop for their weekly visit. When Grayson had tossed out his payment of the club entry fee in exchange for the work she'd done on his computer, his look stated louder than the offer that he wanted to be the one to continue her education into kink. Since that was what she wanted also, she needed to show up prepared to stay on his good side, and that meant finding something suitable to wear.

"Sure. What's up?" Sydney agreed without hesitation.

"Clothes. I only have jeans and tops and need something that will pass the club rules." She shrugged self-consciously. "I'm not exactly skinny, or sexy and never needed much else in the way of clothing."

"Master Grayson seemed pleased enough with your figure," Nan tossed out from behind the counter. "I knew he could entice you into returning."

"And I sure as heck wouldn't mind some of your curves." Sydney's pointed look at Avery's chest slid down to her own.

Avery giggled. "To use Nan's words, Caden seems happy with what you've got."

Sydney's face brightened. "Yeah, he is. I'm in. We'll run down to the boutique when we leave here and find something that will knock Master Grayson back a step."

"Not too far," Avery chided. "The idea is to keep his attention."

Concern clouded Nan's brown eyes. "Enjoy him, Avery, but don't get attached or read too much into his attention. He's not the staying type."

"I disagree," Sydney argued with a shake of her head. "Caden was a confirmed bachelor before I showed up and now look at us." She wiggled her glittering ring finger. "I've seen the way Grayson watches you, Avery. A hawk couldn't maintain such intense interest."

Avery didn't mention she feared that interest stemmed more from unearthing her secrets than her sexual education into BDSM. She didn't need Nan's warning; she knew there was no future for her here, or with a man like the dominating but caring sheriff.

"Like you both have told me, Grayson is a good tutor, and that's all that is between us. I don't want to be punished the minute I step inside the club Friday night." She winced.

"You never know, you may like it," Sydney returned with a sly look in her eyes. Stuffing the last bite of blueberry muffin into her mouth, she washed it down with a sip of tea before saying, "Let's go shopping."

Friday night, Avery parked in front of The Barn again, this time knowing what to expect. So, why were her palms just as clammy and her heartbeat racing just as fast as last week when she slid out of the car? She wanted to be here, that much she knew for certain. Last week, Master Grayson had expanded on what he'd started during their phone conversation, opening up something inside her, a part of her she never imagined existed. If only she could get past the fear of putting her trust into the wrong man again. That barrier kept her from fully relaxing around the one man whose complete sexual dominance she could envision herself welcoming. Geeks were not brave or adventurous, at least she'd never been.

With a tight grip on the bag holding her change of clothes, she dashed inside the double doors before she could chicken out. Avery relished the rush of heat as she hung up her coat, wishing she had asked either Nan or Sydney to meet her in the foyer again. Squaring her shoulders, she recalled the way Grayson had brought all her senses alive with that simple example of bondage and one, searing kiss. *Yes!* she crowed silently when her nipples grew taut just from the memory. *That's why I'm here, what I want more of along with his trust.*

Slipping into the restroom on the other side of the foyer from the coat closet, she changed out of her jeans and into the calf-length, pleated gray skirt she'd chosen over Sydney's pick of a much shorter, tighter black one. As she exchanged her sweatshirt for the red camisole top that didn't allow for a bra, she wondered why she'd caved to her friend's insistence on this garment. When she'd tried it on in the shop, she didn't remember seeing every bump on her areolas outlined by the satin or the noticeable sway of her full breasts as she moved. *Nothing I can do about it now*, she thought. With a deep inhale, she padded barefoot back out to the foyer and entered the club, not expecting the surge of excitement tickling her abdomen at hearing the tormented cries of slapping flesh and soft moans of pleasure wafting down from the dimly lit loft and breathing in the pungent mingling odor of leather and sex.

Avery paused in the doorway, scanning the lower floor for a familiar face when her eyes landed on Grayson, the sight of him seated by a table, bringing his hand down with blistering force on Sue Ellen's bare butt freezing her in place. The poor woman's husband, Master Brett stood to the side in a rigid stance of anger, arms folded, a dark scowl on his face. Avery couldn't budge or look away from watching a side of Grayson she hadn't witnessed before. Even though Sue Ellen's buttocks were already glowing bright red from his spanking, he continued to smack the abused globes with repeated swings of his arm, not leaving one inch of skin untouched.

She cringed and took an automatic step back as he moved to the under curves, his swats so hard they shoved the tormented girl forward, almost landing her on her head, she dangled over so far. Sue Ellen's hair obscured her face, but Avery had no trouble seeing her white-knuckled grip on the chair legs or hearing her sobbing breaths.

That is not what I want, who I want. Just as Avery made that acknowledgement and pivoted to leave, Grayson halted his punishing hand, his face softening as he gently lifted and turned Sue Ellen on his lap. Tipping her face up to his, the look of remorse on Sue Ellen's face instead of reflected on Grayson's, as she would have expected, confounded Avery. After whispering a few words to her followed by a soft kiss, he nudged Sue Ellen up. She wobbled, and he aided her with a tight hold on her hips and that same piercing, steady gaze of close scrutiny that had ensnared Avery when they first met at the diner and then again up in the loft last week. When Sue Ellen steadied, Grayson nodded and turned her toward her husband, baffling Avery further as the woman slid to her knees and bowed her head.

Confused and unsure of both herself and this harsher side of Master Grayson, she decided to leave, but Grayson looked over and snagged her in his vivid gaze and she found herself unable to look away as he pushed to his feet. His face etched with purposeful intent, he ate up the space between them with long, determined strides.

OF ALL THE FUCKING LUCK, Grayson groaned when he released Sue Ellen to finish making amends to her Master and husband and caught sight of Avery standing near the entrance. He'd been so immersed in first, administering the submissive's punishment as directed by Master Brett because he'd been too angry with her to risk raising his hand, and second, with ensuring Sue Ellen's well-being before turning her back over to Brett that he'd forgotten to keep an eye out for Avery's arrival. He didn't have to guess at what she was thinking; her expressive face depicted her every thought and emotion. Uncertainty backed by a sliver of fear clouded her eyes, her face turning even paler as he moved to stop her from running away. He couldn't let her leave now, not without explaining the difference between his friend's twenty/four seven, sub/master lifestyle and what he could, and would introduce her to here.

He reached her as she gave in to panic and pivoted, but he halted her with a one-word command. "Stop." The sexy thin top couldn't hide Avery's delicate shudder or the instant rigid outline of her nipples. A foot away from her, he waited for her to face him and then held out his hand. Patience was a trait he'd mastered years ago, but at that moment, it took every ounce of his control to keep a hold on it. "Good girl," he murmured as she slipped her trembling fingers into his grip, the extent of relief easing his tense shoulders better left for later to analyze.

"Let's talk." Peering around, he opted for the privacy corner for what he had in mind following their discussion. A four-foot, half wall topped with an array of indoor plants partitioned off the cozy nook from the rest of the room. Other than the one, open side where people could enter or get a glimpse of who needed a quiet moment of aftercare, the secluded space offered a combination of privacy and risk of exhibitionism that suited his purposes.

"I didn't notice this last week," Avery whispered, as if speaking louder would land her in trouble.

Grayson paused in front of the small sofa to give her time to look around before tossing a small pillow on the floor. Taking in her skirt and breast-clinging top, he found the sight of her bare feet peeking out below the hem both sexy and cute, kind of like her.

Settling on the sofa, he was aware of the fine line he was straddling between showing Avery his preferred, stricter dominant self as opposed to the milder instructor he'd portrayed last week while alleviating her misconceptions about the scene she'd just witnessed. Pointing, he watched her face as he instructed, "Kneel there." His cock stirred as she faltered and then obeyed, sinking to her knees at his feet, her skirt spreading around her bent legs. She opened her mouth then clamped it shut before shifting her eyes away from his.

"No." He used two fingers under her chin to turn her face back toward him. "Talk to me, I insist. I might be stricter than you first thought or care for, but I want any sub I play with to feel free to express her concerns, and her pleasures without fear of reprimand. I'll let you know when I want you to remain quiet." Releasing her chin, he sifted his fingers through her loose hair, enjoying the way the dim lighting brought out the red and blonde streaks woven in with the light brown.

Fisting a handful of the thick mass, he tugged her head back. "You witnessed a punishment scene just now, and yes, I made sure Sue Ellen would hurt for the next few days, just as her Master and husband asked me to. I will treat any woman who puts herself into my hands the way her submissive nature demands, and that sometimes might be at odds with what they think they want. That's where trust comes in." He released her hair and reached down to haul her onto his lap. With one arm wrapped around her waist and the other draped across her lap, he held her close enough to see the rapid flutter of her pulse in her neck and feel her warm breath tickle his neck. "I can see the questions in your disbelieving eyes. Ask."

"Okay, why? A husband is supposed to love his wife." Avery's quizzical tone had turned accusing with the second line, her slim brows dipping into a frown behind her lens.

"Why, because she'd done something before arriving tonight to displease him so much, Master Brett was too angry to discipline her himself. And, he does love her, very much. Did you see her struggling to get away from me, hear her cry out for me to stop or run away when I released her?"

Avery shook her head and Grayson knew the second she remembered the look of chastisement crossing Sue Ellen's face as she knelt in apology before Brett. It's too bad she missed the contentment the other woman exhibited when her husband lifted her for a hug.

Watching her closely, he slid his arm over her thighs and down her legs, sliding his hand underneath the skirt to inch it up. "Last week, you watched two other subs getting spanked on the benches, but this time was different because it was me, the one you agreed to explore your interest with. Correct?"

"I… guess that was it," she admitted in a subdued tone. "It… you took me by surprise. You looked so…" She shivered and clenched her fists, her eyes following his hand gliding along her leg under the soft material. "Mean, I guess is what I want to say."

"There's a difference between mean and strict. Doms can look formidable, but that doesn't make them mean. You know I'm not, right?" He reached her thigh and kneaded the tight muscle.

Avery tried to shift her leg, but he clamped down, holding her still. "Answer me, Avery."

"If you want honesty, then… I'm not sure. You've been nothing but nice to me, but people aren't always what they appear."

He nodded. "You're right."

"I am?"

He squeezed her soft leg, getting a kick out of the astonishment lacing her reply. "You are. Actions speak much louder than words. In fact, a demonstration of the difference between a punishment spanking and a playful, stimulating one is in order."

Grayson didn't give Avery time to think, just flipped her over his lap, pinned her legs with one of his and pressed her shoulders down. "Relax," he coaxed, rubbing his hand over her ass in a soothing caress. "You know the safeword. Use it if you have to. I'm betting you won't, though."

Chapter 7

One minute Avery was conversing softly with Master Grayson, enjoying the steady beat of his heart beneath her ear, the corded strength of his arm around her waist and his calloused palm trailing up her leg, and the next found her looking down at the wood floor, his hard thigh muscles contracting under her fluttering abdomen. Her thick, unruly hair fell over her face, a curtain blocking out everything except the few inches in front of her.

His explanation of the side of him she'd just witnessed had worked to soothe her worries but didn't prepare her for the heat rushing through her veins as he exposed her thighs and panty-covered butt. A wave of uncomfortable self-awareness sent goosebumps racing across her skin, her breath stalling as her heart skipped a beat waiting for the unknown. Instead of the sharp crack of his hand landing on her vulnerable backside, as she'd expected, her breath exhaled on a *whoosh* when he explored her buttocks with casual caresses interspersed with tight squeezes.

"Sir?" Avery's voice quivered with the surprise and uncertainty his light touch produced. She'd expected pain, not the pleasure sweeping through her, never imagining her butt could be such an erogenous zone.

"Feels good, doesn't it, sugar?"

Grayson squeezed her right cheek, this time a tad harder than before. The discomfort ignited another startling burst of heat that spread to include her pussy. "And a little uncomfortable?" He soothed the throbbing flesh with another caress.

"Yes. But…" Avery struggled to lift her shoulders and turn her head, but he pressed harder on her back, keeping her pinned in place. She wasn't sure if the blood rushing to her face was because of her dangling position or the surprising thrill his control stirred up.

"Just because it's new or unexpected doesn't make it wrong or unacceptable." He swatted her left cheek, the sudden sting wringing a cry from her throat, the instant warmth drawing a shiver down her spine. "Some women get off on a touch of pain." The next smack heated and stung her right buttock, leaving behind dual sensations of soft, pulsing flesh. "Even a few on much harsher torment."

Avery damn near flew off his lap as Master Grayson cupped his hand between her legs and pressed up against her damp flesh. Smugness laced his voice as he said, "You're wet, which proves you like that small agony. Let's see how much you can take, shall we?" Nerves skittered under her skin, but embarrassment and curiosity kept her quiet until he demanded a verbal reply in a dark, displeased tone that unnerved her further. "Red or green, Avery. Answer me now."

She felt his fingers at the waistband of her panties and pictured the way her bared butt would face the open side of the nook and the possibility of others seeing, watching. Her sheath clenched at the image in her head and aching need overruled insecurities and mortification with little thought. "Green, Sir."

"Excellent."

Oh, God. It wasn't the slightly cooler air teasing Avery's naked buttocks that caused her to shiver as he lowered her panties to rest at mid-thigh, but the sheer decadence of lying over his lap in such a vulnerable pose. Her nipples puckered, pressing against the satin camisole, another reminder the only part of her he exposed were the rounded globes of her fleshy, white butt.

"Nice." Grayson stroked her bare cheeks, the difference between his hand touching over her panties and now without that thin barrier shockingly acute.

The first few slaps did nothing more than tingle and warm her skin, stirring the results of the previous swats. Avery blew out the breath she'd been holding, relaxed and embraced the oddly arousing sensations coming to life with this new experience. She soon forgot about the risk of being seen, her mind centered on his hand connecting with her backside in a steady volley of titillating smacks that warmed her both inside and out. He stopped to rub her pulsating flesh, lulling her into further complacency she should have been leery of. Her sigh of pleasure ended in a gasping lungful of air as he resumed with a harder swat that stung briefly before disappearing. Shifting her hips against the instant burn, she groaned in frustration of a nameless yearning as his leg tightened over hers.

"Lay still," Master Grayson admonished, delivering another smack hard enough to bounce her buttock.

"I'm trying," she snapped and then cried out as he showed his displeasure with her tone by administering a smarting blow on the under curve of one cheek. "*Sheesh!*" Avery wasn't sure if her startled exclamation stemmed from the blistering pain of that reprimand or the way her copious juices oozed from her empty pussy as a result, her response rattling her. Latching onto his leg for added support, he rocked her body forward with two more butt covering swats, each one a touch harder, turning heat into fire.

"Try harder. I love your ass, sugar." He tapped a sore area, the lighter touch emphasizing the burn again. "So soft and malleable." Cupping the plump roundness of her right buttock, he kneaded the flesh he'd just smacked. "And responsive to my touch." Releasing the tender globe, he again smoothed his palm over her backside, leaving none of her reddened skin untouched.

A nervous giggle slid past Avery's compressed lips. "I don't know what to say to that. No one's ever…"

"Never?"

She shook her head, wishing she had the guts to look back at his face. "Nope, never."

"Idiots. You're better off without them. You like a touch of pain."

Avery knew where he was going when he brushed the pads of his fingers over her throbbing buttocks then down to her crotch. She whimpered with the single-digit glide up her seam, moaned as he kept going, dragging the slick juices he'd encountered up her crack, and shuddered from the light press against her back orifice. Embarrassed and appalled at the spark of pleasure she never expected from such a taboo part of her body, she put more effort into shifting away from his hand.

"Give me a color, Avery," Grayson demanded, his voice calm and implacable.

"Um, yellow?" She didn't want him to give up on her but wasn't sure what that touch was leading to.

"Good enough." Pulling up her panties, he said, "Up you go."

GRAYSON FLIPPED Avery over and held her pressed against his chest, catching her wince when her well-spanked ass came to rest on his denim-covered thighs. Her face was almost as red as her butt, her eyes glazed behind the glasses she was nudging back in place. "I'm surprised those stayed on," he commented, flicking the corner of the black frames.

"Me too." She leaned her head against his shoulder, a sign she wasn't put off by that light demonstration.

Reaching up, he cupped one full breast, enjoying the poke of her puckered nipple through the soft satin and the shape and size of her. He couldn't remember when he'd delighted in a spanking for titillation and tutoring so much, her responses boding well for her acceptance into submission. Taking advantage of her bemused state, he pushed his agenda to get her to open up by asking, "You're a long way from home, sugar. What brought you to Willow Springs?"

She stiffened, and he tightened his arm around her waist, scraping his thumbnail over her nipple to keep her teetering on that edge of arousal the spanking had brought her to.

"I… does it matter?" she answered with an indrawn breath as he circled the turgid tip with his finger, tracing over the bumps of her areole.

"You tell me."

"I needed a change, is all. My job… I wasn't happy there anymore."

Grayson moved to her other breast, toying with that nipple as he said, "From your computer skills, I'm guessing you weren't waitressing."

Avery paused long enough to push into his exploring hand with a small shudder before replying, "No, I… I'm a certified IT tech."

It should make him happy she was talking, but instead he found himself frustrated by the bits and pieces she kept tossing out with the evasive replies. Deciding it might be best not to push her for more answers tonight, he nudged her up from his lap. "We've hidden behind here long enough. Come on."

Snatching her hand, Grayson led her around the half wall and toward the bar, surprised to see Dan filling drink orders instead of Connor, who usually took the early shift bar tending until later in the evening, when he was ready to play. Ever since his breakup with Annie, though, Connor had been spending more and more time behind the bar and less time with a sub.

"A little early for you to be taking over, isn't it?" he asked Dan as he slid onto a stool, pulling Avery in front of him and caging her in between him and the bar top.

"Connor's a no-show tonight. But I'm good. Caden will relieve me in an hour when you're up for monitor upstairs," Dan reminded him.

Grayson nodded, removing the toothpick as Dan set his usual whiskey in front of him. "Got it. Thanks."

"You look like you could use a drink, Avery. What can I get you?" The lawyer's dark eyes missed nothing as he took in her flustered appearance and distended nipples.

"A light beer, thanks." She squirmed against Grayson, shifting her eyes away from the knowing glint in Dan's assessing gaze. Smart girl to suspect the other Dom knew about and might have caught a glimpse of her first spanking.

Grayson pressed his arm against her lower abdomen, pulling her ass against his pelvis, her soft buttocks providing a nice cushion for his erection. After taking a sip of his drink, he turned her face to meet his mouth and let her taste the liquor on his tongue. She sank into the kiss, her hands clutching his forearm as he took his time exploring the inner recesses of her mouth, their teeth gnashing as he went deeper with it.

The clank of Dan setting the beer bottle down drew them apart, the return of Avery's glazed expression leaving Grayson satisfied. "Take a drink, sugar. I agree with Master Dan. You look like you could use it."

Grabbing the bottle, she gulped down a hefty swallow, her eyes watering from the long drink. Dan chuckled and reached over to give her hair a friendly yank. "I don't think you need to worry about this one hiding what she's thinking, or feeling, Master Grayson."

No, just everything personal about herself and her past, he thought.

"She can be an expressive little sub," he returned, not surprised to see that cute frown appear between her eyes. Those small signs of irritated rebellion against an observation by him or someone else contradicted the way Avery continued to cower away from verbally revealing too much about herself. He liked that spark of fire as much as he disliked her reticence about her past. Time to test that fiery streak and work on knocking down a few more barriers.

Reaching up, he lowered the narrow strap of her camisole until the scooped, lace-trimmed neckline snagged on her nipple. "Problem, sugar?" he taunted, pinning her other hand down on the bar top as she attempted to readjust it.

Avery bit her lip, indecision written clearly on her face as her eyes flickered between him and Dan. "I'm right here, you know," she returned, her peevish tone at odds with the consternation she exhibited over her potential public exposure.

"Yes, we can see that, and want to see more." Grayson nodded to Dan who took over shackling her wrist so he could return his arm around her waist. Figuring she didn't need another reminder about using the safeword option to stop him, he tugged on the lowered strap, dropping the top and baring her breast. Her deep inhale lifted the enticing, plump mound, her nipple tightening into an even harder pinpoint under his and Dan's gazes.

"Very pretty, Master Grayson." Dan followed his compliment with a wink at Avery as he stated, "Thank you for sharing."

"My pleasure." Grayson relented under Avery's heated blush and downcast eyes, lifting her chin to take her mouth again, this time in a softer kiss designed to encourage and put her at ease.

He palmed her breast as he slipped his tongue past her lips, the soft fullness as enticing as her delectable ass. Thumbing her rigid nipple, he swallowed her low moan and relished the way she leaned back against him in surrender. He loved testing a sub's limits as well as his own, but he'd only just begun with Avery and every time he touched her, he felt his control slip another notch. The urge to take, possess and ravish kept growing stronger instead of lessening the more he was with her. And *fucking A* but he wanted answers, both to what she was running from and to ending the constant nagging sense of familiarity continuing to plague him.

MASTER GRAYSON RELEASED Avery's mouth, leaving her lips to tingle along with her nipple. She couldn't recall doing anything as difficult as sitting there with her breast bared to two men, and anyone else mingling around who happened to glance their way. She also couldn't think of anything in her sexual experience that had been as erotic or as arousing as her current exposed state or the men's eyes on her nakedness and Master Grayson's hand on her flesh. This time when he scraped a nail over her nipple, the absence of the thin satin resulted in an electric charge zinging straight down between her legs. She shook from the instant pleasure, biting her lip to swallow a low moan begging for release.

Master Dan moved away to serve someone else, which helped ease her tension and get her mind off Master Grayson's earlier personal questions. When he touched her, she forgot everything, including what was at stake if she revealed too much too soon. What if *Sheriff* Monroe refused to cross the blue line after she told him about Darren, or started checking into her allegations and Darren or his partner found out? What if he stood by the law instead of by her if she admitted to hacking to show him her proof? She shuddered to think what would happen in either case.

Picking up her beer, she took a sip, but the cold brew did nothing to counteract the heat of Master Grayson's hand casually exploring her breast.

"What are you thinking?" he whispered in her ear, kneading

the full softness of her left breast. The activity and sounds resonating around the room fell to the wayside under the rising tide of arousal until he sank his teeth into her earlobe. The sharp nip distracted her as much as his hand until he demanded, "Avery, answer me."

The whole truth, or a portion of it? She made the decision to err on the side of caution and went with door number two. "I don't like how easily I answered your personal questions earlier." Which was true, she didn't, but had to admit he didn't push very hard or for much.

"Sugar, you are anything but easy." With a sigh, he covered her breast and she twisted on his lap enough to watch his tanned throat work as he tossed back the rest of his drink. "It's my turn to monitor upstairs. Come keep me company."

"Okay," she agreed, thrilled he still wanted her company and with the chance to learn more about him by watching him work without his distracting touch. Little did she know how good he was at doing two things at once.

Over the next hour, Master Grayson kept Avery close to his side as he alternated between strolling around the lofts on both sides of the barn and leaning against a wall to observe in silence, all the while never wasting a chance to brush his fingers over her nipples or trail his hand down her thigh, stopping to press against her mons. She discovered he liked nipping along her neck, hard enough to sting and make her gasp with a delicate shiver. As if she hadn't already suspected, she learned he enjoyed a butt fetish and didn't miss an opportunity to fondle her cheeks or trail one finger in between, pushing the material of her skirt and panties to rub against her anus. Avery still couldn't get over the surprising tingles of pleasure those touches produced. By the time his shift as monitor ended, he'd reduced her to a quaking mass of edgy, pulsing arousal, leaving her nipples aching and her swollen pussy needy.

Avery couldn't think about anything except easing the ache

he'd caused as Master Grayson escorted her back downstairs, and wondered how far he planned to take her, and where and how. Despite her desperate need for relief, getting stripped and fucked in public left her uncomfortable, at least more so than others she'd witnessed tonight who appeared to enjoy the exhibitionism as much as their orgasms. But she swore she'd combust if he didn't end her torment soon.

Which was why she was both confused and disappointed as he led her toward the front doors, saying, "I'll walk you out. I've given you a lot to think about tonight, a lot to decide before I take you further."

Okay, damn it, that made sense, and was considerate of him. Damn it again. Still, she ached and didn't relish going it alone, not after having his hands on her all night. Of course, she wouldn't tell him that.

"Thank you. I had a good time."

He must have read something on her face because his lips quirked, and his eyes crinkled with humor. "Don't fret, Avery. I'm not going anywhere yet. Drive safely."

Once again, she resisted the urge to look back as she drove out of the parking lot, her mind at odds with her body's cravings.

On Saturday, Avery learned how fast word spread in a small town when Bill Wojick, the barber asked for her assistance in updating his computer with new software when she waited on him at the diner. After agreeing to stop by the next day, Harvey Loggins, who owned the feed store, waylaid her to inquire about setting up his accounts online.

"It's time I quit fighting it and get on board with paying my suppliers and other bills online," Harvey sighed, the disgruntled look crossing his weathered face a sign he wasn't happy about twenty-first century technology.

Avery patted his shoulder while refilling his iced tea. "I promise, it won't hurt for long," she teased.

They thrilled her with their requests and the opportunities to use her mind and skills again. Her job logging evidence onto the computer had just been a stepping stone while waiting for an opening in the precinct's IT department, but she'd often done personal side jobs, keeping up with the rapid changes and honing her talents. When Caden and Sydney entered without Grayson, both her smile and lighter heart faltered, making her realize she'd been keeping one eye on the front for his usual appearance.

"Hi," she greeted them once they took their seats in a corner booth. It took every ounce of willpower not to ask about the sheriff, but that's where her strength ended. She tried and failed to keep from wondering if he was already at the club enjoying someone more experienced, ready and willing to indulge him in all his kinks. How he'd known just how far to push her the last two weeks she didn't have a clue, but at the time had appreciated. Now, not so much. She didn't care for the images in her head or the tightness around her chest they caused.

"Hey." Sydney returned her smile with a puzzled look in her eyes. "I didn't get a chance to talk with you much last night or see you leave. Everything go okay?"

"Uh, sure." Avery shrugged. "Some things take time getting used to."

Caden smirked. "You could take lessons from Syd. She caught on real quick."

"Would've been quicker if you hadn't been so stubborn," she muttered.

Avery enjoyed their easy banter with each other; it was obvious how happy the two were. Another pang clutched at her chest. At one time, she'd imagined herself that happy with Darren. Just how pathetic did that make her? "Just the two of you this evening?" she asked, hoping her desire to hear about Grayson wasn't obvious.

"Just us and I'll take the chili even if it's not as good as Sydney's," Caden answered. It hadn't taken Avery long to hear what an awesome cook Sydney was and how much the Dunbar hired hands adored both her and the meals she prepared for them. "If you'd like, I'll open the doors at The Barn to let you in after you get off tonight," he offered, eyeing her with a probing look similar to those Master Grayson gave her.

Must be a Dom thing, Avery mused, shifting her gaze away from his. "Thanks, but I'm more than ready to rest by the time I leave here." He didn't need to know that wasn't the entire reason she turned down his invitation, or even the mitigating factor. Despite mentioning taking her further and that he wasn't going anywhere yet, she hadn't heard from Grayson all day. Since she couldn't imagine herself submitting to anyone but him and wanted no one else except the sheriff, there would be no point in exposing herself to the potential embarrassment and heartache of entering the club only to see him with someone else.

"Sydney, do you know what you would like?" Poised with her pen above the pad, she prayed her friend wouldn't push for more.

Sydney nodded, her green-eyed gaze both shrewd and knowing. "I'll have the same, thanks. What are you doing tomorrow?"

Taking their menus, Avery breathed a sigh of relief at the change of subject. "No plans yet. Why?"

"It's supposed to reach a balmy forty degrees by two o'clock and Caden promised I could accompany him and Connor on their afternoon ride to check on the herd. I'm told the weather is due to take a turn for the worse anytime, so I want to take advantage of any outdoor time I can clock. Come along," she invited with a coaxing smile.

"Oh, I couldn't," Avery answered with a shake of her head. "I've never been on a horse. Heck, I've never even owned a pet of any kind."

"You can ride up with Con. He'll enjoy the company. One o'clock." Caden's low, insistent voice and direct, blue gaze added to the unwavering resolve she heard behind the casual words.

"Okay, I'll go. Leave me directions." She ripped off a page

from her notepad and laid it on the table. "I'll get your order turned in." Maybe the excursion would keep her mind off Grayson, and the growing ache for more from her dominant caller.

GRAYSON LEANED against the end of the bar, his current mood as dour as a late spring snow warning. He'd been nursing the same drink since he arrived at The Barn an hour ago, and now the lukewarm whiskey had lost its appeal. He found the loud music as annoying as the interested looks aimed his way from willing submissives. He should have stayed home, or better yet, waited until Avery's next evening off and then issued another invitation for her to accompany him.

The temptation to pull her secrets from her was as strong as the one prodding him to fuck her. Yet, he refused to indulge either her or himself until she trusted him enough to open up about herself. He could do a little discreet digging on his own, run her license plates for one thing, but wouldn't take that back-stabbing route unless she left him no choice. Betraying her now would undo everything he'd accomplished the last two weeks.

"Heads up," Connor murmured from behind the bar, his blue eyes on someone behind Grayson. "Cassie is making a beeline straight for you."

"*Fucking A*," Grayson growled, snapping his toothpick in half when he bit down on it. He was in no mood to deal with the pushy, clinging sub. Removing the splintered pieces, he tossed them down and fished another one out of his shirt pocket and stuck it in his mouth. He'd picked up the habit in the military-it had given him something to do with his mouth while struggling to keep silent and still while holed up on some Godforsaken hill, watching for insurgents.

Dan, perched on the stool next to Grayson, raised one brow,

a sardonic look to match his tone as he asked, "Why don't you boot her out of here? It's your club, and it's not like we don't have a selection of other subs to play with."

Grayson shrugged. "Others like her, and she'll soon tire of the game."

"I suggest you prod her along toward that end," Connor urged.

"Master Grayson! I've been looking for you," Cassie gushed as she latched onto his arms and dug her nails into his skin.

With a thunderous scowl she ignored, he removed her hands with an admonishment. "You're interrupting, Cassie, and you know better than that. Go away."

"Aw, come on, quit being so grouchy," she cajoled, leaning forward in a blatant move that offered him a peek down her sheer, white blouse at her unfettered breasts. "Am I being a bad girl?" she teased, rubbing her breasts on his arm.

Grayson swore under his breath as a small smile played around her mouth. He knew what she thought as he straightened with a cold, hard look. With a quick nod of agreement from Dan, he was about to show her how wrong she was. Cassie enjoyed pushing Doms into punishing her and got off on the harsher pain, but she didn't care for the humiliation of a discipline scene. Too bad. She had earned this lesson.

"Bad girls don't get what they want. Just the opposite, in fact."

The satisfied glint in her eyes increased as he yanked her over his arm and rucked up her ass hugging skirt to reveal her bare butt. "Master Dan, I suggest you don't hold back."

"What?" Outraged that it would be another Dom meting out her punishment stained her face red as she lifted her head to glare up at Grayson. "I want... *ahh!*" she screeched as Dan blistered her right buttock with a forceful blow. She blubbered again, wriggling against Grayson's arm until he wrapped his other arm around her back and held her still.

All three men ignored her wails—she would yell the safeword red if she needed or wanted to—as Dan laid into her ass with a volley of fast, pain-inducing smacks that turned her lily-white buttocks crimson. His swats were so effective, he stopped after a mere three minutes, not offering the chastised sub the comfort of a caress over her blazing cheeks or a hug when Grayson lifted her. Despite the pain he knew Dan inflicted, he suspected the tears streaking her face were due more to frustration than the throbbing discomfort. Neither of them had missed the glistening proof of arousal dripping from her pussy.

Before he could warn her of losing club privileges, she stomped her foot and poked him in the gut, stirring his annoyance anew. "You've had your fun." She flipped Dan a cold look before all but demanding Grayson's personal attention. "You can't seriously mean to leave me hanging like this? What kind of cruel Dom are you?" Trailing her fingers up his chest, his rigid stance and cool disdain forced her to try a new tactic by turning coy. "I apologize, Master Grayson. There. Now, can we play?" She stroked her fingers up his corded neck to run one around his ear.

Fed up with her, he drawled in a deceptively soft voice, "Play, Cassie? I don't think so. Come with me." Snatching her hand, they both heard Connor quip, "Sucks to be her," as Grayson hauled her over to the corner spanking bench, bent her over and wrapped the center strap around her lower back, pinning her down. "Again," he whispered in her ear, "I don't reward disobedience and rudeness."

Whipping off his belt, he delivered three bruising stripes across her already bright red, tormented ass, her cries loud and long, but revealing no safewords, either the club's or her own. Returning his belt to his waist, Grayson released her, noting her swollen, damp labia. But if she wanted relief, she would have to look elsewhere. He was done with her.

He held her long enough to ensure she was steady, her eyes

clear before releasing her with a final warning. "Find someone else to sink your claws into, Cassie. You knew before we hooked up I wouldn't commit to anything more than a few scenes." He spun on his heels, missing the daggers she shot at his back as she yanked her skirt down over her throbbing buttocks.

Grayson was so ready to head home; he just waved to Connor and Dan as he passed by the bar on his way out. Without bothering to don his coat, he walked out to the parking lot just as Caden and Sydney were coming in.

"Leaving already?" his friend asked, cocking his head.

"Yes. Been a long day."

Caden nodded, took Sydney's elbow and started around him, tossing out, "We invited Avery to join us tomorrow for a ride. Just so you know."

With a huff, Grayson climbed into his SUV and slammed the door. Sometimes, having someone know you so well, for so long could be a pain in the ass.

Chapter 8

A very was just about to leave for the Dunbar Ranch the following afternoon when an unexpected knock landed on the door leading to the outside staircase behind the diner. Since she wasn't expecting anyone she answered with all the caution ingrained from growing up in the city with the highest murder rate in the country.

Cracking the door only as far as the safety chain allowed, her eyes widened when she saw the sheriff on her doorstep, his sheepskin-lined leather jacket doing little to disguise the breadth of his shoulders, his lowered black Stetson revealing only a gray/green sliver of his eyes. The respectful title of Sir trembled on her lips without conscious thought as she swung the door open in surprise, and she needed a moment to get her jumbled reaction under control.

"Are you ready?" Grayson asked. At her puzzled silence, the corners of that sexy as sin mouth curled. "I'm headed out to the ranch as well. No sense in both of us driving, and you may have trouble finding it."

Excitement warmed Avery against the chill of standing in the open door without a coat. It wasn't another invitation to join him at the club, but she wasn't about to turn down the opportunity to spend time with him in any capacity. Being with Grayson in yet another environment would give her more insight into the type of man she was still debating over how far to trust.

"Okay, thanks, that's… nice of you," she replied lamely, flustered and thrilled all at the same time. Pivoting, she reached with a jerky hand for her coat and knocked her purse off the small table next to the hook. "Crap, sorry. Come on in while I…"

Grayson's large body stooped down next to her as she scrambled to pick up the fallen items out of her bag, his voice rough and close enough she could feel his warm breath on her neck as he said, "Relax, sugar. You should be more at ease with me by now. Is there some reason you're not?"

You mean other than having to deal with the sexual frustration you're responsible for along with wondering how far I can trust you to help me return home safely? At least she could answer him this time with complete honesty. "I'm sorry. A bad experience has taught me to take my time getting to know people."

Grayson handed Avery her purse then they stood at the same time as he replied, "It never hurts to be careful, but don't let one asshole who has made you so wary negate your chances with someone else. If you do, he wins."

"And if it's not a game I can afford to lose?" she blurted without thinking.

Nudging his hat back, Grayson eyed her with grave concern from his towering height. "Then maybe you should let someone else in on it. You never know who can be of some help." When her eyes skittered away from his, his sigh revealed frustration with her, but all he said was, "Let's go. The sun is never up high and warm enough for long once it peaks and I, for one, want to be back at the house before it, and the temperature starts to dip. Is that your warmest jacket?"

"Yes. I'll be fine in it." Avery couldn't very well tell him she'd packed so fast trying to flee before Darren came by her apartment looking for her that she'd grabbed the closest coat at hand on her way out. Although lined, the denim jacket was better suited for fall than winter.

"You'll ride up with me, so I can be sure."

It was on the tip of her tongue to argue over the high-handed order, but the fact he'd issued the dictate with her welfare in mind and with him was exactly where she yearned to be kept her quiet.

Forty minutes later, Avery stepped inside a working ranch's barn for the first time in her life, the mingling odors of hay and manure tickling her nose as two collies came bounding straight up to Sydney. The beaming redhead greeted the dogs with scraps of bacon and sausage as Caden released an exaggerated huff of disapproval, which she ignored. Four horses stood near the open back doors, saddled and ready to ride, but as Grayson tugged on her hand, prodding her toward them, she slowed her steps the closer she came to the huge animals. "They're uh, bigger in person, aren't they?" The sleek black stallion tossing his head and nudging Grayson with his long nose towered over her, just like his master.

"That was my first thought too." Sydney smiled, patted the collies and then stepped up to the large bay to stroke its muscled neck. "But they're sweet, aren't you, baby?" she crooned. Caden swatted her butt and rolled his eyes behind her.

"Anything covered with fur, and walking on four legs is sweet to Sydney," Connor drawled as he swung up into the saddle of a stunning Palomino. "I have to say, Avery, I'm sorry you won't be riding with me."

"Deal with it," Grayson returned.

Avery flushed, unused to rivalry between two men over her, even friendly, innocent banter. Before Darren, she mostly went unnoticed by the opposite sex, and the lesson she'd learned from his sudden attention was still keeping her at arm's length from

Grayson even though she trusted him now more than anyone else.

"I'm sorry, Connor." She frowned at Grayson. "He didn't give me a choice."

Connor winked and turned his horse, tossing back, "As it should be, sweetie," before trotting off.

Ignoring them, Grayson followed Caden in mounting up and then reached a hand down to Avery, his eyes steady on her face as he said, "Trust me."

Those simple words curled around her heart and she took his hand before she could talk herself out of it. She never hesitated to admit what a coward she was. With a strong tug, he drew her up in front of him, her butt shifting around on the definite bulge between his legs as he turned her to straddle the horse and pressed her to lean back against him.

Daring a look down, she muttered, "*Sheesh*," before cringing back from the height and sudden movement as he nudged the steed to follow the other three.

"Not so bad, is it?" Grayson murmured in her ear, tugging hard on her braid. "I prefer your hair down but can have fun with it pulled back too."

The quick yank on her scalp drew a frisson of tickling goosebumps down her back, and Avery found herself grateful for the distraction as Grayson kicked the horse into a faster trot. Gripping the arm wrapped around her waist, she sucked in a deep breath of cold air, all the while conscious of the way the jarring pace bounced her up and down on his lap.

"Hold tight, sugar. Here we go."

They took off with another booted heeled nudge to the horse's sides, the ground and trees blurring as the chill whipping her face soon warmed from the sheer exhilaration and sense of freedom sweeping through Avery. She laughed outright, drawing Connor's grin from up ahead and a thumb's up from Caden who rode alongside Sydney. The clomp of pounding hooves against the dried earth and the horse's heavy exertions echoed in her ears, the sounds so different from the constant cadence of traffic and crowds she was used to.

She could feel the heaving, muscled sides of the animal against her legs and the thick bunching of Grayson's thighs against the back of hers. Between the comfort of his big body and the sun shining down on her face, she barely felt the nip of winter anymore, and when Grayson slid his hand down to press between her legs, a burst of fiery heat shot up her core, reigniting the quivering of unfulfilled lust he'd lit Friday night.

"Problem, sugar?" he asked. She shuddered against his wide chest as he slowed them down to a trot as they approached a small group of black cattle.

Swiveling her head around, Avery nudged her slipping glasses back into place, replying in a breathless tone, "You enjoy toying with me, don't you?"

"I want answers. After I get them, I'll enjoy toying with you." Nudging her head back, he kissed her fast and hard, leaving her lips tingling along with her scalp by the time he released her and turned his attention to Caden's interruption.

"More tracks that look similar to the others we've found." He pointed down as Grayson and Connor joined him.

"Fucking bastards," Connor swore, his congenial mood vanishing. "I've counted three head missing and one calf. God damn it, now they've gotten brave enough to hit us closer to home."

"Calm down, Con. They could have just gotten separated," Caden stated. "Let's fan out but stay within sight of each other. I'll phone Jim and get him to round up this group and bring them closer in."

"Is someone stealing their cows?" Avery asked Grayson as they veered north at a slower pace.

"Cattle rustling never goes out of style. These guys have been plaguing ranchers for over a month now, despite our best efforts to catch them in the act."

Avery remained quiet as they rode, not wanting to interrupt his concentration. She'd come to know how seriously he took his job as sheriff, an admirable trait and one that urged her to trust him with her secrets, as he kept asking. A shout from Caden reached them ten minutes later and as they trotted toward him and Sydney, Avery spotted a small calf lying down, its back leg stretched out at an odd angle. The mournful lowing the poor thing emitted caused her muscles to tighten and a lump to form in her throat. It sounded so pitiful.

The ice-cold rage in Connor's eyes when he joined them didn't bode well for the young animal. Swinging down, he dropped the reins and stooped to caress the calf's head before running a light touch over the limb. Even that gentle probing caused the young male to kick out in pain. "Broken," he clipped, pushing to his feet.

Caden responded to his brother's diagnosis with a curse and disgusted sigh before giving Grayson a pointed look. "Take Avery and Sydney back to the ranch, would you?"

Avery didn't understand the glance the three men shared, or the tears welling in Sydney's eyes, not until Grayson turned their horse around, Sydney's mare falling in step with their mount. As they put distance between them and the injured calf, she jerked in shock from the sudden report of a gunshot reverberating in the air.

"There was no other choice," was all he said, tightening his arm around her.

GRAYSON DROPPED the girls off at the front of the house and returned both horses to the barn to unsaddle them and rub them down. *Fucking A.* He'd been enjoying Avery's company, her soft body swaying against his and the light of appreciation shining in her eyes as they rode, as well as a return of Connor's good-humor. He swore heads would roll once he caught the callous bastards. Taking his time, he lingered in the barn until the brothers returned, the calf's carcass draped over Connor's horse. As cold as it sounded, they bred cattle for either sale or the butcher shop and he knew neither Dunbar would let their anger sway them from getting what they could from the tragic end of the young animal's life.

"I'm ready for a beer and a big serving of whatever Sydney's cooking," he said as the three of them strolled up to the house.

"You and me both. She had potato soup already warming before we left." Caden opened the front door of his sprawling home, releasing the tantalizing aroma of freshly baked home-made bread. "God, I never tire of that smell."

They went straight to the kitchen where Sydney set down her stirring spoon to give Connor a silent hug before telling all three, "Five minutes. You have time to wash up." She shooed them out with a wave of her hand.

"She's gotten bossy lately," Grayson quipped, looking around for Avery.

"I give her leeway in the kitchen in exchange for bigger servings." Caden nodded toward the den. "She's sitting by the fire."

Connor remained sullen and quiet even though his face had softened when Sydney embraced him. With a mental head shake, Grayson padded into the high-ceilinged great room, his gaze zeroing in on Avery huddled before the blazing fire, holding her hands out to the heat, sadness reflected on her expressive face. He hoped she never lost the appeal of wearing her heart on her sleeve.

Bracing his forearm on the mantle, he stood next to her, liking how she looked kneeling at his feet, her eyes lifted to his, shining with both wariness and pleasure. The only thing that could make it better would be if she were naked, her soft flesh bared for his eyes and use, his to do with as he pleased. Soon, he vowed, and then it would be no holds barred between them, a surefire scene to prod her into spilling her secrets.

"What are you thinking about with such a solemn look?" he asked.

She hesitated a fraction of a second before answering. "I'm wishing I were a braver person."

Pleased with her honesty, he held down his hand, squeezing hers as she clasped it and then pulled her to her feet. "There's hope for you yet, sugar." He kissed her and then pushed her toward the kitchen with a hand on her ass. "Come on. I'm starving."

AVERY ENTERED the sheriff's office connected to the courthouse the next morning, a thread of excitement prodding her forward. Not as much from getting yet another opportunity to use her IT skills as for the chance to spend more time with Grayson. His request to update the office computers when he'd dropped her off last night had pleased her so much, she'd been able to set aside the pang she still felt over the tragic death of that poor calf. With her mind on both the work and the sheriff, she missed catching sight of Cassie across the street, and the jealous glare the other woman leveled at her back as she slipped inside the two-story, brick building, the small bronzed plaque next to the double doors dating it back to the 1880s.

A wide foyer separated the courtroom from the police station and she pushed open the glass door marked Sheriff's Office. A middle-aged woman seated behind the first of four desks looked up and greeted her with a smile.

"You must be Avery." Rising, she held out her hand with a friendly smile. "I'm Rebecca. The sheriff's waiting for you." Leading the way, she tossed over her shoulder, "We'll all be forever grateful if you can get our computers up-to-date."

"I'll try my best." Eying the monitors, Avery wasn't so sure they wouldn't be better off starting over new.

The forty-something receptionist nodded to the three young men wearing khaki police uniforms and deputy badges, offering a short introduction. "Adam, Jase and Doug, our deputies." With one sharp rap on her boss' door, Rebecca opened it a crack, announcing, "Avery is here."

"Send her in."

Would she ever stop responding with a warm gush every time she heard that deep voice? As Rebecca pushed open the door and stepped aside, Avery took one look at Grayson and doubted it. "Thank you," she told her, entering the brick-walled office. As she crossed the tan carpeted floor toward where he sat behind a massive, wooden desk, he pushed to his feet and her entire body went molten under that penetrating stare.

Surely he didn't intend for this meeting to go beyond her computer help, she wondered as he strode toward her, his face revealing the same intense regard as he'd shown at the club while tormenting her in one way or another. When he reached her, he raised his hands to push the door closed and she heard the distinct click of the lock turning. Bracing his hands against the door, he caged her in, his body held inches away from hers and yet she could still feel his heat.

Swallowing past the sudden lump in her throat, she mumbled, "Um, Grayson, uh, Sir... I mean, Sheriff..."

A wry grin twisted his lips. "Again, Avery, relax." After subjecting her to a close scrutiny, he nodded and stepped back. "Why don't you start with my console and then we'll see how much time you have left. I don't want to monopolize your entire day off."

Funny, she mused, thinking she wouldn't mind if he did even though he enjoyed flustering her with just a look or touch. Or by locking a door just to watch her reaction to being closed in with him while he kept others out. "Okay. I'll need your passwords."

She padded over to the desk, breathing easier until he replied with emphasis, "No problem. I trust you."

Avery flicked him an uncertain look before taking the chair he'd vacated. "I see them here, thanks. I'll... I'll just get to work."

He nodded, reaching for his hat and coat on a stand. "I have highway patrol and will be gone for a while. Rebecca can answer any questions you have. Thank you, Avery."

"No problem. I enjoy the challenge of troubleshooting and updating."

"Then have fun. I'll be back."

She wasn't sure if his parting comment was a promise or threat. Settling down to work, she vowed to put him, and her decision to reveal who she was to Master Grayson out of her mind. She was still more comfortable talking to the man she'd met over the phone than the law officer.

Avery became so immersed in her work once Grayson left she didn't hear him return until another click of the lock caught her attention. Peering around the computer, she saw him leaning against the door, arms folded, his gray-green gaze on her.

"You have good timing," she greeted him, glancing at the wall clock. "Two hours? I'm sorry; time flies whenever I get online. Almost everyone I've assisted in this town has had the same problem, outdated hardware and software, but I have you updated for now." Pushing back, she rose and ran her suddenly damp palms down her jean-clad thighs, his slow, purposeful steps and predatory look in those enigmatic eyes sending her pulse skyrocketing.

"Excellent. I believe you could use a break now." He crooked a finger, beckoning her to come around the desk to him.

Her gaze skittered to the door and back to him. "What kind of break did you have in mind?" she asked as she obeyed the silent order without thinking about it.

"A fun one. Don't worry, no one can enter. As long as you're quiet, they won't hear anything either." His look stole her breath; his next command robbed her of speech. "Bend over my desk." Gripping Avery's hips, he turned her and, with a hand pressed between her shoulder blades, urged her down. "I decided not to wait until Friday night at the club to continue your education. Ever play with beads?"

He held up two purple beads attached on a slim cord about a fourth of an inch apart. Avery shook her head, her mouth going dry as Grayson slipped his other hand around to undo her jeans. He didn't hesitate to yank them and her panties down, the sudden naked exposure pulling a gasp from her. Her stomach muscles contracted as the cooler air wafting over her bare buttocks popped up goosebumps and pebbled her nipples into prominent pinpoints brushing the desktop from where she leaned on her elbows. Excited and uncertain all at once, she stuttered, "I… don't know about this. What if…"

"Let me worry about the what if's," Grayson interrupted her as he skimmed his fingertips across her butt, Avery's cheeks clenching in automatic response to the light, stimulating touch. Setting the beads on the desk in front of her face, he trailed his other hand up her inner thigh and traced the damp seam of her pussy with his fingers.

"*Sheesh!*" she exclaimed in a whispered huff, shocked at her instant, fiery response to the 'barely there' grazes. "Grayson… *ow!*" The pinch he delivered to her right buttock stung but, just like other erotic pain he'd introduced her to, the small throbbing burn it left behind worked in her favor instead of against it.

"We're in a scene, so it's Sir, or Master Grayson, even though we're not in the club. And, I suggest you keep your voice down," he warned.

Avery swore under her breath, noticing his lack of remorse over causing her outcry. Just like at The Barn, his touch stripped her of all willpower and tossed her into a heightened state of unfulfilled ecstasy. Praying for relief and enough composure to keep silent with it, she laid her head down and bit her lip as he explored her pussy and inched into her rectum with slow finger jabs that ignited the sensitive nerve endings along her inner walls. She could feel her cream seeping down her thighs, hear the damp slurp of his now three fingers moving in and out of her sheath as he worked a second digit into her ass. Discomfort gave way to pleasure as he initiated a tandem rhythm between the two orifices that drove her crazy.

"Sir, *please.*" She quivered as he scraped her swollen clit with a nail then slid away too soon for the small contractions that touch produced to burst into an orgasm.

"I think you're ready for the beads," he drawled, withdrawing his fingers to pick up the toy. "I brought two sets and want you to wear them home, and then for thirty minutes every day between now and Friday night without climaxing." He tugged on a few curls of pubic hair. "And I want this gone. Understand?"

He pushed the beads inside her pussy, nestling them deep. Avery shifted her hips, moaning as they rolled around, teasing the already inflamed tissues anew, the strange sensations racking her body with shivers of arousal and distracting her from that last dictate. "I... what if I can't?"

"Then I won't finish what I've started." Grayson's hard, implacable tone revealed how serious he was. Spreading her buttocks, he pushed two greased balls into her rectum with a soft warning. "And Avery? I'll know."

As he refastened her jeans and helped her upright, Avery looked up into his chiseled face and didn't doubt he could take one look at her and know if she'd indulged in an orgasm. Taking her elbow, he relieved part of her unease when he said, "You can come back another time to work on the rest of the computers. In the meantime, I'll have Rebecca cut you a check..."

Avery stumbled against him, her knees almost buckling when walking stirred the toys into small vibrations, both his offer of payment and quick steadying reflexes jarring her into responding in a rush. "No… I mean, thank you, but I don't want payment." She wouldn't risk cashing a check until she talked to him, so there would be no point in taking payment. He must have read something about her dilemma on her face, his look reminding her how astute he was.

"This is something else we need to discuss, but it can wait as I have to get back to work. I'll pick you up on Friday."

Grayson didn't give her time to argue as he ushered her out of his office and it took all of her concentration to keep from groaning against the warmth spreading from her crotch up to her face. Afraid of what Rebecca and the one deputy still at his desk might see, and think, she waved while keeping her face averted.

Out on the sidewalk, he gripped her nape, holding her head still for his kiss before releasing her with a pat on the butt. "Remember my instructions."

Grayson pivoted, and as Avery stood in bemused stupefaction, watching him go back inside while leaving her a jumbled mess of frustrating sensation, she again missed seeing Cassie's frigid look as the other girl came out of the beauty shop across the street.

Cassie clenched her hands into fists as soon as she recognized the look on Avery's face. It wasn't bad enough the bitch continued to monopolize Master Grayson's attention at The Barn, but now he was welcoming her at work, and from her red-faced appearance, he'd lavished his dominance on her. Since she'd never known him to do that outside of the club, her jealousy and anger toward the interloping newcomer escalated several more notches. Vowing revenge, she stalked off, her dallying making her late in returning to work.

IT WAS a good thing the military had taught Grayson discipline, he mused as he returned to his office and the mountain of paperwork he could now deal with a lot easier with his smooth running computer. Otherwise, he would have found himself ruled by his dick right now and risking his position as sheriff by fucking Avery over his desk. Her slick heat still coated his fingers, a reminder of how her snug pussy gripped him and of the little ripples along her damp inner walls he could produce with just a few strokes. He hadn't been with anyone in the past two weeks, not since he'd first invited her to the club, and if he didn't get relief soon, he would combust.

Why those rapid responses added to his suspicions of knowing her from somewhere, Grayson couldn't imagine. He sure as hell had never fucked her before; that experience and her expressive face would have been unforgettable. After discovering how much he'd enjoyed spending the afternoon with her at Caden's ranch, he'd decided to push faster and stronger for more answers. If any other woman would have been so evasive with him, continued to hold him at arm's length and revealing nothing personal about herself, he would have walked away long before this.

Grayson insisted on honesty from the subs he spent time with, and from himself. If he could admit it was more than his concern as sheriff for Avery's welfare that had him itching to drag everything there was to learn about her from her stubborn, wary head, she could damn well come clean with a few suspicious issues. And he was prepared to do whatever was necessary to get the answers he needed.

Chapter 9

Chicago

Detective Darren Lancaster spotted his partner at the corner table in the popular cop hangout a block from their precinct. Gritting his teeth, he maneuvered through the Friday night crowd, irritated with Chad for his constant harping over Avery's whereabouts. Yeah, her abrupt disappearance after Chad had discovered her snooping was suspicious and both miffed and concerned him. While he wouldn't hesitate to arrange an accident if she proved to be a risk, as he'd mentioned when Chad had first alerted him to the girl's computer searches, he wasn't about to gamble calling more attention on either of them with the tragic death of a city employee he had ties with unless it became necessary. Now, if he could just get Chad to chill, maybe he could enjoy the fruits of his illegal endeavors.

Dropping into the vacant chair, Darren frowned at his irritating friend from across the table. "Now what?" he growled, not bothering to hide his annoyance at this summons.

Chad leaned forward, bracing his arms on the table, his eyes darting around before he snapped in a low voice, "Did you know Avery hasn't contacted her guardian in Florida since the day she walked off the job and disappeared even though her supervisor told me she left because of a family crisis?"

Closing his eyes, Darren counted to ten to get his anger under control. Opening them again, he whispered back in disbelief, "Please tell me you weren't stupid enough to call Marci Devers again. I told you to let me handle her."

"It wasn't so stupid since I found that out, now was it? We both know Avery is hiding, just as you must realize she's smart enough to hack any information she might go looking for, info that could send us to jail for a long fucking time, partner." Chad leaned back and grabbed his drink, tossing back the half-full glass of scotch in one gulp.

Darren shook his head. "Look, just chill until after the sting goes down tomorrow night. We've busted our asses to take down this ring, and the stash we might grab from it will add a nice cushion to our accounts. Then we can talk about hunting her down. Until then, let her lie low a little longer. She's such a fucking coward over everything, I'm not worried in the least she'll do an about face and get up the nerve to turn to an illegal activity like hacking just because of one anomaly between a witness and the evidence we turned in." His tone turned smug as he stated with confidence, "Odds are, as I've said, she's probably more upset over the possibility I was using her than by anything illegal she thinks I may have done. She fell for every line I fed her without questioning my sudden interest or even considering I may have an ulterior motive for sleeping with her."

"I'm not a risk taker, partner. After tomorrow night, we go after her." Tossing down a few bills, Chad stood and stalked out without another word or a backward glance, leaving Darren to wonder if it was time to end their lucrative thefts, and their friendship.

WILLOW SPRINGS

AVERY MADE it through her busy shift on Friday with just one clumsy stumble and one tray mishap that resulted in a spilled glass of water. That was quite a feat, she surmised, given her frustration level and the unaccustomed sensations teasing the bare flesh of her labia every time her panties brushed against the newly exposed skin. She had no idea why she had obeyed Grayson's order to insert the beads for thirty minutes each day the past four days and shaved her pubic hair that morning, or why she'd held back from getting herself off and relieving the constant ache his devious commands had resulted in. It wasn't like it would be the first time she'd resorted to attaining her own pleasure due to a lack of other options. But something inside her stilled her hand every night as she'd lain in bed quivering after removing the tormenting objects. Grayson's face etched with disappointment kept popping up, his deep voice laced with disapproval intruding on the dark silence.

He'd done her a huge favor weeks ago, when she'd been so desperate, afraid and alone. That favor had led her here, to him and the other wonderful people whose friendship now brightened her days. But this new, contented feeling couldn't last, she knew that. When Grayson had asked her what she'd been thinking as she'd sat in front of the fireplace at the ranch following their ride, she'd been remembering the rent payment coming due at her apartment, wondering about who had taken over her job and if anyone missed her, and desperately wishing she wasn't such a coward.

There had been something about the way he'd gazed down at her from where she'd been kneeling, as well as the way he'd taken her over the minute she stepped into his office the other day that settled something inside Avery she hadn't been aware needed calming before she could reveal both how he knew her and her troubles. Whatever the unnamed emotion was, it opened her up to taking that final step toward giving him her complete trust. Tonight, when they left the club, she would reveal who she was, and enlist his advice on how to get back home safely.

"No broken dishes tonight. There's hope for you yet, girl." Gertie's gruff voice coming up behind Avery made her jump. "Even with your head in the clouds," she grumbled as she reached for an order.

"I'm not a total lost cause," Avery returned with a smile. She'd grown fond of her brusque employer who kept her on her toes.

"I would say not." Ed winked at her as he set another steaming plate on the ledge separating them. "At least Gertie is giving credit where it's due. That's a plus."

"You." Gertie pointed at Avery. "Clock out. I saw the sheriff pull up and I'm assuming he's here for you and not my food. And you." She glared at Ed. "Get me that fried chicken order. We've got a line forming."

Guilt forced Avery to offer, "I can stay, if you need me. It's no problem."

"Shoo, girl. I've got all the help I need. It's just a matter of keepin' 'em goin'."

Grayson walked in just then, sealing her fate with one look at his face. Dressed in his usual black shirt, jeans, Stetson and coat, he looked every inch the rugged, cowboy lawman as well as the dominant Master ready to put her through her paces. As usual, a warm rush traveled through Avery just from one glance out of those piercing eyes. She only prayed he still regarded her with such intense promise after tonight.

"Hi." Coming around the counter, she said, "All I need to do is grab a change of clothes and I'll be ready."

"Don't bother," he replied, taking her elbow with one hand

and snatching her jacket off the coat rack with the other as he steered her toward the door. "You won't stay dressed for long once we get to the club, so I can excuse your jeans."

She looked up at him as he held open the passenger side door of his SUV. "I honestly don't know what to say to that."

"Good. Get in."

The man knew how to rattle her while at the same time putting her in a state of heated anticipation. He spoke of mundane topics, such as their continued search for the rustlers and how well his office and staff were functioning with the updates she'd done; and distracting her from where they were headed and what they would be doing by placing one large hand on her thigh, close enough to her crotch to keep her focused on his not-so-innocent touch.

As he pulled to a stop at The Barn and turned off the engine, Grayson turned to her with a complete change in conversation and demeanor. "Did you insert the beads every day, as I instructed?"

Grateful for the darkened interior, Avery flushed and nodded. "Yes, and that wasn't very nice of you."

"No, but necessary."

She followed him inside, wondering at the dark edge to his tone, the one that sent a shiver of unease trickling down her spine while her pussy clenched in a spasm of damp awareness. As soon as they entered, Cassie waylaid them before they could reach the bar and Avery didn't understand the cold glare the other woman gave her before a sly look came into her eyes as she shifted them to Grayson.

"I see the newbie still hasn't learned the dress code. I guess you'll be delivering her punishment, won't you, Master Grayson?"

"Since *my* guest is dressed as I instructed, no. Excuse us, Cassie." Grayson's frown and the icy bite in his voice sent Cassie back a step.

Avery couldn't remember when a man had ever stood up for her, and the warm glow she experienced as Master Grayson escorted her away from the disgruntled shrew had nothing to do with arousal and everything to do with a pop of pure happiness. When they reached the bar, he lifted her by the waist onto a stool next to Sydney and ordered a light beer for her from Caden, who was bartending.

"Visit with Sydney for five minutes. I'll be right back."

He didn't give her time to question him before trotting upstairs and disappearing from view. Shaking her head at his abrupt departure, Avery clasped the cold bottle Caden set in front of her and sighed. "I swear, that man keeps sending out mixed signals until I don't know what to think."

"Then I'd say he's doing his job well," Caden drawled before shifting down to take another order.

"Caden did that when we met. I knew he wanted me. He was just too stubborn and rigid with his rule of not mixing his pleasures with his employees to admit it or act on it," Sydney said with a twinkle in her eyes as she watched her fiancé.

Avery took a sip before asking, "And how long did it take you to wear him down?"

Her friend's smile turned wicked. "Not long after Connor volunteered to help."

Looking around, Avery didn't see Sydney's soon-to-be brother-in-law. "Is he not here tonight?"

A look of worry crossed her face. "No. All he said at dinner was he had something else he needed to do. He's been distant since having to put that calf down last week and Caden's worried he'll do something rash. He's always been one to stick up for the underdog, including animals it seems."

"That's an admirable trait but I hope he's careful," Avery replied, concern coloring her tone.

"Who?" Nan asked, inserting herself between their seats.

"Connor." Sydney sighed and scooted over.

"Yeah, I noticed his distraction the last time we played, and that is so not like him. It's these rustlers, isn't it? I don't know why they can't find the bastards."

Avery frowned at Nan. "Grayson is trying. He and his deputies are out every night looking."

Nan flicked her a teasing grin. "Sticking up for our sheriff, are we? Relax, I know that. I was just saying."

"Who was sticking up for me, and why?" Grayson demanded from behind Avery, startling her with his sudden reappearance.

She jumped, swiveled and lost her balance, sloshing beer on the bar top as he reached out a hand to keep her from toppling off. "Me, but I won't do it again if you sneak up on me like that again," she groused, pushing her glasses back up.

There wasn't a hint of repentance in the curl of his lips as he plucked her off the stool and took the half-empty beer from her hand. "I'll remember that. Come with me."

Stumbling behind him, Avery responded to Grayson's urgency with a thrill of expectation. Between the tormenting use of the beads and her craving for more of what he'd introduced her to already, and of him, she vowed not to hesitate at whatever he had planned.

That promise lasted until he led her upstairs and over to a secluded corner and a dangling chain bearing two cuffs on the end, tossing over his shoulder one word, "Strip," with a backward wave of his hand.

Avery cast a quick glance around the loft and saw no one not engaged in their own scene. *Okay, I can do this.* Keeping one wary eye on Master Grayson as he padded over to a cabinet against the wall, she pulled her long-sleeved tee over her head. Her stomach muscles contracted when he turned holding several objects that sent her pulse leaping. Her hands flew to the waist of her jeans as he eyed her clothes and approached her with a scowl.

With her eyes on the objects, she shimmied out of her pants, asking, "What are those?" even though she had a good idea.

Grayson wiggled two fingers at her bra and panties and then held up the blindfold. "Self-explanatory. This," he dangled the three-foot bar with cuffs on each end, "is a spreader bar for your feet. And this," he twirled what looked like a hand-held massager, "is a Hitachi wand."

He didn't offer further explanation as he took her bra and panties and turned to lay them atop her jeans and shirt on a chair and Avery noticed the black, multi-leather strands swinging against his thigh for the first time. The wicked looking flogger sent another ripple of unease slithering under her skin, but she refused to cave to the cowardice itching to take over. She wanted him, and that meant giving him the trust he kept asking for and his proclivities a try.

That proved much easier to do when Master Grayson faced her again and Avery's entire body flushed under his intense, molten stare. Excitement intertwined with nerves to start her trembling as his eyes lingered on her naked folds before he beckoned her to stand under the dropped chain. Her nipples pebbled into taut peaks as her breasts swayed with each step, her buttocks clenching as she imagined the eyes of others behind her shifting their way.

"Wrists." Master Grayson held out his hand, his dominant persona having taken over the minute they'd entered the club.

Avery kept quiet while he secured her arms into a taut stretch above her head, the lined cuffs comfortable and somehow lending her a sense of security as he cut off her vision of the activities and people around the loft with the black silk swath. His clothed body brushed against her skin as he knelt at her feet, the brief contact tingling and warming her exposed flesh. He tapped the inside of her right calf, issuing a silent command to spread her legs she didn't think to disobey.

"*Sheesh!*" she gasped, swaying in the restraints as he finished securing her ankles.

"Deep breath, sugar. You're okay," Master Grayson soothed, his voice a deep rumble as he ran his hands down the insides of her arms until he cupped her heaving breasts. "I do like your tits. Soft and so fucking squeezable." His thumbs rasped her nipples, the calloused touch drawing the nubs tighter, his warm breath blowing in her ear as he pressed against her with a warning or a promise, she wasn't sure which. "Time to play."

Avery didn't know what she expected him to do next, but it wasn't to trail the supple leather strands of the flogger over her quivering breasts and nipples as he tugged the band at the bottom of her braided hair off. He sifted his fingers through the mass of thick, unruly waves while tickling her abdomen with the narrow strips next, the dual pleasure of soft tugs against her scalp and caresses along her body lulling her into leaning toward him with a relaxed sigh.

"There you go," Grayson murmured, brushing the leather up between her legs, that simple graze against such sensitive flesh enough to pull a low moan from her constricted throat.

A sharp nip on her neck spread a wave of heat throughout her body that intensified as he shifted behind her and snapped the flogger across her buttocks. Tiny pinpricks of pain came and went, leaving behind stripes of warmth. Avery drew a deep breath, thinking after the next swat that the instrument wasn't so bad, and then quickly changed her mind with the third stroke.

"Thought that might get your attention," he stated in a smug tone from behind her.

Even though she couldn't see him, Avery turned her head and muttered, "You could have warned me," referring to the heated stings that strike elicited.

"And here I thought you knew me better than that," he replied with humor.

She sucked in a deep breath seconds before he delivered

another blistering swat, this one leaving her cheeks throbbing along with the heat encompassing the fleshy globes. Her entire body quaked as he treated her thighs to the same burning cuts, her breasts jiggling each time she jerked against the restraints and the blows that were slowly working to suffuse her with pleasure. He trailed the flogger around to the front of her body, softening the strokes over her waist as he moved up to her trembling breasts. With a talent that spoke of experience, he struck the fleshy underside of her left breast, hard enough to sting but not hurt for long. He gave her right fleshy mound equal treatment before catching her nipple with the end of one knotted strand.

Avery flushed and mewled with the onslaught of arousal as each sting made her crave more of the fiery lashes even though through it all her pussy remained empty, untouched... needy. She whimpered for more without realizing it, thrusting her hips forward, pleading without words for what she yearned for the most. He caught her other nipple on the next strike, leaving both nubs to pulse in swollen discomfort that fed her need as he snapped his way downward.

"Tell me something, Avery," Grayson demanded as he again brushed the strands over her labia. "Do you trust me yet?"

"Yes, of course," she rushed to answer without having to pause or think it through, her body shivering as her core filled with expectant heat.

"Let's test that, shall we?"

She held her breath, knowing what was coming, waiting for it, wanting it and yet dreading it at the same time. When he struck the most delicate part of her body, inflaming the tender flesh, Avery shook in the bonds, shocked at the way her pussy swelled and dampened from the heated pain. Master Grayson's curses warmed her even more, a hint her response had caught *him* off guard as well. She heard the flogger drop to the floor, a deep moan pushing past her lips as the soft brush of feathery strokes over the lingering pinpricks across her stomach jumbled her thoughts.

"Where did you get that?" she gasped as he tickled the fleshy underside of her breasts next. That was one object she'd missed seeing in his tormenting arsenal.

"I snuck it over." Grayson twirled the feather around her breast, avoiding her nipple as he arched her head back with another tight grip of her hair.

The tug on Avery's scalp elicited another tremble, or did she quiver because he continued to tantalize the lingering discomfort from the flogger with light brushes over her striped skin? "You've run me a merry chase since coming into town, sugar, one I'm not altogether happy about."

The deep displeasure reflected in Grayson's voice was at odds with the soft caresses over her nipples and yet bothered her just as much. "I didn't mean to."

He released her hair and shifted behind her before she felt the touch of his lips on the side of her neck and the sweep of feathers across her throbbing buttocks. "That's beside the point. You say you trust me but refuse to give me more than your body."

There was no time to formulate a reply as he ran the feather between her cheeks, the glide over her anus sending ripples of arousing shudders up and down her swaying body. The darkness enhanced her other senses, working to focus her attention on Master Grayson's voice and movements as he reached around and plucked at one nipple while whispering in her ear.

"But you'll find I don't give up that easy, Avery." He punctuated that remark with another stroke between her buttocks and a tight pinch to her already throbbing nub, blurring the sensations until she couldn't differentiate between discomfort and pleasure.

It was on the tip of her tongue to say she was glad when the response dried up on her tongue as he reached around in front of her to tease the pulsating flesh of her labia next. "Oops, looks like I'll have to either toss this feather or keep it as a souvenir now," he taunted after pressing the feathers between her folds far enough to tickle her needy clit.

"Please, Sir." The whispered plea escaped before she could think to hold it back.

Master Grayson stepped back with a low curse, shifting around in front of her a second later, the whirr of the wand startling Avery as he positioned the curved, vibrating end between her legs and covered one tortured nipple with his mouth. The soft buzzing against her clit sent a firestorm of sensation straight up her pussy. Avery's breath caught in her throat as she fell headlong toward a mind-shattering orgasm that encompassed her whole body with mind-fogging ecstasy. Writhing in the bonds, she gasped for air like a drowning person breaking the water's surface as pleasure unlike anything she'd experienced before washed over her.

SHOCK SLAMMED into Grayson with the ramming force of a two-by-four. He *knew* that catch in her voice, the same sound that had haunted his dreams for weeks, ever since he'd heard it over the phone. All the nuances about Avery he'd found so familiar since meeting her came back in a rush to leave him reeling from finally figuring out where he knew her from. Disappointment, curiosity and a kernel of anger replaced his need to be inside her bucking body as he held the wand against her clit and pulled up on her nipple before releasing it. Her soft cries were a shade off from the ones he remembered, and he surmised now she'd held something over the phone to disguise her voice. But nothing could hide that cock-tugging catch in her throat as she climaxed.

He'd always enjoyed the intricate dance of negotiating a scene with someone new, but with Avery, he'd wanted to turn caveman and just take from the moment she'd stepped foot inside the club. Her wary skittishness, evasive answers about anything personal and those hints of familiarity had driven him to consider using his cock to pummel her depths for answers tonight. Now that he'd seen her naked and her lush body strung up, writhing in acceptance of his torturous commands and dampening in arousal, he knew she was perfect for him in all ways except the most important. She'd lied by omission.

Grayson brought Avery down by slow degrees from the pleasure racking her body, removing the wand and replacing the strong vibrations with calmer strokes of his fingers. Her hot, swollen bud still pulsed, her abundant cream pouring from her puffy lips with each shuddering breath. Leaning forward, he licked over each erect, reddened nipple and heard her sigh. His disgruntlement wouldn't allow him to fuck her right now, his need for both answers and relief rivaling each other until he decided answers had waited this long, they would keep a little longer.

His lust couldn't.

Whipping the blindfold off, Grayson slid his hand under Avery's hair and clasped her nape. Looking down at her flushed face, he waited for her eyes to focus so he could ensure she saw the displeasure he refused to hide. Let *her* wonder for a change.

"You continue to surprise me, sugar. I wonder if you realize what secrets a woman's naked body can give up when she's bound and vulnerable as she's brought to orgasm." He reached up and released her wrists and then stooped to free her ankles. Pushing to his feet, he caught her as she swayed, the feel of all that soft, slick skin tempting him to take her here and now. His displeasure over her duplicity and years as a Dom and the lessons learned from playing with subs who weren't forthcoming with crucial personal information kept him from sinking into her hot depths. Looking down into her eyes, he noticed her furrowed brow, a sign he'd confused her with his abrupt tone. Good.

"Are you steady?" Grayson waited for her nod and made sure

her focus was clear before reaching for her shirt and panties and handing them to her. "You can put these on." Without waiting to see if she complied, he gathered up the spreader bar, blindfold, flogger and wand, returning the first three to the cabinet and tossing the toy in a bin for items needing sterilization before being put away. He tucked the feather with its damp plumes in his back pocket then turned to see her pulling the shirt down over her panties. Avery's face clouded with confusion as he snatched her hand and tugged her toward the stairs.

Stumbling behind him, she asked with breathless concern, "Is something wrong?"

Grayson paused at the top of the stairs to swivel his head and reply, "Not a thing now, sugar. Come along. I need a drink."

Chapter 10

Grayson was glad to see Brett seated at the bar with his wife, Sue Ellen, conversing with Caden. Since he'd spotted Dan at the spanking bench, in the midst of a scene with Mindy, a cute, curvy blonde who had been a regular for a few years now, he would enlist Brett's assistance. He craved Avery's lush mouth on his flesh more than his next breath, and it was time his sub learned to see to his needs.

"Your sub looks a little dazed," Caden remarked, his blue eyes twinkling as he took in Avery's flushed face and round eyes as he poured Grayson a whiskey.

Settling on a stool, Grayson pulled her between his legs, her back to him, her ass snuggled against his bulging erection. "The results of the two F's: flogger and feather."

Brett smirked. "Just the two?"

"Yes," he returned without explaining why he hadn't fucked her. "Thanks." Nodding at Caden, he took a sip of the fortifying liquor. Tightening his arm around her waist, he pressed his cock between Avery's buttocks and felt a shudder go through her soft body. "Problem?" he drawled, reaching up to cup one full breast through the shirt, rasping her nipple until the pouty bud stiffened again.

Avery shifted her eyes away from the other two men, her gaze landing on Dan, who was now fucking Mindy with her legs over his shoulders, his hips pumping with vigorous plunges. She shook again, this time with a small sigh and he knew she was wondering why he hadn't ended their scene by fucking her.

"No... Sir," she tacked on after he pinched her nipple in reminder.

"Some subs deserve their Dom's cocks, isn't that right, Master Brett?"

"That's the way it's always been." He winked at his wife who returned his smile. "Then again, some subs enjoy pushing buttons and having to work for it."

"And some," Grayson returned, hardening his voice in Avery's ear, "push buttons and deserve to wait. But," he pinched her other nipple, "that doesn't mean her Dom should suffer along with her."

Turning her in his arms, he held her wary gaze as he slowly lowered his zipper and freed his throbbing cock, the sudden exposure to cooler air a soothing balm wafting over his inflamed flesh. Fisting a hand in her hair, a hold that was rapidly becoming his favorite, he ordered with direct bluntness, "Put your mouth on me, Avery."

THE SILKEN THREAD of steel underlying Master Grayson's words gave Avery pause, as did the uncomfortable awareness of the other eyes on her. Something had changed, and for the life of her, she didn't know what. The flash of disappointment she'd seen in his eyes when he had released her from the bonds had cut her to the quick. It hurt to think she might have caused him to become disillusioned with her. She wanted to see that light of approval in his eyes again and get back into his good graces, and if that meant meeting the challenge in that penetrating gaze, then so be it. Even though she had little experience with fellatio and wished he'd chosen another way to press whatever point he wanted to make, she almost drooled at the thought of tasting the hardened flesh he clutched in his hand. It helped she could still feel the imprint of his jutting cock against her butt, the scratch of his denim-covered thighs against the back of her legs teasing anew the stripes left from the flogger.

He'd been stricter tonight than the previous two times she'd joined him at the club, but she'd relished the take-charge, firm commands that had stripped her of all decision-making and worries. His control had enabled her to embrace the new experience with bondage and light pain, and with any luck, she would continue to benefit from it as she tried her best to bring him as much pleasure as he had gifted her with.

"I… I'm not very good at this," Avery felt compelled to warn him, her hands pressed upon his thighs to brace herself as she bent at the waist.

"I'll guide you." Master Grayson's guttural voice sent a wave of longing through her as she watched his hand tightened around the base of his thick length. Aiming his rigid erection at her mouth, he prompted, "Open for me."

Closing her eyes, she wrapped her lips around his cock head, blocking her mind to everything except pleasing him. Hard and hot, his flesh seared her tongue as she stroked over the smooth crown and tasted his tangy seepage. That small sign of his aroused state emboldened her to take more, and with the aid of his hand guiding her head, she slid her mouth down several more inches. She licked a circle around his girth, the thick veins pumping under her tongue, his skin tightening over the iron rod stretching her lips.

Master Grayson tugged on her hair. "You weren't honest with me, sugar." Avery tightened her lips, wondering why she thought that statement held a hidden meaning. "You're better at this than you said and that means a challenge is in order. Master Brett, could I enlist your help?"

Avery only had time to suck in a shocked breath as Grayson clasped her head and pulled her mouth up his shaft. Her lips clung, out of fear of what they intended or the need to keep him close, she wasn't sure. Holding her face, he kept his eyes on hers as Master Brett grasped her wrists and drew her arms behind her back, shackling them together in one hand. The awkward position had her struggling against their grips. "Gray... Sir..." Tightening her mouth, she shuddered as Grayson brushed his thumb over her lips.

"Still don't trust me, huh?" Disappointment laced his voice and tears welled in her eyes as she tried to shake her head.

"I do..."

"Prove it," he demanded, cutting her off and lowering her mouth to him once more.

Once she let go, put herself in his hands and concentrated on pleasing him, she was surprised by how easy it was despite the awkward, uncomfortable position. Opening wide, she took him deep, sucking hard as he maneuvered her head up and down on his cock. The back of her shirt rode up, and when a light swat jiggled her butt, the instant warmth urged her on. She traced a path under the rim of his cap, repeating the stroke when he jerked. A swipe over his crown and slit drew his low moan, so she did it again. Another tap landed on her opposite cheek and it was her turn to moan as she slid back down and used her teeth to trace those pumping, bulging veins. She came close to smiling when he swore and tightened his hands on her head, holding her still for his pumping, throat nudging invasion.

The spanks turned harder, came faster as Master Grayson held her head still for his use. Her mouth ached and her butt burned, the whole scene taking a decadent turn, one she found disconcerting because of how arousing it proved to be. Either she'd fallen deeper into submissiveness than she'd ever imagined, or there was little he could do that she would balk at simply because it was coming from him, or in the case of Master Brett's tight hold and swats, stemming from Master Grayson's orders.

"Let go if you don't want to swallow."

Grayson's low, gravelly voice broke through the fog of concentration and pleasure enveloping Avery and she quickly tried to shake her head against his hands. She wanted this, all of him, any way he desired, even if she had never gone that far before.

"So be it. I warned you," he huffed before another groan rumbled from above her and the smacks turned to soothing caresses over her throbbing buttocks.

His cock jerked again, his seed spilling onto her tongue, his thigh muscles bunching under the brush of her nipples. Avery shook along with him, moaned in tune with his grunts of release, and basked in knowing she had passed whatever test this had been. Now, if she could just figure out what brought it on.

"IS THERE anything else I can get you?" Avery asked the older couple after handing them their check.

"No, thanks, hon. Everything was delicious, like always," the balding, seventy-something man returned with a smile that should have warmed Avery but didn't.

"Great. Thanks for coming in." Pivoting, she ran into Barbara for the third time that evening. "*Sheesh*, I'm so sorry, Barbara!"

With quick reflexes, the other waitress righted her tray before anything slid off. "I've got it, Avery." As they stepped away from the table, Barbara whispered, "Is everything okay? You seem distracted, and a little upset."

Avery stifled the urge to confide in her co-worker. If she

couldn't figure out why Grayson had entered The Barn last night appearing pleased with her company and interested in continuing her introduction to his proclivities and ended the evening with an abrupt coolness and displeasure in his eyes, then Barbara wouldn't be able to make her feel better. His change of attitude had kept her from going through with her plans to reveal how they'd first met, but she still ached to get everything out in the open between them.

"I... I didn't get much sleep last night, is all. I'm sorry, I'll try to do better."

"Foods not going to get to the tables by itself," Gertie snapped as they stepped up to the counter. Flicking Avery a shrewd glance, her boss added, "Deputy Jase was in this afternoon, said as how Sheriff Grayson gave him the night off from patrol, took his place instead. Now, quit dawdlin' and git back to work."

Barbara giggled and winked at Avery. "You heard her. You've got nothing to worry about."

Oh, Avery had plenty to fret over, but thanks to Gertie knowing everything that went on in Willow Springs, and, it seemed, with her, her sly comment lifted part of Avery's unhappiness. At least she could quit wondering if Grayson was spending the evening with someone else at the club. She knew she didn't have a personal hold on the sheriff, or any right to expect him to forgo playing with others just because he'd befriended her. Even though it pained her to admit it, there was no future with him, or for her here, and she needed to remember that.

But that didn't prevent Avery from continuing to agonize through the night over the way Master Grayson had driven her home in silence last night and left her at her door with a cryptic, "Lock up," as a goodnight. If only she could figure out what she'd done to displease him, then she wouldn't have spent another sleepless, restless night and woken to the gray-cast dawn with a sense of foreboding. Stumbling out of bed Sunday morning, she rubbed her tired, gritty eyes, wishing she hadn't volunteered to fill in for one of the waitresses this morning.

As soon as Avery entered the diner's kitchen from the back door, she knew something was wrong from the looks on Clyde and Gertie's faces. Her stomach cramped and a cold chill crept under her skin as Gertie slammed a pot down, mumbling, "Damn fool boy, going and getting himself shot."

Avery gasped with the painful talons of fear gripping her insides. "What? Who's been shot?"

Gertie's silver-haired head whipped toward her with both concern and anger swirling in her blue eyes. "Connor Dunbar, the idiot. Out all night by himself and then tries going after those shit-faced rustlers. He's damned lucky they didn't blow his fool brains out."

"Now, Gert, young Connor was just trying to protect what's his," Clyde put in, his face lined with worry despite his words defending Connor.

Conflicting emotions of relief and concern muddled Avery's thinking. She couldn't help the surge of gladness at hearing they weren't talking about Grayson while bemoaning the thought of Connor injured in such a way. He'd always been so nice to her and she could see why so many at the club found his easier going, sexy dominance tempting.

"Where is he? Will he be okay?" The need to check on him and be there for Sydney and her family pulled at her. A quick peek out at the dining room showed few customers had ventured out this cold morning, but Gertie beat her to it before she could ask to take off to be there for her friends.

"Go on, girl. Weather's coming in this afternoon, which is keeping people home or tending to chores early before it hits. Heard they took him to All Saints Hospital in Billings. But," Gertie shook a finger at her, "don't you be gone long. That rattle-trap you drive won't get you back here on slick roads."

"I won't. Thanks, Gertie."

After looking up directions on Gertie's office computer, Avery pulled into the hospital parking lot an hour later and found Sydney in the emergency waiting room, sitting with several people she recognized from either the diner or the club, including Nan. Wondering where Grayson was, she tried to push aside the ache to see him as she gave Sydney a brief hug before asking, "What have you heard?"

"It's not bad, at least not as bad as it could have been," Sydney answered, her eyes red-rimmed, her lips trembling. "The bullet went through the fleshy part of his shoulder but may have damaged the muscles. They won't know until it heals and they can do physical therapy. Caden is *so* pissed."

"Not to mention Grayson," Nan injected with a grimace.

Dan came strolling in from the hall carrying a tray of paper coffee cups. "He'll catch the bastards," he said, handing out the steaming brews to the girls first.

Avery shook her head. "I just got here. I can go get…"

"Take it." he stated, holding out the cup, his tone as hard and implacable as if he were at the club.

"*Sheesh*, are all you guys always so bossy?"

"Yes, always," Grayson said from behind her.

She whirled around, sloshing the hot liquid over her hand. He swore, snatched the cup and pulled her red, stinging fingers under the water fountain. "Damn it, can't you be more careful?" he demanded without looking at her.

"It's fine, it wasn't that hot." Avery pulled out of his grasp and dried her fingers on the napkins Sydney held out to her with a compassionate look.

"We're all on edge, isn't that right, Sheriff?"

Sydney's cool rebuke bounced off Grayson as he turned from Avery with a shrug. "Just watch yourself."

Feeling both chastised and left out as the small group huddled and began trading stories about Connor, Avery took a

seat and waited in quiet solitude. It was so easy to see the closeness they shared, hear their fondness for not only their injured
friend but for each other as they joked around to ease the
tension of waiting. *That is what I want.* Not just to be friends with
a few women, but to be considered part of them, and their
community. Her refusal to divulge anything of a personal nature
about herself had kept her at arm's length from fitting in, and
from getting too close to anyone, including Sydney and
Grayson. The tightness clutching her chest was of her own
doing, her reticence possibly the result of Grayson's disfavor
with her as well.

The question still remained; what to do about it? By the time
Caden brought Connor out, his brother's face ashen, his right
shoulder bulky from the bandaging under his shirt, Avery had
come to a few conclusions. She *yearned* to get back into Master
Grayson's good graces, see that probing, intent gaze focused on
her again, hear that deep voice commanding her to let go, and to
trust him. Past disappointments taught her not to expect
anything more from this relationship or the interest and time he
had gifted her with, but that didn't mean she couldn't try for
more of both.

She *needed* to confide in Sheriff Monroe about what she knew
about Darren and his partner and take him up on his offer to
help her. Her safety and future depended on seeing them
punished for what they had done.

And she *longed* to find a place for herself among these people,
far away and so different from everyone she knew and everything
she'd grown up with.

But before any of that could be even a possibility, she *wanted*
to shove her cowardice aside enough to help herself first. Pushing
to her feet on legs gone rubbery with her decision about taking
the next step toward those goals, she ran shaking hands down her
thighs and sucked in a deep breath as Grayson moved
toward her.

"He can go home?" she asked, her eyes lingering on Connor's disgruntled, pain-lined face.

"Doctor finally agreed after realizing how stubborn the son-of-a-bitch is," Grayson grumbled, warming Avery's insides with a direct, heated look that curled her toes until he issued an order that rubbed her wrong. "Go back to Willow Springs, Avery. A storm is blowing in soon that'll turn the roads slick, and we're warning people off them until tomorrow."

Stepping back, she averted her suddenly watery eyes, wishing his concern was for her rather than just another citizen in his county he'd sworn to protect. "Don't worry, Sheriff. I know what I need to do." She started to turn and happened to glace over at Connor as he looked her way and winked. Nothing could have hardened her resolve to take this first step as much as that silent gesture of gratitude and friendship. Feeling Grayson's eyes following her, she left the hospital; first stop, the library.

SWEARING UNDER HIS BREATH, Grayson watched Avery walk out of the hospital, her eyes bruised with fatigue, reflecting both uncertainty and hurt that ate at him, and pissed him off. He didn't believe in coincidence, at least not of this magnitude. There was no doubt in his mind she was his troubled mystery woman, the soft voice over the phone who had haunted his nights these past weeks, driven here because of his offer to help her. So why hadn't she revealed herself to him? Was she feeling him out, getting a sense of how much she could trust him? Possibly. Even likely. But that didn't mean her subterfuge sat well with him, only that he could understand her reserve. Now, what to do about it?

"We're heading back. It looks like that storm is moving faster than predicted," Caden said as he and Sydney stood on each side of Connor, waiting to help him if he needed assistance.

"Are you sure you don't want to bunk here tonight?" Grayson didn't like the gray cast to Connor's skin or the grimace of pain when he moved despite the meds he'd been given.

"I'm sure. All I need is a little recovery time and I'll be back up." The younger by a year Dunbar nodded to his well-meaning friends as they all headed out to the emergency room parking lot. "It wasn't necessary, but thanks guys."

"It was necessary," Sydney told him, squeezing his forearm. "You'll be staying with us for now. I hope you've learned your lesson, though, about chasing after these guys by yourself."

Dan snorted as he grasped Nan's elbow. "I doubt it. Our Connor may be easy going most of the time, but he's also the most stubborn."

"Bite me," Connor returned, his voice clipped, but his lips curled up at the corners.

Laughing, Dan slapped him on the back as they reached their vehicles. "I'll save that for the subs you will enjoy tormenting right back. Grayson, give me a call once this storm passes and I'll ride out with you. I lost three head last night, despite Connor's best efforts." He opened the passenger door for Nan and ushered her in, out of the cold wind.

"I'll take you up on that next time you're at the club, Connor." Nan smiled and gave them a finger wave as Dan shut the door.

Grayson nodded, wrapping his gloved hand on the door handle of his cruiser. "Will do. Let's hope this weather keeps the bastards from returning any time soon."

Shoving aside worry over his friend now that Connor was in good hands with his brother and over-protective, soon-to-be sister-in-law, Grayson's thoughts switched back to Avery. He would make her wait one more day and then confront her about her identity, he decided on the drive back to Willow Springs. Tonight, he would be busy monitoring weather and road conditions. After returning to the office and logging in a report on

Connor's shooting, he planned to spend the evening in front of a blazing fire with a good book until his duties required him to ensure crews were out clearing the roads and no one had gotten stranded by the storm once it passed.

It was going to be a long, unpleasant night with only his irritation and thoughts for company.

AVERY HUDDLED in front of the library computer, her finger shaking as she hovered over the send key, her stomach churning with nausea over what she was about to do. Even though she'd set up a temporary, dummy e-mail account to use this one time, she didn't doubt Internal Affairs would eventually suspect her of sending them these conflicting reports. Pressing that button would start the ball rolling on an investigation, but where it would lead, or who it might end up pointing to was up in the air. Darren and Chad were cagey enough, smart enough to have gotten away with their evidence theft so far, and she'd bet they had amassed a sizable sum from their lucrative crime spree. Enough money to get them out of the country and leave her the one in the hot seat, answering all the questions.

But what other choice did she have? If she hadn't heard that conversation in the parking garage, if she had been brave enough to stay and come up with a plausible excuse for her snooping that would have kept her safe from their threat instead of running like the coward she was, she wouldn't be stuck in limbo right now, sweating this decision. After sending a message to her landlord to rent her furnished apartment to someone else following his message threatening eviction because of non-payment, she now had no home or job to return to in Chicago. She knew Marci would help her, but there was no way she would repay her kindness and support by embroiling her in this mess or risking her safety.

After overhearing their conversation, Avery wouldn't put anything past her ex and his partner.

Before she could talk herself out of it, she hit send and then took down the e-mail. A good hacker could find it again and trace it to this library, but that would take time, and not necessarily lead to her. Shoving back from the computer, she prayed Grayson not only meant it when he offered to help her but could come up with a solution that would protect her.

The air held a hint of moisture with the darkening clouds as she dashed to her car and flipped on the heat, for what good it would do. She was still shaking when she reached the highway, whether from the inclement weather or fear, she didn't know. Gripping the steering wheel, all she could think about now was getting to Grayson. She not only wanted Sheriff Monroe's help but found herself needing Master Grayson, and what he could do to her in a way she'd never needed from another man.

The anonymity, her loneliness and stress had made getting off over the phone under his command easier. She appreciated Master Grayson's slow introduction into the BDSM club scene, but now that he'd broken her through the ice and she had not only experienced the pleasures giving up control offered but witnessed the close bond of everyone she'd met that extended outside of the club, she wanted more. She craved everything he had to offer, desired everything he was willing to give her. *If* he was still willing to continue with her sexual education. His cool attitude at the end of Friday night and again today didn't bode well for that, but now that she had unearthed a small iota of hidden bravado, she intended to milk it for all it was worth.

All he could do was say no, to either her request for help or to continue on with her, right?

The sudden shrillness of sirens coming up behind Avery caught her unawares, and a quick glance at the speedometer pulled a low groan from her tight throat. With her mind whirling in trepidation over so many things, she hadn't been paying attention to her speed. To add even more misery to her day, the first spittle of sleet pelted the windshield as she pulled to the side of the road and prepared to face the consequences for her inattentiveness.

Five minutes later, she was back on the road, this time crawling at a snail's pace, fighting both her nerves over getting a ticket and driving on the rapidly icing road. Since she intended to go straight to Grayson's cabin, she wouldn't have to travel all the way into Willow Springs, which shortened her trip by about ten miles. At this point, she would take what she could get.

Avery was less than a mile from the turnoff to his place and was priding herself on making it without further mishap when she hit an icy patch just right, sending the car sliding in a slow, uncontrollable glide toward the embankment. Never having driven in such treacherous conditions, she didn't know to turn the wheel into the spin and did the opposite, compounding her situation until she came to a jarring stop with the front end of her car pointing down toward the small ditch, the front tires spinning uselessly.

Tears of frustration and despair welled, blurring her vision as she looked around at the deserted road behind her and dense woods in front. If memory served correctly, and she prayed it did as she struggled out of the vehicle and freezing rain stung her face, Grayson's home wasn't far. Holding her jacket closed with her hands tucked inside and face down, she trudged up the road until she recognized the turnoff.

Ten minutes later, her face and feet were numb, her teeth were chattering, and she was so miserable, aching for warmth, she didn't hear the SUV coming up behind her until Grayson pulled to a stop. Flinging open the passenger door, Avery had never been so glad to see his scowling face or hear his commanding voice.

"Get the fuck in here."

GRAYSON COULDN'T BELIEVE it when he spotted Avery halfway up the road leading to his place, her hair plastered to her face and neck in frozen tendrils, her face pale, her lips blue when she looked up at him. Anger warred with concern as she struggled to climb inside the cruiser until he leaned over and hauled her up himself. She should have been home two hours ago, not out in this weather, stranded without a car. He was so pissed he didn't trust himself to say anything else yet. Flipping the heat on high, he sped down the road, anxious now to get her warm before hypothermia kicked in.

"I… slid o… off the… road…" She waved a shaking hand backwards, indicating the highway through her chattering. "I… w… was…"

"Quiet," he bit out. "I already gathered you didn't go straight home after I warned you about the storm. You're really racking up the infractions."

"B… but…"

"Avery, I swear to God, if you don't shut up, I'll stick a ball gag in your mouth the minute I get you inside. I'll let you know when I'm ready to hear your explanation." Grayson pulled into the garage and closed the door before cutting the engine, saying, "Wait there. I'll help you."

Coming around to the passenger side, he lifted her and carried her straight into his bathroom, his first intention to get her out of her cold, sodden clothes, the second to get her warm enough to start answering questions.

Chapter 11

A very wasn't sure what a ball gag was, but the image that popped into her head prompted the tight clamping of her trembling lips together. Being carried by Grayson would have been a pleasant experience if it weren't for the cold expression on his face adding to the shivers already racking her body. She wanted to explain she'd been coming to him, and why, but the small amount of bravery she'd managed to conjure up back in Billings seemed to have deserted her in the face of his wrath. His displeasure with her continued to bother her on one of those indefinable levels she didn't understand. Regardless of their limited relationship, she wanted back in his good graces.

Grayson kicked the door to the master bath shut, set her down and reached into the glass enclosed tiled shower. As he flipped on not only the middle overhead rain shower head but both side sprays, instant, billowing steam started seeping into her bones. And then he turned back around, yanked off her sodden jacket, tossed her glasses onto the double-sink counter and reached for her sweatshirt, making her forget to stay silent.

Lifting shaking hands to his, she whispered, "I can do it."

Grayson's eyes snapped to hers. "You won't be sitting comfortably for a week if you keep it up."

A slow curl of anger tightened Avery's abdomen, but she pushed back the temptation to question him about his mood. She got that his current pissy attitude stemmed from her getting caught unawares by the weather and ending up in physical jeopardy because she hadn't listened to him about heading straight home from the hospital. But his ire had kicked in Friday night, two days before today's fiasco.

He whipped the damp shirt over her head, tossed it on the floor and didn't hesitate before ridding her of her bra. Her nipples, already puckered from the cold, went tighter under his heated inspection. Taking a deep breath, she breathed in the steam as it slowly warmed her icy skin.

"Hold on to my shoulders," Grayson instructed after loosening her jeans.

His muscles bunched under her grip as he bent down to work her wet pants, shoes and socks off before removing her panties. She found herself warmer naked, without the cold, clinging dampness of her clothes, his nearness, piercing eyes and the steam all working to envelop her with much-appreciated heat.

Grayson checked her pulse while looking her over with a critical eye. With a nod and one hand on her butt, he pushed her into the shower. "I'll be back," was all he said before closing her in under the pelting, hot water that struck her cold body with stinging force. The fact he hadn't let his irritation with her keep him from ensuring her well-being perked her up.

Avery yelped and then sighed under the heated deluge, thawing the rest of the way, barely hearing the bathroom door snick shut. Sinking down onto the small bench, she leaned her head back against the wall and just sat there, soaking up the humid warmth and praying the hot water lasted forever. Without realizing it, she drifted off only to jerk into instant awareness when Grayson returned and stepped into the shower naked, the sight of his jutting cock making her pussy go damp.

Grabbing her wrists in one hand, he pulled her to her feet and grasped her chin. "Are you with me, sugar?" She nodded and watched his eyes blaze as she leaned against him. "Excellent. Now you'll talk to me."

"Fine, what…" She sucked in a breath as he raised her arms above her and made quick work of shackling both wrists in a terrycloth wrap attached to a short, dangling chain. "*Sheesh*, do you have those things everywhere?"

"Yes." Sliding his palms down her neck to her breasts, he cupped the heavy weights and rasped her nipples with his thumbs, his eyes on hers as he said, "You haven't been honest with me, sugar. And I don't like that." Releasing her plumpness, he circled the puckered tips with his forefinger then grasped each nub between fingers and thumbs. Applying pressure Avery could feel straight down to her pussy, he shocked her with his next words. "Tell me something. How did you do with other callers after you and I ended our first conversation together? You remember, don't you? The night you climaxed for the first time under my commands."

Gasping as he tightened his grip on her nipples, she stuttered, "You… you know?"

"I do now. It was that little catch in your voice when you went off like a firecracker the other night that gave you away." He released her pinched tips, and she gasped again as the blood rushed back into her engorged, numb nipples.

Before she could adjust to the pinpricks of pain and tingling pleasure, he spun her around to face the wall, running those large hands over her quivering stomach, down the insides of her quaking thighs and then around to cup her clenching buttocks. Bending his head, he pressed his water-slick body against her back, his cock between her cheeks and his lips to the side of her throat. His chest hair tickled her skin, his teeth delivered a sharp nip and his hands a painful squeeze to her globes.

"From the moment we met at the diner, you knew who I was, and all I asked for was honesty. Why couldn't you give me that?"

Avery shuddered, regretting the underlying disappointment she caught in his voice. He released her buttocks, cupped one hand between her legs and pushed the other between her cheeks, holding her in a tight clamp by the crotch as he waited for her answer. "I… I'm sorry. I needed to know…" She groaned as he slid two fingers inside her pussy and one past her puckered back entrance. "Sir, please," she begged, surprised by how fast she reached the boiling point of need.

Gripping her hair, he pulled her head back, his voice low as he drawled slowly, "Oh, I don't think so, sugar. Not yet." Stepping back, he turned her around, and she shivered at the look on his face, his tight-jawed disapproval contrasting with the light of possessiveness in his eyes as he ran one finger over the bare flesh of her labia. Going to one knee before her, he kept his gaze on her face as he instructed, "Spread your legs."

He didn't need to repeat the order; Master Grayson's look alone commanded her obedience. Avery's first glimpse of this side of him had caught her unawares but left her interested in seeking more of both him and a sexual lifestyle new to her. The second, longer, up close look as he'd disciplined Sue Ellen had shaken her; the lighter demonstration he'd given her of the same act had left her with a needy ache. And then, just a few days ago, he'd brought out a part of her she'd never known existed and left her craving more of his strict side. Now, even wary and unsure, she thrilled to be on the receiving end of his complete dominance.

With a delicate shudder, she shuffled her feet apart, unsure about his mood, intentions and what was to come, yet craving him with every fiber of her being. Avery now knew why he'd been so put off with her following their scene the other night, never dreaming he could identify her by such a small sound, one she'd never known she made. As he used his thumbs to spread her tender folds and expose her swollen clit, she shoved aside that revelation to deal with later.

Being enclosed in the steam-filled room with a naked Master Grayson required Avery's full concentration, especially since he wasn't happy with her. Scraping her clit with a nail, she arched against his hand in helpless surrender to whatever he wanted.

"You were scared, needed to be sure of me before revealing yourself." He brushed his lips over her labia before sinking his teeth into the soft flesh. "I get that."

"Oh, God." Avery shook in the bonds, that sting seeping into her sheath, drawing more dampness.

"But I proved my trustworthiness the first night you came to The Barn, didn't I?" He punctuated that question with another bite.

"I… yes, but… everything was so new… unexpected… and I was… am so…" The quick thrust of his tongue kept her from forming a coherent thought to the rest of her reply. She whimpered as he added two fingers and circled her clit with his tongue before pulling on the tender piece of flesh with his teeth. Yanking on her arms, she thrust her hips into his face, allowing her body to do the begging for more. Ignoring her pleas, he fucked her pussy with tongue and fingers, bringing her to the cusp of orgasm before pulling back, not once but twice and then three times.

Instead of delivering what she ached for, he tormented her until she was swollen with edgy need, writhing in the bonds and grinding against his marauding mouth. With his lips wrapped around her throbbing clit, pulling on the puffy nub with strong suctions, he reached out, and with a hard yank on one shower-head hose, sent it toppling down to grab the handle. Pulling back from his feasting, he turned the spray between her legs.

"Afraid?" he continued his questioning, switching the light

spray to one of harder pulsations. "Of me, or the circumstances that sent you to me?"

Grayson didn't give Avery time to answer, or even think. Her cry resounded in the small space as he aimed the jets on her aching flesh, unleashing fiery sparks of pleasure to convulse the slick walls of her pussy only to pull away, once again stalling the final explosion of ecstasy.

"Either way, you should have been able to come clean with me before I found out on my own who you are." Holding her labia wide open, he held the spray right on her clit until her entire body jerked from the small contractions of an impending orgasm. As soon as she let loose with that telltale sign, he pushed to his feet, returned the showerhead above and then lifted her right foot onto the seat. Reaching to the shelf behind her, he plucked off a condom she never saw him place there. Sheathing himself, he growled, "You'll tell me now what you're afraid of, who caused you to have such mistrust, won't you?"

The silken-softness of his voice didn't fool Avery; that was a definite, steel-edged command, not a polite request. "Watch me take you," he ordered next, reaching behind her to clasp her buttocks in a tight grip, holding her immobile for his slow invasion into her trembling body.

Biting her lip to keep from moaning, she eyed his thick length as he sank by slow measures inside her, stretching her wider than anything or anyone who had come before him. Her vaginal lips clung around his thick girth like a soft glove, sucking him deeper, each slow glide brushing against still quivering muscles, releasing small tendrils of pleasure along the way.

"Jesus, but you're tight," he muttered, pushing a little harder, working inside her slick depths as he pressed her pelvis closer to his. "And so fucking hot you may burn me up."

Water sluiced between them, a misting curtain that lent an intimacy to the carnal fucking. With one leg still propped up on the seat, spreading Avery wider, the only reason she could maintain her one-legged stance during his tortuously slow assault was because of her bound hands and his firm hold.

Grayson pulled back, dragging his rigid flesh over sensitive, swollen tissues, his breathing as harsh as hers as he pushed her for more. "Tell me, Avery. What is it you've been too scared to talk about?" Another deep surge drew a shudder. "What drove you so far from home, made you so desperate for cash?" A repeated slow withdrawal accompanied his attention-forcing stare, one she couldn't break even if she wanted to.

"Please, Sir," Avery pled as he thrust back inside her with enough force to bump her womb and set off another round of small contractions heralding an orgasm.

"Not until you talk to me," Grayson ground out, sinking his fingers tighter into one malleable globe as he released the other to press between her cheeks and invade her ass with a two-fingered jab past the puckered rim.

Avery lost herself in the steamy confines of the shower, in the closeness of Master Grayson's naked strength, the tickling brush of his chest hair over her nipples, his breath in her ear, his teeth scraping her neck, his pummeling cock and pumping fingers. Aching need too long denied coupled with weeks of fear-induced stress burst through the last of her resistance and shattered her will. With tortuous sobs, she poured out her plight in stuttering gasps as he continued to drive her up, leaving nothing out from the time she'd stood hidden in the precinct's garage and over-heard Darren and Chad to losing control of her car on the ice today.

By the time she finished, pleasure rivaling everything she'd experienced before burst upon her with the jarring jerks of his ramming cock, filled her with incredible ecstasy and crumbled the weeks-long dam keeping her emotions in check along with her body as she fell into his arms and continued to let go.

GRAYSON REACHED up and turned off the shower heads, keeping a tight hold of Avery's shaking body with one arm wrapped around her waist. He still shook from the riotous force of his own climax, but nothing could have cleared his mind so fast as the outpouring of her confession. *Fucking A.* Going up against two dirty Chicago cops would not be easy for anyone, let alone a young woman whom one had betrayed with such callous disregard. His girl often bemoaned her lack of bravery, but from where he was standing right now, he thought her the most courageous woman he'd ever met. And damn it, he was still fucking pissed at the time she'd taken to come clean with him and the risks she'd taken today, both with the anonymous Internal Affairs contact and with the weather.

Despite her muddled, emotionally messy state, she felt good against him, all that damp, abundant, soft flesh cushioning his hard body, her muscles still shaking from her climax, her breathing still ragged as her tears blended with the water wetting his skin. Driving a woman into a crying binge with his dominance didn't bother him, but listening to Avery's gasping sobs brought on by her ordeal tore into his gut with sharp stabs and gripped his chest in a vise.

He waited until she quieted and then ushered her out of the shower, wrapping her in a large, heated towel before drying himself and slipping his jeans back on. Gripping her chin, he lifted her ravaged face, pleased to see her eyes were clear despite being red-rimmed.

"Are you steady enough to dry your hair on your own, or do you want me to do it?" He suspected she would need a few minutes alone to get herself under control, and he didn't mind giving them to her as long as she was capable of handling herself. But only a few. They still had issues to settle before they sat down and discussed where to go from here.

Avery nodded against his hold. "I'm… okay. I can do it."

"Meet me in the den when you're done. Make sure you're

dry, including your hair before coming out. I'll have the fire going, but I still don't want you to get chilled again." Releasing her, he gathered up the still damp clothes and left her staring after him in bemusement. Good. Keeping her off guard would continue to work in his favor, and eventually, hers.

Grayson rummaged through his bedroom toy stash before padding down the hall and into the den. A glimpse out the wide front window showed the sleet had stopped and now the trees and ground glistened with an icy sheen. Once the sun popped back out tomorrow, as predicted, he knew the remnants of this quick storm would melt away, but tonight would remain treacherous for drivers. He heard his hair dryer come on as he stoked the fire into a hot, crackling blaze and deemed he had just enough time to make a quick call before Avery joined him.

He had just ended his conversation with Gary Ayers, who owned Willow Springs' twenty-four-hour tow service and repair shop when he looked up and saw her standing at the entrance to the hall. Taking his time, he enjoyed a leisurely inspection of her naked body, a rosy tinge now replacing the goosebumps covering her white skin when he'd first stripped her. Wearing nothing but her glasses, she shifted under his inspection, dropping her hands to cover the enticing view of her bare pubis.

With a silent crook of his finger, he beckoned her forward, satisfied when she didn't hesitate to obey. Cupping her chin, he lifted her face, noting her clear but wary eyes. Excellent.

"We will take a look at your copied files and discuss your options later. First, there's the matter of dealing with the consequences of your foolish disobedience. I can understand and forgive your reluctance to tell me how we first met until you got to know me better. But I can't and won't dismiss you ignoring my instructions to hightail your ass back home to avoid the incoming storm, thus putting yourself in physical jeopardy. Christ, sugar, you took ten years off my life when I saw you."

"But…"

"Quiet." He pinched her chin and almost smiled when she fisted her hands and narrowed her eyes but clamped her lips together. "I've been operating under your terms regarding this relationship since day one of your arrival in Willow Springs and that stops now. We will move forward with our relationship under my terms now and that means obeying not only my sexual commands, but any orders I issue that involve your safety and well-being."

"We will?"

If he wasn't mistaken, the light in her eyes, breathless voice and pleasure softening her expressive face reflected happiness about that statement. Cocking his head, he asked for verification, just to be sure. "You're good with that?"

Avery nodded against his hand, the relief now shining on her face unmistakable. "Yes."

"Excellent." A surge of heat swept through Grayson as he dropped his hand and stepped back, pointing to the thick, braided rug spread in front of the fire. "On your knees, face to the floor, arms stretched out in front of you."

A look of consternation crossed her face, but she sank to her knees and assumed the position he'd ordered. Picking up the new butt plug he knew she hadn't spotted sitting on the couch end table along with the wooden paddle, he coated the rounded silicone with a liberal dose of peppermint oil. Spreading her buttocks, he prodded her anus with the greased plug.

"Deep breath, Avery." He pushed past her tight sphincter. "The tingling and warmth you'll feel are from the peppermint oil, which is perfectly safe and often used to enhance sensation." With one more nudge, he inserted the toy inside her ass until the flat, round base held it in place. Running one hand down her smooth arched back, he reached behind him and picked up the paddle next, caressing her upturned butt with the smooth wood, feeling her body shiver under his light touch.

"Sir?"

He addressed the quiver in her voice first. "You trust me, sugar, or else you wouldn't have been coming to me. That's what you were doing when you lost control on the slick highway, wasn't it?"

Avery turned her head and peeked up at him out of one eye. "How... how'd you know? You wouldn't let me explain."

"If you'll recall, some of my first words to you were how good I am at reading women. Deep breath." He brought the paddle down across both buttocks, the snap against bare skin almost as loud as her gasp as she buried her head face down again between her arms. Her hips swayed, and he swatted her again, enjoying both the movement and the bright red swath against the paleness of the rest of her flesh. "My heart must've stopped for several seconds when I saw you trudging up my drive, soaked and freezing wearing nothing but that jacket." *Whack!* *Whack!* "I'm too old to suffer such stress." A tiny laugh shook her shoulders before she cried out with the next blow. "It's not funny, Avery. You've led me on a merry chase, and that ends now." *Whack! Whack!*

"I... I'm sorry, Master Grayson!" The apology sounded wrenched from her throat, her use of his title prompting him to toss aside the paddle and reach for the condom off the end table.

"I believe you, sugar," he rasped, kneeling behind her crimson ass. A low moan and another shift of her hips accompanied the slow rub of his hand over her burning backside, her glistening slit drawing his eyes and his cock as he worked to sheath himself with one hand. "Another deep breath," he instructed. Latching onto her hips, he drove into her, fast and deep, slaking a thirst too long denied and not yet appeased.

Another cry spilled from the cocoon of her buried face as she squeezed her hands together and rocked her hips against his thrusting pelvis, joining him in the age-old dance of carnal fucking. Along with the crackling, spitting flames, their hips pounding together, the ramming strokes of his rigid flesh into her accepting, wet pussy, his heaving grunts and her mewling whimpers reverberated in the room. The plug made her even tighter, the snug confines of her pussy threatening to end this way too soon.

"*Fucking A*, you just might be the death of me," Grayson grunted, Avery's slick heat a burning vise as the tight grip of her vaginal muscles clamped around him. She cried out, her whole body shaking as she gushed over his pistoning cock with the release of her climax, pulling his orgasm from his balls and up his erection.

Arching his head back, he shut his eyes and basked in the pleasure of her surrendering, spasming body. His thumbs dug into her hot, reddened buttocks for more anchorage against the mind-numbing ecstasy she wrought, and he prayed he survived the onslaught enough to take her again soon.

AVERY'S BUTTOCKS throbbed from the abuse Master Grayson had heaped upon them, her body shook under the force of his slamming hips and her pussy and rectum quivered around his cock and the plug. The warmth and tingles running up and down the walls of her butt clenching around the plug matched the pulsations in her sheath rippling around the steel rod of his stroking shaft. She basked in his rough possession as much now as she had in the shower, pleased with herself for having passed his test of leaving her with nothing to don after their shower, giving her no choice but to face him in a state of vulnerable nakedness as he laid out the terms for their relationship going forward.

As she crumpled onto the rug in a heap of blissful ecstasy that challenged her sanity, he covered her prone, shaking body with his, scraping his teeth over one shoulder. "I don't think I can feel my toes."

Avery felt Grayson lift and twist as he replied, "Don't worry, they're still there. Let me know when you're able to get up. I'm starving."

Her stomach took that announcement as its cue to let out a loud rumble, revealing her own state of hunger. She huffed a quiet laugh. "I didn't realize I am too until now."

"Be right back."

Grayson slid to the side, removed the plug and then pushed off her. She rolled over to see him hiking up his jeans as he strolled down the hall. Lying in front of the fire, her body still pulsating from head to toe, she tried not to think about the clutch around her heart that kept growing tighter the more she was with him. Yes, she trusted him with her knowledge of Darren and Chad's crimes and the fears that came from having that knowledge, but that didn't mean she believed she meant any more to him than the other women he had taken up with. His offer to help her stemmed more from protectiveness toward those facing peril than from personal feelings, and she needed to ensure she didn't forget that.

He returned carrying one of his black tee shirts, a small smile curling his mouth as he tossed it down on top of her. "You can slip that on for now. Stay here where it's warmest and I'll bring over something to eat." Walking toward the kitchen, he asked over his shoulder, "A steak and potato okay?"

"More than," she answered, her mouth watering at the thought.

After slipping on the shirt, she scooted around until her back was to the fire and she could watch him in the kitchen. Light smoke billowed upward into the overhead exhaust above an indoor grill as he placed two huge steaks onto the heat. He looked as comfortable and at ease flipping meat shirtless in his kitchen as he did wearing all black and exerting his control at the club. Avery found the different facets of his personality fascinating and the sheriff, the Dom and the considerate host equally likable. Grayson's casual acceptance of her troubles and willingness to examine the files she'd run off with had gone a long way toward lightening that burden but now she hoped they could put off coming up with a possible solution. She would like more time with him here in Willow Springs before having to say goodbye.

"What's that look for?" Grayson asked, carrying over two plates and silverware.

Avery hesitated only a second before giving him more of the trust and honesty he kept insisting on. "I was just wondering how much longer I'll be here, in Montana." *Near you.*

Settling on the rug in front of her, he handed over one plate, those observant eyes focused on her face as he replied, "That will be up to you once I ensure your ex and his partner are no longer a threat to you."

"And what if you can't do that?" Her breath burned in her lungs as she waited for his answer.

"I will," he returned in a hardened tone. "Eat."

Digging into the thick steak, cooked medium rare and tasting better than anything she'd ordered out, Avery answered Grayson's probing personal questions about where she really hailed from and then about her life growing up in Chicago. He steered clear of what she'd overheard between Darren and Chad until she'd eaten every bite of steak and potato and he rose to take her plate.

With a tug on her hair, he stated, "I cooked, you do dishes while I look at your flash drive and check in with my deputies."

"Don't you want me to look at it with you?" Standing, Avery shivered as she stepped away from the fire to pick up her purse where he'd tossed it onto a chair.

"No. I want to read through it without your input as IA will do." He pointed to a door off the kitchen. "Laundry's in there. Your clothes should be dry."

Handing him the drive, she swallowed past a sudden lump in her throat. "Thank you. Even if... whatever happens... I appreciate..."

Grayson cut off her stumbling gratitude with his mouth, swallowing her low moan as she leaned on his strength and let him take her over. She would take whatever she could get, for as long as she could, she vowed as he slid one hand under the shirt to grip her sore butt. God help her but she loved that possessive hold, and so many other things about him she was beginning to realize.

"Give me twenty minutes," he said after releasing her and taking the flash drive, leaving her standing there with tingling lips and a throbbing buttock, watching him go into the first door on the right in the hall.

With another shiver, Avery went to pull her clothes from the dryer and get dressed before returning to the kitchen to load the dishwasher. A sound on the front porch drew her gaze out the window as she was wiping down the counter and she spotted the scrawny wolf/dog, Lobo pacing back and forth. She looked down at the two bones left from their steaks and pulling on the small ounce of bravery she'd unearthed earlier that day, she grabbed them and dashed to the front door.

"Okay fella, be nice," she murmured, standing half in, half out of the doorway. Lobo stood cocking his head but didn't attempt to come closer. "There, that's a good boy." Holding out a bone, she resisted the temptation to toss it to him. If she ever returned to her life in Chicago, or faced Darren, she needed to work on building her courage. Damn it, she sighed as the animal took the treat from her. There went that pang again, the one that always seemed to grip her whenever she thought of leaving.

Avery waited until he settled down under the same tree in the yard where she'd first seen him before tossing him the second bone. Stepping back, she closed the door, turned and saw Grayson standing a few feet away, arms crossed over that wide, muscled chest, eyes glittering with an unnamed emotion that curled her toes inside her warm socks.

"What?" she squeaked as he approached with slow, measured

steps, her heartbeat ratcheting up along with the heated rush of her blood.

"You surprise me, sugar. Sometimes in ways I don't care for. Others, in ways I like, a lot." Reaching for her hand, he pivoted and pulled her behind him. "Come on."

"Where? I thought we were going to discuss..."

"Later," Grayson tossed over his shoulder as he hauled her into his room and gave her a friendly push onto the bed. Coming down on top of her, he growled, "Much later." Avery giggled, the sound easing the last of his strained emotions since discovering who she was two nights ago. Watching her hold out a shaking hand to Lobo, her face pale but taut with determination, sent a wave of uncontrollable lust through him as his heart rolled over in his chest. *So this is what it feels like to topple into love*, he mused, not at all displeased with the revelation.

"I thought men your age needed more time in between..." she bucked her hips under him, "starting up again."

He narrowed his eyes and softened his tone to a silky purr. "Minx. You should know better by now not to push me."

"And if I don't?" she gasped as he stripped her jeans off.

"Then suffer the consequences."

Chapter 12

"Thanks for coming over." Grayson closed his office door behind Dan and gestured to a chair in front of his desk before resuming his seat behind it.

"No problem. What's up? Does this have to do with the rustlers, or Connor?" Concern shadowed the lawyer's eyes, something Grayson shared with him only he had more on his mind this morning than his injured friend and cattle thieves.

"No, another problem. Avery's got trouble."

Those dark eyes sharpened even though Dan assumed a casual pose of leaning back in the chair and crossing one booted ankle over his opposite knee. "Legal trouble?"

"Maybe, if it gets that far. I prefer this to stay between us for now. Caden has enough to deal with with his brother laid up." When he got Dan's nod, Grayson revealed Avery's story, leaving nothing out. "Before I start snooping around the Chicago police department, I need to know what she can be charged with, considering everything."

A low whistle blew past Dan's lips as he removed his Stetson and hung it on his bent knee. "Depends on if, and how well these assholes frame her. If it ends up being just hacking, we can always plead extenuating circumstances. I can get her off on that charge if we can take these guys down. As far as she knows, right now it's just he says, she says, correct?"

Grayson nodded. "Yes, but she's been gone for over six weeks. No telling what the bastards have been up to in that time."

Dan shrugged. "Maybe nothing. Even if her ex was suspicious of the way she took off without a word or thought she knew more than made him comfortable, he would have been a fool to jump the gun and come after her in any way that called more attention to her, or their relationship."

"That's my thought. If he played it smart, he'd show concern about her whereabouts or make up a story about them splitting up. But if IA now questions him and his partner?" Grayson's jaw went rigid as he thought of the jeopardy Avery had placed herself in by sending those files to IA. Despite the risk of that department suspecting her right from the get-go, she had alerted Lancaster and Banks she was through with hiding.

"I can tell by your face you know the answer to that. They may not be willing to ignore her any longer. Best case scenario – the two of them cut their losses and leave the country."

"That would make this too fucking easy to resolve." Grayson sighed, running one hand through his hair.

Dan slapped his hat back on and got to his feet. "Do some discreet investigating and get back to me. I'll help in whatever way I can. She's a sweetheart, and much braver than I would have labeled her, considering everything."

"Yeah, she is, and I'll make sure she stays safe."

With a thumbs up as he pivoted to leave, Dan returned, "We both will. Later."

CHICAGO – two days later

. . .

DARREN SLID into the passenger seat of Chad's car, slammed the door and threw the bag of cocaine and money on the floor in a fit of temper. "Fuck!"

Starting the car, Chad pulled out of the apartment complex parking lot as he bit out, "What now?"

"Her apartment has been rented out to someone else following, I'm sure, a thorough cleaning. Since the landlord stored her things, I couldn't very well stash the stuff now. Bitch," he swore.

"I warned you," Chad reminded him.

"Shut up. Hell, I never imagined that meek mouse would get up the nerve to contact IA, not with the chance it could backfire on her."

Surprise and fury didn't begin to describe what both Darren and Chad had felt when Internal Affairs called them in that morning and asked them to look at the contradicting reports e-mailed by an anonymous sender over the weekend. Wesley, the detective in charge of investigating both the source and the discrepancies, hadn't appeared suspicious of either them or Avery, but that meant nothing. So far, they hadn't drilled Darren on his relationship with Avery or questioned him about her abrupt resignation, but that was only a matter of time.

"We either need to split the country and retire early or track her down, and I, for one, am not ready to cash in. Close, but not yet, not if I want to have enough to spend the next thirty years on a warm island with no extradition back here," Darren said. "I'll start combing through airline and bus rosters, see what I can find."

Chad turned into the parking garage of their condo building where they each enjoyed their own place. "No need. Pack up and get ready for a long drive on Friday. We're going to Montana."

"What the hell for?" Darren snapped, not bothering to stifle his worry and irritation.

"Because that's where I traced your fucking girlfriend. She got a speeding ticket heading west on the highway between Billings and some bumfuck place called Willow Springs. We start there. Since we're off on Friday due to the stakeout tomorrow night, that will give us just enough time to drive there, take care of her and get back here late Sunday night."

Darren sent his partner a questioning frown as they walked toward the elevator. "She doesn't drive, or at least not since I've known her. I didn't even know she had a license let alone a car."

"It seems there's a lot you don't know about Avery Pierce," Chad shot back.

Darren punched the number for his floor without commenting. Damned if Chad wasn't right. Again.

FOR THE FIFTH morning in a row, Avery awoke in Grayson's bed, spooned with her buttocks nestled against his groin as he rubbed his cock between them. She pushed back, loving the feel of his rigid hardness gliding up her damp seam to spread her juices along the sensitive path and over her rear entrance.

"You're almost ready to take me here," he whispered in her ear as he thrust his cock head against her anus, his deep voice and tight hold around her waist drawing a shiver.

"So you keep saying." She wasn't sure if she was looking forward to that new experience or dreading it, only that she was tired of waiting.

"I'll fuck your ass when I think you're ready and not before. In the meantime…" Rolling her beneath him, he shackled her wrists above her head and crushed her mouth with his, swallowing her breathy moan.

Avery bucked beneath him and he pinned her hips with his, dipping his head to one straining nipple. The sharp sting from his bite fed her arousal as much as his tight hold, making it easy for him to slide his now sheathed erection between her slick folds. She wrapped her legs around his hips and locked her ankles, his lower back muscles bunching under her heels as he reared back and began the steady, pounding rhythm she had come to crave.

I love waking this way. The idle admission slithered past the slow fogging of her brain as he drove into her quivering sheath over and over. He'd surprised her Monday morning when he'd driven her into town to pick up her car at the tow shop and she discovered he'd paid for new snow tires to replace the worn treads. A warmth had invaded her chest when he'd announced she would stay with him without offering her a chance to refuse or putting a time limit on it. Happiness she hadn't felt in ages, if ever, filled her with joy when he'd taken her out to eat at the steakhouse, the only pricey, fine dining establishment in Willow Springs. After lots of wine and a decadent filet mignon topped with an even more decadent chocolate cheesecake, they'd driven out to Caden's to play cards with him, Sydney and Connor who was still bunking at their place. He'd been so attentive, overprotective and demanding the past few days, she didn't know whether to bask in his undivided attention or smack him for not sparing her time to make a move without him or his permission.

Avery tightened her thighs, her breathing turning shallow as he plowed into her quivering pussy with heavy grunts of exertion. Small contractions clutched at his invading flesh, her abundant cream easing his way as his shaft jerked against her clamping muscles.

"Fucking yes. Now, Avery," he demanded, huffing as he took her harder, faster.

Yes, now... now... now They splintered apart together, their groans mingling, their slick bodies straining as they toppled over the precipice into blinding ecstasy. As she lay shivering under him, Avery wondered when, or if her response to his controlling possession would ever lessen. God, she hoped not.

"Come on, sugar. We need to get going." After giving her a

soft kiss, Grayson pushed off her, yanked her out of bed and swatted her ass. "Into the shower. I'll bring you in a cup of coffee."

Avery rubbed her butt as she padded toward the bathroom, looking back over her shoulder to see him strolling out, his jeans left opened, a small smile curling his mouth. Her heartbeat kicked up, and she found herself in the precarious position of teetering on the edge of falling in love. Yesterday, he'd told her his digging had revealed Darren and Chad had been questioned by IA, that small tidbit offering her the first ray of hope since she'd fled Chicago. But now the thought of leaving Willow Springs, and Master Grayson dimmed that beckoning brightness.

Shaking her head at her growing, contrary dilemma, she slipped into the bathroom, praying her heart stayed intact in the upcoming days.

GRAYSON PULLED his gaze away from Avery where she sat wearing nothing but his black silk shirt and her glasses, twisting on the barstool to face Dan as he took the seat next to him. The activities already taking place in The Barn didn't command his attention as much as she continued to do. Watching her had become his favorite pastime, even when she was doing something mundane, such as talking to Sydney and Nan at a table a few feet away, her soft face showing less strain, those whiskey eyes sparkling with the humor portrayed by her smiling mouth.

"Anything new?" Dan asked with a lift of one brow as he glanced from Grayson to Avery.

"No. I did a little more snooping today but couldn't pick up any movement by Chicago IA toward Avery."

"But that doesn't mean they're not," the lawyer finished for him.

"I know and I can only dig so deep without sending up red

flags. I'm tempted to agree to Avery's suggestion she hack into their personal finances."

"I wouldn't do that, at least not yet," Dan advised. "One, they're sure to catch wind of it and two, anything she found couldn't be used against them. Best to give it more time, see if IA goes so far as getting a warrant to do the same thing."

"Are you two talking about Avery's scumbag, crooked cop?" Caden asked as he joined them from behind the bar.

"You know?" Surprise colored Grayson's voice.

Caden nodded toward the three girls. "She told Sydney and Nan the other day and gave Syd the okay to tell me. Given my girl's experience with being on the run, Sydney said Avery seemed relieved to have it out in the open."

Avery had kept that conversation from him, which was no big deal, Grayson admitted. So why did it rub him the wrong way, as if she still wasn't comfortable speaking openly with him about any and everything like he wanted her to be? "That's good," he murmured, taking the beer Caden handed him. "How's Con? Still cranky?"

"Not as much." Caden shrugged. "He knows he screwed up going after cattle thieves by himself, without backup or telling anyone what he was up to, and how much worse it could have been." Concern clouded his friend's blue eyes. "I sure hope he doesn't end up with permanent damage to that shoulder."

"He's tough and determined," Dan put in. "He won't let a gunshot injury keep him down for long. I hear the clinic's hired a physical therapist, so maybe he won't have to drive into Billings for therapy."

"Let's hope." Caden sighed before cocking his head at Grayson. "So, you're pitting yourself against two crooked Chicago cops?"

Scowling, Grayson replied in a deep rumble, "*Fucking A*, I'll go up against the whole Chicago police force if I have to."

Shaking his head with a smirk, the rancher who should know

stated, "They slip under your radar when you least expect it." Caden reached across the bar and slapped Grayson on the shoulder. "Welcome to the downfallen, buddy."

"Shit." Dan hopped off the stool. "Keep away from me, both of you. Whatever is going around, I want no part of it." He took off, stopping at a sofa where two unattached subs sat and held out both hands to them.

"Lucky bastard," Grayson commented when the girls accepted his invitation to play.

"So are you and I."

Looking back at Caden and then over at Avery and Sydney, Grayson nodded in agreement. "Damn right. I'll be back to relieve you in an hour."

"No hurry. Have fun."

He intended to. Reaching the table, he snatched Avery's hand and pulled her up, raising one brow as she wobbled and leaned into him. Her face reddened, likely from the sudden shift of the larger plug he had inserted before leaving the house. "Please excuse us, ladies."

With a breathless laugh he loved, Avery recovered enough to stutter behind him as he dragged her toward the stairs. "Wh… where… are you hauling me?"

"Upstairs." Turning his head around halfway up, he inquired with a small smile, "Do you have a problem with that?"

Her reciprocating grin lit up her face. "Nope, not in the least."

"I love your eagerness, sugar." Grayson led her to the corner swing where he'd first introduced her to bondage. Dropping her hand, he ordered her to strip as he reached for the long strap dangling on a hook in the wall behind the webbed contraption. Seeing her standing there naked, her eyes darting around the loft to check who might be watching as she fidgeted with her fingers, he nodded in approval. "Excellent." Clasping her soft waist, he lifted her onto the swing and smiled when the apparatus rocked and she made a frantic grab for the lines attaching it to the ceiling. "Relax. I haven't let you fall yet, have I?"

"There's a first time for everything. This thing feels so flimsy."

"It's not. As for there's a first time for everything, that's true about a lot of things, but not me failing to ensure your safety. But it does apply to this scene."

Avery's eyes turned wary as Grayson issued an up gesture using two fingers above her right knee, but she obeyed the silent command without balking. Wrapping the end of the strap right above her knee, he fashioned a loop by velcroing it closed and then brought the strap around her shoulders, lifting her bent leg up to her chest as he went, gesturing for her to raise her left leg to meet the opposite end.

"*Sheesh*," she muttered in consternation after he bound her other leg in the same folded back and out position.

Standing between her splayed legs, he offered a token to ease her embarrassment. "Between the dim lighting and my position, it'll be difficult for anyone to get as close a look at your pretty pussy and uplifted ass as me." He ran his hands over her quivering thighs until her tight grip on the lines eased and she strained towards him with a tiny whimper. "There you go, sugar. Breathe." As soon as she inhaled, he removed the plug and tossed it aside. "So fucking wet," he growled, thrusting two fingers into her sopping pussy and swiveling them around until they were well-lubed with her juices.

"Oh, God." Avery's eyes flew from his face down between her splayed legs as she watched him pull his fingers from her vagina and slowly breach her back orifice, prepping her dark channel for his cock using her own abundant cream.

"Bear down and don't tense up. I'll go slow, and only so far. I know what I'm doing, Avery," Grayson assured her with a light caress down the inside of her left thigh.

She nodded on a long exhale and didn't shy away from

watching him release his cock and sheath himself in a lubed condom. Pulling his fingers from her ass, he reached for her right hand and brought it down to her gaping pussy. "Finger yourself as I take you." He didn't give her time to think or balk at the order as he pushed two of her fingers inside her while fisting his shaft and working into her puckered rear entrance. Avery bit her lip, zeroed in on her clit as he pressed forward, filling her with half his length before pausing and then retreating until just his cock head remain buried inside her snug rectum.

"Sir... Master Grayson... *please*," she whispered, lifting eyes drenched in need up to his face.

"Tug on your clit and keep tugging as I fuck you." Grayson's breathing grew as harsh as Avery's as he jabbed back and forth inside her tight ass, feeling the small contractions in her pussy through the thin wall separating her fingers and his invading cock. As hot as her pussy, her ass gripped his girth with spasmodic clutches, her mewling cries and arching hips pushing him past the point of slowing down after a few, shallow thrusts. Clasping her buttocks, he lifted her hips higher to meet his deeper, faster plunges, all the while her fingers plucking nonstop at her swollen, crimson bud, her juices dribbling down her crack to aid in his possession.

"Fuck, fuck, fuck," Grayson ground out, wishing he could have made this last longer as he spewed his climax into the condom and saw stars. He heard Avery's cry of release, felt it rippling along his cock even with the barrier between the orifices, and swore nothing had ever come close to rivaling the sensations her climax pulled from him.

AVERY LEANED on The Barn's bathroom counter, hardly recognizing herself in the mirror. With her thick, unruly hair falling around her face and shoulders in a tangled mess and her face, neck and upper part of her chest exposed by the open buttons on Grayson's silk shirt flushed and damp, she looked... ravished. Heck, she mused, with the muscles lining her rectum and pussy still contracting and her body still pulsating, she *felt* ravished. But that wasn't what had prompted her hasty dash from the loft and into the restroom as soon as Master Grayson had released the binding strap she could still feel wrapped around her shoulders, holding her knees up and out, leaving her exposed in a lewd, decadent position.

Shaking her head, Avery wondered why she hadn't seen her downfall coming. Tonight wasn't the first time he had maintained his stern dominance and need for control while that inner core of protectiveness and decency prompted him to alleviate her insecurities first. But after choosing an apparatus in a secluded corner instead of one out in the open for her initiation into public fucking and anal sex and then easing her embarrassment over her displayed body by shielding her, how could she help taking that last step into falling in love with him?

With her mind whirling from that revelation and her body humming in sated bliss, she didn't notice someone else entering the bathroom until Cassie's mocking voice interrupted Avery's musings and her cold face appeared in the mirror.

"Well, well, well, look what the cat dragged in," she sneered with an insolent look up and down Avery's disheveled appearance. "Enjoy it while you can, hon, because it won't last."

"What are you talking about, Cassie?" Avery managed to ask with a semblance of calm despite her racing heart. It was no wonder the woman had few friends as she rarely offered any friendly overtures to females, only men.

The attractive blonde snorted and shook her head, crossing her arms in front of her. "Shit, you can't be that stupid, can you? Do you honestly think a man like Master Grayson wants anything more from you than that ass fucking he just gave you? Hell, you're not even his type. Trust me, you'll be history soon, just like every submissive who's come before you and will follow you."

Avery surprised herself by shooting back, "Like you?" despite the coldness invading her body from the other woman's cruel taunts.

Cassie laughed and stepped up to the other sink, running her fingers through her long hair. "Oh no, not me. You see, I'm the only one he returns to, time and time again. He can't get enough of me," she lied.

Moving toward the door on rubbery legs, Avery dug up enough bravado to toss over her shoulder, "And yet he continues to seek others. *Mmm*, I wonder why?" *I am really liking this new streak of courage I've found*, she thought as she opened the door with a shaking hand. Too bad her bravery only lasted long enough for her to get away from the other woman. Uncertainty assailed her as soon as she stepped back into the club room and saw Master Grayson leaning against the bar, talking around the toothpick in his mouth, those piercing eyes zeroing in on her with the quick, laser sharpness of a radar beam.

Was Cassie right? Maybe she'd read too much into Grayson's solicitous attention since she'd come to town, injected too much hope into the signs of caring and concern he'd been lavishing on her. She'd never felt at ease around men like most women did or was good at reading them. Just look at what an idiot she'd been with Darren. Why hadn't she remembered that hard-learned lesson these past few weeks?

Avery could tell the moment he read something on her face that drew his suspicions. Pushing away from the bar, he said something to Caden before striding toward her, nailing her in place with an unbreakable, intent stare. Wiping her clammy hands down the sides of his silk shirt, she pressed her bare toes into the wood floor, tried calming her ratcheting pulse and struggled to hold herself in check and prevent him from seeing anything else.

Fisting his hands on his hips as he reached her, Grayson cocked his head, asking, "Everything all right, sugar?"

Remembering his accurate astuteness, she answered with as much honesty as possible at the moment. "I'm a bit… overwhelmed right now, with all this," she waved a hand around the room, "along with everything else I'm trying to work out in my life."

Master Grayson nodded but his eyes remained sharp and assessing. "Understandable. Do you want to head back to my place now, or would you rather visit more with Nan and Sydney?"

Avery blinked rapidly against the moisture blurring her vision. Damn the man, why did it have to be someone so unattainable who did it for her in every way she'd ever dreamed, and ways she never imagined? "I'll stay. I know you're needed at the bar now."

"I am, but there are always exceptions allowed for needy subs. Are you sure?"

"I'm sure." She smiled, not wanting to appear needy.

"Then come keep me company." He frowned as Cassie came through the foyer door and flicked Avery a smug look before beaming at Grayson as she walked by.

"There's Nan," Avery rushed to point out before he could question her again. She recognized the suspicious look crossing his face as he eyed Cassie's retreating back. "I'll go sit with her while you tend bar." She pulled away from him and wound her way over to Nan's table, feeling those eyes now following her until she sat down.

It was after ten the next morning by the time Avery roused, showered and found Grayson on the phone at the kitchen counter. She must have been more tired than she thought to sleep so long; either that or the tossing and turning she'd done all night as Cassie's words kept replaying in her head was responsible. It wasn't until Grayson's muttered, frustrated swearing pre-empted his hard arm clamping around her waist to pin her against him that she settled down to a few hours of sleep.

"I'll head out shortly and get back to you." Snapping the phone shut, he nodded toward the full pot of coffee. "I refilled it when I heard you moving around. I'm sorry," he said, coming around the counter to drop his mouth onto hers for a quick kiss. "Today was my day off, but Caden called to tell me a neighboring rancher spotted the same truck Connor went after. I need to get their statement, but it won't take me long."

"No problem. I planned to go into town anyway and pick up a few things. I'm… not sure if I'll be back before I go to the diner." Avery held her breath, praying he didn't read more into her plans than she wanted him to. She needed to put space between them, figure out how to keep her heart from crumbling when she returned to her life in Chicago, or went back on the run. The best she could figure, those would be her only two options once IA finished their investigation and Grayson informed her he'd done all he could.

"I'd rather you returned here by early afternoon and let me drive you back to work. The forecast calls for snow by then and you suck at driving in bad weather." He softened his criticism with a teasing smile that didn't erase the doubt darkening his eyes.

"Thanks to you, I have snow tires, so I should be fine." She averted her eyes and inched around him, turning her back on his scrutinizing gaze.

"But, because it concerns your safety, which falls under my control, you'll do as I suggest, won't you, sugar?"

She whipped her head around as she reached for the coffee pot, the implacable, hard edge to his tone a sure sign he wouldn't back down. A curl of resentment festered inside her as she thought of him moving on to the next submissive woman who caught his eye after he finished with her. Avery tamped down the urge to lash out, which would get her nowhere, shrugging with an evasive reply as she poured her coffee. "I should be done by then. I hope you get another lead on those rustlers this morning."

"We'll get them; it's just a matter of time." Snatching his Stetson off a hook by the door, Grayson stepped out with a parting shot that heated Avery from head to toe even as it sent a ripple of unease slithering down her spine. "I'll introduce your ass to both sides of my hairbrush if I don't see you back here in a few hours."

"That's just wrong," she mumbled, her buttocks clenching and her pussy spasming as she imagined how the bristles on his brush would feel scraping over skin reddened after he applied the wooden side. "Huh, it might be worth it to ignore his order, in more ways than one."

Chapter 13

C had Banks pulled the pickup rental into a parking space in front of the Willow Springs library and cut the engine, turning to his partner as Darren warned him for the umpteenth time, "Remember, don't go off half-cocked so people will recall the two strangers in town after she disappears."

Gritting his teeth, he snapped, "If you had listened to me in the first place, we wouldn't have to make this desperate attempt to track her down and take her out. We could have planted evidence in her apartment right after she fled and led IA right to her."

"So sue me. I never thought the bitch would have the guts to do anything with just a few suspicious files, let alone managing to attain more." Opening the passenger side door, Darren slid out and looked up and down the quiet street with a sneer. "If she is here, or has been since getting that ticket, someone should have seen her. People in small towns like this are up in everybody's business since there's not a God damned thing else to do. Call or text me if you get a lead and then we'll come up with a plan."

Chad didn't wince when Darren slammed the door in frustration and stomped into the small library in the town's center square. As far as hubbubs went, his partner was right; the cobbled street and covered sidewalks running in front of the hundred-year-old buildings housing a mixture of city offices and small shops presented an idyllic picture of Hometown, USA. Like Darren, he would take the crowds, noise and traffic of the big city to this nauseating blast from the past of life back in the fifties. Yanking his coat around him, he stepped out into the cold bite of fresh mountain air he appreciated no more than he did Avery Pierce's jeopardizing interference into their tidy, profitable enterprise.

Thirty minutes later, as the first soft snowflakes started falling, Chad left the mercantile no closer to subtly unearthing any knowledge of Avery than when he'd first started out. With his head tucked down against the damp weather, he trudged toward the corner diner, intending to text Darren as soon as he sat down. Thinking about getting something hot to eat and what plan B could be, he wasn't paying attention and bumped into someone exiting a tea shop.

"Sorry." He looked into a pair of blue eyes that showed an immediate spark of interest as a slow smile curled the attractive blonde's full mouth.

"Oh, absolutely no problem, sir." Cocking her head, she gave him an easy opening to pry for information. "You're not from around here. Can I help you with something?"

"As a matter of fact, maybe you can," he answered, tired of tiptoeing around people for information and getting nowhere. "I'm looking for my… sister," he improvised on the fly. "She took off a few weeks ago after a fight with her boyfriend and my parents are worried sick about her. The last time I spoke with her, she mentioned staying in a small town outside of Billings." Pulling out the only picture Darren had of him and Avery, Chad showed it to the young woman whose expression hardened as she looked at it.

Much to his delight, she proved to be lousy at hiding her

knowledge of and animosity toward Avery. *Fucking perfect*, he thought with satisfaction as she answered with a calculated gleam replacing the friendly light in her gaze.

"She's here. Works at the diner and lives above it." She pointed right to where Chad had been heading to next. "I hope you find her. I'm sure she'll be happy to see someone from home. She doesn't fit in well around here. Sorry if that offends you." Handing back the picture, her expression said she was anything but sorry.

Chad knew his smile revealed elation at her reply and didn't care. "That doesn't surprise me. Thanks for your help."

———

CASSIE WATCHED THE TALL, good-looking stranger stroll toward the diner at a fast pace, delighted at the opportunity to rid herself of Master Grayson's new interest. It was unlike her favorite Dom to spend so much monogamous time with one sub, and she'd never known him to be interested in such an inexperienced, naïve one. It had irritated the hell out of her when he'd turned his back on her desire to hook up with him again, and the more he did it, the more time and undivided attention he lavished on the mousy nerd, the more annoyed she'd become.

She never did take kindly to being told no. But now she'd gotten a little payback. She only wished the stupid interloper would know it was she who had informed Avery's family about her whereabouts that with any luck, would result in her being hauled back home, where she belonged. Far away from here and out of Cassie's way.

———

CHAD WAS PULLING out his phone as he neared the diner

when he spotted an older sedan coming around from behind the building. Even from a distance, he recognized Avery's pulled back hair and black-framed glasses. Fearing losing this chance, he snapped his phone shut and dashed back to the truck parked across the street. With no plan in mind, he hopped behind the wheel and whipped around to follow her, the thrill of a chase mingling with anger that had been festering inside him these past weeks.

The snow fell thicker now, but still soft enough not to cause problems on the roads yet as they both picked up speed once she hit the highway leading out of town. Wondering where she was headed and hoping for a chance to pull her over and snatch her, he set aside his frustration and stayed a safe distance behind for now.

AVERY CLUTCHED the steering wheel tighter, her breath burning in her throat as dread clawed at her abdomen. She would never forget the instant, icy fear that had gripped her the moment she'd glanced out the diner's front window and spotted Darren's partner, Chad talking to Cassie, or the satisfaction etched on her nemesis' face as she pointed toward the diner. The heartbreak over Cassie's cruel words last night that she'd been struggling with all morning took a backseat to the sudden need for not only Grayson's protection, but the comfort his nearness always seemed to envelop her in. She'd known last night her feelings went beyond sexual pleasure and had seeped into her soul, and the trust he'd been asking for is what gave her the nerve to flee back to him without a thought as soon as she'd seen Chad's threatening presence.

His sexual interest in her might be temporary but she trusted in his friendship and offer of protection enough to believe he would set aside his irritation with her for not returning before the snow started as he'd instructed. She hadn't counted on Chad seeing her and following. Jitters danced over her skin and nausea churned as she glanced in the rearview mirror again and saw the truck continuing to barrel down on her despite the snow now falling harder. As she neared the turnoff leading to Grayson's house, she prayed she was wrong, and that wasn't him, but when she chanced another quick look back, Avery knew with sickening clarity she was in trouble. With the truck now riding her bumper, she could clearly make out Chad's cold, determined face.

"*Oh, God,*" she gasped, slowing only enough to make the turn before the jarring impact coming from behind sent her careening toward a stand of snow-blurred trees. A cry wrenched from her throat as she struggled to control the inevitable impact and prayed Grayson would once again prove to be her miracle out of another untenable position.

With a hard yank on the wheel, she side-swiped the trees instead of hitting them head-on, but the impact still threw her against the dash. Glass shattered and pain blossomed across her head before the blinding white filling her vision went black.

CHAD SLOWED and pulled off the main road, stopping out of direct sight of any other vehicles passing by the turnoff. With a hard push, he opened his door against the increased wind and snow and trudged toward Avery's car wedged against three trees, the engine sputtering and dying as he approached. He could make out her slumped form, see the bright red trail of blood running down the side of her face and that she wasn't moving. He doubted she would have made this easy for him by dying on impact and refused to leave anything to chance. As he reached for the door handle on the passenger side, a low, menacing growl came from his right and froze his hand before he could grasp it.

A shiver of trepidation snaked down his spine as he turned his head and came almost eye to eye with a teeth-baring wolf the size of a very large dog. With the animal's fur standing up along the back of his nape, ears flattened and quivering body crouched, ready to attack, Chad didn't dare move. Swearing under his breath, he stood rooted in place, wondering how long this stand-off would last. With no other option he could think of, he inched his hand down, intending to go for his gun tucked into the back of his pants.

Before he got halfway to his goal, Avery stirred and her cry of pain laced terror drew the wolf's attention and incited his anger. With a snarling leap, he launched himself at Chad, his sharp teeth sinking into his arm, through his coat, breaking skin and drawing blood as Chad fell back with a shout against the animal's attack.

GRAYSON STORMED out of the house, letting his annoyance with Avery's deliberate absence before the snow started to propel him with angry strides out to his SUV. He wouldn't wait another minute for her to get over whatever had been bothering her since they left the club last night. Slamming into his vehicle, he turned around and headed down the drive thinking it had been a mistake not to pull answers from her before they parted company this morning. He knew her well enough to know a stubborn streak went along with her insecurities. When he tracked her down, they were going to iron out a few things, the least of which would be admitting their feelings for each other. *Fucking A*, if he could do it, so could she, damn it.

As he neared the end of the drive before reaching the high-way, Lobo's distinct howling growl rent the air followed by a sharp human cry, the unexpected sounds interrupting his thoughts and intentions. Worry over who had drawn the hybrid's irritation sliced through him seconds before he stomped on the brakes upon spotting Avery's wrecked car. Jumping out, fear for her wrangled with concern for the man Lobo had pinned down with a tight, vicious clamp on his arm. The fact the wolf drew blood showed he meant business and added to the frisson of alarm skating through Grayson. With regret, he pulled his rifle from the back of the SUV, praying the wild dog wouldn't force him to use it. The need to see to both the man and Avery took precedence over his fondness for the animal he'd befriended since he was a pup.

"Lobo, back!" Grayson commanded, approaching with slow, cautious steps and then halting mid-stride as he recognized the pale man who had pulled his own gun out from under him. Lifting his rifle, fury unlike anything he'd experienced before filled him with an icy hot rage. "Drop your fucking gun, now!"

The man Grayson recognized as Chad Banks from the photos he'd pulled up of both him and Avery's ex, Darren Lancaster gave him a pain-filled, incredulous look before snapping back, "Are you fucking kidding me?" and lifted his gun toward Lobo's head.

"No!"

Both men and Lobo jerked toward Avery's strident cry as she all but fell out of the wrecked car, the blood caking on her face sending another wave of fear and uncontrollable fury through Grayson. Knowing the history between the two, it didn't take a genius to look at the vehicles and deduce what happened here.

Before his girl could do something else foolish, Grayson swung out with one booted foot, connecting with Banks' gun-holding hand as Lobo let go of his arm and trotted over to Avery's shaking, outstretched hand.

"What the hell?" Banks gaped, clutching his arm, his eyes skittering between Avery and Grayson as he rolled to his feet.

Unable to resist, Grayson sent him sprawling back onto the

cold, snowy ground with a fist to his jaw. Pulling out handcuffs, he made short work of snapping them on with a low-voiced warning in the bastard's ear, "*No one* harms my girl and gets away with it, you son of a bitch."

Turning from him, Grayson's heart clutched and his breath stalled in his throat as he saw Avery hugging Lobo, tears swimming behind her broken, askew glasses, her swelling, bruising forehead still oozing a trickle of bright red blood down her pale cheek. "*Fucking A*, sugar," he rasped, reaching for her and petting Lobo before scooping up a handful of snow. Holding the frigid, damp wad against her injured forehead, he hauled her against him with his other arm. "If I didn't love you so much I'd tan your ass right here and now for the scare you gave me."

———

STARTLING disbelief followed by stunned joy enveloped Avery in a warm embrace that rivaled the feel of Grayson's arms drawing her up and enfolding her against his solid, rock-hard body and dispelling her cold shivering. She heard Lobo huff and giggled; she listened to the rapid beat of his heart beneath her ear and breathed her first sigh of relief. When she'd roused, looked out the shattered window and saw Grayson's face taut with fury and concern, her heart had rolled over. But it wasn't until she watched him put together a mental picture of what had occurred and immediately rush to her defense that she let herself believe everything might be okay.

With his declaration ringing in her ears, she asked, "How did you know?"

"I didn't, or hell, maybe I did. Who knows? I was coming to look for you after you didn't return by one. Chad Banks, right?" He ran a light-fingered caress over her aching forehead, lingering rage and worry darkening his eyes.

"Yes." She nodded against his chest, refusing to look at the man who tried to kill her. "But that's not what I meant." With a deep, fortifying breath, she peeked back up, her face heating as she clarified, "How do you know you... you love me?"

His tone turned as dry as the look on his face. "Sugar, when a virtual stranger knocks you for a loop the moment you meet and then she invades your thoughts twenty-four-seven, you know."

"Oh, then that must mean I've been in love with you since I first heard your commands over the phone," she admitted, this time without shying away from his probing stare.

Lobo's low growling broke them apart and Grayson swore as he snapped at Chad, "Don't take another step or I'll let him have you."

Chad halted halfway to his truck, hatred spewing from his eyes and coloring his voice as he ground out, "You're aiding and abetting a criminal and I'm a Chicago cop. Do you really want to go down with her?" He jerked on his hands bound behind him with a nod toward Grayson's police marked vehicle. "You might be with the force in this backwoods Podunk town, but you don't stand a chance against me."

Grayson pulled back his coat to reveal his badge hooked on his belt buckle as he pulled out his phone. "I am the *head* honcho of my force in *my* Podunk town and entire county, and I beg to differ." Taking Avery's arm, he led her to the cruiser while putting the phone to his ear and calling ahead to the clinic in Willow Springs. "Hang on while I get him secured in the back," he told her after getting her ensconced in the front and flipping the heat on high. "I'm taking you to the clinic first where they can tend to both of you and then my deputy will meet me to escort him over to the jail. He can just stew there until you feel up to giving me a statement about what happened here."

Avery gripped his arm before he shut the door. "If Chad's here, Darren can't be too far away. They stick together."

"I've already alerted my deputies, and they have his picture. Sit tight."

The shock, cold and mountain of events that had transpired in the last twenty minutes had kept Avery from feeling the pounding ache encompassing her head, but as she settled against the seat and warmth seeped into her bones, her vision blurred from the throbbing ache. At least the packed snow Grayson had applied worked to stop the bleeding and numb some of the stabbing pain. Closing her eyes, she willed an end to the chapter of her life that had sent her fleeing.

One month later

Giddy excitement prompted Avery to pop up out of her seat the moment the *fasten your seatbelts* sign clicked off. The early afternoon sun shining outside of the small airplane window brightened her mood even more as she grabbed her bag from the overhead compartment. Her week-long visit with Marci in Florida had gone a long way in easing the stress of the previous three weeks. She doubted her ability to have gotten through the grueling process of returning to Chicago to speak with IA without Grayson sticking like glue to her side the whole time. When he'd announced Dan would accompany them as her attorney, she'd broken down in tears of gratitude. The burden had still lain heavily on her shoulders given the years both Darren and Chad had been on the force, but when they factored in Chad's attempt on her life, all suspicion had shifted to further investigation of the two cops.

By the time Grayson had dropped her off at the clinic and taken Chad into custody, his deputies had had Darren in handcuffs, having cornered him right on the street just a few feet from the police station. Upon hearing about his partner's attempt on Avery's life, Darren had clammed up, but his silence wouldn't keep him out of jail. As for Cassie's inadvertent part in putting Avery in jeopardy, all Grayson would tell her was he'd set her straight on her error and banned her from the club. But from his tone and look in his eyes, she'd experienced a stab of pity for the other woman whose jealousy had cost her everything.

Avery had gone to Florida without Grayson at his insistence and was glad he had seen, better than she, what she had needed by the time the department cut her loose from questioning. The time away from everything and everyone associated with the fear and stress of being on the run had helped clarify what she felt for Grayson wasn't based on those emotions. Her determination not to make another error in judgment because she was a needy, lonely geek had paid off because she now knew for certain her happiness centered on hearing his voice, seeing him looking at her with that gleam in his gray/green gaze and embracing his hard-edged dominance.

Avery's pulse spiked as she strode down the exit tunnel leading from the plane to the terminal, picking up her pace as she spotted a group of people waiting on passengers to disembark. She saw Grayson's coal black head first and then, as she emerged into the Billings airport, her eyes widened upon seeing Sydney, Nan, Dan and the Dunbar brothers were also there for her. Surprise and pleasure caused her to stumble over someone's bag, muttering, "*Sheesh*," as Grayson caught her next to him with an amused chuckle.

"*Fucking A*, but I missed you, sugar."

He bent his head and kissed her with the pent-up lust she also felt, his hands latching onto her butt and pressing her pelvis against the rigid shape of his erection. Pulling away, Avery cast an embarrassed look around before greeting her friends. "Hey, everyone, thanks for coming." She smiled, her face as flushed as her dampening pussy. Grayson slung an arm around her shoulders and Caden snatched her bag from her hand as they answered in unison.

"Welcome home, Avery."

The End

BJ Wane

I live in the Midwest with my husband and our two dogs, a Poodle/Pyrenees mix and an Irish Water Spaniel. I love dogs, spending time with my daughter, babysitting her two dogs, reading and working puzzles. We have traveled extensively throughout the states, Canada and just once overseas, but I much prefer being a homebody. I worked for a while writing articles for a local magazine but soon found my interest in writing for myself peaking. My first book was strictly spanking erotica, but I slowly evolved to writing erotic romance with an emphasis on spanking. I love hearing from readers and can be reached here: bjwane@cox.net.

Recent accolades include: 5 star, Top Pick review from The Romance Reviews for *Blindsided*, 5 star review from Long & Short Reviews for Hannah & The Dom Next Door, which was also voted Erotic Romance of the Month on LASR, and my most recent title, Her Master At Last, took two spots on top 100 lists in BDSM erotica and Romantic erotica in less than a week!

Visit her Facebook page
https://www.facebook.com/bj.wane
Visit her blog here
bjwane.blogspot.com

Don't miss these exciting titles by BJ Wane and Blushing Books!

Single Titles
Claiming Mia

Connect with BJ Wane
bjwane.blogspot.com

CPSIA information can be obtained
at www.ICGtesting.com
Printed in the USA
LVHW011514010320
648615LV00001B/166